A JAMIE AUSTEN

SAVE

— THE —

GIRLS

TERRY TOLER

Save The Girls
Published by: BeHoldings, LLC

Book Cover: BeHoldings Publishing
Contributing Editor: Donna Toler

For information email: terry@terrytoler.com.

Our books can be purchased in bulk for promotional, educational, and business use. Please contact your bookseller or the BeHoldings Publishing Sales department at: *sales@terrytoler.com*

For booking information email: booking@terrytoler.com.
First U.S. Edition

ISBN 978-1-7352243-5-0

This is a work of fiction. All of the characters, organizations, and events portrayed in this novel are either products of the author's imagination or are used fictitiously. Any resemblance to actual persons, living or dead is entirely coincidental.

OTHER BOOKS BY TERRY TOLER

Fiction

The Longest Day
The Reformation of Mars
The Late, Great Planet Jupiter
The Great Wall of Ven-Us
Saturn: The Eden Experiment
The Mercury Protocols
The Heart of Pluto
Save The Girls
The Ingenue
Saving Sara
Save The Queen
No Girl Left Behind
The Launch
Body Count
Save Me Twice
Powerful Enemies
Deadly Games
Don't Be Careful
Wintervention
Saving Alex
Cliff Hangers: Anna
Cliff Hangers: Mr. & Mrs. Platt
Cliff Hangers: The Quarterback
Cliff Hangers: Macy
Cliff Hangers: Not, Not Guilty
The Blue Rose
Triggers
The Book Club
The Book Club Murder
The Book Club Rescue

Non-Fiction

How to Make More Than a Million Dollars
The Heart Attacked
Seven Years of Promise
Mission Possible
Marriage Made in Heaven
21 Days to Physical Healing
21 Days to Spiritual Fitness
21 Days to Divine Health
21 Days to a Great Marriage
21 Days to Financial Freedom
21 Days to Sharing Your Faith
21 Days to Mission Possible
7 Days to Emotional Freedom
Uncommon Finances
Uncommon Health
Uncommon Marriage
The Jesus Diet
Suddenly Free
Feeling Free

For more information on these books and other resources visit terrytoler.com.

Thank you for purchasing this novel from best-selling author, Terry Toler. As an additional thank you, Terry wants to give you a free gift.

Sign up for:

Updates
New Releases
Announcements

At terrytoler.com

We'll send you an eBook, *The Book Club*, a Cliff Hangers novella, free of charge.

Dedicated to the many men and women who are on the front lines and risk their lives to save the girls from the horrors of sex slavery.

1

The cell phone alarm went off at the worst possible time.

The alarm meant Jamie Austen was more than twenty minutes late. She should've already grabbed the package and been long gone from the closet of a storage room she'd been hiding in for the last forty minutes.

If someone heard the alarm and came to investigate, she'd have to improvise, and who knows what would happen. She had wanted to get in and out without anyone knowing she was ever there.

Get out without killing anyone.

I can't believe I forgot to turn off the alarm.

A rookie and possibly deadly mistake.

Jamie listened carefully for anyone who might be coming. The only sound she heard was the rhythmic moaning of the disgusting man in the room next door, having his way with a fifteen-year-old-girl. She grimaced when she heard the faint and fake moans of the girl, pretending he was somehow giving her pleasure, which was impossible.

There's no way she felt pleasure from any of these men. Any feelings she might've ever had for men were permanently damaged and left her for good several hundred men ago.

The man was the reason Jamie was late.

Why is he taking so long?

What Jamie really wanted to do was walk right into the room and snap his neck, or better yet, kick him between the legs so hard he'd never be able to do what he was doing with anyone again for the rest of his life.

But he wasn't the target. The girl was. She was the package.

Jamie hated calling the girls packages. A demeaning and impersonal code name. Necessary though. If the authorities were listening to their cell phone conversations, which was a possibility, they wouldn't know who or what package they were talking about.

The girl's name was Chang which meant elephant in the Thai language. Ironic since the girl weighed less than a hundred pounds soaking wet. Jamie had no idea if Chang was the girl's real name or someone's idea of a joke.

She'd been sold into the sex trade by her mother when she was only thirteen-years old. The misfortune of being born to a poor family in Thailand where parents routinely sold their young girls to the highest bidder. For more than two years, Chang had been forced to service as many as ten men a day, seven days a week. It'd probably been more than a year since she'd had a day off.

More than twenty million women and girls were exploited in sex trafficking worldwide, and Jamie was risking her life for just this one.

The starfish on the beach.

The story goes that a boy was walking along the beach and throwing as many starfish as he could back into the ocean. Someone told him he was wasting his time. He couldn't possibly make a difference with so many of them stranded on the beach. The boy said he was making a difference for that one.

Jamie understood the deep meaning of that parable. She was risking her life for this one, and the danger was worth it to her. Chang may only be one in twenty million, but Jamie could make a difference for her.

Her thoughts were interrupted by a loud and disgusting moan signifying the man had finished, and it had finally, mercifully, come to an end for Chang. Time to get out of there as quickly as possible.

Hopefully the man was thinking the same thing. The scumbags usually didn't hang around long after the deed was finished. Like a robber fleeing the scene of the crime. Take the money and run. In this case, leave the money on the table and run.

Jamie heard the man say, "You did good."

"Definitely American," Jamie said under her breath.

Thousands of American men came to Thailand every year for cheap thrills and the availability of young girls. Sex with minors was illegal in the United States. Illegal in Thailand as well, but the authorities generally looked the other way, as long as they got part of the action.

The American had probably paid about 600 Thai Baht, approximately twenty dollars for the thirty minutes. Brothel girls were the lowest quality of girls in Thailand. The locations were seedy and not well maintained.

The higher end girls were in the gentlemen's clubs and escort services and could bring as much as 2400-5000 Baht depending on the length of time and beauty of the girl. The "giks" were the higher-end girls who were considered mistresses and were available at a man's beck and call. They demanded the most money.

Chang was the bottom of the sex food chain in every way.

Jamie felt like she needed a long shower after hiding in that closet. A bath filled with disinfectants might be more necessary. She thought she had dressed appropriately. Long pants and long sleeve shirt. A hazmat suit would've been better.

Thinking about it caused her to shudder. The best she could do was try and take her mind off what disgusting creatures might be in the closet with her.

Whatever she was going through didn't compare to the torture Chang had to endure.

That's why Jamie was there. The giks and other girls, while exploited, had a choice, were treated better, and made some money selling their bodies. Chang was a sex slave. She'd never see any of the twenty dollars, but her mother would. Her family got a meager check once a month, as did the crooked cops whose pockets were greased once a month as well.

Chang got nothing but deplorable room and board ... and constant heartache.

Jamie would have to move quickly once the man left the room. Chang would only have fifteen minutes to clean herself up and prepare for the next man. Jamie moved quietly to the door and cracked it enough to see a three-hundred-plus-pound man lumbering down the hall and out the door.

No wonder it took him so long.

Jamie was unable to manage even the slightest grin at her joke.

She waited to see if anyone came back in through the same door. She caught herself holding her breath.

When she was satisfied no one was coming, she slipped into the hallway and into the adjacent room. Chang was lying on the bed in a fetal position, sobbing. Allowing herself a few of the fifteen minutes to let her pain out, so she'd have the strength to do it all over again.

Chang sat up in the bed, startled. Her eyes widened in a look of disbelief as she saw a young, blonde, American walking toward her. Jamie put her finger to her lips imploring her to keep silent.

Jamie sat on the side of the bed next to her and said in Thai, "I have come to help you get out of here. We have to hurry."

No response. The girl just sat there with a dazed look on her face.

The girl might not go with her. As horrible as her plight was, her family needed the money, and Chang was their major source of income.

Jamie opened her backpack and pulled out some clothes and a pair of sneakers.

"Here, put these on," she said with a sense of urgency in her voice.

"I can't go," Chang said meekly in English.

"I'm not leaving here without you," Jamie said strongly, surprised but glad she spoke her language. "Trust me. I can help you."

"They'll kill my family," the girl said with a little more resolve.

A lie. They always threatened to kill the girl's family, but they wouldn't. Harming their supply chain wasn't good for business. The other parents might not be so quick to sell their girls if they thought there might be potential danger down the road.

An idle threat, but the girls didn't know that, and often refused to leave, or worse, they did leave and returned after a few days. If they came back, they were severely beaten, and some were even killed; made an example of for the other girls.

Very few girls escaped on their own. Where would they go? They had no money and couldn't go back to their families. The authorities wouldn't help them. Most just stuck it out until they were so damaged the men didn't want them anymore and preferred fresher meat. That usually happened around their twenty-fifth birthday. Chang would have ten more years before her nightmare would be over.

I can't leave here without her.

"They won't hurt your family," Jamie said. "I promise. You have to trust me. I can help you, and I can help them."

"I can't," Chang said. "My family needs me."

Her eyes darted back and forth, and she kept looking at the door. Jamie felt the same angst. Someone could come at any time.

"I can get you out of here," Jamie said a little more forcefully. "I took a great risk to help you. You don't have to stay."

Chang laid back down in the bed and curled into a ball. Jamie thought about making her go, which she could easily do, but if Chang screamed and caused a commotion, they'd both be in grave danger.

This wasn't the first time a girl refused to go and wouldn't be the last. She needed to cut her losses and get out of there while she still could. Jamie touched Chang's hand and squeezed it. A slight consolation but maybe one she'd remember.

She put the clothes and sneakers back into her backpack and went to the door where she cracked it slightly. Convinced the coast was clear, she slipped out the door and down the hall the opposite direction the man had gone.

A back entrance opened into a dark alley. Always locked, Jamie had easily picked the lock and entered the building through the same door about an hour before. She had left it unlocked for a quick get-away.

As she reached for the door, she heard a noise. Already on edge, Jamie turned around ready to strike.

Chang!

She was in the hallway coming toward Jamie.

"Can I still go with you?" she whispered.

Jamie gave her a quick hug and said, "Of course you can. Put these clothes on."

She took everything back out of the backpack. Chang stood there in only a tee-shirt. The clothes would fit perfectly. Most of the girls were generally the same size, and Jamie had this process down to a science, including what they would wear to be as inconspicuous as possible on the outside.

The pants were black, one-size-fits-all leggings, and the shirt was a black pullover that stretched to fit any sized girl. The shoes were slip on, and ended up being too big for Chang but would have to do.

They snuck out the door undetected and into the alley. Not out of danger but out of the building. The dark alley was a blessing. Jamie had left an older model motor scooter around the back of the building behind a garbage dumpster. She climbed onto the scooter, helped Chang get on behind her, and told her to hang on.

Jamie didn't bring helmets. They could slow down a getaway. She waited until the girl was securely on before starting the motor bike. Chang wrapped her arms tightly around Jamie's waist.

The noise would likely draw attention, and Jamie wanted to get out of there as quickly as possible. She prayed it would start. It did. An older model, it had seen better days but at least it worked.

She revved the engine and took off. The bike wasn't fast but quick enough to get them out of there before anyone could react. The perfect getaway vehicle. Thousands of them were on the road, and it also allowed for maximum maneuverability. Jamie could steer it through a traffic jam, or even drive it on the sidewalk if they really needed to get away from someone chasing them.

Jamie looked in her side mirror. Her heart was beating in her ears. She half expected to see someone with a gun pointed at them.

She took in a deep breath once she was satisfied no one was there or following them.

She'd already planned out the route and had made several practice runs. Meticulous planning had saved her skin on more than one occasion. One left, then a right, and then two lefts when the roads ended. After the last left, she went one mile where a small SUV was parked on the side of the road.

They quickly jumped off the scooter, and Jamie rushed Chang into the back of the waiting SUV.

The young girl looked up at Jamie with tears in her eyes. She mouthed the words, "Thank you" as Jamie closed the door, banged on the roof signifying all clear to go.

As the SUV sped away, Jamie wished they were all that easy.

2

Somewhere in the Caribbean

Jamie sat by the swimming pool on the upper deck of a massive cruise ship, with headphones covering her ears. A large, thick hardback book rested open on her lap, and a refreshing nonalcoholic drink was in her hand. While enjoying the sunshine, she was oblivious to everything else around her.

The headphones weren't playing music—they were for show so no one would try to talk to her. Twenty-five years old, this was her first cruise, and she'd already decided it would be her last.

An occasional look out at the pristine Caribbean Sea provided a gorgeous view of the sun glistening brightly off the turquoise, almost green, silky, smooth water. Jamie barely noticed. The sea was boring to her. The water looked the same every time she bothered to look that way. Nothing exciting about it, at least compared to her last three months in Thailand.

The horrific memories and images were still seared in her mind. Of course, that was the purpose of the cruise. To relax and be bored for a while after living on the cutting edge of danger almost daily for three straight months.

Yet, she couldn't help but think about the girls who were going through unspeakable pain at that very moment while she sat in the sun enjoying the life of luxury. The guilty feelings overwhelmed her. That's why she refused to allow herself to enjoy it.

This would be one of the few times she had disobeyed the orders of Brad, her CIA handler. He'd given her strict instructions to get away for some R & R and not to think about anything but men, sun, and fun.

Jamie admitted to herself that she needed the break. She was in a beautiful, exotic location, surrounded by hundreds of people laughing and having fun, and she was thinking about the girls in Thailand and what they were going through.

She also had trouble sleeping at night. More evidence the job was getting the best of her.

Jamie was a CIA officer. A spy really, trained in special operations. Tasked with rescuing girls from sex trafficking. Waging a war against some of the most ruthless tyrants in the world. She was sent to Thailand to work with a Christian organization called *Save The Girls*. Jamie freed the girls, then handed them off to the organization who provided the victims with food and shelter and helped reintegrate them into society. Preferably in another country.

She remembered every girl rescued and recorded it in a journal. She had successfully rescued more than one hundred twenty girls in the three months. Considered by her supervisors a remarkable achievement considering the constant danger.

A twinge of disappointment shot through her heart like a dagger. She was angry it hadn't been more and that she had to leave the theater and put her mission on hold. Couldn't be helped. After a while, the sex traffickers were on the lookout for a blonde, American woman infiltrating their operations and stealing their girls. The danger became too great, and Jamie needed a break anyway.

Even someone as strong as her couldn't take the stress indefinitely.

She'd been ordered on a vacation and told to let her hair down and have some fun. Fun was not something that came easily for her. She'd been there for three days, and while her long, blonde hair was down, she couldn't stop thinking about the girls.

Jamie's cell phone unexpectedly lit up startling her.

Only four people in the world knew the number. Her best friend Emily back in Arlington, Virginia, where she lived. Brad. Curly, the man who had spent months training her on every aspect of special operations. And a cute guy she'd given the number to the night before at dinner.

She stared at the phone, hardly believing what she was seeing.

The cute guy.

What! Why is he calling me?

Her heart was suddenly racing. Like it did when someone had a gun pointed at her. Her mind started processing all the possibilities.

The night before, Alex had nervously sauntered up to her table and asked if he could join her. Before she could say no, he sat down and began talking. Initially, she was taken aback. Thought it rude. After it was over and she was back in her room, she admitted to herself that she'd had a good time.

Even told him as much when she gave him her number after he asked for it.

Now she regretted it. Curly's words resonated in the back of her mind. *No emotional entanglements. They will get you killed.*

When she shook Alex's hand after dinner and said goodbye, she had hoped that was the end of it, and that he wouldn't call.

Dang it!

Why had she given him her number? Why had she put his name in her phone as a contact? Why didn't she block the number? So many questions. So little time to answer them all.

Jamie made a snap decision to let the call go to voicemail. The wisest thing to do.

Her mind and heart were not in sync.

"Hello, this is Jamie," she said instead, answering the phone impulsively.

Why did I do that?

"Hey, Jamie. It's Alex. You know from last night . . . Are you alone?"

"No, I'm not alone," Jamie answered, with a slight laugh. "I'm here at the pool with about four hundred fifty other people."

Alex stammered slightly. "What I meant to say is . . . if you aren't doing anything, maybe I could come and join you for a few minutes."

No. Absolutely not. I need to cut this off now.

"Sure. I'm not doing anything. Come on over."

The words came out of her mouth like a burp. Before she could stop them.

"Great. I'll see you soon."

The line went dead.

Jamie sat there stunned at her lack of self-control. She couldn't stand it when others let emotions trump their good sense. Now, she'd done the same thing and was upset with herself. She'd let her feelings overtake her will.

A weakness she didn't realize she had. Alex gave her attention, which was flattering, but she shouldn't fall for it. With her life, how could she possibly have a boyfriend, much less get married and have kids?

Relax, Jamie. He's not coming to ask you to marry him. He just wants to hang out.

Within two minutes, she spotted him across the pool walking her way. Her skeptical CIA investigative mind kicked into action. She began processing information like a supercomputer.

How did he get there so fast?

He'd probably been standing somewhere in the pool area, watching her, getting up the courage to call.

Was he stalking her?

How else could he have gotten all the way across the large cruise ship in two minutes?

Come to think of it, he hadn't even asked which pool she was at. The ship had three of them. He already knew she was at this one.

Jamie saw right through the ruse.

Her training caused her senses to heighten. Something instinctive inside of her. That's what she did for a living. Investigations. Spying. She was highly trained to spot inconsistencies. To notice everything. It's what made her a great operative. The best in the business according to Curly and her handler.

I shouldn't trust him.

Stop it! You're not a spy on a mission. You're a tourist trying to have fun.

She let out a huge sigh and scolded herself for being paranoid.

I do need a break.

It wouldn't go away easily. Curly taught her to constantly be on the alert for any danger. Even if she wasn't on a mission. Her mind was always analyzing every situation. At dinner last night, she sat with her back against the wall. Something she was trained to do so she could see the whole room. So, no one could sneak up on her.

Why was that necessary on a cruise ship? The most danger she was in was possibly getting a bad sunburn.

Alex was getting closer. Her shoulders tensed.

Try to relax. He's not a stalker.

She took a deep breath, closed her book, and put a smile on her face.

That's better.

Then the angst returned when she remembered the uneasy feelings she had struggled with the night before.

His name was Alex P. Keaton which seemed strange to her. He explained that his parents loved the 1980's sitcom, *Family Ties*. Jamie vaguely remembered watching a few reruns of the show on TV.

Alex's mom and dad had always wanted to name their son Alex P., so when his mom became pregnant and they learned they were having a boy, the hope was that he would turn out just like the character on television.

The Alex approaching her was nothing like the one on the show. He was approximately six foot four, two-hundred-plus pounds, movie-star handsome, and athletic. The *Family Ties* Alex P. Keaton was five foot four, one-hundred-twenty-two pounds. He was a staunch conservative. She didn't know this Alex's political views.

The whole story seemed odd at the time. Something about it didn't ring true. No time to analyze it now. Being tall and athletic, Alex crossed the pool area with large strides. He sat down at the end of her lounge chair.

A mistake.

Jamie didn't like her private space invaded and started to say something but decided to give him a pass since all the chairs next to them were taken.

Alex ran his hand through his styled hair, and she couldn't help but notice the muscular definition of his biceps. He had brown eyes, thin lips, with two dimples bookending them. Broad shoulders. His legs were as muscular as his arms.

"You look fantastic," Alex said, interrupting her thoughts while trying not to be too obvious as he looked her up and down.

She hoped he hadn't noticed that she was staring at his buff body as well.

Jamie looked away, embarrassed. She was tall and thin, muscular in a feminine sort of way. She was wearing an all-black one-piece bathing suit. Sexy, but she wanted to send the message, "I don't have to show you everything in order for you to notice me."

Not that Jamie wanted to be noticed. CIA operatives wanted to be unremarkable. To blend into the environment. Jamie almost wasn't hired for that reason. Beauty was a liability in the field. Her testing and evaluation scores were off the charts, so she was hired anyway.

Curly trained Jamie how to downplay her looks and to use them to her advantage when necessary. On vacation, Jamie wasn't too worried about that. All she wanted was to be left alone. Not noticed at all. Hence the modest bathing suit.

The one piece also hid a scar on her left side from a bullet that had grazed her on one of her missions.

Alex smiled. He was gorgeous. Jamie wondered what their kids might look like.

Quit thinking about kids and marriage. You don't have a future with this guy.

She wanted to say something quickly, to get those thoughts out of her mind.

"I see you have your Superman shirt on," she said with a grin.

Alex was in a blue swimsuit—long, stopping just below his knees— with a white tank top, a large red *S* on the front.

Alex laughed while pulling the shirt out from his chest looking down at it. "No, that's Stanford University. That's where I got my undergraduate degree."

Jamie wanted to say something else but couldn't think of anything. An awkward silence followed. On a mission, she never had trouble getting into a role and talking to people. This seemed different. Like a date. Real life with real feelings. With her job, she didn't have many opportunities to date. It had been a long time since she'd even been on one.

What was his excuse? He probably had girls falling all over him.

Alex finally broke the silence. "What ya reading?"

Jamie held up the book. " *The History of the Breakup of the Soviet Union,*" she said, embarrassed.

Alex laughed.

Belarus was another hotbed for sex trafficking, and Jamie wanted to learn all she could about the area. Brad had said she might be going there.

Right as Alex called, she'd been reading about the Grand Duchy Charter of 1588 where women gained protections under the law. One of the facts she found fascinating about recent social norms was that women were required in most homes to set the table. It's considered degrading for men to perform the task.

A small thing, but a reflection of a bigger problem in her mind. Those archaic rules created an environment conducive for exploitation and human trafficking of women and girls. It made her want to go there.

I know. I'm on vacation. I'm not supposed to be thinking about those things.

Alex looked at the book and had a curious grin on his face. She knew what he was thinking.

"Just a little light reading," she said, responding to his obvious amusement at her choice of reading material on a cruise ship.

"I'm reading *War and Peace* back in my room," Alex said. "I should've brought it so we could read together."

Jamie stared in silence.

"I'm joking," Alex said, but Jamie still didn't get it.

"Actually, I'm not any better," he continued when it was clear she wasn't going to laugh. "I'm studying for the law exam, and I brought some of my books. I thought it would be fun to come on the cruise and get a break from school, but I can't get away from it."

"I know what you mean."

Another awkward silence.

Alex grabbed Jamie's book, sat it down next to her chair, and said, "Let's go get in the pool."

Jamie disliked it when someone touched her stuff, but she held her tongue. She was acting too uptight. He was going to think she was a crazy person.

Alex pulled off his college shirt, revealing his sculpted pecs and six pack stomach. He jumped right in the pool, forming a cannonball and splashing a lot of the unsuspecting patrons lounging nearby. Several gave him dirty looks. One woman even said something rude. He couldn't have heard it because he was underwater, but Jamie heard it clearly.

Come on people, lighten up. We're on vacation.

And with that thought, Jamie did loosen up.

She took the headphones, hid them and her book under a towel, and walked over to the edge of the pool. Slowly, she stuck her foot in the water, letting herself get acclimated. She was one of those who got in the pool hesitantly, first testing the waters and then easing herself in when she was ready. She was determined to do that in their relationship as well. Go slowly.

She was amazed how fast it moved once she let her guard down.

Alex and Jamie swam around like kids splashing each other. They grabbed a volleyball and hit it back and forth. With each laugh, Jamie could feel the tension leaving her body. The physical exertion wasn't with purpose like when she was working out. This was fun, exhilarating, and exciting.

Things were going really well until Alex came up from behind and tried to dunk her. She instinctively turned toward him with her fist closed, stopping herself before she smashed it below the bridge of his nose.

He looked shocked and quickly backed off and said, "I'm sorry."

Jamie composed herself and said, "No. It was my fault. I'm sorry. I don't like being snuck up on."

Jamie splashed him in the face to ease the tension.

He splashed her back.

She swam over to him, jumped out of the water, and put her hands on his head, easily dunking him. When he came up, they were both laughing. He put his arms around her, and she let him dunk her as well. She came out of the water and pushed her hair out of her face. They were very close to each other. For a moment, they were about to kiss, but Jamie turned away.

After several more minutes, they went back to the lounge chairs, dried off, gathered their things, and went inside to find a quiet place to talk. A lobby just off the pool was fairly private. They sat in two of four chairs that surrounded a wooden coffee table.

Alex asked the question Jamie knew was coming but dreaded.

"What do you do for a living?" he asked.

So, let the lies begin.

3

"What do you do for a living? Alex had asked.

"I work in women's healthcare," Jamie responded with a lie.

Lying was second nature to her. Every mission was a big lie from start to finish. Called a cover story. Her cover was always different. Sometimes she was a computer programmer. One time she was an accountant. Other times, a college student. Once she had to play a married couple with another operative. She always saw it as playing a role, like an actress in a movie.

It never bothered her, until now. This wasn't a movie. Or a mission. This was real life, and she liked Alex. She hated having to lie to him.

Curly always said that when you lie, try to keep it as close to the truth as possible. Women's healthcare was all she could think of on the spot. She was in women's healthcare. Sort of.

"Are you, like, a doctor?" Alex asked, with an inquisitive look.

"No. I'm a consultant." Jamie nervously changed positions in the chair.

A consultant in women's healthcare was sort of the truth. Jamie rationalized it to herself so she could make it sound believable.

What difference does it make?

A lie discovered in the field could mean death. What was happening with Alex was important to her, but in the end, it didn't matter if he knew she was lying as long as he didn't know the real truth.

It still bothered her. Deep down, she didn't feel good about this conversation.

"How did you get into that line of work?" Alex sat across from her with his feet up on the wooden table.

"I was recruited right out of college," Jamie said. "A booth was set up at a job fair at my school. I signed up on the spot."

The truth. Sort of. Actually, a Senator, a friend of her father, had pulled some strings to get her an interview. She saw the booth at school, and it reminded her to call him.

While in college, she had taken out a terrorist who was about to fire a missile at a spacecraft that would've killed tens of thousands of people. Including her father who was an astronaut on that spacecraft.

A long and complicated story, she was not about to bring up now.

The Senator had encouraged her to sign up with the CIA or Homeland Security when she graduated from college. He offered to help. All she had to do was call him. Which she did. She had an interview within a week.

"Where do you work?" Alex asked.

What's with the interrogation?

"I work overseas a lot," Jamie said, a fake company name not coming right to mind.

A good answer in case they did start dating. She'd be out of touch for weeks or months at a time. Easily explained by her job that took her out of the country. Jamie already had some excuses ready in case this developed into a relationship.

There's no cell phone service here.

We're in a different time zone.

I got delayed.

I won't be back in the states for three months.

Why was she thinking about a relationship? She couldn't let this go beyond the cruise. Not even beyond this conversation.

While the CIA didn't forbid romantic relationships or marriage, it wasn't encouraged. Curly downright told her she'd be a fool for ever getting involved with someone. His words echoed in her head.

If you want a two-story house with a white picket fence and a bunch of rug rats running around, choose a different profession.

Curly was not a subtle guy. He didn't mince words. In fact, many of his words were very colorful. Of the four-letter variety. Jamie filtered those words from the remembered conversations.

She looked around the lobby, wondering if she could come up with an excuse to leave but something else Curly had said was thundering around in her head causing her to pause.

Have all the sex you want; just make sure it doesn't mean anything.

Jamie looked away so Alex wouldn't see her blushing. She definitely wasn't going to have sex with him. She hoped that wasn't his intention. Fortunately, Alex's next question was the jolt she needed to get rid of those thoughts.

"What led you to want to work in women's healthcare?"

The truth. *I killed a man. Stole his sex slave right out from under him and was immediately hooked.*

She bit her tongue to stop herself from saying the reason why she had volunteered to help in the sex trafficking division of the CIA. Jamie was sent to Columbia to take out a drug lord who'd been smuggling cocaine into the United States. Jamie had to sneak into his home, past a dozen men with machine guns, find his room, kill him, and then get out undetected.

Things were going smoothly. The drug lord was dead, and Jamie was about to leave when she heard a noise in the other room. The noise was coming from a seventeen-year-old girl half-naked and beaten because she hadn't performed up to the man's expectations. She'd been made his sex slave, and Jamie couldn't just leave her there.

Jamie had a difficult enough time to get out of there by herself. More complicated with the girl. They got out, but not without a gun fight. Jamie was grazed by a bullet. The reason for the scar. They both barely escaped alive. From that moment on, she knew she wanted to spend the rest of her life helping girls get out of the sex trade.

"I went to University of Virginia in Charlottesville and got a degree in kinesiology," Jamie said, truthfully. "I didn't want to be a doctor. Kinesiology is the study of motion."

Alex nodded as if he already knew that fact. The look on his face told Jamie he was genuinely interested and listening intently.

"I've always loved motion and adventure," she continued with more excitement in her voice. "Bungee jumping. Racing bikes. Paragliding. I've always been a risk taker. Used to drive my mom crazy."

She felt a twinge of hurt. Her mom was dead, and she never knew her father. How was she going to navigate through that conversation if Alex asked about her parents?

Her father was never in her life. Except for about twenty minutes. For the first eighteen years of her life, she thought her father was dead. That's what her mother had told her. Her mother died of cancer when Jamie was eighteen. A year later, she learned she did have a father.

Unfortunately, she learned the truth too late. The day he left on a one-way mission to space.

She tried not to wince thinking about the losses. If Alex noticed, he didn't say anything.

Jamie was close to giving him insight into her soul. At least it felt that way. Fortunately, he didn't ask about her parents. The next few questions were superficial. She didn't directly answer the question he asked, but she kept the conversation moving, giving him only the information she wanted him to know.

She used every pause to turn the questioning back on him.

"How about you? What did you study at Stanford? I'm assuming law of some kind."

"Criminal justice. My dad's a lawyer. He's always wanted me to take over his firm when he retires. I'm not sure that's what I want to do with my life." Alex spent the next ten minutes telling her all about his childhood, school, and now graduate school.

Jamie suddenly hated her secret life. Not the work but the secrecy. Alex was sharing the details of his life, and all she could do was tell him a made-up version of her life. She felt like a fraud.

"Do you like what you do?" he asked, turning the focus back on her.

A ping pong match of questioning had broken out between them.

"I love it," she said emphatically. The most truthful thing she'd said since the conversation began. She loved what she did for the girls. Even loved the risk. The thrill. The danger.

After the situation in Columbia, she volunteered and transferred to a section of the CIA that focused on sex trafficking—one of the most dangerous assignments in all the CIA for a female operative. In order to be successful she had to infiltrate some of the seediest of all the underworld. The girls were their capital, and the traffickers protected their investments with whatever means necessary.

"My job is important. I help a lot of women. And young girls."

That was an understatement.

The biggest challenge was infiltrating the sex trafficking groups. Standard procedures for most undercover agents in the CIA was to make contact with a group, earn their trust, and become part of the inner circle. That strategy wasn't an option in the area of sex trafficking. A female operative couldn't become a part of the group because she would have to become a sex slave and endure everything the girls went through.

That was against CIA policy. They had strict rules of engagement. Women weren't allowed to work as prostitutes, and men weren't allowed to have sex with the trafficked women, even if it did allow them into the inner circle.

They had to look for more creative ways to bring down the groups. They had to get the girls out by essentially kidnapping them or making contact somehow and convincing them to leave voluntarily. Women were more effective with the girls than men for obvious reasons, and Jamie was more effective than anyone else had ever been.

Her unique skills allowed her to go into the depths of these operations undetected where no one else could go and get the girls out without being spotted or captured, and successfully fight her way out if she was.

She wanted to explain her job to Alex but couldn't. She resisted the urge to tell him everything.

Why did she feel so comfortable talking to him? Even if what she was saying was a lie. She felt like they were getting close. Getting to know each other. Of course, he wasn't getting to know her at all. Just what she wanted him to know.

It's complicated.

They talked about it in training. Some operatives had been married for thirty years and their spouses still didn't know what they really did for a living. Curly didn't recommend it.

"My job has its challenges like any other," she responded, "but I love everything about it. I know you don't feel the same way about law, but is there anything you are passionate about like that?"

"I'm pretty good with computers."

Jamie didn't know much about computers and didn't know what to ask. Alex changed the subject before she could think of anything.

"I played football at Stanford. I love it with a passion. Do you like football?" he asked.

Jamie noticed that Alex always finished his sentences by asking her a question. Turning the conversation back toward her.

"Sure," Jamie said hesitantly. She hadn't watched a game in years. She hadn't spent three hours in front of any television watching anything for as long as she could remember.

"What position did you play?" she asked, realizing she was doing the same thing.

Alex explained that he was the starting quarterback for the Stanford Cardinals football team who lost to Alabama in the national championship game a few years before. They didn't lose because of him. The defense gave up a last-second touchdown. He would've been the game's Most Valuable Player had they won. Now he was just a footnote—the losing quarterback of another Alabama championship.

"Did you watch the game?" he asked.

She shook her head.

Alex went on to explain that he was drafted in the first round by the San Francisco Forty-Niners, but hurt his knee in training camp, so his NFL career was short-lived. She had noticed the scar.

Jamie could see a hint of sadness in his eyes. A lost dream.

"When my football career was over, I enrolled as a law student at Berkeley since I already lived in the Bay Area."

Hmm. Berkeley. Probably not conservative politically. Not like the Alex on the television show.

"I don't really fit in there," Alex quickly added. "Not with their crazy radical views."

It's as if he was reading her mind.

"You look like an athlete," Alex said.

"I'm into martial arts," she blurted out, immediately regretting giving out that much information. She was now walking a fine line between the lies and revealing her true occupation. She had to be careful.

Into martial arts was an understatement. She knew how to kill a man with her bare hands in a hundred different ways.

Curly was the best martial arts trainer in the world by most measures. She never learned why he was called Curly since he didn't have a single hair on his head and hadn't had any for more than twenty years. She once jokingly said it was because he reminded people of Curly, one of The Three Stooges. He wasn't amused, and Jamie paid a price for the joke that day as he worked her so hard, she literally had to crawl into bed that night.

"What kind of martial arts? Should I be worried?" he asked jokingly.

"You should be worried," she said.

Curly taught Jamie skills such as hand-to-hand combat, martial arts, and Krav Maga which was the Israeli form of self-defense. She was put in every conceivable situation and taught how to fight her way out of it. He trained her on every weapon including guns, knives, swords, machetes, daggers, brass knuckles, batons, and tasers among other things.

She was taught how to withstand torture without disclosing any information, pass a lie detector test, endure waterboarding, and how to survive without food, water, and sleep for long periods of time.

Curly said she was the best recruit he'd ever trained. After a few months on the job, she was considered the most lethal female assassin on the planet. There may be one or two men who were better, but they hadn't proven it.

Jamie had proven her credentials. She was sent on the most dangerous assignments and had always managed to get out of each of them mostly unscathed.

"I'd better keep my hands to myself then," he said with a sly smile.

"Yes, you should."

Jamie immediately regretted the threatening tone.

"Do you want to have dinner with me tonight?" Alex asked, changing the subject again.

She was relieved he hadn't pressed the subject more but was suddenly nervous because he clearly wanted to take the relationship further. If she said no, that would effectively cut off the relationship, and he would probably get the hint and leave her alone. If she said yes, she might start something she wasn't sure she could finish.

He seemed like a nice guy. She didn't want to break his heart. They hadn't even started talking about past relationships. Who knew where that conversation might lead? What would he think when she told him she was a Christian and saving herself for marriage?

What were his intentions?

"I'd love to have dinner with you," she said, not giving the argument in her head a chance to come to a final conclusion.

They had dinner and every other meal together for the rest of the cruise. Jamie had gone back to her own room at night, though. Well, except for the one night when she fell asleep on his couch while watching a movie. She woke up the next morning covered with a blanket.

That was sweet and thoughtful. She couldn't remember the last time she had slept so soundly as she did that night, with no nightmares of girls in bondage and no people shooting at her.

In fact, that whole week she felt like a real person and not an international woman of mystery. It felt good. His law books and her *The History of the Breakup of the Soviet Union* were not picked up again for the rest of the cruise.

4

Jamie hadn't heard from either of the two people she expected a call from—Brad and Alex.

Brad not calling wasn't totally unexpected. Several weeks between missions wasn't unusual. They'd let her know when they had something for her. In fact, it was better he hadn't called. Jamie needed the three weeks to regain her edge.

She'd just finished a fast-paced, five-mile run and was starting to feel more like herself. She was still burning off the voluminous amount of food she ate at the buffet on the cruise ship. After meeting Alex, she had lost even more of her edge emotionally when she allowed herself to get too close to him.

Why hasn't he called?

He's probably just busy.

A debate raged in her head. The internal conversation had an angry tone to it. Part of her was upset. The less emotional side was searching for a logical explanation.

Alex said he was studying for the bar exam. While she didn't know everything involved in preparing for the exam, she imagined it would consume most of his time and energy. She had many all-nighters in college, cramming for a test, gulping down cups of coffee to stay awake.

Casual relationships were the last thing on her mind when she was trying to pass a test.

That had to be it. He was busy.

How long did it take to make a phone call? Send a text message? Ten seconds!

He didn't want to talk to her, or he would have called by now.

Oh well. It's for the best.

She got up from the bar stool in the kitchen and walked over to the couch intending to remove his contact information from her phone. Instead, she picked up the phone and started to dial his number and then abruptly stopped.

What are you doing? Jamie Austen, you have lost your mind!

She sat the phone down on the coffee table. Alex had to make the first move. She was old-fashioned that way. She wasn't going to chase after a guy. Especially one she had just met and who was on the other side of the country.

She had never made the first move with a guy in her life, and she wasn't about to start now. If he didn't want to talk to her then it was his loss. She needed to let it go. This was what Curly meant by emotional entanglements. He had told her in no uncertain terms that pining over a boyfriend on a mission was a distraction that could get her killed.

It made sense now. The whole situation was messing with her mind, and she wasn't even in harm's way. She needed to let it go. Not care so much. If he called, he called. She'd end it for good when he did.

The phone rang. Jamie jumped. She lunged for the coffee table and grabbed the phone.

Is it Alex?

Her heart sank a couple of notches in her chest when she realized that Emily, her best friend, was calling.

"Has he called yet?" she asked excitedly, not even bothering to say hello when Jamie answered the phone.

"No," Jamie said, followed by a deep sigh.

Emily was well aware of the whirlwind romance. She had about fallen out of her chair when Jamie told her the story. Emily had been trying to find a man for Jamie since they met. A year after Jamie graduated from college.

She was probably more emotionally invested in Alex calling than Jamie was.

"His loss," Emily said, with exasperation.

"He obviously didn't like me that much."

"Not possible. You're the best."

"Thanks. He must not think so."

Jamie sat down on the couch and crossed her legs. Trying to figure things out. The whole week on the cruise had played out in her mind several times like a movie. More like a broken record stuck on one song.

The whole thing was her fault. She had played hard to get. A little aloof. Kept her distance. It seemed like the right thing to do. She thought guys liked the pursuit.

"You should move on," Emily said. "There are more fish in the sea."

"I already have."

Maybe if she said the words out loud, then she'd believe them.

"I don't think you should even take the call even when he does call you. That'd serve him right."

"What if something happened to him?" Jamie asked. "He could have a good reason for not calling. Maybe his grandmother died or something horrible like that."

"Maybe he's married!" Emily said. "He can't call because he's back home with his wife and kids."

"Why would he go on a cruise without his wife and kids? That doesn't make any sense."

"I don't know. You hear all the time about men with two wives and two families."

Emily let out a gasp.

"What?"

"I saw a miniseries the other day where a woman was married to a man who said he was a CIA agent. He had five wives. A perfect cover for a secret life. None of the wives knew about each other until he died. Maybe Alex is a CIA agent married with two kids!"

Jamie's heart skipped a beat when Emily mentioned the CIA. The conversation was starting to hit too close to home. She was the one lying. She was the CIA operative. They weren't called agents. Emily wouldn't know that.

Emily didn't know she was in the CIA either. Couldn't know. She needed to change the subject.

"I don't think he has a wife, and I know he doesn't work for the CIA," Jamie retorted. "He's just a jerk. A pretty boy football star who's used to getting any girl he wants. Well, he couldn't have me, so he's moved on to bigger and better things."

The whole saving-herself-for-marriage-thing probably turned him off.

My body, my choice.

"There are no bigger and better things than you," Emily said kindly.

"Thanks, girlfriend. You're a good friend. You're right. It's time for me to move on."

"Good idea. Take your pictures of him and burn them."

There were no pictures. As an operative, Jamie was instructed to make sure no strangers ever took pictures of her. While on the cruise ship a lady had come up to them with a camera. She worked for the cruise line and offered to take their picture.

Jamie was glad Alex strongly objected as well. Made it easier for her. She didn't have to explain why she was adamant about not having her picture taken.

"I think I'll just block his number," Jamie said.

"Good idea. Forget about him. He's not worth the mental energy. I gotta go," Emily said suddenly.

She was probably at work.

Jamie hung up the phone and scrolled through her contacts, debating whether or not to block his number. She hesitated. She stood and walked back to the kitchen, thinking. Finally, she put the phone down on the counter and walked away.

She didn't want to block his number in case he did call. If he didn't have a good excuse, she could give him a piece of her mind and block him then. After having the satisfaction of hanging up on him.

A sudden sadness came over her. A loss. A pain in her heart. Tears formed in her eyes, but she fought them back. As hard as she had tried not to develop feelings for him, she clearly had.

Then the anger returned. It's how she survived in the field. Curly warned her in training that she'd see unspeakable things that would break her heart. He said to channel those emotions into anger.

That's what she needed to do now. Her fists were balled. The best thing to do was get back in the field and hit someone. A bad guy. A good remedy for a broken heart.

All of those thoughts were interrupted by the ping of her phone, notifying her she had a text message.

Alex!

She rushed across the room in anticipation. The message was from Brad.

"My office. 4:00 sharp."

So that was that.

Her vacation was over and so was her little fling or whatever it was called. If it didn't mean anything to Alex, it wasn't going to mean anything to her either.

As Curly said, *have all the sex you want, make sure it doesn't mean anything.* There was no sex, and Jamie decided that it didn't mean anything either.

Fun while it lasted.

Time to go to work.

***

CIA Headquarters,
Langley, Virginia

Jamie walked into the reception area of Brad's office at fifteen minutes to four. She always gave herself extra time, because the fastest way to get on his bad side was to be late. The second fastest way was to not follow his instructions in the field. Jamie often did the second, so she made sure to never do the first.

Considered a bit of a "loose cannon," Jamie liked to think she was improvising based on what was happening on the ground. Going with her gut. Curly said to always trust her instincts over those of the suits. They weren't the ones getting shot at.

He also said it was better to ask for forgiveness than permission. So far, Jamie had never had to ask for forgiveness. Things had always turned out for the best and her instincts had mostly been right.

Like when she rescued the girl in Columbia. Totally off mission when she brought the girl back with her. Brad was furious until he learned the girl was a treasure trove of information. Being a sex slave, she'd overheard all kinds of conversations that turned into actionable intelligence.

Brad said she was lucky; Curly said it was a good call. Brad said never do it again; Curly said to keep up the good work.

Brad's secretary, Connie, had the phone to her ear. She held up her hand signifying to Jamie she'd be right with her. In less than a minute, Connie hung up the phone and said, "Hello, Jamie. Welcome back. Did you have a good time on your vacation?"

"I did," Jamie replied.

Or at least I thought I did.

An image of Alex in his swimsuit popped into her mind. She tamped it down.

"Brad is in a briefing room," Connie said, interrupting that thought. "The meeting has already started."

Jamie looked at the clock on the wall. Did she get the time wrong?

"He said to meet him here at his office at four. I'm early."

"Right. Director Coldclaw is attending the meeting, so they moved it to a secure room. They are in room 4B. You can go on down."

"What's so important that the Director has to be there?"

Connie shrugged her shoulders.

"I'll know soon enough," Jamie said, turned and walked out of the office after a friendly wave.

In the hallway, Jamie took a right turn and went down a long hallway and made another right stopping in the ladies' room. A quick check of the cell phone confirmed Jamie had gotten the time right and that it needed to be turned to silent.

She couldn't help but notice there were no messages from Alex.

Quickly putting that thought out of her mind, she began an inspection in the mirror immediately regretting she was dressed so casually. She ran her hands through her hair thinking she needed more makeup. Makeup was not something she carried around in her small purse, so the little she had on would have to do.

While she looked good in her black jeans and a green chiffon V-neck blouse with long sleeves, rolled up just above her elbows, the Director of the CIA was going to be in the meeting. Brad would be in a suit and tie. Business casual was fine for an operative attending a meeting with the Director, but Jamie was straddling the line between casual and business casual.

Brad never cared what she wore when she met with him. Shorts, sneakers, and a tee shirt were fine with him. Jamie was only this dressed up because she thought she might go out to dinner afterwards. Emily had invited her to go out. Maybe to a happy hour. To meet some men.

Her way of getting back at Alex, Emily had said.

At the moment, Alex was the least of her worries. This was a high-level meeting. She needed to pull things together right away. Brad must not have known the Director would be there or he would've warned her.

The first time she met the Director she was dressed even less appropriately. Having just come from a long workout at the fitness facility at Langley. Hadn't even bothered to take a shower. Brad was walking with the Director in the hallway and flagged her down. So she could meet Jamie.

Jamie had been furious. Only one chance to make a first impression.

Two times in a row had her concerned that she wasn't making a good impression at all. To make matters worse, she knew that Amy Coldclaw would be dressed to the hilt.

The Director had only been on the job for six months and was confirmed by one vote in the Senate after a contentious confirmation process. Jamie admired her. She'd started at the CIA right out of college and had made it all the way to the top by being the toughest and smartest person in the room most of the time.

A tough woman in a department dominated by men. Like Jamie or at least what she aspired to be. Sort of. Director Coldclaw was a top-notch analyst. Never worked in the field. To Jamie's knowledge, Director Coldclaw had never been shot at.

That didn't mean she wasn't tough as nails. She exuded confidence in everything she did. Excellence was her driving force and was reflected in how she dressed.

Jamie wanted to exude that same image when she walked into the room today. That's why she stopped in the bathroom. To make sure she was in the right frame of mind. Not thinking about some pretty boy in California.

After a little pep talk, Jamie left the bathroom and walked toward room 4B with a purpose. Practicing the greeting in her head.

Good afternoon, Director Coldclaw. I'm pleased to see you again.

Handshake needed to be firm.

Jamie wished she had the Director's last name. Coldclaw was a perfect name for a "spook." The name Coldclaw struck fear in people. Jamie Austen sounded too much like Jane Austen, the author who

Jamie couldn't stand. She'd once read the book *Pride and Prejudice* and thought it a waste of time.

"Elizabeth Bennet was a fool to fall for Mr. Darcy," Jamie had concluded after forcing herself to finish it.

Then she remembered, *Who am I to talk? I was equally a fool to fall for Alex.*

She was at the door. Jamie quickly turned her thoughts back to the meeting. If the Director was there, it had to be something important, and she wanted to be on the top of her game.

She put on her most serious face, knocked politely, opened the door, and walked in. Six people were sitting around a conference table. The Director and her assistant, Brad and one of his analysts, and two people she didn't know.

No one even acknowledged she had entered the room. One of them was talking and giving a presentation at the front of the room so all eyes were in that direction.

Finally, Brad looked her way and simply nodded toward where he wanted her to sit.

The screen on the wall had a map of Belarus displayed on it. At that moment, Jamie wished she had finished *The Breakup of the Soviet Union* rather than wasting her time with Alex.

Why did everything remind her of Alex? When was that going to end?

5

Jamie took a seat at the back of the conference table. All eyes were on the man at the front of the room. He was in the process of giving a brief history of Belarus. It seemed like the meeting had just started.

"Belarus is a former territory of the Soviet Union," he said.

Of course, everyone in the room already knew that.

He gave a number of seemingly inconsequential facts. Population is 9.4 million people. Russia is the most commonly spoken language. Minsk is the capital.

Jamie knew that information before she joined the CIA. Learned even more detail in the book she was reading on the cruise.

Before I was so rudely interrupted and wasted a week of my life.

The man continued. "We recently learned that Alexander Lukashenko, the President of Belarus, is negotiating a secret deal with Russia to buy its natural gas when the new Russian pipeline is finished."

Jamie knew from the news that this was a major issue in the west. The undersea pipeline would carry natural gas from Russian fields to the Baltic coast. The pipeline was in direct competition with American natural gas production. The concern was that European companies would become dependent on the cheaper Soviet gas rather than what was called the "freedom gas."

"This is a problem for obvious reasons," he said.

Several around the room nodded in agreement. Jamie knew what those reasons were. He expounded on them.

"The Russian companies are filled with corruption and the fear is that the gas line will line the pockets of mafia types and might even get into the hands of terrorists."

Director Coldclaw spoke up.

"It would certainly make Russia stronger and broaden its financial influence, giving Kuzman more money to flow into his military apparatus. It ultimately makes Europe less safe, but some leaders are more concerned about short term savings than long term security."

Nitikin Kuzman was the Russian President.

While all this was interesting, Jamie had no idea what it had to do with her. Hopefully, he would get to that soon.

He did.

"As you know, Belarus has been a leader in fighting sex trafficking."

Jamie thought that statement was laughable. No leaders of any communist countries were serious about fighting sex trafficking.

At least he might be getting around to why she was there. She sat forward in her chair.

"The foreign minister of Belarus recently gave a speech at the United Nations documenting his country's success in fighting sex trafficking. A speech very well received."

Jamie had read the transcript of the speech. In reality, Belarus was barely making a dent, but they were doing more than most if the substance of the speech could be believed.

Director Coldclaw voiced what Jamie had been thinking.

"Even then, the US State Department's Office to Monitor and Combat Trafficking in Persons placed Belarus as a Tier 3 country," she said. "That means they aren't doing as much as they should be doing."

She looked back at Jamie and smiled. Jamie nodded politely.

"Tier 3 means that the government did not fully comply with the minimum standards and wasn't making significant efforts to do so," the Director added.

"Belarus is confusing in a way," the man continued. "While they pay a lot of lip service to cracking down on sex trafficking and they have certainly taken some steps to curtail it, many think it's just lip service, and that they aren't really serious about it. Prostitution is a major problem in that part of the world."

Jamie was one of those not impressed with the efforts of the Belarus government. As far as she was concerned, none of the countries did enough, including the United States. The world needed a lot more action and less talk from all of the countries of the world. The problem could be completely eradicated, at least in the free world, if everyone would join together and get serious about the problem.

The man still wasn't giving any clue as to what any of this had to do with Jamie. Was she going to Belarus or was this just a briefing?

Why was the Director there?

Finally, Jamie's impatience got the better of her.

"That's not new information," she said. "Prostitution has always been rampant in all of the eastern bloc countries."

If they weren't going to let Jamie know why she was there, then she would press the information on her own.

Brad frowned at her.

"That's true," the man at the front of the room responded. "But there's been a shift in focus. It used to be that the poorer women in the low-income regions of Belarus were recruited to serve as prostitutes in Minsk. They were mostly single, unemployed women between the ages of sixteen and thirty. While their lives weren't great, they weren't really forced into prostitution and were free to leave and go back home if they wanted. Some of them actually made good money and wanted to work there."

Jamie still considered that sex trafficking. Even if a woman was caught up in it voluntarily. They were still being exploited.

"What's the shift in focus, Forrest?" the Director asked. Jamie now knew the presenter's name.

Brad answered for him. "We recently uncovered intelligence that there's a trafficking pipeline that's originating in Belarus. By pipeline, we mean women are being recruited into the legitimate sex trade in Belarus and then transported as slaves to other countries."

"What other countries?" Director Coldclaw asked.

"Mainly Russia, but also Turkey and Poland."

Interesting.

Brad continued. "When gambling became illegal in Russia, Belarus opened several casinos in Minsk and the demand for prostitutes increased as Russians came over the border in droves to frequent the casinos. Demand increased even more as the Russians gained a greater appetite for Belarus women."

"That's when an underground group started the pipeline and started exporting the women to Russia where they become sex slaves," Forrest said. "The women thought they were going to Minsk, but they ended up in Russia, or worse, in Turkey."

Director Coldclaw interjected, "Why doesn't Lukashenko shut that operation down? If we know about it, he obviously knows about it as well."

As expected, the Director was smartly dressed and extremely well spoken. She was wearing a black pantsuit and white blouse. Her hair was up in a tight bun. The men were all in suits and ties. Fortunately, no one noticed or seemed to care what Jamie was wearing.

"He doesn't shut it down because of the gas pipeline," Forrest answered. "He doesn't want to do anything to jeopardize that deal. He's getting the natural gas at a discount and so he looks the other way when it comes to the women."

"They're trading their women for natural gas?" the Director asked, skeptically. "I don't understand why he would worry about losing a natural gas pipeline deal over a few prostitutes. They are a dime a dozen in Russia."

"I agree. They're not tied together. There's no quid pro quo so to speak. It's just that the prime minister doesn't want to do anything to make the Russians mad."

"How many women are we talking about?" Jamie asked.

"We don't know exactly, but we believe they could be transporting as many as three hundred women a month out of Belarus."

Jamie's mouth flew open.

Three hundred women a month was a huge number out of a country the size of Belarus. Unheard of in sex trafficking circles for one country.

"You can't kidnap three hundred women a month, and no one knows about it," Jamie said. "Family and friends and local law enforcement would be in an uproar, even in a communist country."

"Somehow, they are getting away with it."

"Any young girls?" Jamie asked.

"Not that we know of, but that might be right around the corner."

"How did Turkey get involved in this?" Director Coldclaw asked.

"That's where it gets even more disturbing," Brad said. "A terrorist group is buying the girls and reselling them to fund terrorism against the United States and its allies."

Now Jamie understood why the Director was in the meeting. Mention terrorism, and it goes higher up the food chain. The only thing higher than the Director on the chain was the President himself. If he didn't know about it, he would shortly after this briefing.

"That *is* disturbing," the Director said.

Brad nodded in agreement.

"They sell the girls for a substantial profit in the Middle East," Brad said. "Of course, there's plenty of money in Saudi Arabia, Oman, Qatar, and other Middle Eastern countries to pay top dollar for them from oil money."

Jamie had her doubts. She knew what was going on but didn't say. It's not so much that they made enough money off the girls to fund terrorism, as much as the girls were used as rewards for those who were involved.

Regardless, she could barely contain her excitement. She might be going to Belarus. To fight an organization with terrorist ties.

"What do you want me to do?" Jamie asked. She had to know and didn't want to wait for them to get around to talking about it.

Everyone looked at Brad. Which made sense. Since he was her handler.

He hesitated. Clearly deep in thought. He had probably intended on going over the mission with her privately after the meeting. Jamie was glad she brought it up now.

"We need more intelligence on the pipeline," he said. "We want you to go to Belarus and find out everything you can about their operations. We want names, locations, scope, and particularly the pipeline route if you can uncover it. We're sending someone to Turkey to see what they can find out there."

"Are we sending Jamie to Belarus alone?" Director Coldclaw asked.

Jamie hoped the answer was yes. She worked better when she was alone. Brad looked at Jamie like, "Don't say anything."

"We think it's best if she goes alone," Brad said. "We're sending her there on a tourist visa under an assumed name. We can't let the government know she's there, or they might tip off the people running the pipeline."

"That sounds dangerous," the Director said.

Brad shook his head.

"Not any more dangerous than usual. We want Jamie to hang around the casinos in Minsk and hopefully someone in the pipeline might try to recruit her. Then she can ask questions acting like she might be interested."

She'd done that same thing many times. That's where her beauty would be helpful to the mission.

"She can also keep her eyes and ears open and make friends with some of the prostitutes who were recruited into the pipeline but were fortunate enough to stay in Belarus. They might know some of the girls who were shipped off to Russia or Turkey."

"Something seems strange to me," Jamie said, thinking out loud. "I don't see how these girls go missing and nobody reports it."

"Something doesn't seem right to me either," Director Coldclaw said. She looked at Jamie when she said it.

"I don't like it. Jamie makes a good point. How do these people get away with it? The cover up must go high up in the government. Probably even to the top. I don't like the mission. Going in with such little information."

"That's why Jamie is going. So we can get more information," Brad said.

Director Coldclaw tapped a pencil on a writing pad for several seconds, then said, "Jamie should have someone there with her for backup support. If the government knows she's there, they'll protect her. They wouldn't dare hurt one of our assets. But if they don't know she's one of ours, she might get caught up in something. How would we find her and get her out?"

Brad replied, "We have an asset on the ground. Jamie will meet with him, and he'll give her the information she needs to get started. He's a local and an important asset high up in the government. He's the one who tipped us off to the problem."

"I'm aware of him," Director Coldclaw said. "The Belarus government doesn't know anything about him, so we have to protect him at all costs. It took years to infiltrate that high in the government and we don't want to lose him."

"Of course. Jamie will be discreet," Brad said. "She's very well trained for this kind of mission. You are aware of her recent success in Thailand."

Brad's encouraging words warmed her heart.

The Director persisted. "We're talking Russian pipelines, which are controlled by oligarchs," she said with a concerned look. "Possible terrorism ties. Hundreds of missing women. This sounds like a lot for Jamie to take on by herself."

"I'll be fine." Jamie retorted confidently.

"I think so too," Brad said.

"What are my rules of engagement?" Jamie asked, trying to change the subject before the Director changed the plan.

Going to Belarus was the perfect mission to put Alex behind her. She realized that was the first time she had thought of him since she walked into the room. Getting back to work was exactly what she needed to make him a distant memory.

"You're not to engage other than to gain information," Brad said, sternly. "You're not authorized to take any action against the group. You just gather intelligence."

Jamie started to protest, but Brad stared her down and added, "We can talk about that later in my office. We don't need to waste the Director's time. You and I can come up with a plan."

Jamie and Brad had a running battle about that very topic. Jamie argued that if she got close enough to gather information, she was close enough to help the girls. She couldn't just walk away and leave them in their misery when she had the power to do something about it. He always said it was his call and she needed to follow his instructions.

Jamie thought what she always thought, *I'll do whatever I have to do*.

Director Coldclaw turned to Jamie and said, "I agree with Brad. This operation is too big for you to try to take down alone. Find out what you can and get out of there. Brad, you make sure everyone knows she has my full support on this. I don't want her hanging out there on a rope by herself. She's too valuable to lose on an intelligence gathering operation."

The Director's words sent a warm feeling through Jamie. A lot of the higher ups were against Jamie being allowed to transfer and stay in sex trafficking. Everyone wanted her in their divisions. Her successes made her bosses reluctant to let her stay in what was a minor division.

Sex trafficking was low on the totem pole of priorities. Many thought it was too great a risk to send her into dangerous situations for such little rewards as saving a few girls from sex trafficking.

Mostly, their objections were self-serving. She had more successful missions under her belt than any other operative and made Brad look good. That made them jealous. But Jamie insisted and Brad continued to go to bat for her. He made the case that her skills were perfectly suited for snatch and grab.

So far, the missions had been a success, and a record number of girls were being rescued. A small dent in the overall problem, but progress, nonetheless. Jamie had won over most, if not all, of the skeptics and more resources were being allocated to her program. Especially since many of the operations ended up revealing bigger and more important security risks like drugs, arms trafficking, and terrorism.

The mission to Belarus might be her biggest opportunity yet.

The Director suddenly stood, and everyone knew the meeting was over. She made a direct line for Jamie and extended her hand. Jamie shook it.

"Be careful over there," Director Coldclaw said. "Belarus and Russia are a lot different than Thailand. These organizations are dangerous."

Jamie looked her directly in the eyes and said, "So am I."

6

Jamie had been in Belarus for less than two hours and was already being followed.

She'd actually been in Belarus for six hours if she counted the four hours of interrogation at the airport by custom's officials. Not a surprise. Jamie expected trouble getting into Belarus. A single, young, American woman traveling alone on a tourist visa to a former Soviet bloc country would garner scrutiny. That would be suspicious in most eastern countries.

The CIA made sure everything was in perfect order. The fake visa said her name was Allie Walker. Allie was twenty-five, five foot ten, and a hundred fifty-five pounds. The last part was Brad's attempt at humor. Adding fifteen pounds to her visa was his way of letting Jamie know he had noticed she'd gained a little weight on the cruise.

While she did gain nine pounds, by the time he'd seen her, most of the extra pounds had been sweated off in the gym with an intense regimen of kick boxing and running. She'd give him a hard time about the visa the next time she saw him.

The passport showed four stamps. Jamie memorized the dates and locations in case she was asked about them.

She was.

"Tell me about your trips. Where all have you been?" the man had asked, her passport in his hand, head down waiting for her to answer.

She had been flagged at customs and taken back to a smoke-filled room. An armed guard stood at the door. The only thing in the room was a table, two chairs, and a picture of the Prime Minister of Belarus on the wall. She wasn't offered anything to eat or drink.

"I went to Costa Rica a few years ago with some girlfriends for spring break," Jamie said.

The official didn't look up, he just waited for her to continue. The man was heavy set. He sat in a chair facing her with his legs spread, his belly hanging over his too small pants, and her papers in his hands in front of him. Each inhale and exhale were more like a wheeze than a breath.

The door opened and another guard entered. To add to the intimidation.

Alone in a room with soldiers would be intimidating to any young woman traveling alone. Jamie tried to show the right amount of nervousness, even though she wasn't the least bit concerned. Periodically, she'd let her eyes dart, anxiously not furtively. She'd rub her hands together. Crack her knuckles. Fidget with her jewelry.

Not like she had anything to hide, but like she was anxious. Unsure about the situation. The appropriate response. She'd spent weeks perfecting it in training and had used it a dozen or more times on missions.

"I went to London with my parents," Jamie continued. "Rome was where I studied for one semester." She looked up and to the right like she was thinking. Jamie was careful not to give the signs that she was lying.

"What did you study? What university did you attend? Where did you stay?" The questions came slowly and methodically. The man did not ask accusingly. He played the role as perfectly as she did. He wanted her to let her guard down. To become frustrated. Make a mistake.

He didn't bother to write down her answers because the whole thing was being videotaped. Jamie had spotted the hidden cameras almost immediately. Her answers were being scrutinized by someone on the other end of the camera, so Jamie had to make sure there were no inconsistencies.

"Mexico was when I crossed the border for a day trip to Tijuana. I was in San Diego with my boyfriend, Alex."

Jamie wanted to slap herself in the face. Why did she say Alex was her boyfriend? She had not heard from him and didn't expect to. She broke down and called him two days before she left. The call went right to voicemail. Her message was friendly but short.

"Hi Alex, this is Jamie. I hope you had a good trip back. Just checking in."

She tried to sound casual. Indifferent. She really wanted to yell in the phone and say, "Why haven't you called me, you jerk?"

It had been four weeks. He'd obviously moved on. He hadn't even bothered to return her call.

She tried to put Alex out of her mind so she could concentrate on the questions. That was the last thing she needed—to get thrown in jail in Belarus and ruin the mission because she was mad at him.

The interrogator asked the same questions over and over again. By the third run through of her passport Jamie decided to show some impatience. Like she had gained some confidence through the process. No one would sit there for four hours of interrogation without showing some signs of annoyance.

Jamie kept looking at her watch. Fidgeting in her chair. She asked to use the restroom. They didn't let her. Asked a couple of times how much longer it was going to take. Yawned a few times, like she was tired, which she actually was.

This was an important time in the interrogation. If she was hiding something, they wanted her to lose her edge. Forget her previous answers. Mix up the order of the trips. Say something like, "Costa Rica was first, then London. I studied in Florence, not Rome. My boyfriend's name was Andrew, not Alex."

Jamie was too smart, too well trained, although she wished she could go back and change the answer on her boyfriend's name.

"Excuse me," she wanted to say, "My boyfriend's name is Andrew, not Alex. Alex was never and will never be my boyfriend!"

She just bit her tongue. But she was ready for it to be over.

In some countries, a few dollars under the table to the custom's official could avoid all the hassle. Bribery was not an option in Belarus. It was the quickest way to get thrown in jail. Jamie had read a lot about the jails in Belarus, and they were someplace she wanted to avoid. So, she just stayed calm and patient and waited it out.

It also gave her a chance to practice her lying skills.

"What is the purpose of your trip?" the man asked in broken English.

"I'm a graduate student. Writing a thesis on Belarus. I came here to conduct research."

"How long do you intend to stay?"

He smelled of vodka. It was early afternoon.

"Three weeks. But I might extend it longer if necessary."

"Where are you staying?" He spoke in a slow monotone voice.

"The Monastyrski Hotel."

"Are you meeting anyone?"

"No. I don't know anyone in Belarus."

"Can I search your luggage?"

"Of course."

As if Jamie had a choice. Had she said no, she would've been immediately detained and taken to headquarters for further interrogation. Searching the luggage was usually the last thing. It meant the interrogation was about over. They didn't expect to find anything. Very few people were stupid enough to carry anything illegal into Belarus. A weapon could get you thrown in jail for years with no chance to explain.

Jamie wanted a gun. The CIA had ways to get her a weapon once she was in the field, but Brad had said, "No guns. If you have a gun, you'll be tempted to use it."

It was against the law for foreigners to carry guns in Belarus. Jamie wasn't going to spend three weeks in Belarus without a weapon regardless of what Brad said. She'd find one on her own.

Jamie asked the officials for a map while her luggage was being searched. She wanted to see their map in case it had been updated. It was an older map. The CIA, as usual, had the most updated information. She looked it over anyway.

The eight hour and forty-three-minute flight had taken twelve hours due to a delay from JFK airport. Jamie didn't mind the extra time. She had spent it learning about Belarus. Particularly studying maps. She wanted to learn every road around the hotel. Look for alleyways. Choke points. Escape routes. Memorize facts about the culture. Practice her Russian. Analyze the risks.

She didn't find many risks. That made her nervous. Every place had risks. She liked to know about them beforehand so there were no surprises.

Belarus was a lovely place and a relatively safe place to visit, she had read. Minsk in particular was modern, clean, with fashionable cafes, many restaurants, crowded nightclubs, and beautiful architecture and art galleries. However, tourism from the western world had never really caught on. Russia had millions more tourists every year than Belarus.

Most attributed it to the strong police presence. Soldiers were everywhere in downtown Minsk, on almost every corner of the tourist areas. It could be unnerving to an American traveling there for the first time, but they were mostly there for their protection.

The benefit was a low crime rate. Even petty crimes were strongly prosecuted, and sentences were harsh and prison conditions even harsher. That made the streets relatively safe to walk, even at night, as long as you stayed in the populated areas.

Tourism was encouraged by the Prime Minister. He wanted some of the revenue that was going to surrounding countries. As long as you were careful not to make any political statements against the "last remaining dictatorship in Europe," a traveler could have a wonderful trip to Belarus.

The police presence was Jamie's biggest concern as well. She liked to be able to move around freely. Avoid scrutiny. Be seen only when she wanted to be noticed. That made it harder when soldiers were on every corner. They'd look her over just because she was a young pretty blonde woman.

She'd read that the soldiers were ordered not to stop and interrogate tourists unless there was a strong reason to be suspicious. Another reason not to carry a gun in Belarus. If she was stopped and frisked for some reason, it could create a huge problem for her. A huge problem meaning twenty years of hard labor in a prison camp with no hope of parole.

"You're free to go," the man finally said. He handed her passport and visa back to her along with her luggage.

"I hope you have a pleasant trip."

"Thank you," she said and quickly gathered her things and walked out of the room.

After she had cleared customs, she took a taxi for the forty-five-minute drive to her hotel. The Monastyrski Hotel was in downtown Minsk. If you counted the twelve-hour flight, and the four hours of interrogation, she was running way behind schedule and also running on little sleep, with barely enough time to take a shower and unpack.

What she really wanted to do was lie down and take a nap. Not possible. She was to meet her contact at exactly 6:00 p.m. Belarus time. Jamie left the hotel almost immediately not even bothering to unpack her bags or take a shower.

As soon as she left the hotel, she noticed the tail almost immediately. The man was short, thin, dark bushy eyebrows and mustache, wore a trench coat, and a ushanka, a Russian fur cap with ear flaps that could be fastened at the top of the hat or at the chin.

It was early evening and not cold. Being overdressed was the first clue the man was trying too hard to be inconspicuous. The ushanka was a feeble attempt to hide his face. He obviously didn't want Jamie to see him.

Clearly a government intelligence officer assigned to watch Jamie for the first couple of days to make sure she was not up to something nefarious. Her hotel room was probably being searched at that moment as well.

Even though he was not particularly good at his job, his presence posed a problem for Jamie. She could lose him easily enough but had to make it look like she didn't lose him on purpose. An American tourist on a visa would not know how to lose a tail. It would be highly suspicious, if not proof positive, if she used sophisticated and evasive maneuvers to lose him.

Why would a tourist, in Belarus to do research for a school paper, know how to identify and evade street surveillance?

Jamie was encouraged by the man's skill level, or lack thereof. They weren't too concerned about her, or they would have sent someone with more abilities. Jamie didn't think there was more than one of them, but she decided to give it some time to make sure.

She strolled casually down the street, looking in windows, pretending to be shopping. His reflection in the window was what she mainly wanted to see.

Did he have a radio? If he did, he could call ahead and hand Jamie off to another person and then drop off, so she didn't see the same person more than once. She had to be satisfied he was surveilling her alone.

Many unskilled agents lost a tail and didn't realize it was on purpose and they let their guards down not realizing someone else ahead had taken up the surveillance.

The telltale sign you were being followed was when you saw the same person again and again. If it's a good tail you never see him. Jamie was not good at surveilling someone else, because she was too memorable. A tail needed to blend into the environment and not do anything to draw attention to himself.

Jamie was a beautiful blonde American girl walking down the streets of Minsk. That was not something their citizens saw every day. While there was nothing extraordinary about her tail, he was trying too hard not to be seen. Making him easy to see.

Jamie started walking again with more purpose, convinced she could easily lose him. He was across the street lagging behind, struggling to keep up. Jamie noticed a bus stop on the next corner with a bus loading and getting ready to leave. She picked up her pace and at the exact moment when the bus was between her and the tail, she ducked into a store. She quickly made her way to the back of the store where there was another entrance, or exit in this case, and walked out into a small square.

Jamie imagined that the tail was confused. He wouldn't know if Jamie got on the bus, went into the store, or kept walking and went around the corner. He might be suspicious that she had lost him on purpose, but he couldn't prove it and he certainly wasn't going to say so to his supervisor. More than likely, he was going to say that she got on the bus, and he couldn't get on it without being detected, so he let her go.

Jamie hid in the shadows for a moment watching the back entrance making sure he didn't follow her. When she was satisfied, she set off walking again. Jamie was off her route and wasn't sure exactly where she was. She stepped into an alleyway between buildings and pulled out her map to get her bearings.

She didn't notice until it was too late that four young men had her surrounded.

7

Jamie did a quick assessment of the threat.

The four young men appeared to be in their late teens, early twenties, medium to slight builds, and all of them were wearing the same color black leather jacket similar to what gangs in the US wore. There were no insignias on the front, so it didn't seem like they were actual gang members.

Jamie surmised they were just some kids out trying to act tougher than they really were. They were probably as surprised as she was that she had happened upon them.

One of the young men said in Russian "Hey pretty lady."

Jamie pretended she didn't understand him. She contorted her face to look confused.

They formed a circle around her. Jamie put the map in her front pocket. She was wearing black stretch jeans, thin for maximum maneuverability. A dark colored light long sleeve turtleneck sweater came down slightly below her waist. Her black shoes, with a slight heel, were designed like sneakers but with a dressier look. The all-black look made it harder for her to be seen at night, if the need arose.

She glanced at her watch.

Oh great. This is just what I need. I'm already late and these idiots are going to make me later.

She still had time to make it to the meeting with her contact but was starting to cut it close. Her concern was more for missing the meeting than the four-to-one odds confronting her. She'd been in worse situations than this against much more formidable foes. In fact, a quick evaluation of the four kids eased Jamie's mind that these were not organized gang members.

On the plane, she'd read about an ongoing gang war between Belarusian and Russian gangs. A firebomb had recently been set by a gang in front of the Russian embassy starting a street war. While the authorities had tamped it down, Jamie didn't want to get in the middle of one of those battles. She was convinced the four in front of her would never pass the initiation into one of those hard-core gangs.

"Where are you from, pretty lady?" he said sarcastically. "Are you from the US of A? Are you going to make my day?"

Jamie laughed out loud. This guy thought he was Clint Eastwood. She wanted to say, "This is about to become the worst day of your life," but she controlled herself.

"What's so funny, pretty lady?" the obvious leader of the little gang of misfits said.

Maybe I can talk my way out of this.

Her mind was processing all of her options and narrowed it down to two. She could act tough and perhaps scare them away. However, four against one were strong odds and they were probably feeling pretty good about their chances. They didn't realize that the odds were highly in her favor.

Jamie rejected that strategy. If she challenged their manhood, they might feel like they had to fight just to save face in front of their friends.

Her second option was to apologize and act innocent. That would allow them to back off without fighting and still feel like tough guys that didn't have to prove anything. She could pretend they scared her and maybe they'd feel sorry for her.

Curly always said a fight was not the place for an ego. If you can avoid a fight by looking like you lost, even if you know you could've won, then you did win. Anytime you avoid a fight you win.

She liked option two, so she said, "I'm sorry. I'm lost. Can you tell me how to get to Liberty Square?"

Jamie spoke Russian fluently, but she tried to act like she didn't know the language very well hoping they might actually back off and give her directions.

He wasn't taking the bait. His eyes darted around, probably looking to see if the coast was clear and no one was watching them.

"Just give us your money and your phone and you can be on your way," he said strongly.

Jamie took the phone out of her back pocket.

"You mean this?" she waved it in front of them. The boy nodded.

Time for option one.

"No," Jamie said in perfect Russian. "You can't have my phone. I need it. Sorry. You can't have my money either. How about you give me your money and phone? Maybe, I'll steal them from you."

The leader paused for a moment, not sure how to react. Curly always said confusion was good in a fight. Get your opponent thinking about other things. Jamie imagined several questions were running through his head.

Why did she suddenly speak Russian fluently? Why was she saying she was going to rob us? What do I do now? Is this girl tougher than she looks?

At first, he chuckled nervously, then he seemed to get angry. His hands balled into fists. His jaw clenched. Shoulders were raised slightly.

Before he could say anything, Jamie said, " ," It sounded like, yah VYH-zah-voo mee-LEE-tsyh-yoo.

She had just told them she was calling the police. She actually said, *Militsia* which was the name for the police in Belarus. Jamie had read there was a no tolerance policy for gangs in Minsk. These four weren't really a gang. They were just a group of kids, hanging out, not even looking for trouble but they'd be afraid of the police coming.

Of course, they didn't know that the *Militsia* were the last people Jamie wanted to see at that moment and she had no intention of calling them. She hoped they were afraid of the police as much as she was.

Suddenly, Jamie's phone rang. It startled all of them. The phone was still in her hand. She looked down at the screen.

Alex.

A bolt of excitement pulsed through her like an electrical current.

"Oh, for heaven's sake," she muttered under her breath. "Now he calls me. At the worst possible time."

She sent it to voicemail and put the phone back in her pocket.

Now Jamie was mad. They made her miss a call from Alex.

And she wasn't getting anywhere with them anyway and they were wasting her time. Her contact was at Liberty Square waiting for her. She needed to get this over with. Jamie put thoughts of Alex out of her mind so she wouldn't be distracted.

The body language of the four told her they were starting to get antsy as well. Three of them were all glancing at the one guy, the obvious leader. The one doing all the talking. All three had their fists clenched as well, but they weren't going to make a move without his permission.

Eyes glancing around nervously was a sign that something was about to happen.

Jamie was resigned to the fact that this wasn't going to end well for the boys. When faced with a situation like this, most people would think that they were fighting four people. Jamie was only fighting one, maybe two of them.

She would make her first strike so devastating and the injury so visible to the other three that it would have such a psychological effect the others would likely scatter without ever throwing a punch. That sucked for the one she chose to hurt, but it was her most effective strategy to get it over with fast.

Faced with that choice, Jamie would normally attack the weakest of the group. He was the easiest of the four to spot. Standing to her right was the smallest and probably youngest who also wore glasses.

"You don't wear glasses to a fight," Jamie wanted to yell to him like a mother would yell at her kids.

A blow to the face of a person wearing glasses from someone with Jamie's skills, was not pretty. Jamie didn't want to choose him. She felt sorry for him. He obviously didn't want to be there but was trying to act tough around his friends.

He was clueless. One foot was behind the other, and his weight shifted away from her. Like he wanted to run away. His eyes were wide as saucers. His thin fingers in a ball. Not ready to strike but in fear. The boy was scared to death.

She decided to give him a break.

If Jamie wasn't going to go for the weakest, then her other choice was usually to go for the strongest. If you take out the leader with devastating and overwhelming force, the others will think twice before making a move. Also, Jamie thought she saw a slight bulge in the back of his pants which meant he was probably carrying a gun.

That changed the equation and raised the level of danger.

Although he clearly didn't know that it was one of the worst places to carry a gun if you wanted to get to it quickly. Jamie could act so fast she could disable him before he could even touch it.

Plus, she needed a gun. This was the perfect opportunity to get one without much effort.

Jamie took a deep breath. Closed her eyes for a moment and envisioned her plan. A sudden thought came to her, so she deviated from the plan slightly, remembering what Curly said.

Always make the first move and make it totally unexpected.

The element of surprise was one of the best weapons in a fight. An unexpected move would temporarily throw them off their game and cause them to think about how to respond. That momentary hesitation was all you needed to create a visible injury for the rest of the group to see.

And you don't want to let your attackers dictate the action. His words resonated, *Fight on your terms, not theirs.*

Jamie did something highly unusual. She turned her back to the leader. In his eyes, she became more vulnerable, and he might think he had less need to reach for his gun. And she could keep an eye on the other three just in case one or more of them had a weapon.

She knew he would instinctively move toward her and try to grab her from behind thinking he had the advantage. The other three's eyes would tell her when he made his move.

It would come soon.

Jamie lifted her left leg slightly off the ground. He probably wouldn't even notice. When he got closer, Jamie could see him lunge for her out of the corner of her eye. In a split second she rotated her right foot, so she was sideways to him.

This move was more difficult to execute and took more time than some of her other options, but it would do the most damage. Curly taught Jamie to visualize that her foot was like a bullet in a chamber. When in the cocked position, Jamie rotated so that her heel was facing the target.

He had his hands raised to grab her, so they were both high in the air. He was slightly shorter than Jamie, so his arms were above his shoulders. She could easily kick him in the ribs and cause serious damage. A carefully placed kick would break several ribs. Maybe even his sternum.

However, Jamie was afraid that a rib could puncture his lung and be life threatening. She wanted to disable him, not kill him.

So, Jamie fired her heel like a bullet towards his lower body, just below his kneecap. He was moving toward her, so his momentum went right into the kick. When it landed, it shattered his tibia and destroyed all of the muscles, ligaments, and cartilage in his knee.

It hyperextended his knee to the extent that it dislodged from his femur as well. He let out a yell and crumbled in a big heap writhing in pain. The cracking of bone echoed through the alley.

Jamie had kicked him harder than she intended. The boy with the glasses took one look and turned around, running the other way.

The other two had started toward Jamie and it was too late for them to stop. They hesitated. They had a shocked look on their faces as they saw their, not so fearless leader, on the ground, with bones sticking out of his leg. Writhing in pain.

It's hard for anyone's mind to process all of that information quickly enough to change intentions, so they kept moving forward. The closest one took a wild swing at Jamie. He started the punch about two steps too soon.

Jamie could have easily blocked it with her arm, but she needed to avoid contact with her hands or arms. That could leave bruises. Bruises could easily identify her if she was brought in for questioning for some reason. She didn't want there to be any evidence that she had been in a fight.

Hands and elbows were not an option except as a last resort. They could bruise as well. She wanted to use her feet or knees. They didn't bruise as easily, and they would not look at them anyway if she were under questioning.

So, Jamie simply stepped back, one step, and let the punch go past her. With her left hand, she grabbed his shoulder and spun him around, so he was facing her. With tremendous acceleration, she kneed him in the groin. While extremely painful, he was much better off than his leader.

Jamie was really trying not to hurt the other two more than necessary. He probably didn't see her as being compassionate at that moment, but she was. She actually pulled back some which lessened the damage. Jamie could have severely injured his groin if she had wanted to.

Two down, one to go.

In one motion, Jamie instinctively turned to face the third guy. He swung half-heartedly. Jamie grabbed his wrist and bent it backwards. Any further and she would have dislocated the wrist from the hand. Instead, she simply twisted it far enough to sprain it.

She released her grip, and he grabbed his wrist and took off running, crying in pain. He was the luckiest of the three. The other two were still groaning on the ground, but they would live.

The leader would probably walk with a limp for the rest of his life if they could even repair his knee. It would take a highly skilled surgeon to fix the damage she had caused. Jamie hoped he didn't lose his leg, but it was his own fault.

She surveyed the scene and was pleased that there was no blood. She had none on her and the fight had gone about as well as she could have hoped.

She looked around to see if anyone had seen the fight. Fortunately, the alleyway was secluded and dark as the sun was close to setting.

Jamie turned the leader over and pulled the gun out of his pants, inspecting it in the process. It was a Russian made Makarov pistol. A gun widely used by law enforcement, military, and special forces in Russia.

Jamie wondered where a punk like that got such a powerful weapon. She didn't think too long; she was just glad to have it.

Let's just hope I don't have to use it.

8

Jamie got away from the scene of the attack as quickly as possible after making sure neither of the boys had life-threatening injuries. She walked out of the alley and turned right down the road running behind the shops. The only person she saw was a man ahead of her unloading a van almost a block away.

He wasn't paying attention to anything other than his task at hand so she continued walking forward normally, in the shadows, so he couldn't make out her face in case he looked her way.

She glanced around to see if there were any video cameras. There didn't appear to be.

She'd gotten lucky. Nothing could tie her to the attacks. Except the boys, of course. They could identify her but what were they going to say to the police? "We were robbing this girl, and she beat us up trying to escape." That story would incriminate them more than her.

The case for self-defense would be clear. If they said she attacked and robbed them, the story would sound even more incredulous. Why would a young woman attack and rob four men out of the blue? What did that say about them that she was successful?

They'd be embarrassed to tell even their friends what had happened, much less the police. Jamie was fairly confident the boys would keep their mouths shut.

Still, it wasn't as simple as that, she finally decided after much thought. An ambulance would be called. Then the police because it would be obvious there was an attack. The boys would have to come up with some story.

More than likely, they would say they were attacked by a rival gang or a man with a gun. Some incredible story that made them look better. Her only concern was the two younger boys.

They might say something out of fear or fall apart under interrogation. She couldn't see the little kid with the glasses lasting ten seconds under intense interrogation by a seasoned Belarusian detective.

No reason to worry about it now. She needed to get to her contact. If she was brought in for questioning, she'd just have to talk her way out of it.

When she was a safe distance away, she stopped, pulled out her map and plotted the quickest route to Liberty Square. She glanced at her watch. Only five minutes to get there, and the walk would take at least fifteen minutes.

If she ran, she could make it in five but then she would be too conspicuous. If the police saw an American running at night through the streets of Minsk, they would arrest her and ask questions later.

Her contact was instructed to wait for fifteen minutes after the scheduled time, so Jamie could still make it. After that he would leave and assume the worst. Jamie quickened her pace without drawing too much attention to herself.

She needed to get back on the main road and take the most direct route to the Square. The guy who was following her out of the hotel could be on the main road looking for her, but that was a chance she had to take. Hopefully, he wouldn't be. Time was of the essence and losing him again would only take more time.

Jamie touched the outside of her coat which now held the gun in the inside pocket. In the back pocket of her pants was where she had put the phone right before the fight started. Suddenly, she remembered that it rang right before the fight.

Alex had finally called her.

A warm feeling came over her and engulfed all of her emotions which were still heightened from the confrontation with the boys. Similar to the feelings she had on the cruise when she was with him. When they touched, kissed, looked into each other's eyes.

An electricity. An overwhelming happiness was the best way to describe it.

Did he leave a message? She took the phone out of her pocket. The notification read one voice mail message. What did he say? More importantly, what was his excuse for not calling sooner?

At least he called. *Four weeks later!*

The tingling feeling was competing with the anger, for control of her emotions. Which would win out?

Didn't matter at the moment, since she had a mission to carry out. Brad and the Director had been adamant about how important the asset was. She couldn't risk making a mistake because she was thinking about some guy thousands of miles away.

Jamie tried hard to return her focus to the more important task at hand. Listening to the message and calling Alex would have to wait. He made her wait four weeks. He could wait a few hours for her to call.

The thought made her angry all over again. He'd better have a good excuse. For the moment, the anger won out, becoming the best way to get her mind off of him.

What she saw next was all she needed to quickly forget Alex. Jamie came around a building and was on the main road. Two Militsia were standing on the corner.

Her heart about jumped out of her chest.

They were on their radios and seemed a little excited. It probably wasn't related to her, but she couldn't be sure. If it was, then there was a description of a blonde, tall, American girl wearing a light brown jacket who was a suspect in a robbery and attack.

She dismissed the thought. It seemed improbable that word could have spread that quickly. Unlikely that anyone had even found the boys yet, much less pieced the facts together.

She was being paranoid, but there was no reason to take any chances.

Jamie spotted a gift shop still open, and quickly slipped inside without being seen by the police. Once inside, she bought a baseball cap and a red jacket. Red wasn't ideal because it would draw attention to her, but it was the only one that fit and would have to do.

She paid for the items which cost 12 rubles, about six dollars, then slipped on the baseball cap, tucked her hair inside and put everything else in the shopping bag. The bag made her look more like a shopper and less like a special operative of the CIA.

After exiting the store Jamie went the opposite way to avoid walking by the two policemen, beginning to regret having taken the gun. If stopped and searched, and the gun found, she would be arrested on the spot.

When preparing for a mission she always familiarized herself with prisons and procedures. What she read about Belarus made her shudder.

In the best-case scenario, she would be sent to Pishchalauski Castle, more commonly known as the Valadarka, which was run by the Ministry of Internal Affairs of Belarus. It housed all death row inmates and was a pretrial detention center for political activists. Tourists that violated the more serious laws were usually sent there.

If she wasn't lucky, they'd send her to the Amerikanka, which was the other pretrial detention center run by the KGB. It was notorious for its inhumane torture of prisoners to extract information. The European Union actually sanctioned two Colonels and one Lieutenant from the prison a few years before for what was described as "cruel, inhumane, and degrading treatment or punishment of detainees."

The sanctions were lifted after Belarus outlawed torture. But who really knew what went on behind closed doors? No one believed the sanctions caused them to change their practices. They just used them more discreetly.

Even if Jamie wasn't tortured, within a week, she would be sentenced to ten to fifteen years of hard labor either in one of the two women's prison facilities or one of the nine prisons that held the general population.

Claiming she was with the CIA wasn't an option. She couldn't claim diplomatic immunity because she wasn't traveling there on official business. Jamie just needed to avoid all of those scenarios.

The last thing Brad wanted was for her to end up being interrogated by the KGB. If Jamie didn't cave to the torture, which they were all certain she wouldn't, they wouldn't be able to get her out without exposing her as one of theirs.

Unfortunately, the political price would not be worth it. They would deny even knowing her. As an American citizen, the state department would demand her release, but that could take months or years.

If faced with a search, Jamie would likely use the gun rather than let them find it. The words of Brad were echoing in her mind, and she understood them better now. "No guns. If you have a gun, you'll be tempted to use it."

He was right. She wouldn't let them take her to prison without a fight. A gunfight if necessary.

How would she explain it to Alex if she went away for ten years?

What a stupid thought.

That's the least of her worries. Ten years seemed like a lifetime to someone Jamie's age. The best thing was to avoid detection altogether, which she was highly trained to do.

The contact had to be considered as well. His identity had to be protected at all costs. So, she decided to take evasive action to make sure she wasn't under surveillance. If the police were on heightened alert, she didn't want to lead them by chance directly to him. Protecting his identity was paramount to the mission and above even her own safety

Jamie made a number of turns as countermeasures designed to expose even the most sophisticated surveillance. If someone was following her, it would blow her cover as a tourist, but it would protect the asset which was the most important thing. Jamie was probably being overly cautious, but she had not lived this long being careless.

Satisfied she wasn't being followed, Jamie headed directly to Liberty Square. A quick glance at her watch confirmed that all of the distractions had taken too much time. She arrived seventeen minutes late. The hope was that the contact wasn't a stickler for details, or maybe his watch was running two minutes behind.

Liberty Square, also known as Freedom Square, surrounded the town hall in the Upper Old Town of Minsk. It used to be called Lenin Square before the revolution. Built on top of the highest hill, it provided a beautiful view of downtown and the Svislach River which flowed through the center of it. Several beautiful all-white buildings dominated the square including what used to be the old City Hall.

In the middle of the square was a sculpture of a carriage. Jamie was to meet her contact there and then walk over to the Holy Spirit Cathedral where they would rendezvous inside. The carriage was easy to find, and several tourists were admiring it. Jamie pretended to be doing the same.

Two horses were pulling the carriage. One had its head bent down, the other was standing regally, his head in the air, watching all of the tourists. It really was a magnificent piece of art. Carefully crafted out of iron. Jamie made a mental note to come back to the square sometime under different circumstances.

Nearby was actually a museum of carriages which Jamie hoped to see as well. She wasn't sure what the fascination was with carriages in Minsk, but maybe she'd learn that fact at the museum.

There were still people milling around but none she could identify as an agent. Jamie slipped off the baseball cap in case he was looking for a girl with long blonde hair. She shook out her hair and ran her hand through it. All the while scanning the square for any sign of the contact.

Over in the main area, near the church, were a dozen or so benches surrounding a beautiful fountain. A wide sidewalk led to the area. Jamie walked there and sat down on one of the benches. Several kids were playing at the fountain, their parents nearby not paying particularly close attention to them.

One of the kids waved at Jamie and she smiled back. He pointed at the pigeons resting on the ledge on the top of the fountain taking the occasional drink.

Still no sign of the contact.

After a few minutes of waiting, Jamie stood and walked to the other side of the square where the *City of Scales* statue stood. It appeared to be a sculpture of three people conducting business. A product was being weighed on a scale. Plaques on the walls probably described the meaning of the sculpture but Jamie was focused on finding her contact.

She was trying to make an appearance in every part of the square. Just in case the contact wasn't an operative skilled in "meets." The term used for clandestine meetings.

More often than not these flipped assets were not skilled and someone like Jamie had to be careful that the contact didn't lead the authorities right to them. While he might have trouble identifying her, she would spot him immediately. He would be nervously fidgeting. Looking around from side to side.

Jamie knew how to surveil the area without making it look obvious. The choice of the location told Jamie the contact was not skilled. This was not the best place to meet. Too many people were around. The square was open with no place to hide or escape quickly, if necessary.

The only good thing about it was there was no police presence. It seemed like a safe place for a family to bring their kids.

She'd read in her maps that there was an overlook, a viewing point. Jamie made her way to that area hoping to have a view of the entire park. All confidence was gone that the contact was there or would arrive any time soon. If he had been there, he left. Probably unsure what to do but determined to stick to the plan.

She couldn't see as well as she had hoped from the viewing point. Darkness was falling and while there were lampposts illuminating the square, buildings blocked the view to some areas, and the darkness made it hard to see faces.

After thirty minutes, she debated whether to leave or not. It was always a bad sign when a mission started out with so many problems. First the fight, now she had missed her contact.

The agent was supposed to bring her a satellite phone with a secure line so she could communicate openly with Brad. He also had vital information about the pipeline including the name of the person running it, and the address of a safe house if she got into real trouble.

When Jamie spotted two Militsia entering the square the decision was made for her. The hotel was only a short walk, just off of the square. Rather than going directly to the hotel, she stopped by another shop and bought three bags of miscellaneous clothes. Not that she needed them, she just wanted to walk into the hotel with several shopping bags.

The tail would likely be watching the hotel waiting for her to return. She wanted him to report back that all she did was go shopping.

At the hotel, Jamie spotted the surveillance rather easily and skipped through the entrance, carrying her bags like she'd had a wonderful time shopping. Like she didn't have a care in the world.

She had many cares. How would she reach her contact? She had no idea who he was or how to get in touch with him. What about the hurt boys? She wondered if they were okay.

So many things were running through her mind that she had almost forgotten to slip back into the jacket she was wearing when she first left the hotel. Fortunately, she remembered in time and quickly slipped on the brown jacket putting the red one back in the bag.

Once in the room, she plopped down on the bed, exhausted from traveling and from the eventful evening. She checked the drawer on the desk. She'd left a small piece of paper in the back that would dislodge if anyone had opened the drawer. The piece of paper was lying on the floor. Someone had searched her room.

More complications. Especially now that she had a gun. While they wouldn't likely search a second time, it was a possibility.

Even though Jamie was exhausted, she took the gun apart and skillfully cleaned it to make sure it was in good working order. A hiding place was constructed for the gun where it would not be found without a thorough search.

Satisfied, she took the gun and sat it next to her bed. She always slept with one next to her bed at home. A gun was like her security blanket. She felt better having it there.

There were nine bullets in the chamber. She wished she had more, she couldn't just walk into any store and buy some. Nine was better than none and Jamie was a good shot and wouldn't waste a single bullet. She usually hit whatever she shot at and would be careful not to waste any, should the need arise.

Shooting the gun and using a bullet was a last resort.

Some agents actually slept on the floor in the closet. That way if someone came in the room, they'd expect the agent to be in the bed. They'd inspect it first or unload their gun into it if that was their intention. Being in the closet would be the last thing they expected, and the agent could react before the intruder knew what hit him.

Those were extreme measures, unnecessary at this point. Jamie could react quickly enough with the gun by the bedside. Besides, as tired as she was, there was no way she was sleeping on the floor.

She jumped in the shower, brushed her teeth, and fell into bed. Then she remembered her phone call from Alex. The clock read 08:17. Not too late to call him but she was already too tired to even listen to his message.

"Serves him right. He can wait for me to call."

With that last thought, she was asleep as soon as her head hit the pillow.

9

The next morning

Jamie would've been the prime suspect in the savage and brutal beating of two twenty-one-year-old young men in an alleyway behind the *Piatra Brouka Literary Museum,* except that her tail, Detective Fabi Orlov, had become her alibi. After she came back to the hotel, he returned to his office, filled out a report, and then went home.

Rather than admitting he had lost her for two hours, he falsified her movements and claimed he had eyes on her the entire night.

Now he sat in the office of his boss, Lieutenant Nika Petrov, the Senior Investigator for the Minsk Militsia Police Force. Petrov had been a detective in Minsk for twenty-five years. Having moved up the ranks, he was now off the streets and behind a desk managing twelve detectives and forty-seven officers.

Known as tough and unfair, all of his men were justifiably afraid of him.

Fabi had learned of an attack on two boys the night before and had heard a young, American blonde woman was the prime suspect. He'd heard the ambulance and police go by the night before but didn't think anything of it. Certainly, didn't think it was related to the girl he was following.

He had spent two hours frantically searching up and down the streets for her but couldn't find her anywhere. He decided to go back to the hotel and wait and breathed a sigh of relief when she showed up around eight carrying some bags.

She'd clearly been shopping. Probably got on the bus and went to the mall.

He could see two reports sitting on the desk—the police report and his surveillance report. Fabi was dreading the questions he knew were about to come.

Petrov lit a cigarette and stared at Fabi who was extremely uncomfortable but trying hard not to show it. Petrov was five foot seven, a hundred sixty-three pounds and fifty-seven years old. He didn't look a day over seventy.

His gray, almost white hair was mostly bald on top, and his gray beard connected to a thin mustache. A gray suit jacket covered a white shirt and crimson tie with Russian sickles. At eight in the morning, his tie was already loosened, and the collar unbuttoned.

He smelled of vodka. Fabi knew he usually had his first glass of vodka before eight and would likely have his second before the clock struck ten.

Petrov sat behind a black metal desk that had been in that office since the second world war. There were no pictures of family, wife, kids, or grandkids in the room, nothing but an old portrait of Lenin in a cheap frame hanging behind a credenza that had seen better days.

With his right hand he picked up the police report from the night before describing two young boys who were beaten by a blonde, American woman. With the other he picked up Fabi's surveillance report and waved them both at his young and scared out of his mind detective.

"So, your eyes never left her," Petrov said in an accusatory tone.

"Nyet," Fabi said hesitantly. His heart felt like it was doing laps around his body.

"Let's go over this report again."

Petrov set down the two reports, picked up his cigarette, and took a long drag from it, letting the ashes fall on the reports for effect.

"She left the hotel, walked over to the *Insomnia Bar* off of Vulica," he said, not reading from the report, just summarizing what it said.

Fabi nodded. Trying to control his nerves.

"She had an espresso. She walked across the street to the outdoor mall and went in several shops. From there, she walked to the *Chito* restaurant and had dinner and then went to the piano bar where she stayed until she got back to the hotel around eight. Is that correct?"

"That is correct."

Fabi changed positions in his chair, crossing his legs and putting both hands on his knees. He immediately realized it made him look weak. Petrov couldn't stand weakness. Fabi also knew Petrov couldn't stand what had become of the young men of Belarus. He thought they were weak and undisciplined. Punks, he often called them.

He'd try to use that information to his advantage if he got the chance. Petrov would not be sympathetic to the boy's plight.

Petrov continued what seemed like an interrogation.

"One of the boys is in the hospital, the other was kneed in the groin but he talked. He said the attack happened around six. I find it a strange coincidence that two boys were savagely beaten by a young, Caucasian, American woman with blonde hair, and a woman matching that description perfectly is staying at a hotel less than a mile from the place where the attack took place and was eating dinner just a few blocks away. Can you explain that to me, Fabi?"

Fabi shrugged his shoulders. The less he said the better it would be for him.

Petrov reached across the desk and handed Fabi the police report.

"Anything you care to change in your report?"

"There must be two women who look the same," Fabi said, after glancing at the report and then peering over his glasses.

He was past the point of no return. If he admitted he lied on the report, he would be fired and sent immediately to the infamous Hrondo prison in West Belarus where he would stand trial for treason. The trial would be short and unfair. He would be given an attorney, but one who worked for the state.

He'd definitely be found guilty. If he wasn't shot, he'd spend the better part of his life in hard labor. There was no way he could change his story. No one could prove his report was fake as long as he stuck by his story.

He thought briefly about his wife and young child. They'd only been married for three years. When he was promoted to detective, they had celebrated by overindulging in a dinner and drinks they couldn't afford on his salary.

Now, he was wondering if becoming a detective had been a good idea.

He decided to take the initiative and defend himself, "How did a young woman beat up two guys? She's a tourist. She barely weighs 150 pounds. And why would she beat them up? What was her motive?"

Lieutenant Petrov reached across the desk and snatched the paper out of Fabi's hands, clearly trying to intimidate him. He read from the statement.

"She robbed them of 51 rubles. There was no mention of anything else being stolen."

"She's a rich American," Fabi retorted. "Why would she rob them of what amounts to twenty-five American dollars?"

"Why would the boys lie?"

"They seem like a couple of punks."

Fabi decided now was a good time to play on Petrov's biases.

"Maybe they were trying to rob her. Maybe the boys were dealing drugs or something. The deal went bad, and they got whacked. They saw her walking on the street and tried to pin it on her. It definitely wasn't the girl. I never let her out of my sight."

He saw the Lieutenant pause, thinking.

"Wait right here," he said as he stood from his desk and walked out of the room not waiting for a response.

***

Petrov left his office and walked down the hall to see his boss, Maxim Kozlov, the Inspector of the Militsia. Inspector would be equivalent to the Chief of Police in an American city. He explained to the Inspector what had happened the night before.

The Inspector already knew most of the details. Not much happened in Minsk that he didn't know about.

"I would like to bring the girl in for questioning," Petrov said.

Kozlov exploded. "On what basis? Your man says he was on her the whole time."

He started to say he didn't believe him but stopped himself. He didn't want to admit to his boss that one of his detectives would falsify a report. That would make him look just as bad as the detective.

Fabi Orlov was a young detective who had been on the force for seven years but a detective for only two. He started his career on street patrol but had been promoted to detective even though barely competent as an officer writing tickets for petty offenses.

Turnover was high in the Minsk Militsia. The best and brightest were quickly recruited into the KGB. The totally incompetent were fired. The barely competent were promoted.

Fabi was promoted, and while Lieutenant Petrov had little use for Fabi, he always showed up to work on time and hadn't quit which were qualities more important than competence.

Petrov needed bodies, even if they drove him crazy. Regardless, he wasn't going to throw him under the bus with so little information.

"She matches the description," Petrov argued. "How many blonde American girls are walking around Minsk? Not very many."

"We checked her out thoroughly when she went through customs. The girl is legit. We pulled up her birth certificate and matched her social security number. We've seen her college transcripts. She has credit cards and a social media page. She already has pictures of Minsk posted on her social media accounts."

Petrov knew that the Americans were good at creating cover stories for their operatives. His boss would know that as well. Creating fake documents and social media pages were easy enough for the Americans to do.

"I don't know who she is, but why is she even in Minsk, traveling alone?" Petrov argued. "It seems suspicious. She might be a spy or something."

"She doesn't fit the profile for a spy," Kozlov retorted. "We can't hassle her without proof even if she is a spy."

"I don't want to hassle her. I just want to ask her a few questions."

"I'm under intense pressure from the higher ups to lay off American tourists."

Belarus was trying to encourage more Americans to visit. For a number of reasons, Americans avoided Belarus and opted for the surrounding countries instead.

Tiny Estonia had twice the number of American visitors every year and it didn't have near the attractions Belarus had. The President had sent a specific directive that American tourists were to feel welcome in Belarus. Police harassing them did not make them feel welcomed. Petrov knew that his boss was not about to go against that directive without a good reason.

Petrov started on the force after Perestroika, so while the official policy was more openness and reform, the police and military were the last to accept the changes. The police were under constant pressure to maintain order while allowing more freedom of expression.

Contradictions that didn't make sense on the streets where order had to be maintained by those on the front lines, namely men like Petrov and Kozlov. They were old school and longed for the days of communist rule and a police state. When whatever the Militsia said was the law and they could enforce it in whatever way they saw fit.

"Remember the Chinese woman from a few years ago who came here and was seducing rich men at parties," Petrov said. "Government men. She was spying, trying to extract information. She left the country before we could capture her."

"This girl says she has a boyfriend back home. What was his name?" Kozlov thumbed through the paperwork. "Alex. She has a boyfriend named Alex."

Petrov started to say something, but Kozlov interrupted him, raising his voice and getting more annoyed.

"The report says she's doing research for a graduate paper. There's nothing about her in our database that would suggest she's anything other than a college student. You need more proof before you can bring her in for questioning."

"Even if she was a spy," Kozlov added, "I don't think we'd want to bring her in. We'd want to follow her and see what we find. Besides, I'm not buying the boy's story. Why would an American spy attack them on the streets for no reason?"

"I agree," Petrov said.

He had decided not to challenge him again.

"I pulled their records," Petrov said. "They were involved in a few minor crimes when they were kids. Graffiti. Truancy. Little stuff like that. Nothing major. They aren't connected to any gangs."

"It does seem suspicious and highly coincidental, but we don't have enough to go on. Have your man follow the woman for a couple of more days. There's a picture of her in the file that was taken at the customs office. Go to the hospital and see if the kid can positively ID her. Have you searched her hotel room?"

"Yes. But we didn't find anything."

"Search it again. Look more thoroughly. Stop her on the street for a routine check of her passport. Tell your men to be considerate and nice and don't do anything to raise suspicion. Have them search her bag and see if they find anything."

"We can do that."

"If you don't find anything in a couple of days, then cut her loose. I don't want to waste any more manpower on her than we have to. If she's up to no good, you should know it immediately."

"If the kid IDs her, then what?"

"We'll cross that bridge when we get to it. If you find anything in her hotel room or on her person, then we'll turn her over to the KGB. If she's hiding something, they'll find out what it is."

"I think she's more than just a tourist," Petrov said.

"You don't get paid to think," Kozlov said in a huff. "You get paid to agree with what I think. Now get out of here."

He waved his hand dismissively and Petrov left without another word. Back in his office, he found Fabi still sitting right where he had left him.

"I want you to follow the girl for two more days. Don't let her out of your sight. Do you think she spotted you?"

"No. She definitely doesn't know I'm there," Fabi answered confidently.

"Good. Keep it that way. Have her hotel room searched again. This time have them look closer and go through every nook and cranny. Stop her and do a routine search. Check out her passport and visa and make sure it's in order. Have them search her bags. They can even pat her down if they're suspicious. Something's not right about this girl, but I don't know what it is. I want you to find it."

"I think she's just a tourist."

"You don't get paid to think. You get paid to agree with what I think."

"Yes sir."

Petrov took a picture of the girl out of the file and headed to the hospital.

***

Fabi let out a deep sigh of relief and left the office. He called his wife.

"Honey. I'm going to be home late tonight. Don't wait up for me. I'm working on a big case. If I can break this case open, I can get in good with the Lieutenant. I might even get a commendation or a promotion with a raise. Don't tell anyone, but I think I'm tracking an American spy. Wish me luck."

While all this was happening, Jamie was sound asleep in her hotel room.

10

Pinsk, Belarus
A few weeks before

Candice "Candy" Smith sat in her plush office in Pinsk, Belarus, loving life and thrilled with the business adventure that had brought her there.

Pinsk was a quaint town on the southwest side of Belarus in the province of Brest. A far cry from L.A. and the glitz, glamour, and nightlife Candy grew up in as a Valley Girl. But she loved it, nevertheless.

Candy was born in Hermosa Beach, California. She attended UCLA for one year but got bored and dropped out, never able to apply her drive and perfectionism to the pursuit of education.

Her father died unexpectedly of a heart attack when she was nineteen, and she blamed her alcoholic mother, who spent too much of his money and was more interested in her country club friends than in her husband. From that point on, Candy looked for every opportunity to disappoint her mother and get as far away from her as possible.

Pinsk was exactly 6,604 miles from her mom's house in the San Fernando Valley. Just far enough, as far as she was concerned.

Candy sat in a high-back leather chair, idling her time, admiring the view. Two sides of the office were solid windows looking out at the large, white, steeple of the *Franciscan Church of the Assumption of the Virgin Mary and Monastery* that dominated the sky and was the number-one tourist attraction in Pinsk.

While she had no religious affiliation or interest in anything spiritual and hadn't stepped foot in a church in years, she often found herself staring at the church, feeling some type of deep connection. A spiritual oneness with either the Virgin Mary or the female nuns who'd taken vows of celibacy, or perhaps both.

Ironic. Considering her line of work.

"You look nice today as usual," her assistant Jada said, interrupting her thoughts as she brought a file in and laid it on her desk.

"You do as well," Candy responded.

Jada had to look nice. Candy demanded it, and Jada complied. Something necessary, considering their entire business was centered around finding beautiful girls.

Candy remembered the first time Jada came in for an interview. She'd worn a plain-colored brown dress with flats. Except for the fact that she was stunningly beautiful, she would've been kicked right out of the office without a single question. But Candy saw something in Jada and hired her on the spot, transforming her into the gorgeous assistant who stood before her today in a skin-tight, mini, black faux-leather dress, pumps, and a green scarf to accent it. Her long, silky, black hair was thick and shiny. Hair Candy would give anything to have been born with.

"Your first appointment is here," Jada said.

"Have her wait. I'll see her in a minute."

She looked around the office to satisfy herself that everything was in order. The office was modern and stylish. A white, built-in bookcase covered the entire left wall. The books were only for decoration and were neatly arranged by a designer who charged more than $15,000 American dollars to create what was the nicest office in all of Pinsk.

Her handcrafted pedestal desk from Italy was neatly organized with no papers, a decorative lamp, a computer, and a white acrylic statue of a man and woman embracing.

A perfectionist by nature, Candy insisted her office always reflected her attention to detail. Always be reflective of the elegance of the person occupying it.

The desk had a transparent glass top with no drawers and an L-shape return with two drawers. Not having drawers in the front allowed Candy's long, slender, and perfectly proportioned legs to be displayed so that they were the first thing most people saw when they walked into the room.

The second thing they usually saw was her breathtaking beauty.

Although a normal day at the office, Candy was dressed for success. She wore a high-waisted, black-leather designer mini-skirt, tight and form fitting. Her Rio red blouse had a plunging V-neck, the three-quarter sleeves made of perfectly draped, silk fabric.

Her shoes were bright red spiked, closed toe, patent leather Versace stilettos, and were the most expensive item in her presentation, including her jewelry, which was made up of diamond hoop earrings and one classic princess-cut diamond ring which was her grandmother's wedding ring. Something she wore proudly on the middle finger of her left hand.

Her hands and fingers were perfectly manicured with French nails mailed in from Paris once a month.

Candy hit the intercom button on her phone and said, "I'll see her now."

She liked to keep the girls waiting so they would become even more nervous. The girls must both admire and fear her. Something she started instilling in them with the first meeting.

She stood and walked around the desk as a young, nineteen-year-old woman entered, escorted by Jada.

Candy held out her hand and said in a friendly manner, "My name is Candice, but everyone calls me Candy."

"Hi. I'm Olga," she said nervously.

Olga's hands were sweaty and clammy but not shaking, clearly doing everything she could to present a composed manner. Her shoulders were back and her head up. She looked Candy in the eye when she shook her hand. A good first impression—except for the clothes.

Olga was wearing a pink midi-skirt, a white blouse with ruffles, and a knockoff leather jacket whose sleeves came down just below the elbow. Her hair was chocolate brown and shoulder length, parted slightly off the center to the left. Her nails were painted a shade of pink that didn't match her skirt.

Her brown, two-inch heeled shoes were scuffed, and while she obviously tried to polish them before she came to the meeting, they were noticeably worn. As was the dirty brown handbag with a long strap that had seen better days.

Candy grinned slightly. Everything about the outfit was wrong. But Olga had a quality. A girl-next-door beauty. Outfit and styling could be changed. Poise and elegance could be taught. But inner beauty was innate.

A girl either had it or she didn't. If she didn't, she would be rejected immediately. Candy had been doing this long enough to know which girls would be successful in the program and who would wash out. Olga had potential to be one of her best girls.

"How did you hear about us?" Candy asked.

"I saw your website and I filled out an application. Someone called me, and I met with her ... I believe her name was Tatiana. And here I am."

She put both hands out in front of her with her palms up and shrugged her shoulders as a gesture to say this is me. This is what you get. For better or for worse.

The website was called bellesofbelarus.com. Tatiana was one of twelve salespeople—all women—who Candy hired to go throughout Belarus and recruit the women. Within a few months, they had a waiting list of more than twelve-hundred women who were waiting to be matched with men.

They had so many applicants, they also began recruiting women to serve as escorts at the casinos in Minsk. A select few were flown to the Middle East to service the clients there.

She's cute.

Olga was well spoken, confident, and appropriately nervous. Anyone would be in that setting.

Candy flipped through the file. "It says you are nineteen. Are you a virgin?"

Olga blushed and looked down, shaking her head no.

"Tatiana said I didn't have to be," Olga said, her voice shaking.

The answer didn't matter. Candy just wanted to see her reaction. About half the girls she saw were still virgins at nineteen. So, half weren't.

Some American men requested virgins, but most didn't. Some preferred women with sexual experiences. The casinos in Minsk definitely wanted experienced girls. Olga was better suited for the mail-order-bride business even if she wasn't a virgin.

"Why do you want to go to America?" Candy asked.

Olga's eyes began to sparkle as a look of excitement came over her face.

"I want to make a better life for myself. I want to go to school and be an architect."

Olga went on to share about her background and family troubles. Candy let her continue uninterrupted.

Olga was a typical Belarusian woman. The unemployment rate for young, single women in Belarus was more than fifty percent, so there were a lot of women looking for work. Olga had her share of family and work troubles. Unable to afford college, she'd likely end up working for the state, destined to a life consumed by long hours at a demanding and demeaning job.

Candy didn't let herself have emotional attachments to the girls, but that didn't mean she didn't feel sorry for them and their plight. It warmed her heart to know she was helping these girls.

The decision was made. Olga was in.

"Here's how it works," Candy said. "We're going to schedule you for a complete makeover. Hair, makeup, nails, and spa treatments. Then we'll do a photo shoot. A photographer will create a portfolio of pictures for the website."

"I can't afford all of that," Olga said hesitantly.

"It's all provided," Candy said. "We pay the cost. We'll get you a visa, passport, and pay for your plane ticket to America. However, I need to know that you're serious about going. You're going to marry an American man sight unseen. Are you okay with that?"

"I understand. I will grow to love him."

One of the reasons the program was so successful. Belarusian women were notoriously loyal. Subservience to men was ingrained in them from childhood. A philosophy Candy could never accept but admired in her girls.

"What if he doesn't like me?" Olga asked.

"He will. I'm sure of it. But if he doesn't, you'll stay in America while we try to find you another match. If we can't find one, then you'll come back here and go back on the waiting list until we find someone. I don't think you'll have a problem. Once you're married, you'll be a US citizen. You can divorce him after one year and still maintain your citizenship."

Candy took out the file and handed Olga a piece of paper. A confidentiality agreement.

"Read this over. This is the most important thing. You're not allowed to contact your family for a year. You can't tell them anything about the process or who you are matched with. They will not be able to contact you. Before you leave for America, you'll write letters and cards that we will mail to them over the year. Do you understand that?"

Olga nodded yes.

"If an emergency comes up, we'll contact you. If you agree to those terms, sign the document, and we'll get you started on your makeover."

Candy took a pen out of her desk and handed it to Olga. She took the pen and signed the form. Candy called for Jada to come back into the office.

"Olga is going to join us. Get her set up for a makeover."

She turned to Olga. "Congratulations. You're in."

A wide smile came on the girl's face as she let out a little squeal of delight.

"My twin sister is in the lobby. Would you be interested in her as well?"

"Of course."

Candy stood, walked around the desk, and gave Olga a hug.

"You're going to do very well. I'm confident we can find you a husband in America."

She summoned Olga's sister in. If they weren't wearing different clothes, she never would've been able to tell them apart.

That's good. Two sisters. Made her job easier.

***

A couple of months later

The unusual career path started for Candy right after her father died when she was approached by a friend in L.A. who told her she could make good money dancing privately for rich men. Shortly thereafter, she found her calling.

She didn't need the money. She had a trust fund with more money in it than she'd ever need. The thrill and the control she had over men was what she loved. She didn't find it demeaning; she found it empowering.

She signed a contract with a company called VIP escorts and became one of their top women. Men paid as much as $1,000 an hour for her time. Seventy percent of that was her take. Anything extra was negotiated between her and the men.

She quickly earned a reputation for being discreet, beautiful, and worth whatever she cost. When asked to go to the Middle East for $20,000 to meet privately with a real estate developer from Turkey, she agreed. Her father did a lot of business in Saudi Arabia and Oman, so she was familiar with the area, and as a girl, dreamed of meeting a prince or rich Middle Eastern businessman.

The man's name was Omer Asaf.

Eventually, Candy started acting as a liaison and coordinated other American girls to come to the Middle East for what they called "sessions." Omer set up a company, and they shared the profits equally. It became highly lucrative, and Candy started making more than a million dollars a year—tax free—since the money was run through a Turkish company.

The girls were happy because they got a free trip out of it and made as much as they would make in three months in the states.

The money was the scorecard. The more money she made, the more proof she was winning. Omer always seemed happy with the results, so it was a win/win all the way around.

A year before, Omer had approached her about a new opportunity. He wanted her to go to Belarus and set up a company that matched Belarusian women with American men looking for a wife. She jumped at the opportunity.

He set up the office for her in Pinsk and gave her full control of the day-to-day operations. Money was no object. The only expectation he had of her was that she had to recruit three hundred women a month.

The caller ID on her phone confirmed he was calling her.

"Omer, darling! It's so good to hear from you," Candy answered warmly.

"Hello beautiful," he said, the words she always expected to be greeted with when he called.

Omer was nothing more than a meal ticket to her, even though she genuinely admired the man. Not just a real estate developer, he was one of the hundred richest men in the world. The feelings of affection were mutual.

Omer admitted that when he first met Candy, he was mesmerized by her wit, charm, and drop-dead gorgeous looks. He hired her on the spot to become his exclusive girl.

For two years, she accompanied him to hundreds of functions and was on call twenty-four hours a day, seven days a week. He couldn't travel to some places because he was on a terrorism watch list, something he said was a misunderstanding, but he took her to many exotic places, nonetheless.

The physical part of their relationship had been awkward and meaningless to Candy, but she'd played the part perfectly, turning it into a full-time job.

"When am I going to see you again?" Candy asked. "It's been such a long time. You're such a busy man."

"You must come back to Oman some time. I'll arrange it in the future."

Candy knew that wasn't going to happen. Omer had grown tired of the physical relationship as well and had turned his affections to the next girls. For him, the relationship was strictly business.

From Candy's perspective, a business relationship going well for both parties.

"I remember the first time you came to Oman," Omer said. "If I remember right, I paid you $20,000."

"That's right," Candy replied with a chuckle. "You have a good memory."

"You've made me millions since. You might be the best investment I ever made."

"No complaints from me either. I have some ideas on how to make you even more money."

"I'm not surprised. Your mind is always thinking about business. When you were in bed with me, is that what you were thinking about—business?"

"Of course not. I gave you your money's worth, didn't I?"

"You've always been good at both. Sex and business."

Candy laughed.

She got her business abilities from her dad. She wasn't sure where she got her sexual prowess. Not from her mom. Her dad had once confided that her mom was frigid, and he couldn't remember the last time they'd had sex. Their relationship lasted more out of convenience and business than love.

Perhaps that's why sex had become more of a business relationship for her as well. When it came to Omer, they were one and the same to her, sex and business, although she'd never let him know that.

"Come on now, Omer. You know you've always been my favorite. That's why I always kept you for myself. I knew how to make you happy," Candy said, laughing.

"How are things in Pinsk?" Omer asked, changing the subject back to the purpose of the call.

"Very good," she responded, which was true.

"Is the next shipment of girls ready?" Omer asked.

"Almost. They will be ready by next Friday. We'll have five bus loads leaving Pinsk if you'll be ready for them. Three hundred girls."

"We'll be ready."

"Perfect. You're the best."

"No, you are," Omer said. "That's why I love you."

Candy kissed into the phone with two loud smacks and hung up.

She dialed her assistant. "We're on for next Friday. Contact the girls. Tell them to pack their bags and be in Pinsk next Friday at three o'clock. One suitcase and one carry-on only. Tell them to bring their passports and say goodbye to their families."

Candy hung up the phone and said to herself, "I love my job."

11

Palace of the Republic, Minsk

Denys Onufeychuk, the Minister of Transportation for the Republic of Belarus, had been in the position for more than ten years and was one of President Igor Bobrinsky's most trusted advisors. His office was less than a stone's throw to the President's, and he met with him almost every day, even though their relationship had grown more strained over the last couple years.

He had not agreed with Bobrinsky's strategy to become more closely aligned with Russia. He believed they should align with the western world and even petition to join NATO. Something Bobrinsky strongly disagreed with.

The President's affection for Russia ran deep. He spent years in the Russian army rising through the ranks. Before stepping into politics, he ran a *kolkhoz* or what was commonly called a "collective farm." Those were industries of the state run by selected businessmen called oligarchs, who lined their pockets on the backs of the peasants of Belarus. Slave labor really.

Bobrinsky's fortune grew to over an estimated fifty million dollars from his farm.

Once in politics, he was backed politically and financially by the Russians and secured power and had held on to it ever since with the help of the Russians and tainted elections, increasing his influence and fortune proportionately each year.

Denys knew he was fighting an uphill battle and his advice as it pertained to the evils of communism fell on deaf ears, so he mostly kept his mouth shut.

While traveling to Vienna a few years before, he was approached by a CIA operative who recruited him to become an agent for the United States government. A Swiss bank account was set up, and millions of dollars had been deposited into his account as he provided information regarding Belarus, and more importantly, Russian activities.

A path that kept his life in constant danger under fear of being discovered.

Seventy-two years old, Denys felt like the benefits outweighed the risks. He hadn't spent a dime of the money and probably never would. He did it because he loved the motherland and hated what was becoming of it. His wife had died years earlier from a disease, and his kids were grown.

He couldn't leave them the money. There would be too much scrutiny. He could never amass that much money on his salary which was well above average for a Belarusian but not one of which fortunes were made.

As Minister of Transportation, border control was one of his responsibilities. Russia and Belarus maintained an open border, so his main concern was commercial transportation between the countries. Denys had recently alerted his CIA handler that a man with terrorist ties from Turkey had been buying up real estate and setting up businesses in Belarus. He had purchased the *Casino California*, the *Splash* nightclub, and a number of other office buildings in and around Minsk.

Denys also learned that the businessman would be transporting three hundred young women as mail order brides monthly through the Russian border and that Denys and his people were to let them pass without any scrutiny. That directive came from the President himself.

Denys was suspicious that the mail order bride business might be used as a front for sex trafficking or to fund terrorism out of the Middle East.

He was given instructions to meet a CIA operative, a woman, at Liberty Square. He was to provide her with a satellite phone, and the name of the Turkish businessman who was funding the operation. If she didn't show up at the scheduled time, he was instructed to wait fifteen minutes and then leave.

She never showed up.

He was still distraught about missing the meeting because he desperately needed to get her the information. That morning he did some checking and found the woman did come through customs and was checked in at the *Monastyrski Hotel* in Minsk and hadn't checked out.

He sat in his office contemplating his next move.

Why didn't the woman show up? Had something bad happened to her? Was she arrested for some reason? Kidnapped or worse, killed? Maybe she had been followed and aborted the meeting to protect his identity. That made the most sense of all the scenarios he was creating in his mind.

At that moment his secretary walked in carrying a file.

"The Militsia sent a request over for any information we have on an American girl named Allie Walker. What would you like for me to do?"

A jolt of panic went through Denys's body as he struggled not to grimace and give anything away. Allie Walker was the name of the CIA contact he was supposed to meet at the square last night. The one who didn't show up.

"Just leave it on my desk. I'll review it," he said indifferently.

When she left, he immediately picked up the file and scanned it. It didn't say why the Minsk police were asking about her, but he knew it couldn't be a good thing. So far, she hadn't been arrested, but they were apparently watching her.

They had ordered her to be stopped and searched and for her room to be inspected. They had accessed her information from customs and were wondering if his office had any additional information that would be helpful to them.

He called his secretary back in the room.

"Tell them that we don't have any information other than what is in the file. Tell them she came through customs, and everything checked out. The woman is clean."

He handed the file back to his secretary, and she left him alone in his office with his thoughts.

I need to warn her.

She obviously had the proper paperwork since she got through customs without any problem. If the Militsia brought her in for questioning, he could do something about it. He could have her transferred to his jurisdiction. He'd have to come up with a good excuse, so it didn't draw attention to himself.

If the KGB got her, then there was nothing he could do for her. They'd take her someplace secluded, and who knew what they might do to her.

Denys shuddered at the thought. He was getting ahead of himself. So far, she'd only raised the suspicions of the local police. It may be nothing.

He really didn't know how these operatives worked. Did she have help?

Did she have a weapon?

I hope she doesn't have a gun.

His thoughts raced like a bullet toward a target. How could he contact her without raising suspicion? Especially if she was being watched. Another meet with an operative was scheduled for later that day. A man this time. Denys had learned that the same Turkish businessman was trying to acquire a briefcase nuke from Bobrinsky. That meet was even more important than the meeting with the girl.

He hoped this operative showed up. He was taking great risks scheduling meetings with two operatives within twenty-four hours of each other. It was worth the risk. This was the most important information he'd ever discovered.

He had to get both of the operatives the man's name.

They both needed to know that Omer Asaf was a very dangerous man.

***

Minsk Regional Medical Hospital No. 9

Lieutenant Petrov lit a cigarette and walked through the large double doors of the hospital and stopped at the information desk in the lobby. He pointed at his badge to the short, stubby, bald man sitting behind the desk eating a strawberry jam *Vatrushka* and drinking a bottle of carbonated water.

The only reason he knew the pastry was strawberry was because of the smear of jelly on the side of the man's mouth. These type of men disgusted Petrov. They were weak and undisciplined. Barely deserving of any job, much less one important as dispensing information.

"I need Yegor Zoran's room," Petrov said roughly.

The stubby man scrambled to look up the name on his computer, almost spilling his drink. He wiped off his mouth with his hand but then looked for something to wipe his hand on rather than get the jam on his computer keyboard. Not finding a napkin, he just wiped the jam on his pant leg and began typing. The man was probably fifty years old but was clearly intimidated by the police lieutenant.

"Ён у пакоі 427," the stubby man said.

Petrov turned without saying a word and walked to the already-opened elevator, stepped in, and pushed the button for the fourth floor. Upon exiting the elevator, he looked for an ash tray to put out his cigarette. Seeing none, he threw it on the floor, put it out with his foot, and smashed it into the floor.

The nurse at the nurse's station glared at him, then looked down to his badge and turned away, busying herself. Probably thought better of saying anything.

"Which way to room 427?" Petrov asked the nurse.

"Down that hall," she said, pointing. "Then take a left, and it's on your left."

Petrov followed the directions to room 427 and opened the door. Yegor was sleeping and being tended to by a nurse. The nurse explained that he'd had surgery on his knee and was now starting to awaken from his anesthesia. She suggested politely that the detective come back later when Yegor was more awake.

Petrov walked over to Yegor and shook him violently. The young man opened his eyes but was still groggy. The inspector pulled a picture of the woman out of his shirt pocket and showed it to Yegor.

"Is this the woman who assaulted you?"

Yegor closed his eyes.

Petrov shook him harder.

The nurse moved toward them but stopped herself.

"Kid," he said in a loud voice that echoed through the room. "Look at this picture and tell me if you recognize this woman."

Yegor mumbled something and shook his head, but Petrov couldn't tell what he said. It looked like he shook his head yes, but he couldn't be sure. He looked at the nurse, but she just shrugged her shoulders. He walked out of the room and went to the main nurse's station by the elevators.

"There was another boy who came in with the kid in 427. What room is he in?"

"He already checked out," she said.

Petrov stood there for a moment, considering what he should do.

"How bad are the injuries to the kid's leg?" he asked the nurse.

"The doctor's think he'll probably lose his left leg, but they're trying to save it."

"Has he said anything to you about what happened to him?"

"He said that a girl kicked him."

"Do you think a girl kicking him could cause that much damage?"

"No way. I think it must have been caused by a baseball bat or a lead pipe."

Petrov grunted, which was his way of saying thank you. He went to the elevator, pushed the button, and left without saying another word.

Once outside, he pulled out his cell phone and dialed Detective Fabi who was supposed to be staking out the American woman's hotel.

"Have you stopped the woman yet?" Petrov asked.

"She hasn't come out of the hotel," Fabi responded nervously as if somehow it was his fault. "I'm here waiting for her. I have two officers with me, just like you said."

"When she comes out, I want you to stop her and search her. I don't think she's involved, but let's find out. If you don't find anything, we can eliminate her as a suspect."

"Do you still want me to search her room?"

"Of course. When she goes out, search her first, then her room. I want you to follow her around today. See what she does."

"You can count on me. Should I ask her about the boys?"

"You can ask. See her reaction when you mention an attack on two boys. The nurse said a kick from a woman couldn't cause those injuries. She thought they were caused by a lead pipe or a baseball bat."

"I doubt the girl is carrying a pipe around with her, and there wasn't one at the scene. I was with her all day yesterday. She definitely didn't have a baseball bat on her."

"She could've taken it with her and thrown it away. Maybe—"

"Where would she have gotten a pipe or a bat?" Fabi asked, immediately regretting having interrupted his boss.

"How would I know? It might've been laying on the ground. The boys may have had it, and she took it from them. Like I said, I don't think she's involved but we have to consider all options."

"What did the boy say?" Fabi asked. "Did he say it was her?"

"The boy isn't awake enough to give me a positive ID. The other kid has already checked out of the hospital. I'll go by his house and see if he can ID her. I think it's a dead end."

"I'll search her and her room and then get back with you. We'll look for a weapon. If we find one, we'll bring her in."

The Lieutenant hung up the phone and looked at his notes for the address of the other boy. He didn't have it with him. He got into his car and drove back to the office. He'd find the address and then go to the boy's house.

Petrov was frustrated because too many man hours were being wasted pursuing the woman. Eliminating her as a suspect was as easy as showing the boys a picture. If it wasn't her, they could move on to other suspects. Another frustration. They didn't have any other suspects.

The only lead he had was the American woman. He hoped to know if she was involved one way or the other before lunch.

If she was, then he'd make her regret ever stepping foot in Belarus.

12

Lieutenant Petrov went back to his office, poured himself a cup of coffee and a shot of vodka, and downed both within seconds. He opened the police report and searched the file for the name and address of the second boy involved in the alleged attack.

Still "alleged" in his mind because he had no idea what had happened. The boys may have well been the instigators or the victims.

He'd hoped the boy in the hospital would've been awake enough to identify the woman in the picture, either implicating or excluding her as a suspect. He seemed to recognize her, but there was no way to be sure. Clearly, he was too groggy to make a positive ID one way or the other.

This case had him puzzled. If it was her, it would raise more questions than answers. Why would a young American woman attack two boys and rob them of a few dollars? If they attacked her, and she was defending herself, where did she learn the skill, and why didn't she call the Militsia?

Nothing about either scenario made sense. Petrov considered the second possibility as he tried to picture in his mind how it happened. The girl wandered by mistake into the alleyway. The boys tried to rob her, and she put them down, having some self-defense training.

A grin came across his face, hoping that was the case. These punk boys were a nuisance and consumed too much of his time. The girl might deserve a commendation rather than an arrest warrant as far as he was concerned.

But what did she have to hide?

The only explanation then would be that she was an American agent. He looked at her picture again. She didn't fit the profile. Why would she be working alone in Minsk, and what interest would she have in a couple of punk kids?

Maybe she wanted a gun and took one off of them. She obviously couldn't bring one into the country. Although the CIA could easily provide her one. The government knew the US had operatives working covertly in Belarus. Certainly, she wouldn't need to rob a couple of boys to get a gun, and neither of them mentioned they even had a gun on them.

He called his secretary into his office.

"Did we hear back from the Ministry of Transportation about the girl, Allie Walker?"

"Yes," she replied, "I put their response on your desk."

Petrov shuffled through some papers.

The secretary walked over to the desk and found it for him.

He glanced at it reading it aloud to himself, "The girl was thoroughly checked out in customs, and she's clean."

Meaning she wasn't a CIA agent or a known terrorist. The second was obvious. And the Ministry of Transportation would know if the Americans had an operative working in Belarus. A common courtesy afforded most host countries.

Under normal protocol, the CIA would contact the Ministry and let them know an agent was traveling to Belarus and would give them a stated reason. No one was naïve enough to believe they didn't conduct clandestine operations, but what could a girl like this possibly be doing undercover in Belarus?

More questions than answers, Petrov concluded. A mystery easily resolved by showing the boys her picture. But the one kid was out of commission. His only immediate option was the second kid. He pulled out the file to review his information.

Rafael Lipko.

Petrov ran his name through the computer and found no criminal record other than a few minor offenses while a juvenile. However, something about the name rang a bell.

Lipko . . .

On a hunch, he ran the last name through the computer and got a hit for Oleksandr Lipko, He did more research and found him to be Rafael's older brother. Olek was a known gang member. He'd been linked to more serious offenses including the bombing of the Russian embassy.

That's why he remembered the name. Olek had done a couple stints in prison, but they hadn't been able to make any of the more serious allegations stick.

Now, he felt like he was getting somewhere. It made more sense. The attack could have been retaliation by another gang. Perhaps, Olek and his group did something to the Brotherhood, the name of a Russian gang operating in Belarus. The Brotherhood hit back by attacking his little brother. His brother made up a story about a girl attacking them to keep the heat off Olek and his gang.

He searched the computer to see if there were any reports of gang activity in the last few days. Nothing obvious surfaced or that could be tied to a retaliatory hit. Didn't mean something didn't happen, it simply meant this wasn't on their radar.

Petrov debated his next move. He needed to question the boy, but it would be a pain. His morning was already shot, and he had a mountain of paperwork to take care of. He considered sending one of his other detectives but rejected that idea.

This case was a priority to him. He wanted to satisfy his curiosity about the girl. Customs were suspicious when she entered, and that's why they questioned her for four hours. He was suspicious now. Something about her didn't seem logical even with what the Ministry had said.

A gut feeling maybe.

He looked up Rafael's address in the police report and compared it to the one on the computer. They matched.

The two young men lived in the Leninsky District less than three miles from his office. He wrote down the address, 24 vulica Karla Marksa, a street named after Karl Marx in a district named after Lenin.

Petrov grabbed his jacket off the back of his chair, gulped down another cup of coffee, lit a cigarette, and headed back outside. He could've walked but decided to take his car in case he got a lead that took him elsewhere.

Not a house but a three-level apartment building. He pulled up in front and stopped in a tow-away zone right in front of the building. Petrov immediately wondered how the boys afforded such a nice place in such a nice part of town. He took the stairs rather than the elevator to the second floor, found number 24, and rapped loudly on the door.

Olek answered.

Petrov knew it was Olek from the mug shot on the computer. He flashed his lieutenant's badge, looking for a response. Nothing noticeable came across his face. He seemed indifferent as if a detective came to his house every day, which was in and of itself suspicious.

Most people in Belarus would be petrified if a lieutenant of the Militsia knocked on their door unexpectedly. Olek was trying too hard to seem innocent. Petrov had seen it many times. Try so hard to seem like they're not hiding anything, and it becomes obvious they are.

Olek wore a white sleeveless undershirt, black jeans, and expensive tennis shoes. He was muscular with an unshaven, scruffy beard. The computer file said he was twenty-nine.

Anger rose inside of Petrov. He struggled to control it.

He couldn't stand punks like Olek. They were arrogant and had no respect for authority. More importantly, they had no regard for the history of Russia and Belarus and the men who'd come before them who fought wars so they could remain free from the tyranny of the west.

He considered Olek a waste of youth and ability. He should be serving in the armed services rather than roaming the streets causing problems for the authorities.

Petrov ignored his dislike for him and got to the point.

"I'm looking for Rafael," he said, roughly trying to bring the right level of intimidation to the situation.

Olek had his left hand on the door holding it half shut. Almost like he was hiding something inside. Petrov could've forced his way in but wanted to let it play out.

"He's not here," Olek said, becoming noticeably more nervous. A sign he was lying.

"Where is he?"

"He went to the grocery store."

"I'll wait for him."

"He ... may be a ... while," Olek said, stuttering. "I don't expect him back for several hours."

"It takes several hours to go to the grocery store?"

"He had to run some errands ... for our mother. He'll go to the grocery store last."

Now he knew Olek was lying. Petrov had been a detective long enough to know when someone was hiding something.

But what? And why?

He had no intention of waiting around, but he said so to throw Olek off. A clear sign someone was lying was when they changed their story after you poked holes in part of it.

If Rafael was at the grocery store, he'd only be gone for a few minutes. He'd have milk or eggs, or something that needed to go in the fridge. He wouldn't carry groceries around for other errands. If he was going to the grocery store last, Olek wouldn't have answered that he went to the grocery store. He would have said he went out to run errands. Interrogation was an art, and Petrov knew all the tricks.

Olek clearly didn't want him to wait for his brother to return. Probably because his brother was already there.

Petrov debated his next move. He could walk right in. He didn't need a warrant or probable cause. Whatever he wanted to do was enough to warrant a search, and a seizure for that matter.

He hesitated.

If he went in, he'd probably find something. Maybe the boy. That would be the best-case scenario. Then he could find out the truth about the girl.

But what if the boy wasn't there? He might find guns or drugs. That would require him to take Olek down to the station. There'd be paperwork to fill out, and then his afternoon would be shot. The whole day wasted.

Instead, Petrov pulled the picture of the girl out of his shirt pocket and flashed it in front of Olek.

"Have you ever seen this girl before?" he asked.

Olek looked at the picture. "No. I've never seen her before."

Petrov studied the young man carefully. He was telling the truth. At least about the girl. He handed him the picture along with one of his cards with a phone number on it.

"Have Rafael look at this picture and see if it's the girl who attacked him. Have him call the number on the card. He probably won't get me but tell him to leave me a message. Just yes or no. Verify if it's her or not. I expect to hear from him today. Is that understood?"

Olek took the picture and the card but didn't respond.

"Do you understand, Olek?" Petrov said more sternly.

Olek nodded yes and started to shut the door.

"If I don't hear from your brother in the next few hours, I'll be back down here at your doorstep. I don't think you want to see me again, so soon. Are we clear?"

"так, сэр"

"Yes sir," Olek had said respectfully with a hint of fear in his voice.

Petrov turned and walked away and back down the stairs. More confused than before.

What was Olek hiding? How was he involved? Made him more suspicious that the attack was related to Olek's gang in some way. Maybe the girl had nothing to do with it after all.

Petrov wasn't a patient man. He wasn't going to chase Rafael around town and didn't want to make another trip to the hospital. The nurse had said Yegor might need more surgery. He wasn't an errand boy. He'd already wasted too much time as it was.

He decided to go to the hotel and question the girl himself. He'd conduct a thorough search of her and her room. If she was hiding something, he'd find it. If she was lying, he'd know it immediately.

He got back in the car and drove to the hotel, determined to question the girl, and find out if she had anything to hide.

***

Olek closed the door and walked into the bedroom where Rafael was hiding, shaken. He shoved the picture of the girl into his face.

"Is this the girl who attacked you?" Olek asked roughly.

Rafael's eyes widened and a look of fear ran across his face. "That's her."

"Why is a detective involved? What were you doing? You'd better not lie to me, or I'll beat you worse than she did."

"It's Yegor's fault. The girl just happened to walk into the alley. We were hanging out. We weren't doing anything wrong. I promise."

"What happened?"

"Yegor tried to rob her."

"What an idiot."

"He told her to give him her money and cell phone. That's when she attacked him. She broke his leg. I was trying to get away but then she attacked me. Like some ninja or something. Started doing karate and stuff like that. She attacked us before we could do anything. Then she took Yegor's gun. You know, the one you gave us."

"What! She took my gun! I have to get that gun back."

"I don't know where it is. All I know is she took it. I didn't tell the police about the gun."

"You idiot! Why did you talk to the police at all?" Olek said. "Have I not taught you anything? Never talk to them. We resolve these things ourselves. We have ways of dealing with people like her. You call this detective and tell him that's not the girl."

He gave Rafael the card the lieutenant had left for him.

"What if he knows I'm lying?"

"Just deny it. He can't prove it. Tell him that's not the girl. Tell him you didn't really see anything. It was dark. You were in an alley. You were blindsided. You don't even know if it was a girl. You might've been wrong about that."

"Okay. I'll tell him."

Olek put his hand on his little brother's head and pulled it toward him. "Don't worry about a thing. I'll take care of this myself. She has disrespected your honor and the honor of our family. I'm going to make her pay."

Olek took out his phone and dialed the number for the leader of their gang, Kostyantin Vinovoy. The gang was called the Red Spades. They had more than a hundred members—men between the ages of twenty-five and forty.

Many of them were hardened criminals. A number were wanted for various violent crimes including murder. Olek was one of the more prominent leaders. One of Kostyantin's right hand men. He could count on his brothers to help him find the girl and make her disappear.

Kostyantin answered on the first ring.

"Kosty. This is Olek. I need your help."

***

Petrov drove the short distance to the *Monastyrski Hotel*. It took a while to find a parking space on the street. He didn't want to park right in front of the hotel and perhaps spook the girl. He found Fabi and the two uniformed Militsia in no time.

Something that frustrated him. Fabi was not supposed to let the girl see him. If he could easily see Fabi, then so could she. He said as much right after he walked up to them.

"What are you doing, Fabi?" Petrov said.

"We're watching the hotel. Waiting for the girl."

"You're doing surveillance. She's not supposed to see you."

"She hasn't. I was just—"

"I don't want to hear it," Petrov said in a gruff voice. "Has she come out?"

"No. We haven't seen her."

"That's not surprising. She just got here yesterday. Probably jet lagged. Slept in. She'll come out soon. Are there any other exits?"

"There are, but they all lead to this street. When she comes out, we'll see her."

"Fabi, you stay in the shadows. I want you to keep following her, but don't let her see you."

He told the two uniformed policemen to stop the girl and search her bags and her body. Make sure her papers were in order and that she wasn't carrying a weapon.

He'd give her thirty minutes. If she came out, the men could search her while he searched her room. If she didn't come out, then he'd knock on her hotel room and surprise her. Even if she was asleep.

An even better plan. Catch her off guard. Do a search of the room with her present and before she had time to hide anything.

Petrov was satisfied. He finally had a plan.

"Allie Walker. Let's see if you are up to no good," he said quietly to himself.

13

Jamie slept past noon.

She felt much better, except for an uneasy feeling in the pit of her stomach. She would've slept later, but the feeling woke her up. At first, she thought she was hungry. Then she realized the feeling came with anxiety.

A sense of dread. A sixth sense like danger was lurking.

She sat up in her bed, analyzing the situation, searching for the source of her angst. It had to be one of two things—the fight with the boys or her contact not showing up. She decided she was most troubled about the boys.

While she was concerned about the contact, the boys had complicated her mission. At first, she thought they wouldn't talk. They'd be too embarrassed to admit they'd been beaten up by a girl.

If they'd belonged to a more sophisticated gang, that probably would've been the case. But these were young kids, inexperienced, who would never be able to keep their stories straight.

If she hadn't hurt the one boy so badly, then they would've probably kept their mouths shut. The one kid with the hurt leg would have to go to the hospital. The police would be called.

Even if they made up some story about another gang or being attacked by some unknown assailant, their stories wouldn't hold up to interrogation. One of them would cave and say it was an American girl with blonde hair.

The Militsia would show them her customs picture and they'd identify her. How many young American girls with blonde hair were running around Minsk? Her tail would also acknowledge he'd lost her for two hours, and she'd have no alibi.

Her word against theirs, and she could talk her way out of it, except . . .

Except she had their gun.

The gun was problematic. No way to talk her way out of having that. It tied her directly to the boys and to the attack.

Although the attack would be the least of her worries. The gun would blow her cover. Any story she came up with wouldn't matter. If they found her with it, they'd arrest her and not care whether she got it from the boys or not.

They wouldn't even care about the attack at that point. The gun would be their biggest concern.

Jamie evaluated her options. She couldn't leave the gun in her room. It would be searched again. Her hiding place was good, but not that good. Not worth the risk.

She couldn't carry it with her because if she were stopped, she'd have to use it. No way would she let them arrest her. That was why Brad said she couldn't take a gun with her.

His words echoed in her head. *No guns. If you have a gun, you'll be tempted to use it.* She hated to admit Brad was right, and she was wrong.

She couldn't be captured in Belarus with a gun. She'd be locked up for years, and the CIA wouldn't do a thing about it. They'd rather let her rot in jail than admit they had an agent working undercover in Belarus.

But would she use the gun?

If she was stopped by a policeman, and the gun was discovered, Jamie also knew that she wouldn't use the gun against him. She didn't want to wound or perhaps kill an innocent policeman who might have a wife and kids in order to save her own skin. It didn't bother her to kill bad guys, but she wasn't going to kill an innocent man just to protect herself.

She might use it to get away, but what if the policeman pulled his gun? She didn't want to have to pull the trigger in self-defense. Local police would be no match for her. She was much more highly skilled, and she didn't want to put herself in a situation where she'd have to make a split-second life or death decision.

If it came down to shoot and escape or don't shoot and go to prison for fifteen years, she'd have to choose the first option.

She decided to get rid of the gun. The trash at the hotel was an option, but if discovered, the authorities would assume it was hers. The exits in the hotel scrolled through her mind. She'd memorized them when she first checked in. Just as a precaution. They weren't an option either. The only way out was the main entrance in front. Other exits had fire alarms attached to them.

Jamie got out of bed, went to the bathroom, and proceeded with her daily routine. She put on workout clothes and put the gun in a fanny pack which she attached around her waist. She checked the room to make sure she left nothing incriminating. She also booby-trapped it so she would know if it had been searched.

Satisfied, she carefully looked out the door and scanned the hall-way of her hotel room floor. No one was there. Not wanting to get trapped in an elevator, she took the stairs, stopping on the second floor where there were meeting rooms. Fortunately, no one was meeting in the Bernardin room, and the entire area was vacant.

The meeting room overlooked the front of the hotel and had big windows with half-closed blinds. Jamie walked over to the windows, careful not to be seen. She quickly spotted Moe, the name she gave the man who tailed her the night before. He reminded her of one of the Three Stooges, and Moe was her favorite Stooge.

Her fears were confirmed. Standing next to Moe were two uni-formed policemen and another, older man who looked like he could be Moe's boss. He appeared to be giving them instructions.

They were already onto her as a suspect.

Jamie considered her options. If she left through the fire exit, the alarm would sound and would provide a distraction. However, there were cameras at the exits, and they would easily see she was the one who set the alarms. She'd have no logical explanation. Looking out the windows again, a different plan came to mind.

She took the stairs to the first floor and walked through the lobby to the entrance.

Moe and the men were standing to the right of the entrance. Jamie went out the door, turned left, and started running like she was going for a jog, hoping they wouldn't see her. Even if they did, she had the element of surprise, and it would take them a few seconds to react.

Unfortunately, Moe saw her. He let out a squeal, and Jamie saw him pointing at her out of the corner of her eye. She kept a steady pace to make it look like she was just going for a run.

She had to maintain her cover if at all possible. If she had to make evasive moves and blow her cover, she would. That would make things more difficult. She'd have to go dark, and everything would be undercover. With the police and KGB looking for her.

She just needed to keep her cool and execute her plan.

Jamie looked back slightly without slowing her pace and saw the two policemen jump in their car which was in front of the hotel but facing the wrong direction. She was already a couple blocks away.

Car doors slammed and the tires squealed. They turned on their lights, made a U-turn, and headed her way.

Far enough away that they couldn't see her, Jamie quickened the pace. She needed to lose them, and make it look like she didn't lose them on purpose. She made the next left, pretty sure they hadn't seen which way she went. She had the advantage of mobility, but they had the advantage of being able to cover ground much quicker than she could.

Fortunately, she didn't have to go far. The Svislach River ran through the center of Minsk and was only a half mile from her hotel.

The most direct route would be the one the policemen would likely take.

She ran through the map in her mind, trying to predict which way they'd go. They'd definitely take the same left she took.

She ran past a restaurant with some patrons sitting at tables on the sidewalk eating their meals. She stepped onto the street.

Not the place to be. The policemen could easily spot her.

An alley was just ahead on the right. Jamie ducked into it and waited as the policemen sped by. She then took off running the opposite direction the way they'd come.

She had a slight risk that her path would intersect with Moe's. He wasn't dressed for a run and wasn't in shape, so she could lose him if she should happen upon him.

Jamie could run a five-minute mile, so even if he was in shape, she could outrun him. She figured the boss man was probably searching her room at that very moment and wasn't an immediate threat.

Jamie crossed the street, so she was running on the sidewalk across from the restaurant patrons. Hoping the policemen didn't see her in their rearview mirror. She crossed a major thoroughfare, fortunately timing the light just right so she didn't have to stand on the corner waiting.

She didn't see Moe but didn't look that closely.

She ran past the Museum of Carriages into a cul-de-sac and toward the riverbank.

The police had slowed and were circling around behind her. They'd turn back her way shortly.

She bolted off the street into an open parking lot. This was the most dangerous time. When she could most easily be spotted.

She also had to hurry because it would be hard to explain why she was down by the river with no running trail, and the embankment was steep. She bolted into a sprint.

She ran down the hill to the edge of the river. It was too open to get rid of the gun there. She continued running along the bank toward the Maksima Bridge which was just ahead. Once there, she ran under the bridge where she was hidden from any cars that might be driving above her and the policemen on the street looking for her.

The gun was wrapped in a towel. She took it out of the fanny pack, careful not to touch it. She had wiped it clean of fingerprints back at the hotel. She flung the gun as far as she could into the river while hanging on to the towel. Then she took off running back the way she had come, staying along the river until she could break out into the open and not be seen until she was back on the pavement.

Once on the street, she wanted to be seen and searched.

She slowed her pace. The policemen were on the next block over. They circled the block, spotted her, and then pulled up from behind, blaring their siren so she knew they were there.

Jamie dutifully stopped. Breathing hard, more from the chase than from the actual running. Relieved the gun was gone.

Out of the corner of her eye, she spotted Moe running down the hill, clearly out of breath. He saw Jamie and stopped suddenly, pretending not to be looking her way. She giggled at how obvious he was. Trying so hard to not be seen.

She was growing fond of Moe.

The two policemen exited their vehicle and walked toward her.

" *Prvvitannie Aficeram.*—Hello Officers," Jamie said with a smile.

" *Adkryicie zapliecnik.*"

One of the men had ordered her to open her fanny pack. Jamie complied and unzipped it.

They asked for her papers.

She pretended to rummage through her fanny pack, found the documents, and handed them to the officer. He scrutinized them for almost a minute and then went back to the car and seemed like he called it in.

Customs had screened that passport and visa more than these policemen ever could, so Jamie wasn't worried. She hoped that they didn't take her in for questioning or tried to say that she was running from them.

There was nothing left in her fanny pack but the towel and some money. She took the towel out and kept it in her hand to wipe sweat off her brow in case there was any residue from the gun on it.

They didn't think to look at it, or if they did, they didn't ask to.

Jamie assumed they were under orders to search her, but she wore a tight, form-fitting running outfit for that purpose. Nothing to search. She obviously had nowhere to hide anything on her body. Even patting her down would be fruitless. She half expected them to do it anyway, for the cheap thrill of it.

Moe watched the proceedings a safe distance away. The policemen were done.

" *Vy volnyia isci*. You're free to go," he said.

" *Dziakui*," she responded, thanking him. Not sure what she had to thank him for but trying to be polite, nonetheless.

She decided not to head straight back to the hotel. If Moe's boss was searching her room while all this was happening, she wanted to give him plenty of time. She was also hungry for breakfast even though it was already after lunchtime.

Jamie stopped at a little café called *Coffee Berry* where she ordered porridge with fruit, a croissant, and a latte, all for 10 BYN, or roughly five American dollars. They were also serving fresh cocktails that early in the morning.

She remembered reading that Belarus had the highest alcohol consumption rate in the world, a fact she was seeing firsthand as most people were having a drink with their lunch.

After she finished eating, Jamie headed back to the hotel. The walk back was mostly uphill. She had to wait for Moe who struggled to keep up with her. Back in the room, Jamie breathed a huge sigh of relief that she'd rid herself of the gun in the nick of time. She checked her booby traps. The room had been searched.

After a shower, she got ready to go out again, reset her booby traps, and left the hotel, making sure Moe saw her.

She spent the rest of the day sightseeing in Minsk. Her cover was that she was a college student, but she wanted to make sure Moe reported back that she was doing touristy things.

She decided to make it tough on Moe. Her pace was fast enough for him to keep up but not too fast that she would lose him. By the end of the day, she wanted him to feel like he'd been through a hard workout.

Minsk was a hilly city, so she had to stop periodically to give him time to rest. Jamie saw the City Scales Sculpture, Lenin Square, and walked through Gorky Park—a children's park with sports and recreation facilities, children's rides, and an open-air amphitheater.

The day was sunny with a slight chill in the air. Tourists wandered everywhere. Jamie would disappear for a moment and then suddenly appear to Moe after giving him a few minutes of panic.

Just to mess with him.

She was actually enjoying Belarus. The Azgur Memorial Studio was an interesting museum with many of the works of Zair Agzur, a famous Belarusian sculpture of the twentieth century.

She toured the National History & Central Museum which gave Moe a long break. He waited outside for her.

The Cat Museum was not one of the places she visited. Jamie was allergic but found it interesting that they had an entire museum dedicated to those creatures. She walked past the museum and decided to head back to the hotel.

Suddenly, she stopped in her tracks.

Someone else was following her.

Not Moe. Another person.

She could feel it. Someone who was good.

At first, she dismissed the feeling as being paranoid. Her senses were heightened from the stress of the last few days, and she might be imagining it.

Then she felt it again. She scoured the crowd. Looked in every direction. Something was off. Someone was there. A familiar feeling. She was definitely being followed. By an expert in surveillance techniques.

She headed back to the hotel, careful not to look around too much, to make it too obvious she'd sensed the other tail.

That complicated things further. She had two tails to concern herself with. The second she couldn't lose without that person knowing she was an operative. Maybe he already knew. He or she. She sensed it was a man.

She'd seen his face in the crowd, and it had registered in her subconscious that something was off. She would search her mind later for the images.

When she got back to the hotel, she waited in her room for a few minutes to give Moe time to leave. Certain he needed a break and time to check in with his boss. Satisfied he was gone she slipped out of the hotel and caught a cab to the airport.

There she rented a car and drove back to the hotel. She took several evasive moves to see if she had a tail following her. She pulled off at an exit and then got right back on. She made four right turns in a row. There weren't any cars following her.

Having a car would give her more freedom. She could leave anytime, and Moe would have no idea she was gone. He wouldn't be looking for her to leave in a car.

An even bigger problem was that she had been there two days now and had made no progress on the reason she was there. She was basically starting from scratch. The meeting with the contact never happened, and she had to assume it wouldn't. She would have to create her own intelligence.

She needed to find out who was behind the sex trafficking operation.

Where do I begin?

14

Jamie had a bite to eat in the hotel restaurant and then went to the business center to use the one computer with an internet connection and a printer. Fortunately, no one was on it, so she sat down and logged in as a guest and began surfing the web to see what she could find.

Anything that might give her a place to start her investigation. She wasn't going to sit around and wait for the contact to reach out to her again.

In preparation for the trip, she'd been given a complete briefing on prostitution and sex trafficking in Belarus. According to the information, there were more than two thousand prostitutes and fifty brothels in Belarus. Minsk, as the capital city with the highest population, had the largest percentage of prostitutes and brothels.

Strange that she hadn't yet seen any signs of it.

She mentally thought through all of the places she went that day. Jamie pulled out her phone and started scrolling through the pictures of tourist sights she visited in Minsk. While scanning through them, she also looked to see if perhaps she might have caught an image of her second stalker.

No such luck. He was too smart to be caught on camera.

Why did she think it was a he?

She'd almost convinced herself she was imagining it. Looking at the pictures made her realize she wasn't. The same feeling came over her while looking at them as it did when walking around the city.

Someone was definitely following her.

But who?

After a few minutes, she gave up and went back to searching on the computer. She then remembered something. A light on her phone reminded her she had one unheard voicemail message.

From Alex.

She'd been so busy getting rid of the gun and taking Moe on a sightseeing trip, she'd forgotten he called. She hit play and the familiar voice came over the phone.

"Hi Jamie. Good to hear from you. Sorry I haven't called. I lost my phone then had to get another one. Couldn't find your number. It's a long story. Talk to you soon. Call me."

Hearing his voice brought a huge smile to her face.

He finally called!

And he had an excuse for not calling. As lame as it was, at least it was something to give her hope that he wasn't blowing her off.

A clock on the wall read five-fifteen p.m., Belarus time. Eight hours ahead of Washington, DC and eleven hours ahead of California time.

Six-fifteen in the morning.

If she did the calculation correctly in her head.

Jamie let out a chuckle.

It would serve him right if I woke him up.

She thought better of it and made a note to call him before she went to bed. She turned her attention back to the computer screen which had articles written about Belarus, sex trafficking, brothels, and prostitutes. Most of them not good.

But where are they?

Maybe the government crackdown was working. The numbers seemed to be getting better. According to the last available statistics, arrests for prostitution had dropped from five hundred forty-six two years ago to one hundred thirty-five last year.

The CIA acknowledged the drop but weren't sure if the authorities were more successful in fighting the sex trade or if they weren't trying as hard to prosecute it. Maybe that was why she didn't see any. They forced it underground.

That will make it harder to find.

Not possible. If hard for her to find, it would be even harder for customers to find. Prostitution didn't survive long without customers.

Most men knew the usual places to find them. Jamie had tried those. Minsk didn't have a red-light district like Amsterdam or Bangkok. The city had no seedy areas where someone would normally find prostitutes. No street walkers and no obvious neighborhoods where prostitution would thrive. No social media posts advertised services, and Johns weren't posting recommendations on where to go for sex.

"Welcome to a communist country," she said to herself.

Whatever a communist government decided to crack down on, they were usually successful at.

How was someone trafficking three hundred women a month out of Belarus with no one knowing about it and successfully avoiding the government efforts to curtail it? That didn't seem logical.

After about an hour of searching, Jamie left the financial center and walked down the street to a shop that sold electronics. She purchased a throw-away burner phone, walked out of the shop, and made a couple evasive moves to ensure to herself no one was following her.

Moe was definitely gone. Probably soaking his feet from the strenuous day's activities. The thought brought a grin to her face.

Her second stalker wasn't there either, but as a precaution, she walked down to the Svislach River to a large open park where she could see in every direction. She pulled out the burner phone and dialed a number she knew by heart.

A man answered on the second ring.

"Hello, Mr. Denworthy," Jamie said.

"Very funny," Brad retorted.

The number was a direct line to Brad that only operatives in the field possessed. Fictitious names were used just in case the calls were being listened to by the local government. Not likely in Belarus, but Jamie wasn't taking any chances.

She chose Denworthy because Brad had a slow southern drawl, and she often joked that he sounded like the comedian Mark Denworthy. Brad hated the nickname and let her know it every chance he got.

"I'm just checking in," Jamie said. "Unfortunately, I don't have much to report. My friend never showed up yesterday."

"That's not good. He's never missed a performance before."

"He may not have missed it. I might've been late. There may have been an incident." Jamie said the last sentence hesitantly.

Silence on the other end.

"I hate to ask," Brad finally said.

"Don't then. It's handled."

"Does it have to do with a couple of boys attacked in an alleyway?"

She was continually amazed by the reach of the CIA. She had no idea how Brad already knew about the boys. She'd have fallen over if he mentioned four boys.

"Maybe. Like I said, better if you don't ask. Couldn't be helped."

"Thought that might've been some of your handiwork. Have you found anything of interest?" Brad said, changing the subject.

One thing she appreciated about him. He didn't make an issue about things he couldn't do anything about. If the mission went well, he'd probably not ask anything more about the boys. If it went bad, he'd bring it up several times and tell her everything she did wrong.

"What I *haven't* found is very interesting," Jamie said.

"How so?"

"I haven't found anything. No red light districts. No street walkers. No websites. How is that possible in a country the size of Belarus?"

"I know you've only been there for two days," Brad continued, "but you always say you're the best, Ms. Perez."

He said the name sarcastically.

Brad's awkward stab at humor. Mona Perez played *Superwoman* in the latest movie version. Better than his other nickname for her, *Miss March*. Depending on the context, he used it to refer to her as either the dominating woman from the book *Little Women* or a March centerfold of an adult magazine.

Neither of which she cared for and gave him an equally hard time about it. Although, if truthful, she enjoyed the banter. Made her feel like one of the boys.

"This isn't like Thailand," Jamie said, not giving him the satisfaction of responding to his quip. "There aren't brothels on every corner. I haven't seen a single prostitute."

"What about strip clubs and casinos?"

"I was getting to those."

"Go get dressed up in your sexiest outfit and go to the strip clubs and casinos and get noticed. Flash your wares. That will get some attention."

"I think that comment borders on sexual harassment."

"Those laws don't apply when you're in another country. I already checked."

"I was reading about forced government labor," Jamie said, his comment about government laws sparking something she'd seen on the internet and wanted to ask him about.

"Do you know anything about that?" Jamie asked.

Nothing was mentioned about it in her briefing, but it was something very prevalent in Belarus.

"We know about it," Brad responded. "It's in the ILO report."

The ILO report listed "forced labor" as one of the reasons for Belarus's low Tier 3 score. A law allowed Belarusians suffering from alcohol or drug dependency to be interned in medical labor centers for a period of twelve to eighteen months.

"I read where more than 6,500 people are in those centers. Somebody could be trafficking some of those workers. I didn't find any evidence. Could the government get away with that without the CIA knowing about it?" Jamie asked.

"I don't think so," Brad said. "If the government was behind it, I think we'd know about it. Besides, there's not enough money in it for the government to get involved. They might look the other way, but I don't think they'd let their state-controlled factories become a front for sex trafficking. They can make more off the girls by forcing them to make products."

"I read something unbelievable."

"What's that?"

"Did you know that in Belarus, if parents have their kids taken away from them, they have to work in a government job? If a person is unemployed and gets a disability or something, they have to work for the government. Seventy percent of their wages are taken from them. Not like the US where you can draw unemployment or disability for months or years. Just the opposite here."

"I know. There are no government safety nets in Belarus. You are punished if you fall on hard times and don't get out of it right away."

"That would certainly create an environment that might force women to turn to selling their bodies rather than working for the government."

"Possibly."

"How would I infiltrate government run operations if they were the ones behind trafficking three hundred girls a month?"

"I wouldn't waste my time running down that rabbit hole. That's communism. Nothing you can do about it. Has nothing to do with sex trafficking. Let's make the eradication of communism your next mission."

She almost heard him chuckle to himself. Not quite. But almost.

"I hear you," Jamie said, somberly. "I was thinking the same thing."

"Casinos and strip clubs," Brad said again with emphasis. "You need to go pay them a visit."

"What about my friend?"

"You'll just have to wait until he schedules the next performance."

"That reminds me. Do you have another person working here?"

"Why do you ask?"

"I'm being followed. By a professional. I wondered if it was one of ours. Are you checking up on me?"

"I'll get back to you on that."

Brad's way of saying he wasn't going to answer that question. Or he didn't know.

The line went dead without another word.

The way he usually signed off signaling the conversation was over.

15

Jamie was getting frustrated. She paused to think through the information as she walked back to the hotel. This was going to be harder than she thought it would be. The prostitution and sex trafficking in Belarus were either deep underground and in the shadows . . . or right in plain sight.

She considered that possibility. Looking at the obvious places wasn't getting her anywhere. She needed to think outside the box. Consider possibilities she'd never considered before. Nothing immediately came to mind.

She went back to the hotel and logged back onto the computer and continued searching but this time focusing on how the government was fighting sex trafficking to see if there were any arrests or initiatives that stood out to her.

The fight against sex trafficking was in plain sight. The government had funded a campaign and placed billboards around the city of Minsk warning women about sex trafficking. She had taken a picture of one and saw it again when she was scrolling through her saved photos. A good idea. One the US should consider.

The government of Belarus even had websites to fight sex trafficking. They warned women to be wary of scams. They listed some of them. Women were warned of the promise of high-paying jobs in foreign countries. When they arrived for the interviews, they were kidnapped and sold into slave labor.

Another website warned women not to fall for a telemarketer calling to say they had won a free trip, all expenses paid. One woman in Germany did fall for it. When she got to Egypt, she was kidnapped and sold into the sex trade. Her dead body was discovered after the press got hold of the story. Women didn't go missing while traveling abroad without the national press drawing attention to it.

Jamie remembered Shelly Howell, a young American girl traveling to Belize on vacation with her friends. She went missing, and a lot of people speculated she was a victim of sex trafficking. Turns out she was killed by a boy she left the hotel with. Didn't have anything to do with sex trafficking at all.

That was the point. Kidnapping and trafficking were hard to pull off and continue as an ongoing operation. Certainly not to the extent of three hundred women a month. Everything Jamie read about Belarusian women was that they were sophisticated and well educated.

Sex trafficking generally preyed on the poor and uneducated.

Awareness of the dangers of sex trafficking was actually taught to young girls in Belarusian schools. So much so that most women didn't fall for those scams anymore. And while they can be effective to a certain extent, it's only for a short time. People catch on to them quickly, and certainly three hundred women a month wouldn't fall for something so simple.

If they were being kidnapped, where were the police reports? She only remembered seeing one article about the one missing woman in another country.

Jamie thought about a twenty-eight-year-old woman named Amaliya Farhod she rescued in Thailand. Amy, as Jamie called her, was born to an impoverished family in Uzbekistan. Her mother died when she was young, and it left her with the responsibility to care for her four siblings since she was the oldest.

Her monthly wage was twelve dollars. A woman approached her and told her she could make a lot of money in Bangkok, Thailand, making cellular phones. The woman said she would arrange all of the transportation. Amy eagerly said yes.

When Amy got to Thailand, the woman destroyed all of her documents, passport, visa, and entry paperwork. She gave her very little food and no money and forced her to work as a prostitute on the streets of Bangkok. Amy had to pay her back for her travel expenses, and then she would be allowed to go to work at the factory.

She was forced to have unprotected sex with dozens of men each week. If she didn't, the woman told her she would never get to work at the factory and would never see her family again. Amy calculated she made more than $10,000 a month for the lady and had more than paid her back.

She tried to tell a policeman on the street about what the woman was making her do. He stood there with Amy until the woman came to pick her up. Instead of arresting her, the policeman told the woman what Amy had told him. The woman took Amy back to her house and beat her nearly to death.

Amy was trapped and didn't know where to turn.

Jamie met her outside a hotel where she had just completed a trick. She was crying. Jamie asked her what was wrong. At first, Amy didn't know if she could trust Jamie. Finally, she opened up. Said she was angry because a woman had tricked her into coming to Thailand and then tore up her passport. The woman beat her and made her have sex with men. All she had were the clothes on her back.

Jamie asked her if she was waiting for the lady who had brought her to Thailand. Normally, Jamie would've taken Amy to a shelter and got her help, but she saw an opportunity to get the sex trafficker arrested.

When the lady arrived, Jamie detained her and called the police. At Jamie's insistence, the woman was arrested. Amy couldn't leave Thailand to go back home until she testified against the lady. It went to court, but Amy was so scared to see the lady, she was afraid to testify. With the language barrier, she had a hard time answering the judge's questions.

The trafficker was freed on bail and disappeared. To Jamie's knowledge, she was never prosecuted. The organization, *Save the Girls*, did pay to have Amy sent back to Uzbekistan and gave her some money to get back on her feet.

As she thought about that story, Jamie didn't think Belarusian women were vulnerable enough to fall for such a scheme. And the large numbers involved gave Jamie pause. Most of the time, sex traffickers could successfully kidnap one or two victims a month.

Jamie was missing something, and she didn't know what it was. One link kept coming up in her searches, sparking Jamie to investigate further. An ongoing tie between Turkey and Belarus.

In 2009, a Turkish citizen was arrested and sentenced to seven years for organizing sex tours to Turkey. His accomplice was captured and sentenced a year later. The article said the funds from the sex trafficking pipeline were going directly to Turkey to fund terrorism. That article described something similar to what she was looking for.

Why Turkey? Turkey was one thousand, one hundred twenty-five miles from Belarus with the Black Sea between the two countries. People had to travel through several other countries to get there. That seemed implausible, and yet the ties were there.

On a whim, she looked up newspaper articles about business ties between Belarus and Turkey. She noticed a Turkish businessman recently had been making significant investments in Belarus. He purchased a hotel, a casino, and a nightclub. All three of those could be viewed as fronts for prostitution.

Jamie's instincts told her to dig further. One of the articles had a picture of the man standing next to the President of Belarus.

The man's name was Omer Asaf.

Had she heard that name somewhere before? Seems like it, but she couldn't remember where. She made a mental note to ask Brad the next time they spoke. Googling his name brought up more information about him.

Asaf was number sixty-four on the list of the world's top one hundred richest men. His net worth was estimated at 13.2 billion dollars.

Jamie let out a slight gasp.

The business tycoon made most of his money in real estate but also had interests in wholesale trade and personal grooming products. Did he have any investments in the US? She searched but couldn't find any. Strange that a man that wealthy had no obvious business dealings in the United States.

She studied his picture carefully. Omer Asaf was short, probably five feet six inches tall, good looking, and wore expensive clothes in the picture. He'd never been married but was said to be a playboy. He must be a very important man to get his picture taken with Lukashenko.

She dismissed the thought. Why would a successful businessman like Asaf traffic in women? He obviously didn't need the money.

Jamie googled Belarus women and sex.

A link to a website called Belles of Belarus came up. A mail order bride business run out of Pinsk, Belarus, owned by an anonymous Turkish businessman.

Asaf?

The business matched Belarusian women with American men. Hundreds of pictures of ladies came up on the website. All in glamorous poses, well dressed, and made up to look attractive to American men. The company was doing a big business to have that many girls signed up.

She scrolled through the pictures of the women and was stunned by the natural beauty of Belarusian women. Most had blue or green eyes, and beautiful faces. They were all generally slender and curvy. She was also struck by how modest they appeared. They didn't wear too much makeup and didn't dress provocatively, even though they were obviously trying to attract a husband.

The women on that website, if they were representative of all women in Belarus, didn't seem like they would be easily fooled into a sex trafficking scam.

She scanned the net for any reports of any mail order brides who were reported missing. Nothing came up.

Another dead end.

She logged off the computer, somewhat frustrated. The only leads she had were the nightclubs and casinos. And at least one nightclub and one casino had a tie to Turkey, which had a tie to sex trafficking in the past.

Not much to go on, but she had to start somewhere. She'd start with the ones owned by Asaf.

Jamie went back up to the room, showered, and changed into nice clothes. A tight, mini, LBD with high heels. A faux-fur, leopard-print, half jacket over it. She looked in the mirror and was satisfied that she was dressed for the part.

For two days, she'd been trying to stay under the radar and not be noticed. Tonight, she wanted to make sure she was noticed.

Follow Brad's instructions and show off her wares.

She looked at herself in the mirror one more time.

I will definitely be noticed.

The question was noticed by who?

16

Denys, the Minister of Transportation, stood in the *Cathedral of the Holy Spirit* in Old Town, at Liberty Square, waiting nervously for the CIA operative who was to meet him there at six p.m.

He always felt uneasy at these meetings but particularly so for this one, considering the woman CIA operative he was to meet the night before hadn't shown up. He looked at his watch which read two minutes after six and wondered if the second operative would be a no show as well.

He took a deep breath and let it out slowly, allowing himself a few moments to take in his surroundings. Not a religious man, it had been years since he'd been in any church. A little boy since he had been in this one, even though it was one of the most famous historical landmarks in Minsk, and one his mother had attended religiously back when she was alive.

A number of people were in the cathedral, some saying their evening prayers. A large number of tourists were taking in the baroque architecture and its beautiful frescoes and artwork. The church contained two holy relics the pilgrims and tourists alike traveled miles to see—the relics of Princess Saint Sophia of Slutskaya and the Mother of God icon.

Princess Sophia lived at a time when orthodox faith in Belarus was forbidden and persecuted. She and her father had refused to convert to Catholicism. Documents verifying her refusal to deny the faith were stored in a shrine in the cathedral.

She was granted sainthood after a number of women were reportedly miraculously healed at her gravesite. Many people believed the shrine with her documents stored at the church contained miraculous healing powers as well.

Denys always wondered why the Princess could not heal herself if she had such powers. Something he never voiced to his mother so as not to face her wrath.

Also, at the cathedral was the Mother of God icon, a painting of the Virgin Mary that had been in Minsk since 1500. Legend said the evangelist Luke was the actual author of the icon. More than four and half feet tall and three feet wide, Denys admitted it was an amazing work of art along with a religious icon.

Legend had it that the icon was captured by a Tatar in 1500 and was thrown into the Svislach River in Kiev. It was supposedly found floating in the river near Minsk and fished out of the river by some peasants who placed it in safe keeping until it eventually became part of the church.

It also was purported to contain miraculous powers, and people came from all over to pray for the sick at the icon. Denys's mother, a deeply religious woman, often came to the cathedral and prayed at the relics when she or a family member was sick.

Perhaps that was why Denys was not a religious man. His sister died of a lung ailment at age forty-six, her mom's prayers to the patron saints and relics having gone unanswered.

He tried to put the thoughts of his mother and sister out of his mind. The operative was ten minutes late. Something was going on.

Anger began to rise inside of him. He was the one risking everything to meet with them. He had vital information to share. On time for each meeting, they needed to afford him the same courtesy or he would not continue to take such risks.

He processed through the instructions for the meet in his mind. He was to enter the church and stand on the far, right side in front of the first shrine. At six o'clock p.m. He was to wait no longer than fifteen minutes. If the operative didn't show, then he was to leave immediately. That meant something happened.

Maybe this operative was in danger as well.

Denys was worried about the girl. He knew she was under scrutiny by local law enforcement. He'd learned she was a suspect in the beating of a couple of boys in an alley behind the Piatra Brooka Literary Museum. The attack occurred about six o'clock p.m. the night before.

Right about the time they were scheduled to meet. The obvious reason why the operative didn't make it. He hoped this meeting took place so he could get a message to her. Maybe the man he was meeting with that night knew the girl and could warn her for him.

Apparently, that meeting wasn't going to happen either. At exactly six-fifteen, Denys decided to leave. He suddenly felt a presence behind him.

A man's voice said quietly, "Don't look back. Just keep your eyes focused ahead of you."

"What time are services?" the man asked.

"The last one was at five o'clock," Denys responded.

The code phrase matched Denys's instructions. The man was the person he was to meet with. A slight grin came across his face.

When he first became a spy for the US, he thought it would be like the movies. James Bond and the like. Phrases would be sophisticated like "the chickens have flown the coop." The response, "The silver fox is chasing them."

Instead, the code phrases were simple, everyday simple sentences in case someone overheard them.

He didn't get much training, only the basics. When he met with an operative, he was instructed to relax. Talk normally. Say phrases that most people would say in that setting. It made sense to him, but he thought his role would be more glamorous. It had all the danger for sure, except without the mystery and intrigue he expected.

"What is your name?" Denys asked the question he was supposed to ask next.

"Mike Seaver. You can call me Mike."

"My name is Denys."

He assumed the operative had given him a fake name. He wasn't instructed to do the same.

"The girl I was supposed to meet with last night didn't show up," Denys continued. "I need to get her a message. I think she's in real danger."

Denys wasn't sure why he mentioned the girl first. The information he had for the man was even more important. Yet, he felt a real affinity for her. Wanted to protect her. Maybe because she was a girl, and he'd seen her picture. She was young and stunningly beautiful. Like a sister or the daughter he never had.

Perhaps, because he knew what the KGB would do to her if they caught her as a spy. They wouldn't care that she was a girl. Must be related to his own fondness for his mother and two sisters. All of whom were already gone.

"You should just wait for her to contact you," Mike said.

"She doesn't know who I am," Denys said. "I know who she is and where she's staying. I can contact her."

Denys could sense the man move closer to him. The cathedral was starting to get crowded again. He was now inches away from his ear. A very clever move in a church. His lips could be moving, and most people would think he was praying, but also, Denys could hear him more clearly.

He now understood why the man wanted to meet him in the church.

"You have information for me?" Mike asked.

"A Turkish businessman named Omer Asaf may be trying to buy a nuclear briefcase from us."

During the breakup of the Soviet Union, four nuclear briefcases went missing. Three of them ended up in Belarus and were under Lukashenko's control. Denys had already given that information to his CIA handler. He'd been given instructions to contact them immediately if anything happened to them. They didn't want them to end up in terrorist's hands for obvious reasons.

"You said 'maybe.' You don't know for sure?"

"I've just heard rumors. I'm going to do more checking."

Suddenly, the man was gone. Denys felt the movement but didn't dare to turn around and look. A jolt of panic pulsed through his body.

What happened?

He stepped to the side and back against the wall so he could look out over the entire Cathedral. He could see everything from there and scanned the small room for the man, even though he didn't know what he looked like.

He appeared to be tall from what he could tell from their brief encounter. The thought occurred to him that he might want to say an actual prayer while he was there in the church. Something had spooked the CIA man.

Am I in danger, too?

He saw what had startled Mike. Two KGB agents had walked in through the front entrance and were walking on the left side of the Cathedral. They were in traditional blue military dress. Their shoulder boards were marked GB meaning state security. Their hats had the KGB insignia on them. The men were in their forties, meaning they were more senior officers.

For a KGB agent to enter an orthodox church was very unusual. Something brought them there. What was it? Denys didn't want to draw attention to himself, so he continued to pretend to pray but kept his head up and eyes opened so he could see what they were doing.

The men walked to the front of the church and then down the right side. Their eyes scanning to the left and then to the right. It took all of his self-control to keep from running away as fast as he could. But that was the worst thing he could do.

He could have left but was curious and wanted to see if he could figure out why they were there.

Did they see him meeting with the American? It didn't seem like it.

Were they looking for him? He wasn't sure but couldn't think of why they would be unless they got word of a meet happening there.

His heart was racing out of his chest. He needed to calm his nerves. The KGB were trained to spot unusual behavior.

He considered his options. He was, after all, the Minister of Transportation. One of the most powerful men in Belarus. Except for his life as a double agent, he had no reason to be afraid of the KGB. One call, and he could have *them* detained on his command.

He was doing nothing wrong. Just praying in his mother's church. That's what he would say if questioned. He came here often to remember her and pray for her soul.

Emboldened, Denys straightened his coat and tie and walked to the center aisle toward the men rather than away from them. The two agents were just a few yards ahead of him.

" *Zdymi sapki,*" he said.

"Remove your hats," he had said with authority. "You are in a place of worship."

The two men looked at each other, then stared at Denys.

He took out his credentials and flashed them at the two men.

" *Ciapier.* Now," he implored them.

The two men took off their hats.

Denys turned and walked out of the Cathedral, emboldened. His hands were shaking, but he suddenly felt confident. Important. He was a meek and humble man. He rarely used his authority over others. It felt good for a change.

He turned and walked two blocks to the Monastyrski Hotel. He got a piece of paper from the front desk and scribbled a note then took the elevator to the third floor and slipped the note under the door of Room 307. Allie Walker's room.

Friday night. Same Time. Same place.

The streetcar is not running.

The code phrase for danger.

For the first time since he started his life as a double agent, Denys actually felt like a spy.

***

Detective Fabi stood outside the Monastyrski Hotel drinking a cup of coffee. Lieutenant Petrov had told him to go home and end the surveillance of the American girl. He had defied orders. He felt certain Allie Walker wasn't just an American tourist, and he was determined to prove it.

So far, she hadn't left the hotel for the evening, but he was going to stay for a few hours just in case she did. He was so focused on looking for Allie coming out of the hotel, he almost didn't notice the man walking in.

The Minister of Transportation. One of the most important men in Belarus.

What was he doing at the hotel?

At first, he dismissed the thought. Then his imagination took over, and he started contriving all kinds of scenarios in his mind. What if the Minister was an agent and was there to meet with Allie?

Fabi walked to the entrance of the hotel, careful not to be seen. The Minister was at the front desk, writing a note.

Was it for Allie?

The Minister turned and started walking toward the elevators. Fabi quickly turned away when the Minister looked his way. That seemed suspicious. Like the Minister was nervous. Trying to make sure he wasn't seen.

Maybe he was meeting a lover. It was a hotel, after all.

Fabi started to go back to his spot and wait for Allie. Then he noticed the elevator stopped at the third floor. The same floor as Allie's room. He started to go in and take the stairs but thought better of it.

The Minister of Transportation was a very powerful man. Fabi wasn't even supposed to be there on surveillance. His boss had told him to stand down and meet him in his office tomorrow morning. If he was right and the Minister was an agent for the CIA, Fabi would be a hero.

If he was wrong, he'd be shot.

He decided to go back across the street and watch.

A short time later, the Minister walked out of the hotel, looked both ways, pulled his coat tighter around him, and walked down the street past where Fabi was hiding in the shadows and disappeared around the corner.

He thought through his options and decided not to follow the Minister. He was cold so he went into a coffee shop.

As he was leaving the shop, Allie appeared at the entrance of the hotel. She exited, looked his way, and then walked the other direction.

What do I do now?

Adrenaline pulsed through him like electricity pulses through an electrical cord.

Was she going to meet the Director?

Do I follow her? Do I search her room?

Whatever he was going to do, he had to do it soon.

She was almost out of his line of sight.

17

Jamie sat on the edge of the bed in her hotel room thinking about the note she'd found on the floor. It must have come when she was in the bathroom drying her hair and didn't hear the person slip the note under the door because of the noise from the blow dryer.

She was distracted, getting ready to go to the nightclub, and almost didn't see it. Fortunately, she had turned on the light in the hallway as she was leaving, and there it was. On hotel stationary.

Strange.

The instructions were clear. Friday night. Liberty Square. Six o'clock. Danger was lurking.

All kinds of thoughts went through her head. Was it from her contact or was it a trap? Why would the contact risk being seen on the security cameras at the hotel to give her the note? How did he know a maid wouldn't find it and throw it away, or worse, turn it in to her boss?

What was the danger? He must have something extremely important to tell her or he wouldn't have gone to that much effort to contact her.

What could it be?

Before touching the note, she had checked it for "spy dust" to make sure it wasn't tainted. Spy dust was a chemical compound the KGB used to mark a person for surveillance. Once it got on a piece of clothing, face, or hands, an infrared camera could pick it up, and the person would never even know they'd been marked.

The note was clean. More evidence it was authentic and not from the KGB.

Jamie had already destroyed it. She lit it on fire and flushed the ashes down the toilet. A bit of overkill, but she wasn't taking any chances that the note could be found. She'd studied the handwriting before destroying it. Definitely a man's writing. No unusual marks. Nothing to give away that it was forged.

A contrived note had a certain look. Loops in the center of lower-case a's and o's, signified the writer was lying. Large loops that crossed identified a pathological liar. A slant variation from left to right in the same sentence showed a dual personality. In other words, the person was writing it as if he were someone else.

This writer wasn't lying. He was just nervous. His hand was shaking when he wrote it.

A hint of anger rose inside of her. The contact took an unnecessary risk leaving the note in her room. Not the way she would've made contact. If discovered, it could've blown her cover.

She was always so careful about every detail. She'd hate to get arrested because of someone else's stupid mistake.

At the same time, he deserved a break. He wasn't a trained spy. This seemed like a move he would make. He was probably as freaked out about her not showing up as she was about missing the meet.

All evidence pointed to the note being from him. That's what she needed to focus on. However clumsily, he made contact, the most important thing. They could now meet. She could get the information. A name.

But the phrase gave her pause. "The streetcar is not running," meant that there was an emergency. Jamie had memorized the phrases in her briefing.

"What time is the train leaving the station?"

Either of them could start with that line.

A response, "It has already left" meant the coast was clear.

"It leaves at three o'clock" or whatever time was said, meant they were being watched at that position on the clock, and the meet was canceled, and he or she should keep going.

"The streetcar is not running" meant something horrible had happened, and time was of the essence and there was a change of plans.

The person who wrote the note obviously knew the code phrases. Did the contact write it, or did he give it up under torture? The note wasn't the context to use the phrase. Was he trying to warn her about something, or was it just his way of saying he had something important to tell her?

Either way, Jamie had to find out.

She suddenly wished she hadn't thrown away the gun. If she was walking into a trap, the KGB would be armed, and she would be helpless against their overwhelming force. Even if she had a gun, she would be outmanned, but at least she'd have a fighting chance.

Jamie rued the fact that nothing about the mission was going as planned. That wasn't unusual. Missions seldom did. But she'd been there more than a week and had no leads and nothing to show for her efforts. She was no closer to finding the pipeline than when she arrived.

Now, she might be walking into a trap with no way of knowing until she got there.

She thought about calling Brad, but she didn't really have anything else to report. She could hear the conversation in her head.

"Have you gone to the casinos and strip clubs?" he would ask.

"Not yet. I'm going there tonight."

"Then why are you calling me?" he would say dismissively. "Go to the clubs and then call me. When you have something."

He probably would want to know about the note. But the meet was in two days. She'd have time to tell him. After she found something. That was another reason to meet with her contact. Hopefully, he would bring the phone and the name of the person running the pipeline. That would make her job so much easier. She could quit chasing a ghost.

"I'll go to the meet," she said to herself. "Then decide what to do next."

Satisfied with her plan, Jamie exited the hotel room, looking both ways down the hall. She went downstairs and out the front entrance. She decided to go to *Splash* nightclub first, and then tomorrow night, she'd go to the *California Casino*.

They were both owned by Omer Asaf, the Turkish businessman. Though a flimsy lead, it was all she had, and she was going to go with it. Jamie knew from experience that even if chasing a false thread, she sometimes fell into the right intelligence just by doing something.

If she did nothing, then she was guaranteed to find nothing. If actually doing something, she usually benefited from the fruits of her labor. Jamie hoped that was the case this time.

She was at least confident she would find some evidence of trafficking at the nightclub or casino. Prostitutes for sure, at both places. She just didn't know if they'd lead her to the pipeline.

She wasn't optimistic. The girls at those establishments were high-end call girls who were not forced slave labor. It would be hard to keep a girl in slavery in a casino with thousands of people around.

Most girls in sex trafficking were kept in dark, seedy, underground establishments, isolated from the rest of the world. They ate, slept, and worked in the same place and were watched every minute of the day.

As she exited the hotel, she looked around for Moe but didn't see him. She wondered if he finally gave up or had taken the night off. Then she saw him out of the corner of her eye, frantically exiting the coffee shop across from the hotel, spilling coffee or tea on his shirt. Obviously caught off guard by Jamie's sudden appearance.

She felt sorry to interrupt his break. Not really. She was enjoying playing this game with him. If only in her mind.

Surveillance was a difficult mind game and hard to keep focused. Jamie had always admired secret service agents who guarded the President and had to pay maximum attention to their surroundings for hours at a time. Of course, they were never alone and had other agents who could give them breaks. Poor Moe was on his own.

Jamie had a long walk to *Splash,* so she decided she'd take the time to call Alex back. She pulled out the phone and started to dial the number, but then paused. "What am I going to say?"

She thought through the conversation.

"Hi Jamie. What are you doing?" he would ask.

"I'm on my way to a strip club in Minsk."

"Where is Minsk?"

"It's a city in a communist country right next to Russia."

She put the phone back in her pocket. She didn't want her first conversation with Alex since the cruise to be awkward. The better answer would be that she was in Virginia, and her week had been uneventful.

Not exactly true as a smile came over her face. No way she could tell him the truth.

She'd been attacked by four guys, her room and person searched by communist police, followed for three days by a member of the Militsia, and she disposed of a stolen gun in the river seconds before she would have been arrested and thrown in a prison for fifteen years.

Other than that, she'd had a very uneventful week.

Jamie was trained to lie, so this would be a time when that skill would come in handy. If she was going to successfully make it sound believable.

She pulled her phone out again and took a deep breath.

She dialed the number, and on the second ring she heard a recorded voice say, "The person you are trying to reach has a voice mailbox that has not been set up yet. Please call back another time."

That was strange.

Jamie checked, and she'd dialed the right number. He had a voice-mail message the first time she had called him. She hung up the phone and tried to put it out of her mind. If he had caller ID, he would see she called.

Maybe Alex didn't like getting messages. Or maybe he didn't want his wife to hear them.

"Shut up Jamie. He doesn't have a wife. There's a perfectly reasonable explanation."

He did say he had lost his phone and had to get a new one. That could be why he didn't have his voicemail set up yet.

No time to do an investigation.

One investigation at a time, Jamie.

She turned her thoughts to what she might find at the strip club. One glance behind her confirmed Moe was still on her tail.

Jamie grinned, "You should thank me, Moe. We're going to a strip club. Your surveillance just got more interesting."

She wondered if he would appreciate it. She'd noticed a ring on his finger and wondered what his wife would think about him going into a strip club. Of course, he would say it was part of his job.

Jamie suddenly slowed her pace. She was about to walk by the place where the boys had attacked her. She glanced that way but didn't see anything. No yellow tape or any sign that anything had happened.

She made the first right and Moe was still following her. She needed to get away from that area as soon as possible. As dumb as he was, Moe might realize they were at the crime scene. She didn't want him to associate it with her at all.

She pulled out a map and pretended to be lost. A quick turn and she was facing Moe, walking toward him. He looked into the window of a shop pretending not to be looking her way.

Jamie pretended to act confused. Like she was trying to get her bearings. She knew exactly where she was. From there, she took a left and went two blocks. She rounded a corner and came upon the entrance to the *Splash* nightclub.

Cars were lined up waiting for the valet, and a line of men stretched around the corner with two bouncers guarding the entrance. Jamie knew from experience that a beautiful girl could go to the front of the line and get in right away.

That's what she did and was motioned in.

"Poor Moe," Jamie thought. "He'll have to get in the back of the line."

18

Splash was a theatre of sight and sound. The million-dollar sound system was topped only by the elaborate, over-the-top light display. The size of half a football field, the club was packed with men and about two hundred women wearing the same tight, extremely short, black dresses, slightly off their shoulders.

They were all wearing high heels, bright-red stilettos. The only way someone could tell them apart was their different hair color, height, shape, and facial features. All were gorgeous.

Jamie was wearing her own LBD, and some of the men were confusing her with the other girls. As soon as she sat down, the men descended upon her like a flock of geese toward a child with bread in her hand.

She politely smiled but refused to get caught up in idle chit chat. The men wouldn't provide any information. She wanted to talk to the girls. So she rudely shooed them away when necessary. That didn't seem to deter them as they continued to approach her.

The club had three large dance floors, but no one was dancing. Mirrors were everywhere, including on the ceilings. Three large bar areas provided a constant supply of drinks. Just about everyone had a drink in their hand. The club wasn't dark like strip clubs in America, where everyone seemed embarrassed and afraid to be seen.

Splash was the place where everyone wanted to be seen and seem important. The men were clearly trying to impress the girls as much as the girls were trying to get the guys to pick them.

Some strippers in clubs complained about there being more girls than guys which made it hard to make money and meet their quotas. That didn't seem to be the case at Splash. Business was booming.

Jamie was taking it all in. It certainly was nothing like what she had expected. No girls were dancing naked. There were no poles. Nothing to make anyone think it was even a strip club.

Except for the look on the girls' faces. Jamie had seen that look too many times. She could spot a working girl a mile away. Not that she could pinpoint what it was specifically. Maybe the eyes.

Someone once said the eyes were the window to the soul. A woman who sold her body to men loses her soul almost immediately.

The girls of *Splash* had the same look as the girls in the seediest brothel in Thailand, even though this was a very high-end club, and the conditions were ideal for the girls. If there was such a thing as ideal conditions for a prostitute.

Selling one's body for money felt the same everywhere, no matter how much money was made. You had to have spent a lot of time around these types of establishments to spot it. Jamie was able to see past the façade. The eyes reflected the emptiness of a soul that's dead inside.

The girls were all putting on a good act. They were friendly and flirty. The smiles were big. She observed the girls mingling with the men until an obvious agreement occurred. Once a verbal agreement was reached, they would walk over to a roped area in front of curtains which undoubtedly led to VIP rooms.

That was where the real action occurred.

The look as the girl walked to the VIP room told Jamie how long she'd been working there. The veteran girls had a distant look of acceptance. Just another miserable day at the office. Another sick pervert who was going to get his kicks off on her and was willing to spend a good part of his paycheck for the twenty-minute thrill.

The newer girls felt the excitement of closing a sale, like a car salesman or door-to door vacuum cleaner salesman, now one step closer to quota. But then as they walked to the line for the VIP rooms, the look turned to fear, as they realized what they would have to do for that sale.

Jamie was processing a lot of information at once. It would've been more, if she didn't keep getting interrupted. She was approached by at least twenty men every five minutes.

There were only a few non-working girls there. The establishment obviously didn't want outside girls competing against their own girls. Jamie was surprised they even let her in.

No sign of Moe.

She was thankful when one of the working girls sat down next to her and momentarily gave Jamie a break from the constant stream of men who were trying to proposition her. At first, Jamie was surprised she sat by her. Most places wanted the girls working, but it became apparent they were also tasked with recruiting other girls at this club.

That's why they let Jamie in. She would be a perfect recruit.

Jamie played along.

"Hi. My name is Chastity," the girl said, extending her hand. Jamie shook it.

She found it ironic that her name was Chastity. She wondered if the girl knew what it meant.

Chastity was probably nineteen or twenty, brown hair, shoulder length. Beautiful facial features, although her teeth needed braces. When she talked, she often moved her hand in front of her smile to hide the only notable flaw in her appearance. When she smiled, her lips were closed tightly. Clearly embarrassed.

Jamie doubted the men even noticed. Her other features dominated her look.

"My name's Allie," Jamie said.

"I haven't seen you around here before," Chastity said.

"No. Just visiting from America."

Jamie responded in a friendly manner. She wanted to earn Chastity's confidence.

"My sister is on her way to America," Chastity said, surprising Jamie.

"Really?"

"Yes. She's marrying an American man."

"Oh. Where did she meet him?"

Chastity got a sheepish look on her face and leaned in and whispered, "Actually, she has never met him."

"I've heard about that. Is she a mail order bride?"

Chastity nodded.

"What's your sister's name?"

"Olga. The American picked her off of a website. I had the chance to go, but I was too scared. I can't imagine marrying someone without getting to know them."

"But your sister decided to go?"

"Yes. She's determined. I went with her to the interview to make sure it was all on the up and up. It was. She leaves this Friday. They found me a job here. This is my first week."

"How is it going so far?" Jamie asked.

"Really good."

Jamie could tell she was lying. Not really lying, just afraid to tell the truth. Afraid to admit she'd made a horrible mistake, that she was ashamed. Jamie had seen it thousands of times. It's how they got trapped. They started out feeling empowered because they were so attractive, and men wanted them. The attention felt good. Momentarily.

By the second or third guy, they went from "I am doing a bad thing" to "I'm a bad person." Then they were hooked. They thought they deserved the shame. The shame took control of them and became a chain around their neck. A badge of dishonor.

For this reason, it was hard to get the girls out because they thought they deserved all the pain that came with it. The key was to get the girls to see that they deserved better.

All hope was not lost for Chastity. She still clearly had regrets and wasn't sure she had made the right decision.

Jamie had to be careful. She couldn't go down that road with Chastity. Not yet. Not until she got the information she needed on the pipeline.

"Tell me about the club," Jamie asked, getting back to the real purpose for being there.

Chastity became animated. She was perfect. She liked to talk. She'd be a fountain of information.

"The VIP rooms are behind the curtain," she said, pointing in that direction. After telling Jamie a lot about the area they were sitting in.

"What are the VIP rooms?"

Chastity noticeably blushed.

"That's where we entertain the men. If you know what I mean."

"I think I do."

Jamie wanted to say more. Give Chastity the standard spiel she gave girls to get them out of prostitution. But she held her tongue. She needed information and Chastity might clam up if she realized Jamie had a hidden agenda. There'd be an opportunity later.

"How many VIP rooms are there?" Jamie asked.

"More than a hundred."

Jamie felt her mouth fly open. Someone had sunk a lot of money into this club. There was no way he made enough on the cover charge and alcohol to pay the expenses. The big money was in the rooms. The house probably took seventy to eighty percent of the proceeds from the girls. Maybe more.

A couple came out from behind the curtains that led to the VIP rooms. Both of them had wet hair. Jamie pointed at them. Chastity looked that way.

"Is that why they call it Splash?" Jamie asked. "Do you girls have to get wet?"

Chastity nodded.

"Well ... Not all the time. The guys have their choice," she explained. "They can choose a private room with a bed or couch, or they can add a water feature. If you know what I mean."

It didn't take much of an imagination for Jamie to figure out what those water features were. Chastity elaborated anyway.

"The guys can choose showers, baths, or hot tubs. Those are extra. They can get wet too or just watch us."

Chastity was talking a mile a minute. Barely taking a breath as she explained. Jamie didn't say anything, not wanting to interrupt.

Chastity pulled on the ends of her hair. "They are kind of a pain. Most guys choose a water feature. I'm ruining my hair having to blow dry it so many times."

"I can imagine."

"It's worse for some of the other girls. They work behind the curtains. If you know what I mean."

She kept saying that. Chastity was clearly nervous.

"I don't actually know what you mean."

"There are more curtains in the back."

"What's behind them?"

"Showers and bathtubs. The girls are behind glass windows. The men can watch them taking showers, baths, or dancing under a waterfall. We satisfy the men while they watch, if you know what I mean. I've had to work one of those shifts before. I looked like a prune when I was done."

"Why do you do it?" Jamie asked, trying not to sound judgmental but sensing an opportunity to start her standard rescue speech. At least skirt around the subject.

"The money is good," Chastity said, as if she needed to justify her actions.

The standard answer. That's what most working girls said to that question.

"How much do you make?"

"I'll make about 1600 BYN this month."

Jamie did the math. About $800.00 American dollars. An average Belarusian woman made half that. Chastity even made more than most men. Belarusian women were more educated than men as a general rule, but earned about two thirds what men did even in the same jobs.

"We are always looking for girls, if you're interested," Chastity said. "I get a bonus if I recruit someone. You're a lot prettier than me. So you could make a lot more money."

"You're beautiful."

She blushed.

"Is it safe?" Jamie asked, feigning interest.

Chastity waved her hand dismissively.

"Splash has a lot of security. The worst part is the Russians. Sometimes they're really rough. Especially the older men. And they take forever. If you know what I mean."

Her voice trailed off as she repeated the last statement.

Several guys stood off to the side waiting for them to finish their conversation. Ready to make their move on Jamie once the conversation ended.

Jamie wasn't finished prying for information. She glanced around to make sure Moe hadn't made an entrance. Still no sign of him.

"What was the name of the company that recruited you and your sister?" Jamie asked.

"Belles of Belarus. See that man over there behind the ropes. He's the owner."

Jamie looked to where Chastity was pointing. She'd already seen the area and knew only important people were allowed behind the ropes.

One table had an Arab looking man with two women on his arms, and his own guards standing a short distance away. He must've just come in because Jamie hadn't noticed him before.

"His name is Omer Asaf," Chastity said.

Jamie already knew his name. She recognized him from the picture. The one with him standing next to the President of Belarus.

The Turkish businessman. With possible terrorism ties.

Jamie now had a connection between Asaf and the mail-order-bride business in Pinsk.

The pipeline? Maybe.

Now she needed to figure out how to get behind those ropes and meet him.

19

Jamie didn't have to figure out a way to meet Omer Asaf. Five minutes later, one of the goons who'd been guarding Omer behind the ropes walked toward them.

"Looks like Mr. Asaf wants to meet you," Chastity said, pointing out the man as he made his way across the empty dance floor.

Not necessary. Jamie had already noticed. She was analyzing the situation. The thought had already crossed her mind that she hoped she never had to fight the man. He stood six foot four or five and three hundred plus pounds.

Lumbering was a better way to describe his walk. He looked like a linebacker on an NFL team. She would have the advantage of speed and quickness. He'd have every other advantage including the one attached to his side under his suit jacket.

A gun. Something Jamie had but threw into the river.

"I wonder what he wants," Jamie said to herself not realizing she said it loud enough for Chastity to hear her.

For a moment, Jamie wondered if she was made. Omer had ties to the government. He might've been warned to be on the lookout for her. Might have even been instructed to dispose of her. Quietly.

"He talks to a lot of girls," Chastity explained. Not the least bit worried. She lowered her voice to a whisper though. "I should warn you. I hear he's kind of a playboy."

"I'll be fine. Thanks for the information."

Jamie leaned over and gave Chastity a hug. Almost a reflex reaction. She barely knew the girl and was already feeling terrible about her plight. Wondering if there was a way to rescue her.

Brad's instructions were cleared. *Don't try to help the girls! You are there for information gathering only.*

Brad had another saying that echoed in her mind. *You can't save everyone.*

Besides, she needed to focus on Asaf. He owned a nightclub that employed prostitutes. That much was clear. It didn't mean he was involved in sex trafficking, but it was close enough to explore further.

If her life was in danger, she needed to be ready for anything. Jamie had already memorized all the escape routes.

"Mr. Asaf would like to meet you and welcome you personally to *Splash*," the goon said.

"Who is Mr. Asaf?" Jamie said, feigning ignorance.

"He is the owner of the nightclub."

The man pointed to Omer sitting behind the ropes. Two women were still at his side.

"I don't know . . ." Jamie said, pretending to be cautious. A normal response for a young woman alone in a nightclub in a foreign country.

"He just wants to buy you a drink and introduce himself."

"I already have a drink."

The man was nervous. He shifted his weight from side to side. He was sent on a mission, and Jamie could imagine that Omer would not be happy if he wasn't successful.

"Go ahead. You'll be fine," Chastity said reassuringly.

"Okay. I guess it won't hurt to say hello," Jamie said.

She stood and pulled the bottom of her dress down as if it could go down any further. A nervous habit most girls did. Didn't matter where a girl was. In church or in a nightclub.

Jamie had learned something from that. Women were instinctively modest. Protective of their figure and men gawking at it. Even prostitutes or girls in strip clubs.

Jamie had seen women in the scantiest outfits pull their top up or their skirt or shorts down to cover themselves. As if they knew. Down deep. They tried to cover themselves because they were instinctively ashamed. Embarrassed.

They never quit doing it. Even when they had accepted the shame. It became part of them. That's why she needed to talk to Chastity alone. Maybe there was still hope for her.

Omer's thug motioned for Jamie to lead the way. As she was walking, she suddenly felt eyes on her. There were hundreds of eyes on her as almost every man in the house stopped what he was doing to watch her walk across the room.

That's not what she was feeling. The eyes were familiar.

Moe.

He was standing just inside the entrance.

He made it inside! A smile came on her face at the thought. Moe was scanning the room for her. A pained and panicked look on his face.

I'm right here, Moe.

She was walking across the floor in perfect view of the entire nightclub and Moe was the only man in the club who hadn't seen her. He was looking in the booths. At the bar. Scanning the tables. His eyes went back and forth furtively. Jamie saw a look of relief come over his face when he finally spotted her.

It was all she could do to keep from laughing out loud.

She turned her attention back to Asaf who now was looking her way with a friendly smile on his face. He sent the two girls next to him away and stood from a lush couch that seated three easily. In front of the couch was a table with a glass top.

Several finished drinks were on the table along with a half empty bottle of chilled champagne in a bucket of ice. The bottle would make a good weapon if necessary. Jamie recognized from the label that it was a very expensive brand of champagne.

A shame to break it over Omer's head if necessary.

"My name is Omer," he said, extending his hand.

He was exactly like his picture, only slightly greyer around the sides. A salt and pepper gray. Distinguished. The look was no doubt created by a highly skilled hairdresser. His handshake was firm but inviting.

He pulled her toward him slightly, exerting control over her immediately. She let him. He took her hand and raised it to his lips and kissed the top of it. Smoothly. Gently. Releasing the hand slowly, at his pace. Romantically, even though they had just met.

Jamie pretended to blush. Curly had said fake blushing was something Jamie wasn't good at. He used to tease her and say she looked like she was constipated. He spent hours trying to help her perfect the proper technique. He finally gave up.

He would've given up sooner if not for the amusement it was giving him. Something she didn't appreciate. He told her not to even bother trying to do it in the field.

"It'll get you killed," he warned.

She had practiced it in front of a mirror for hours and had become better at it. Enough that it wouldn't get her killed.

Omer certainly didn't notice. He invited her to sit next to him.

Jamie studied him carefully. To see if she saw any hint of deception. Like he was pretending to be nice to her but had other plans.

She didn't see anything that raised any alarms. His looks were what she would expect from a playboy billionaire entertaining a pretty woman.

"Bring us some more champagne," he commanded, snapping his fingers in the air. A waiter standing in the corner immediately responded.

They took the half-opened bottle away. Jamie thought it was a waste of good champagne and it left her without a weapon.

Curly would disagree. He said she always had a weapon. Her knees, feet, fists, the palms of her hands, could all be lethal in a fight. For that matter, she could take a gun from one of the guards.

Let's hope it doesn't come to that.

"Bring us some Armand de Brignac Brut Rose," Asaf said with a look of satisfaction. "Have them bring some strawberries with it."

Jamie tried to relax while maintaining the awkwardness. She didn't want to appear too comfortable. That'd make Omer suspicious.

"That's very expensive champagne," Jamie said. "As I remember."

Omer waved his hand dismissively.

"I have some bottles in my collection worth over $25,000 each. This one is about $1,000 a bottle."

"French, I presume," Jamie said.

"Of course. I would never drink any champagne that wasn't from France. This bottle is less expensive, but very exquisite. Like you, my dear."

"Merci," Jamie replied.

"You speak French?"

"Not hardly," Jamie said in more of a southern accent, shaking her head, chuckling. "I know a few words. That's about it."

A lie. She could speak it fluently.

"What's your name?" he asked.

"Allie."

"Where are you from, Allie?"

"I'm from America. Omaha, Nebraska."

Jamie saw a hint of anger flash across Asaf's face. He couldn't hide it. His eyes burned with hatred.

She remembered that he had no business investments in America. He'd probably been blackballed. Being from the Middle East, he may have any number of reasons why he might hate America. That one being at the top of his list. He was trying hard not to show it.

Asaf looked away. So did Jamie. What she saw made her angry.

Chastity was standing in the line for the VIP rooms with a man next to her. A paying customer. Jamie couldn't bear the thought of what was about to happen. Unlike Omer, she was careful to make sure the anger inside didn't make it to her face.

Fortunately for both of them, the bottle of champagne arrived. The smile returned to Omer's face as he insisted on opening the bottle. Asaf expertly removed the cork. The loud popping noise echoed through the room as it opened.

It sounded like a gunshot, causing Jamie to catch herself so she didn't jump. Then a crackling, fizzing sound as the champagne bubbled over the top and then swooshed into the glass. Jamie could hear the distinctive sound of hissing, chatter, bubbling that eventually faded away to a whisper.

Omer poured each of them a glass. He swirled the champagne in the glass and then placed it under his nose. Jamie had been taught the proper etiquette but decided to act naïve, unsure of herself. She slowly raised it to her lips as he gave a toast in French. Complimenting her beauty.

She shuddered slightly as the alcohol permeated her body and senses. It rushed to her brain, instantly releasing tension. She felt herself relax slightly. He dipped a strawberry in brown sugar and handed it to her. The taste exploded in her mouth and she felt suddenly energized.

For the next twenty minutes, they drank champagne, ate strawberries, and laughed, avoiding any serious conversations. Omer was charming and sophisticated. Jamie could see why women were mesmerized by his wit and his money.

She was careful not to drink the champagne too fast. She nursed two glasses over twenty minutes so as to keep a clear head.

Finally, Omer interrupted the conversation and said, "I must go."

"Aww..." Jamie said in her most disappointed voice. "I sure had a good time."

"How long are you in town?" Omer asked.

"For three weeks."

"I own the *California Casino*. I'd like you to be my guest this Saturday night. Will you honor me with your presence?"

Jamie pretended to be unsure. She acted hesitant. She definitely wanted to go. Omer was a bad character. She knew it after five minutes talking to him. He was into all types of bad things. She saw right through his playful and charming exterior.

He was a killer. She'd been in the presence of many men like him. Bad actors she was hired to identify and eliminate.

She was determined to find out who he was and what he was into. He might or might not be behind the pipeline, but she now had an in with someone she believed capable of funding terrorism.

Brad might or might not approve of her change in focus. She could certainly justify it as part of her investigative mission.

"It might be the champagne talking, but I think I'd like that."

"Then the champagne was worth every penny I spent on it," Omer said, laughing.

Jamie stood to her feet and caught her balance as the blood or champagne, or both pulsed through her body and caused her to temporarily lose her equilibrium. Omer reached over and took her hands to steady her and kissed her on both cheeks.

"I look forward to Saturday night. How about nine o'clock?" he said.

"How will I find you?"

"Come to the entrance, and I'll have someone waiting. They'll bring you to me."

"Sounds good," Jamie said and turned and walked away as one of the men opened the rope for her. By the time she made it back to her seat on the other side of the nightclub, Omer was gone. Probably out a back entrance.

Jamie sat down and let out a huge sigh of relief. The tension was indescribable in those situations. Every second and every mannerism, every word spoken, every gesture all had to be carefully choreographed to fit her fake persona.

She thought back over the conversation. From what she could remember, she didn't make any mistakes.

Suddenly, the feeling came back over her. Stronger. Intense this time.

The person watching her was back.

He was there. Somewhere in the nightclub. Not Moe. Someone else.

An eerie feeling, a chill, a sense of dread came over her.

Who was it? Where was he?

Jamie scanned the room, careful not to make it too obvious. Moe was over in the corner with a drink in his hand. Probably water. Talking to one of the girls. That was good. He was distracted.

Where she was sitting, she had her back to the wall. She could see the entire nightclub. People were dancing now. The music was louder. The lights dimmer.

She saw Chastity come out of the VIP area. She made her way back into the crowd to talk to other men. A sad look on her face caused Jamie to grimace. She motioned to her and got her attention.

Her eyes lit up when she saw Jamie. Chastity walked over to her table, sat down, and said, "How did it go with Omer?"

"Fine," Jamie responded. "How much is an hour with you in a room?"

"A private room is $100.00 for the men," she answered.

"Come with me," Jamie said with a sense of urgency.

They stood and Jamie led Chastity over to the line for the VIP rooms. Jamie could feel the eyes on her. Following her. Watching her every move. She wanted to stop and look. But it would be too obvious. She didn't want him to know she knew he was there.

"What are we doing?" Chastity asked, shocking Jamie back to reality.

"I want to pay for one hour in one of the rooms with you. It has to be a private room."

A look of astonishment came over Chastity's face. Her eyes widened and her lips curled in confusion.

"You want an hour with me?" Chastity said.

"Yes. We'll work out the price later."

Jamie positioned herself in the line, so she was to the left of Chastity. Looking past her into the entire nightclub. The darkened lights made it harder to see in the shadows. The man could be hiding in any number of places.

Fortunately, they made it through the line quickly and behind the curtains. Out of his sight. She'd be safe in there for at least an hour.

The back of the nightclub was one big room. Like a warehouse, only nicer. No ceilings, but marble floors. Several partitions lined the sides and formed several makeshift hallways.

It smelled of water and chlorine.

"Those are the water rooms," Chastity said, pointing.

Some were behind curtains and others behind doors. Jamie could imagine the showers, tubs, and waterfalls in the viewing rooms.

A door opened to one of the rooms and a man came out. One of the paying customers. A weird look of lust and satisfaction was on his face.

A girl came out right behind him buttoning her shirt, pulling it up to cover her breasts. She straightened her shorts. Pulled them down in the back to cover her butt.

Instinctive.

To the left were a number of additional areas cordoned off with curtains. Most of the curtains were closed. The ones that were open had various accommodations. Some had full-size beds. Others just couches. Some massage tables.

As they walked further to the back, the rooms became nicer. Some had king-sized beds. Lush bedding. Pictures on the wall. Mirrors. She could occasionally hear noises coming from behind the curtains.

"Take us to your most private room," Jamie said, anxious to get away from it all. "One behind a door that we can close."

They turned to the left and back to the far corner where there were two rooms with doors. One was already closed. Chastity led them through the open door of the other one into a large room. Bigger than the others. Better described as a suite.

It was richly adorned with a couch, a couple lounge chairs, and a table where food could be served. In the center was a king-sized bed with a royal-red bedspread covering it. A large painting of a nude woman was displayed above it. It had its own bathroom and shower. TV with porn playing. The light switches had dimmers, and Chastity lowered them some.

Jamie walked over and turned the TV off. "How much is this room for an hour?"

"$400.00."

Jamie took out $1,000 in American bills and laid them on the table.

Chastity took the money in her hands and counted it and said, "I don't understand."

"The rest is for you," Jamie explained.

"What are we doing? Do you want to have sex with me?"

"No, honey," Jamie said. "I want information. Tell me everything you know about Omer Asaf."

20

The next day, Thursday morning, 6:30 a.m.

Chastity got off work and went home. She scarfed down some breakfast then took a quick shower, and decided to call her twin sister, Olga. Normally, it would be too early in the morning, but Olga had texted her and told her she was so excited she couldn't sleep.

She was up packing for her trip to America.

"Daria!" Olga answered on the first ring.

Daria was her real name. Chastity was the name she used at the club.

"They said I can only take one bag and one carry on. How in the world am I going to get everything to fit in one bag? What should I wear on the plane? I was thinking the red dress. And cream-colored shoes. What do you think?"

Olga was talking so fast she was barely taking time to catch her breath.

Daria was happy for her sister. She'd never seen her this excited about anything. Olga was the one who first heard about Belles of Belarus. Daria thought she was crazy. Never in their wildest dreams did they think anyone would pick them.

"Can you believe it?" Olga said. "Out of all the beautiful girls on the website, someone picked me to be his wife. I'm going to make sure he doesn't regret it. I'll be the best wife he could ever have. Better than any of the other girls."

"Yes, you will."

"I'm sorry, Sis. I haven't given you a chance to get a word in edgewise. How are you doing?" Olga asked.

"I just got off work," Daria said in a tired voice. Her voice was hoarse from talking all night over the music.

"It's six-thirty in the morning. What hours do you work?" Olga asked.

"I work all night. Six nights a week. Ten to six. That's the best shift, though. That's when I can make the most money. The club is open all the time. I guess I'm one of the better girls because I got one of the best shifts."

"Of course, you're one of the best girls. I'm going to America!" Olga squealed into the phone.

Daria put the phone away from her ear. "I can't believe it," she heard Olga say enthusiastically.

"I know. I can't either. That was fast too. They said they had a waiting list of twelve hundred girls."

"Someone picked me off the website."

"I'm not surprised. You're one of the prettiest ones."

"You're so sweet."

"Are you nervous?" Daria asked.

"Of course, I am. Excited but nervous. I'm going to be married."

"I always thought I'd be there when you got married," Daria said somberly. "I'm supposed to be your maid of honor."

"I know. I hate that too. It's not going to be the same without you. I bet my guy is rich, though. He has to pay a lot of money for me. As soon as I can, I'll send for you. You can come to America. You can live right next door to me."

"I'll do that. Listen. I won't be able to call you tomorrow. I go into work early, at three o'clock. I'm covering someone else's shift. That's why I'm calling today. And you can't call me at work. They don't let us have our phones on."

"How's it going there?" Olga asked.

All Olga knew was that Daria was working at a nightclub in Minsk. They had applied together at Belles of Belarus to be matched up with an American man to marry. Both were selected for the website, but Daria opted to go to Minsk and work at a nightclub.

Olga chose to become a mail order bride. Daria was wondering if she had made the right choice. Maybe she could have been the one going to America.

I'm going to miss her desperately.

They were the only family each other had. Born to an abusive father and an alcoholic mother, they had both left home when they turned eighteen. As far as they knew, their father was in prison somewhere, and their mother was in the *Republic Hospital for Mental Health.* A fancy name for an asylum.

"I've been worried about you," Olga added.

"It's okay," Daria said, in obvious pain.

"What's going on? Talk to me."

"I mean ... Some people are nice. It's not what I thought it would be like."

Tears started welling up in Daria's eyes. She tried to hide it, but Olga commented that she could tell Daria was crying.

"Actually, I hate it. The guys are disgusting."

"Which club are you working at?" Olga asked.

"Splash."

"Have you met any cute guys?"

"I don't even notice anymore. None of them are cute to me. I pretty much have to do whatever the guy wants. I thought I got to make my own choices. But I don't. It's really hard to pretend I'm enjoying it. I hate every second of it."

"What do you mean, you hate what you have to do?"

Silence as Daria didn't say anything.

"Daria?" she asked more strongly.

"I have to have sex with these guys."

"What?" Olga said in a loud voice. "No one ever told us that. I thought you just had to dance for them, maybe take your clothes off. I didn't know you actually had to have sex with them."

"That's what I thought too. It's horrible. The money's good. But ..."

"Why don't you come home?"

"I can't. I signed a three-year contract. If I leave, I have to pay them back a lot of money. They said they would sue me and turn me in to the government. I'm afraid. These people aren't messing around. I agreed to it. It's my fault. I have to live with it."

The girl, Allie Walker, had said last night she would try to get her out of the contract. Not to get her hopes up, but she'd try.

"Anyway, enough about me. I'll be okay. What about you? Are you excited?"

"I'm nervous," Olga answered. "I mean ... I'm marrying a strange man sight unseen. I guess I'll have to have sex with him too," she said with a nervous laugh.

"At least it's only one guy. You're scared. I understand. But you'll get used to it. You may even like the guy."

"I hope so."

"Do you know your itinerary?"

Daria could hear Olga shuffling some papers. "We're supposed to be at Belles by three o'clock on Friday," she said. "Our buses leave right after that. Our flight leaves Moscow at midnight."

"When will you be in America?"

"I don't know exactly. I think we fly through Germany or something."

"Are you sure you're doing the right thing? I already regret my decision."

"They said I can always come back if I don't like it or if I don't like the guy."

"Did you get the phone I sent you?"

"I did."

"It's an international phone. You can use it anywhere."

"How can you afford that?"

"I'm making pretty good money now. I bought it at a phone store here in Minsk. I put some money in the envelope for you."

"I got it, but they said we can't bring phones or money. I'm not supposed to call you for a year."

"Screw that. You call me. You promise?"

"I promise. I'll call you every chance I get."

"If you don't like it there, call me. You can come back home."

"I will. I'll be fine."

"Call me before you get on your flight in Moscow. I'll be at work, but you can leave me a message. Let me know you're okay."

"I will. We should have plenty of time before our plane leaves. I'm not supposed to have a phone though. I'll have to sneak it in."

"That shouldn't be hard. We had a lot of practice sneaking stuff around mom. She never found anything. Promise me you'll call. Even if it is just for a second. Let me know you're okay. If I don't hear from you, I'll be worried."

"I promise."

"By the way, I met an American girl tonight. Her name is Allie."

"You met her in Minsk?"

"Yeah. She came into *Splash*."

"What was she doing there?"

"I don't know, but I like her. She paid me a thousand American dollars to go back to a VIP room with her for an hour."

"You had sex with a woman?"

"No, silly. She just wanted to talk to me."

"She paid you a thousand dollars to talk to her for an hour?"

"I know, right. It was so strange. She gave me her phone number. Said to give it to you and for you to call her when you get to America. Do you have something to write with?"

"Hold on . . . Okay. Go ahead."

"555-282-3212."

"That's easy to remember," Olga said.

"It's not that easy. You have to dial eight, then wait for the tone. Then dial ten and then one. Then 555-282-3212. Write that down."

"I think I got it. Eight, then wait, ten, one, and then the number."

"Listen to me carefully," Daria said. "I want you to enter the number into your phone as a contact. Her name is Allie Walker. Promise me you'll put her in your phone. You can call her when you get to America. I gave her my number. She's really nice. We can keep in touch through her."

"I will. Thank you."

"I'm going to go to bed now, but please know that I love you."

"I love you to the moon and back."

"Promise you'll call her if you need anything."

"I promise." Olga said.

"I love you, infinity," she said, as the line went dead.

***

8:30 a.m.

Fabi had been summoned to Lieutenant Petrov's office first thing in the morning. Normally, it wouldn't be an issue. This morning, he was tired. He'd been at Splash nightclub until two-thirty in the morning. Allie Walker had stayed there for hours. He followed her from her hotel to the nightclub.

He didn't have his eyes on her for thirty minutes or so when they wouldn't let him in the nightclub. He had to talk his way in. He flashed his badge, but that didn't work at first. They weren't so sure they wanted to let a detective in.

He finally told them he was off duty and not working. So, they let him in but made him pay the cover charge. Half a day's pay. No way he could turn it in as an expense either. The Lieutenant told him yesterday to quit following the girl.

Once inside, he had seen Allie talking to one of the call girls. He had to admit that Allie was the prettiest woman he'd ever seen. She seemed really friendly with the other girl. Like they knew each other. Which was strange. Supposedly, Allie Walker had never been to Belarus before.

Then she went over and met with a middle eastern man. He seemed like a high roller. Like he owned the joint. They drank champagne and ate strawberries. It looked like they were having a good time. This girl got around. She was a real flirt.

Then it got really strange. Allie went back to her table, found the first girl, and then they went into the VIP rooms. He could only imagine what they did back there. He tried to get the man at the ropes to let him go back there, but the bouncer wouldn't unless he was with one of the girls.

He talked to one and she said it would cost 50,000 BYR! More than twenty American dollars. Just to look. A hundred American dollars if he went back there with a girl. No way he could afford that. How would he explain it to his wife? And what would he do once he was back there? Go from room to room searching for her?

He decided to wait in the club for her. That didn't stop him from picturing what they were doing back there in his mind. A smile came over his face as he thought about it again. After about an hour, they came back out. Allie Walker stayed in the club for another two hours.

He intended to follow her back to the hotel where he'd confront her. He now had proof she was behind the attack on the boys. His plan was to interrogate her until she admitted it. Instead, she left the nightclub and got immediately into a taxi. He guessed she went back to the hotel because there was no sign of her when he arrived back there. He hung around for a few minutes but then went home and went to bed.

He wouldn't tell any of this to the Lieutenant until he had a confession from the girl. He figured the Lieutenant wanted to meet with him to give him another assignment. He hoped it didn't take too much of his time.

He was this close to solving the beating of the boys. He was going to go over to the hotel and confront the girl this morning. He walked into the Lieutenant's office and was immediately hit with the musty smell of stale cigarettes.

"We've ruled out the American girl as a suspect," Lieutenant Petrov said.

"Why?" Fabi asked. "I know she's up to no good. I still think she's involved in the beating of those two boys."

"The one kid called me yesterday and left a message saying he looked at the picture and it wasn't her."

The boy was lying. Fabi knew it was the girl who attacked those boys. Yesterday, when he was following her to the nightclub, he saw her look over to where the boys were beaten. It was a quick glance, but it was apparent, nonetheless.

Why would she look down that alley unless she'd been there before? He was determined to confront her. He started to tell the Lieutenant but thought better of it.

"What if he's lying?" Fabi asked. "Have you talked to the other boy? The one in the hospital."

"No, but a nurse said there's no way those damages were caused by someone kicking him. She said they had to be from a baseball bat or a lead pipe. Nothing like that was found at the scene. And I doubt that girl's been carrying a lead pipe around with her. I think it was another gang."

Fabi started to answer, but the Lieutenant gave him a stern glare.

"Go back to doing what you were doing and leave the girl alone. That's an order."

Fabi left the office and went back to his desk with no intention of leaving the girl alone.

***

10:00 a.m.

Denys sat at his desk in the Republic Palace trying to stay busy and trying equally as hard to keep his mind off last night's meeting with the CIA operative interrupted by the two KGB men who had entered unannounced into the church. He was still spooked by how close he came to getting caught.

These meetings were getting dangerous.

He also wondered if the girl had gotten his note. He'd have no way of knowing until tomorrow night at 6:00 when she either showed up or she didn't. This whole thing was getting really complicated. He was beginning to wonder if the risk was worth it.

The good news of the morning was that the Militsia no longer considered Allie Walker a suspect in the beating of the boys. Word was that they were pulling surveillance off of her. That would make it easier for them to meet and easier for her to do her mission. She had to find a way to stop Omer Asaf.

His thoughts were interrupted by the antiquated telephone ringing. It sounded more like a buzzer or an alarm than a ring.

" *Zdravstvujtye,*" he said matter-of-factly. The Belarusian word for hello.

The secretary from the office of the President said in a monotone voice. "The President would like to see you in his office."

"Right now?"

"Yes sir. Right away."

Denys hung up the phone. "What could that be about?"

He suddenly felt like he'd been hit by a truck. He'd been called into President Bobrinsky's office with no explanation. Did it have to do with last night?

The church. The KGB. The meeting.

His imagination was playing tricks on him. Creating all kinds of scenarios in his mind.

Relax. These meetings happen all the time. Sometimes he was called into Lukashenko's office just to share a glass of vodka.

For some reason, he had a bad feeling about today, certain it was more than to share a drink. He stood from his chair, adjusted his tie, and brushed off his suit. He walked slowly down the hall like a man walking to his execution through the doors into the lobby. The secretary motioned for him to go in.

The office was a large and stately room. The President sat behind his desk. He motioned Denys in and said, "I have someone I want you to meet."

Denys hadn't seen the man sitting in the huge high-back chair in front of the desk. A man stood and turned to greet him.

"Hello Comrade. My name is Omer Asaf."

21

"Hello, Comrade. My name is Omer Asaf," the man said as Denys's heart started doing what felt like somersaults in his chest.

Even with the fear his first thought was, *You are not my comrade.*

His emotions were mixed. Vacillating between extreme disdain for the man who was a terrorist working against everything he believed was good for the world, and utter fear as to why he was in the President's office summoned to a meeting with the man.

The best course of action, he decided, was to take his cue from the President and match his tone and manner. Bobrinsky was smiling, so he did the same.

"Hello, Sir," Denys said, as he walked across the room, put his hands on both of Asaf's shoulders and kissed him on both cheeks.

"I am very pleased to meet you," he added. "Our Supreme Leader has many good things to say about you. What brings you to Minsk?"

"We will get to business soon," the President interrupted the usual greeting. "First, we must have a drink."

No meaningful business ever commenced in Belarus before a drink. President Bobrinsky walked over to a cabinet filled with bottles of various liquors. He poured three glasses of Vodka. The drink of choice in Belarus. He handed each of them a glass, his filled slightly above the others.

They stood in a circle.

The President raised his glass and said, " *Vashe Zdorovie.*"

The three men raised and toasted to their health as the President suggested. They each downed the glass in one swallow. The President walked back to the cabinet and poured another shot into each of their glasses. Then he filled his own beyond a shot.

The President looked at Omer signifying it was his turn to make a toast. He raised his glass and said, " *Za Milyh dam.*"

"To lovely women," the other two repeated.

"And to our wives," Omer added.

They all laughed heartily.

"May we have good health so we can enjoy all of them," he continued.

Bobrinsky roared with approval. Denys hated those kinds of toasts which were commonplace. Obvious jokes meant to disparage wives and toast mistresses. Particularly offensive because his wife was dead, and he had been a loving and faithful husband to her for the forty-five years they were married.

A rare feat in Belarus. While the divorce rate in Belarus wasn't as high as Russia, it was well over fifty percent. Ukraine was the highest. Pushing nearly seventy percent. Estonia was well under fifty percent. Denys wasn't sure why.

Denys did what he always did and ignored the barroom banter.

The President topped off the glasses for one last toast from Denys.

Denys set aside his anger and raised his glass high in the air and said robustly, " *Za vstrechu!*"

"To our meeting." The other two mimicked Denys's boring toast.

They downed what was left of their drinks in huge gulps. Apparently satisfied, the President screwed the top back on the bottle, and walked back behind his desk and sat down. Their cue to do the same.

Denys sat in the other high-back chair next to Asaf and across from the President. He tried not to fidget. Still not sure why he had been summoned there.

The President's manner and tone turned serious, affirming his fears. "Gentlemen. Providence has brought us to this moment in time. The Americans are trying to destroy us with their economic sanctions."

Denys wanted to correct the President.

The sanctions are against Russia, not against us.

He dared not open his mouth. Bobrinsky made no distinction. He considered the American sanctions against Russia an act of war. Any war against Russia was a war against Belarus as far as Bobrinsky was concerned.

"Comrade Kuzman has stood up to their aggression. He refuses to give in to their demands. Mr. Asaf has provided us with an interesting alternative that will bring America to its knees."

Denys didn't like where this conversation was heading. All he knew were the rumors he'd heard that Asaf was trying to buy the briefcase. That had to be what they were about to discuss.

A dose of adrenaline shot through him. What if the President had already made a deal? Up to that point, Bobrinsky had been hesitant to part with even one of the briefcases. They were too valuable.

If that were the case, would Denys still be able to set up another meet with the American to give him the information from this meeting? Information they'd paid a handsome sum for. More than a million dollars had been deposited in his Swiss bank account last week.

Not that the money mattered to him. A nuclear bomb in the wrong hands was the most important thing. He'd give that information away for free if it would stop the madman.

He guarded his mannerisms. He couldn't act anything less than enthusiastic while in the presence of the foreigner. He could speak somewhat freely with the President in private, but he knew to never contradict the President in front of a guest.

"Mr. Asaf has agreed to purchase a briefcase," Bobrinsky said.

Before he could stop himself, Denys said, "Are you sure that's a good idea?"

During the breakup of the Soviet Union, four nuclear briefcase bombs went missing. They were hidden in Belarus. So well hidden that only a few people actually knew where they were. Denys knew because he was in charge of transporting them across the border.

At the time, it seemed like a good thing to do. Get them out of the hands of Russia and into safekeeping. The location was some of the intelligence he had given to the CIA, and he'd been rewarded handsomely. Of course, he was the only one in the room who knew anything about that.

The President continued, "Mr. Asaf has been transporting buses of women out of Belarus every month. He has been selling those women to American men. While I don't approve of the practice, I have looked the other way. Mr. Asaf has made it well worth our while by making significant investments in Belarus for which we are very grateful. And now he is making an even greater investment by buying one of our bombs."

"What do you intend to do with it?" Denys asked Omer, afraid he already knew the answer.

By the look on his face, the President seemed annoyed that he was interrupted, so he provided his own answer, "He's only going to use it as a threat. He's going to smuggle it through Mexico and hide it in an American city. He's then going to demand that they leave the Middle East and remove the sanctions against Iran and Russia, or he will activate the bomb."

"America will have no choice but to capitulate," Asaf said. His words were dripping with vitriol. "They have dominated the world for too many years."

"That will start a nuclear war that will result in the annihilation of all of us," Denys said, nervously.

"We have no intention of detonating the bomb," Asaf explained. "Just using it as leverage. As a threat. We will give the Americans proof we have it and the resolve to use it. That should be enough for us to get the sanctions removed."

"What do you want me to do?" Denys asked.

"Make sure they have safe passage with the briefcase through our border into Russia," the President said.

"When are you going to transport it?"

"The handoff will happen on Monday," the President said. "They're going to move it out of Belarus and into Russia next Friday night in one of the buses with the girls in it."

"Aren't there buses leaving tomorrow night?" Denys asked.

"Yes," Asaf responded. "We will have another group the following Friday night. They will go through the border between five and six o'clock."

"You can count on us," Denys said, trying to process all the information in his mind, including trying to determine if there was anything he could do to stop it.

Probably not, but maybe the Americans can. He'd tell the girl about it tomorrow.

"It's settled then," Bobrinsky said, as he stood from behind the desk. He then went to the liquor cabinet and poured three more drinks. This time the glasses were nearly full.

He raised his glass and said, "*Давайте выпьем за успех нашего дела!*" A toast to the success of their project.

Asaf lifted a glass and said something in Arabic. Denys didn't understand until he gave them the translation.

"May our sons have rich fathers and beautiful mothers."

They all drank with a hearty laugh.

It was Denys's turn. "*Давайте выпьем за то, чтобы мы испытали столько горя, сколько капель вина останется в наших бокалах!* May we suffer as much sorrow as the number of drops we are about to leave in our glass."

With that, the meeting was over. Denys hurried out of there. Emotions were pulsing through him like lava in a volcano about to erupt. If he didn't get out of there soon, he would say something he regretted.

He had to meet with the girl. Tomorrow night. Which wouldn't come soon enough.

***

The meeting was over, and Denys had just left the room. Asaf stayed behind to talk to the President alone.

"Are you sure?" President Bobrinsky asked Asaf.

"Positive," Omer Asaf answered.

"Denys has been my friend and confidant for more than forty years. No one has ever questioned his loyalty to the motherland before. I can't believe he's a traitor."

"Two of my men saw him last night. Meeting with an American. At the Holy Spirit Church."

Asaf didn't mention that his men were dressed in stolen KGB uniforms.

"The American could have been anyone," Bobrinsky said. "Why do you think he was meeting with the CIA?"

"The man he was meeting with left the church as soon as my men walked in."

"I need more proof than that."

"I have more proof. It pains me to bring you this information, my friend. I'm sorry the bad news must come from me."

Omer pulled some papers out of his suit jacket. He handed them to President Bobrinsky.

"What are these?" the President asked.

"Bank records. For a Swiss bank account. In Denys's name."

"How did you get these? The Swiss don't give out this information. How do I know these aren't fabricated?"

"Let's just say that the bank values my business more than they do his. I have considerably more money there than he does. But look at the balance. He has more than eight million dollars in the account.

A million dollars was deposited just this past week. Do you know where else he might have gotten that kind of money?"

"No. I don't."

Bobrinsky slumped into his chair and stared out the window.

"I was wondering if you might let me handle this for you," Asaf said. "It could be very embarrassing to you if it came out."

"What did you have in mind?"

"With your permission, I'd like to have my men follow him around. Let me see if he meets with the American again. If he does, I'd like your permission to capture him and question him."

"Just don't kill him. I want him to pay for his treason."

Asaf nodded in understanding and agreement.

"Kill the American, though," Bobrinsky said with anger in his voice.

"Of course."

22

Thursday afternoon, 12:15 p.m.

Jamie sat on the patio of the hotel, having finished eating and paying for her lunch. She picked a table against the wall so she faced out where she could see everyone who entered and exited the restaurant. She had no reason to believe anyone would bother her, but she always took every precaution.

Curly had drilled that into her. His stern instructions were to always take care of the little details. The simple things. Fundamentals. Once in the field, she understood why Curly had been so insistent.

Even though she was only having breakfast, it helped put her in the right mindset when she faced challenges that required split-second decisions. That seemed to be happening a lot on this trip.

She had just devoured a plate full of syrniki. Pronounced SIR-nee-kee. The Y sounded like an I.

Syrniki were Russian pancakes. Almost like crepes or cheese fritters. Light, fluffy, and soft on the inside, slightly crisp on the outside. The restaurant at the hotel had provided several toppings to choose from. Blueberry or maple syrup. Sour cream or cottage cheese. Or plain blueberries.

Jamie chose a combination of all of them even though she had wanted something light. She'd gotten a good night's sleep and was ready to tackle the day. She didn't want to be weighed down by a ton of food in her stomach. Even though she ate everything on the plate, she still felt the right amount full.

She had no idea what the day might bring. She wasn't expecting to run into any threats. That would come tomorrow night when she met with her contact and on Saturday when she went to see Omer Asaf. Today would be spent in preparation.

She had a map in front of her opened to Liberty Square. Her meeting with the contact was tomorrow night, and she wanted to be as prepared as possible. She was looking again at every entry and exit point into the square. There were many.

After lunch, she'd go there and see them in person. For now, she wanted to get as familiar with the area as possible in case it was a trap. She tried to get into their minds, determine what she would do if she were them and wanted to surprise her and take her down.

She didn't even know if she was on anyone's radar at the moment, but it never hurt to consider every possible threat. She was so engrossed in her thoughts she didn't notice the figure approaching her until he sat down at the table.

Moe!

"Hello, Allie."

She tried to look surprised, which wasn't hard to do since she was. "Do I know you? You obviously know me."

She was mentally kicking herself for being so lackadaisical. For letting him sneak up on her. She'd been so concerned about preparing for threats, one walked right up to her without her noticing.

Not that Moe was a major threat.

Still . . .

"My name is Detective Fabi Orlov. I'm with the Minsk Militsia."

Moe flashed his badge. He put both elbows on the table and leaned toward her. Jamie made a quick glance around the restaurant to see if he was alone. A sigh of relief when she realized he was. He hadn't come to arrest her.

It's nice to finally put a name with a face.

Although, he'd always be Moe to her. She made a mental note not to say that name aloud.

"It's nice to meet you, Detective. If you'll excuse me, I have someplace I have to be."

Jamie started gathering her things together to leave. She put her hand on the map and took it off of the table and put it into her backpack. She didn't want him to see what she was doing with the map.

"It will only be a moment," Moe said. "I have a few questions for you."

"Can it wait? I'm in a hurry. I answered a lot of questions when I came into Belarus."

Then she became curious and wasn't so anxious to get out of there.

"Why would you want to question me?" she asked.

"Some boys were attacked over by the library," he said.

He was eyeing her closely, almost comically staring at her to see if there was any recognition in her eyes. It was a good way to tell if someone was lying, and Jamie had used the technique many times before. They were called "tells," and Moe didn't know that Jamie spent hours training on how to lie without giving it away.

"I'm sorry to hear that," Jamie said sincerely. "I hope the boys are okay. What does that have to do with me?"

"The boys said that they were attacked by an American woman with blonde hair."

Jamie flipped the ends of her hair which rested on her shoulders.

"That certainly fits my description, so I can see why you'd want to talk to me, but I know nothing about it. When did the attack happen?"

"Last Sunday night around six p.m."

"Let's see ... "

Jamie pretended to be thinking.

"I had dinner and then I went shopping. I bought a few things."

"I know. I was following you."

"What?" Jamie said, feigning anger. "You've been stalking me? I need to see your badge. I'm going to report this to your supervisor."

A look of fear flashed across Moe's face as his eyebrows furrowed at the mention of his supervisor. That either meant he was under a lot of pressure from his boss to solve the case, or he had gone rogue, and the surveillance was without his supervisor's permission.

Where is he going with this?

"I think you might be the blonde woman who attacked those boys."

At first, she thought he was bluffing. Now, she wasn't so sure. She looked around for a way of escape in case it became necessary.

"I need to see your badge. How do I know you are even a detective?"

Fabi showed Jamie his badge—a mistake on his part. In an interrogation, you always want to be the one in control. The one asking the questions.

Jamie was dictating the conversation and he didn't even realize it.

"If you were following me, then you know that I had nothing to do with it."

"I was following you until you lost me. I think that's when you attacked the boys."

"That's ridiculous. Why would I attack a group of boys? How old were these so-called boys? Are you talking about little kids?"

Jamie wanted to keep asking the questions. Keep him talking. Deflect his questions by asking a question.

"They were twenty-one and twenty-two."

"That doesn't sound like boys to me. Sounds like men. Why would I attack ... How many did you say there were?"

A good interrogator lets someone hang themselves. If Jamie had said something like, "Why would I have attacked four boys?" then he could trap her.

"How did you know it was four boys?" he'd say if he was smart enough to catch it.

Jamie was the one who was too smart for that. She didn't know how many of the boys had talked or how much Moe actually knew about the attack. This was a good opportunity to fish for information. Find out how much the police knew.

"There were two boys."

That was good. They didn't know about the other two boys.

"Look Mr . . . what was your name again? Mr. Olive."

Even though she was taking this seriously, she was also enjoying messing with him.

"Detective Orlov."

"Detective," Jamie said slowly. "I don't know anything about any attack on two boys. I'm just a college student working on a paper. Do you have any more questions for me? I really need to go."

Moe hadn't actually asked a question in five minutes. He leaned across the table, looked around, and cavalierly said, "I saw you look."

Jamie's heart did a lap around her chest.

"I beg your pardon?"

She knew exactly what he meant. When he was following her over to *Splash*, she glanced over at the scene. She didn't think there was any way he could've seen that. Was he sharper than she thought or was he making it up?

It was time to find out. Jamie had to tread lightly. Even though Moe was a keystone cop in every sense of the word, he was still a detective in a Soviet bloc country. He had the power to throw her in jail and hold her for a month if he wanted—or worse, he could turn her over to the KGB.

"Detective Orlov, what do you want with me?"

She would make him play his cards. Tell her what he really knows. Depending on his answer, Jamie was either going to disable him, blow her cover, and spend the next few weeks underground, or he had nothing, and he would have to let her go.

"I think you know more than you are letting on," he said. "I think you know what happened to those boys. I just can't prove it yet. I want you to know that I'm watching you."

He didn't have anything on her, and they both knew it. That was when Jamie realized that he'd probably been told to stand down. This was not how the KGB and Militsia did interrogations. They simply threw you in jail and let you suffer with no food and water or sleep until you answered their questions.

His bosses had told him to leave her alone, and he was trying to be a hero. He might've seen her look. Probably did. His supervisor would laugh him out of his office if Moe went to him with such flimsy speculation.

Now was the time to confuse him further. Jamie leaned in and motioned for Moe to do the same. He leaned over the table closer to her.

"You know what this means, don't you?" Jamie asked in her most serious tone.

"What?" Moe's mouth was wide open in anticipation.

"I'm going to have to kill you."

Moe jerked back in his chair.

Jamie burst out laughing.

"I'm kidding. It's a joke."

She could tell Moe was genuinely scared for a moment. Time to go back to being nice. "Detective, I hope you find the ones who hurt those boys. I really do. But it was *not* me. Now, if you'll excuse me, I hope you have a very pleasant day."

Jamie stood from her chair and walked out of the restaurant. Mad at herself for looking over at the crime scene.

Moe was turning out to be a bigger problem than she anticipated. She hoped it didn't become necessary to actually kill him.

23

"Everyone. Raise your glasses!" Candy, the CEO of the *Belles of Belarus* said.

Three hundred girls raised their glasses of champagne in unison. Candy stood on the steps of the patio outside her office and looked out over the throng of girls standing in front of five large tour buses.

"I have grown to love you girls so much," Candy said sincerely. "I will miss each and every one of you. I want to wish you all a lifetime of happiness in America and many, many, children. Lots and lots of children."

The girls let out a loud squeal of delight and then applauded wildly.

Olga was nervously taking it all in. She could feel the excitement in the air.

Nervousness. Anticipation. Fear. Homesickness. A range of emotions.

"I love you all like my own daughters," Candy said. "I hope you have a wonderful trip and a wonderful life. Cheers!"

Everyone downed their champagne, and an even louder cheer went up. A few bystanders stood off to the side watching the scene. No family members were allowed to see them off. They could come and say their goodbyes when they dropped them off, but they had to leave at least thirty minutes before departure.

"Listen, ladies," Candy said into a microphone that provided some minor amplification. "There's a sign in the window of each bus. There are two red buses, two blue buses, and one white bus. For those of you who don't know, those are the colors of the United States of America."

Another loud cheer rose from the girls.

"You were each assigned a color," she explained. "Your bus is one that matches your color. As soon as I'm done giving instructions, you'll make your way to your colored bus and get in line to board."

Olga had been given a blue card.

"Get out your passports and cell phones," Candy continued explaining. "Give them to the driver for safekeeping. All bags must be in the lower compartment, including your personal handbags."

A groan went through the crowd. Candy held her hand up to silence the girls.

"The bags will be checked when you cross the border. He will need your passports for when you go across the border into Russia. He will give them back to you after everything has been approved by the Russian border patrol."

"Why can't we hold on to our own passports? We don't need them to get into Russia," a woman called out.

"That's a good question," Candy said, trying to silence the girls who were murmuring among themselves. She waited for the girls to be quiet.

Some in the crowd began imploring the girls to be quiet with a loud "Shh."

"The question was asked, 'Since we don't need our passports to cross the border, why will they check them at the border?' You don't need passports to go into Russia, but you do need them to get on the plane. The Russian officials want to make sure everything is in order before they let you into the country. We don't want you getting to the airport without the proper paperwork. You won't be able to get on the plane, and you won't have a way to get back to Belarus. It's for your own benefit."

"Why do we have to give him our cell phones?" another girl shouted out.

"Once you leave Belarus, your phones won't work anymore. You'll be given new phones as soon as you land in America. They use a different cell phone service."

Another murmur went through the crowd as the girls seemed excited about the thought of a new cell phone. Olga figured that most of the girls didn't even have one. Not many people in Belarus could afford that luxury.

She understood from her sister, Daria, that the phone she gave her was an international phone and would work anywhere cell phone service was available. She was nervous about the phone. It was well hidden on her body, but a thorough search would find it. It couldn't be that big of a deal. Why would anyone search her?

"Are there any other questions?" Candy asked.

"When do we get to meet our husbands?" one lady yelled out as more murmuring went through the crowd and then laughter.

"As soon as you land in America!" Candy said enthusiastically. "The man of your dreams will be standing at the airport with a sign with your name on it. That will be the first time you meet him. I hope you're excited. I know the men are excited to meet you."

Another cheer went up among the girls.

"Time to go! Thank you so much and have a great trip. I love you!"

Candy waved to the girls as a loud chatter started echoing through the crowd, and the ladies made their way to the buses, separating into groups by color.

The ladies discarded their plastic champagne glasses into trash cans set out for that purpose. Workers were at the entrance to each bus, instructing the girls and checking to make sure they didn't carry anything onto the bus.

A nervous energy pulsed through the crowd. Olga glanced through the crowd of girls in the line to get on a blue bus. They were of various ages. Some girls looked to be as young as fourteen or fifteen. The minimum age was supposed to be sixteen. Some of the girls must have lied on their applications.

The moods of the girls varied. Some were extremely excited and talked nonstop to anyone who would listen. Others seemed stoic. Accepting of their decision. Others looked petrified.

Olga felt every one of those emotions to various degrees. She tried not to let the fear show on her face and put her arm around one of the younger girls who was crying. Olga tried to comfort her like a mother or big sister.

"What's your name?" Olga asked.

"Anastasia," she said between tears.

"Do you want to sit with me?"

The girl nodded. Olga figured Anastasia to be fifteen, if that. Olga wondered about her story. She'd have several hours on the bus to ask her.

The line boarding the blue buses went fast. Most of the girls obediently followed the instructions and didn't try to carry anything on. It made sense for the drivers to carry the passports. Things would go faster at the border.

Olga gave the driver her passport without resistance. The man didn't seem like the type who would stand for anyone not following the instructions.

He was large and extremely overweight. A striped, short sleeve shirt with a logo on the pocket was loosely tucked into his pants.

Olga didn't recognize the company name on the logo.

His belly hung over his pants that were low on his waist and secured by a tightly fastened belt. Probably forty-five, she estimated. And extremely gruff in his manner. He looked each girl up and down, carefully. More businesslike than lustful as far as Olga could tell.

He asked for her cell phone. A jolt of fear rushed through her body.

"I don't have a cell phone," Olga said.

The phone was tucked into her bra. She made sure it was left on silent. She shuddered at the thought of the driver patting her down, groping her breasts, and searching her body for a phone. She hadn't seen him do that to any of the other girls.

For a moment, she thought about giving it to him, but when he motioned her on through, she breathed a sigh of relief and rushed back and sat down next to Anastasia.

"I can't believe we're doing this," Olga said to herself, not wanting to say it out loud where Anastasia could hear. Ana, as she wanted to be called, was nervous enough as it was. She would make it her job to keep the girl calm.

At that exact moment, an ominous feeling came over Olga. One of dread. Doom. She quickly dismissed it, but it didn't go away that easily.

Everything's going to be all right. You're just nervous.

She kept telling herself not to worry. She wrung her hands together. She tried to remember a song she used to sing with her sister on the school bus.

The wheels of the bus go round and round. The wipers go swish and swish. The doors open and close. The horns on the bus go beep, beep, beep. All around the town.

She struggled to remember all the words. The tune she did remember as it played in her head. She allowed a smile to come on her face as she thought about her sister and how they used to sing that song together. A song their mom had taught them.

A feeling of sadness came over her. She was leaving her home. When would she see her sister again?

She asked Anastasia if she knew the words to the song. Ana matched her smile as she did remember it. They started singing it together. A few of the girls around them joined in.

Olga felt better until the bus fired up and began moving and the sense of dread came back over her.

***

Candy watched the five buses leave from her office. A sense of satisfaction warmed her heart as another group of women were going to America. Omer would be pleased.

She pulled out her phone and dialed his number. He answered on the third ring.

"The buses have left, and the girls are on their way," Candy said enthusiastically. "Three hundred of them. We didn't have a single no show."

"Excellent!" Omer said. "We are prepared for their arrival."

Candy had nothing to do with matching the girls to the American men or with the travel arrangements. All that was handled through a different company.

"I have another request for you," Omer said. "Can you have another bus ready for next Friday?"

"That quickly?" Candy asked.

"Yes. You have a waiting list of girls. We have a waiting list of men who want them. You don't have to have five buses. Can you fill one bus in one week?"

"I'll do what I can. We do have a waiting list, but it takes time to contact all of them. But I'll work around the clock to make it happen. Is that enough time to match the girls with their husbands and make all the travel plans?"

"You don't worry about that," Omer said roughly. "You take care of getting the girls, and we'll do the rest."

"You can count on me," Candy said as they hung up the phone.

One week. That's not much time.

She wondered how the other company would match the men with the girls that quickly. She wouldn't have a complete list until Thursday at the earliest.

And why all the secrecy? Omer wouldn't let her know who the other company was or how they matched the girls to the men. She had several ideas on how to create the most successful matches.

Strange that Omer never wanted her involved in that process. Never even wanted her to have any contact with the girls once they left Pinsk.

"Oh well," she said as she breathed a heavy sigh. She picked up the phone and called her assistant Jada into her office.

"We have a lot of work to do," Candy said. "We need to put together another bus load of girls by next Friday."

24

Jamie had skipped her reconnaissance of Liberty Square the day before because Moe was still following her. She was being more careful after he confronted her in the restaurant at lunch.

She left the hotel in the car which she didn't think he knew about. It allowed her to move freely without him knowing she was gone. She made the occasional appearance out of the hotel to get something to eat, do some shopping, and be seen. Enough to keep Moe guessing about what she was up to.

Certain he had no proof of her involvement in the fight with the boys or she would've already been arrested. Her room hadn't been searched recently either. More proof she was in the clear as far as Moe's supervisors were concerned.

She pulled up satellite images on her phone and used them to familiarize herself further with Liberty Square. Not as good as being there, but it would have to do.

She felt confident in her preparations, even though she hadn't seen the scene again. She'd already been to Liberty Square once and had checked it out the first time, and with her maps and the images, she memorized every square foot of the area.

Five o'clock. Time to leave.

The waiting had been torturous. Jamie felt excitement building inside of her. It felt like tonight was going to be a turning point in the mission. One of those feelings she got when a mission started heating up.

This one had been mostly boring so far. Even the fight with the four boys had barely elevated her heartbeat.

Not that she was complaining. CIA operatives often joked about boring missions, but every one of them welcomed them. As long as they were successful. Not being shot at was a good thing.

When the clock struck five, Jamie sprang into action. She wanted to get to the Square early and into position so she could watch and see if anyone followed her contact into the area. Jamie was confident she was as prepared as she could be.

So prepared, she even ended things with Alex.

Sort of. On the phone. She broke up with his voicemail. Funny, she considered it breaking up with him when they were never really together. He probably already considered them broken up.

He was too big a distraction. They went on the cruise almost six weeks ago, and since then, they hadn't spoken once. She called him four times, and he had called her twice. Every time they both got the other's voicemail.

The first time she tried to call, he didn't have a voicemail. Now he did.

Strange.

This wasn't going to work. As Curly said, *no entanglements.*

Jamie made some mistakes on this mission. Looking over at the scene of the attack was an obvious one. A rookie mistake even Moe had caught. She blamed it on Alex. He was why she couldn't focus. Thinking about him was a distraction.

Is he going to call? Should I call him? Why hasn't he called?

High school stuff. She'd had a good time while it lasted. It was over. The phone call was closure.

It was done. She had to put it out of her mind. End the distractions once and for all.

Meeting her contact demanded her complete focus. In one of her shopping trips, Jamie bought another set of black leggings, another black, long sleeve form-fitting pullover, a black pullover wool hat, dark-colored socks, dark tennis shoes, and a black sweat jacket with inside pockets.

The black would make her hard to spot as it was starting to get dark out. The only thing she had on her was a map and a cell phone. The only thing she wished she had that she didn't was a gun.

Satisfied she had everything, Jamie left her room, went down to the second floor, and looked out the window from one of the meeting rooms, hoping Moe was at home with his family having a nice dinner.

No such luck. He was in his usual spot, looking bored. She hadn't given him much to do over the last couple of days. Scanning the street, she didn't see the other tail, but wasn't optimistic she would spot him.

He was too good.

His identity was still a mystery. She couldn't figure it out. If it was related to a trap at the meet, then why tail her? They would merely wait for her to show up. If the KGB, she would've eventually spotted them.

It wasn't the KGB. They weren't as good as this guy. She thought about leading him into a trap so she could question him but dismissed the thought. Time was of the essence. She needed to lose him right away. She would need all of her skill to do so.

In the lobby, Jamie waited by the front door for the right opportunity to leave without Moe seeing her. At just the right time, a hotel van pulled up in front of the entrance.

A perfect opportunity. Jamie walked out the door and made an immediate right out of the hotel. The opposite direction of the meet, but also the opposite direction of where Moe was standing.

She glanced back and saw him desperately looking at the entrance and the van watching to make sure he didn't miss her leaving. He was looking for a blonde-haired woman, nicely dressed in colorful apparel.

The black outfit worked perfectly. Jamie was out of his sight, down the street, and around the corner before he could spot her. She took off the black cap and shook out her hair.

She stayed around the corner looking to see if the other tail walked past. A simple maneuver—a trap she figured the second tail was too skilled to fall into. Worth the effort, nonetheless. She didn't see anyone who might've been him.

After a couple minutes, she started walking in the opposite direction of Liberty Square. She couldn't lead whoever was following her to the contact. She had to lose him. Jamie quickened her pace and then slowed it to see if anyone was matching her speed.

She made several evasive turns. Unusual paths. In and out of stores. In a store on one side of the street and then out a back entrance.

She went down an alley with no exit and watched to see who might walk by and look that way. She suddenly realized it was in the same area as the alley where the boys had confronted her. Not the same alley but in the same vicinity.

The only thing she saw was a couple kids kicking a ball around.

Jamie walked out of the alley, took a right and then an immediate left by a large statue. She then circled around to a side street that crossed under a train trestle. She remembered this to be a large and long tunnel under the train tracks. If anyone was following her, they would have to enter the tunnel. She'd confront them there. That would be the perfect place to find out this guy's intentions.

A man entered shortly after her. She couldn't see his face, but his intentions were clear. He was coming for her. With a quick glance, she noticed he held a pistol with both hands. That was a good sign. He wasn't as experienced as Jamie initially thought.

Who was he?

The one following her?

He was definitely not KGB or CIA. It also made her wonder if this was a different man. The other tail seemed more skilled. For a moment, Jamie wondered if she had imagined it all. Maybe there wasn't even a second tail.

Her curiosity got the best of her. She decided to slow her pace. She could easily outrun him. He might get off a shot, but the odds of him hitting her outside a distance of eight feet with his gun and his skill level were next to impossible.

She wanted to know who he was. Why was he following her? Was he the one who'd been following her for the last week?

More importantly, she wanted his gun.

She slowed her pace even more and pretended she hadn't seen him or heard him.

He tripped on a rock, making even more noise. Even more proof he wasn't the man who had been following her.

What is it with these guys?

She would name him Curly, one of the other three stooges, then stopped herself. That would have been disrespectful to her own Curly, of whom she had deep admiration.

Jamie couldn't remember the name of the other Stooge right off hand, or she would've named him that.

She was two-thirds of the way in the tunnel. Time to make her move. She came to a complete stop facing away from the man on purpose.

Whoever he was came right up behind her and stuck the gun into the small of her back.

This mission was no longer boring.

Jamie quickly analyzed the situation. She already had some information. The gun in the small of Jamie's back was slightly to the right of her spine, telling her the assailant was right-handed, and the gun was in his right hand. In addition to being right-handed, the man was about two inches taller and thin.

He also wasn't the man who'd been following her for the last few days. That man was a professional. Highly skilled. This man was a buffoon.

It also clearly wasn't a random act. It wasn't like when she just happened upon the kids by accident. He had sought her out. Followed her. And definitely not KGB.

"Padniac ruki uvierch," he said. "Put your hands up."

Jamie raised her hands into the air in a submissive pose. That would buy her some time. She was really positioning her arms and hands for her next move. Of course, he had no way of knowing that. He probably thought he was gaining control. "Put your hands up" sounds good in the movies, and it is good if the person being attacked has a gun in his or her pocket.

If the person doesn't have a weapon, it's much better if their hands are at their sides rather than in the air, free to strike. With Jamie, it didn't make much difference. She could strike effectively either way. That was the advantage of him being close range. She could direct the line of fire by controlling his arm and moving her body. If he were five or six steps behind her, he could potentially have time to fire before she could bridge the distance.

When she did act, it would be swift and violent.

But why was he doing this? Jamie wanted to act and disarm him, which she could easily do, but wanted more to know who he was and what he wanted before she did.

Was he acting alone? If he wasn't acting alone, who was he working for? Did he know about the meeting? Was this related to the pipeline? Was there a bigger conspiracy involved? Gathering that information was worth giving him a few seconds to state his intentions. It didn't take long at all.

"You messed up my brother and his friend," he said roughly. "I'm going to mess you up."

He added a disparaging swear word at the end of the sentence. Trying to sound like a tough guy.

That was all Jamie needed to know. One of the two kids had an older brother who was defending his family's honor. He was seeking revenge and thought he was going to finish what his brother had started. Jamie was ready to act. No need for any more information

Her options were limited. Not that there weren't many different things she could do, it was just that there were only two that made the most sense at that moment. It all depended on whether Jamie wanted to move to her right or to her left. She had trained extensively for both and had used each of them in real-life situations. She was comfortable with either one.

A phone started ringing, and Jamie realized it was hers. That distraction was all she needed. A split second later, she had control of the gun, and he was flat on his back.

She had moved to her right so she could look him in the eye when she struck him. She heard his skull crack when it bounced off the pavement. He would have a severe concussion and likely join his brother or friend in the hospital. Maybe they could share a room.

She disarmed his hand from the gun but not before snapping his finger. Unnecessary at that moment, but she wanted to be sure he would never be able to handle a gun with that hand again.

When someone was threatening to take your life, Curly said there was only one rule. *There are no rules. Whatever it takes.*

"Thank you for the weapon," she said to the unconscious man lying on the ground.

The gun might come in handy in the next twenty minutes.

25

Friday, 5:25 p.m.
Somewhere between Pinsk and the Russian border near Homel

The girls had been told the trip from Pinsk to America would take about twenty-seven hours from start to finish, taking into consideration travel time and layovers. The trip to the border would only take about two hours. Eight more hours to Moscow. Their flight would leave Moscow sometime the next morning.

They were starting to settle in for the long journey. The mood was festive as the girls sang and laughed and played car games. The champagne had taken the edge off, and the nervousness subsided slightly. The conversations Olga overheard were lighthearted and hopeful. They were about America and what it will be like.

One girl talked about shopping on Rodeo Drive like Julia Roberts in *Pretty Woman*. Mostly, everything they knew about America was from the movies. The Empire State Building from *Sleepless in Seattle*. Philadelphia from *Rocky*. San Antonio River Walk from *Miss Congeniality*.

Most had heard of the *Real Housewives*. That's how they knew of New Jersey, Orange County, Beverly Hills, Atlanta, Miami, Potomac, and Dallas. Olga had seen the shows a few times, and it seemed like some of the girls felt like they were about to become real housewives.

They were blinded by the glitz and glamour of the television shows. She knew enough about America to know it wasn't going to be like that for all of them. Better than life in Belarus but not the life the TV depicted.

She didn't say anything because she didn't want to dampen the mood. They'd find out their fates soon enough.

One girl said she was going to get a "boob job" as soon as she got to America. Cosmetic surgery wasn't available in Belarus except for the very wealthy. Most of the girls hadn't even heard of a boob job and were giggling like schoolgirls as it was explained to them.

Anastasia looked up at her with a confused look. She couldn't help but think that the young fourteen-year-old girl was going to have to grow up quickly.

Everyone seemed excited, including Olga. She couldn't help but feel like things were finally turning around for her. The other girls all seemed to feel the same way. She heard them say things like:

"I hope my guy is rich."

"I hope my guy is handsome."

"I hope my guy likes kids."

"I hope my guy likes me."

Hope abounded in the bus.

Olga scanned the bus, checking out the other girls. Most were above average in the looks department. The *Belles of Belarus* had done a good job picking out this group of girls.

Belarus girls were known to make very good and obedient wives. They grew up learning all the skills of a homemaker. Most could cook, clean, and make their own clothes. And they did so enthusiastically.

They were also enthusiastic in pleasuring their men. Belarus women were not inhibited when it came to sex and were playful and willing to try almost anything. They were loyal and faithful and trustworthy and could generally be counted on to keep their word.

That was what made eastern European and Belarusian women so attractive to American men. Olga presumed the return rate on a mail order bride from Belarus was very low. Most wouldn't want out of their contract.

Olga was determined to make her marriage work. No matter what.

As good as the Belarus women were, the men were just the opposite. They were rude and egotistical and drank too much. Women were to be dominated, and kids were not to be seen nor heard. The women were unanimous in agreeing that the American men couldn't be any worse.

Again, she knew that wasn't necessarily true. She was certain some of the men would be hard to live with. But women had more rights in America and could get out of the marriages if the men were abusive.

Anastasia had experienced abuse firsthand. The first hour of the trip, she opened up and shared her whole life story with Olga. Her dad had left the family shortly after she was born. Her mother couldn't raise three girls on her meager earnings. She remained single for several years until she married a man out of necessity.

While the man provided money, he was mean and cruel to the girls and to their mother. Often beating them, always wanting the kids out of his sight when he was home.

When Anastasia suggested going to America, he was all for it. One less mouth to feed. He made her promise to send money back to them from the United States. She would miss her mother and sisters desperately but was certain she had made the right decision. She had to get away from the man and thought the United States was far enough.

Anastasia laid her head on Olga's lap and she was stroking her hair. Ana wasn't asleep. Was just being comforted by the young woman who had suddenly become a mother figure to her in their few short minutes together. While Ana was only fourteen, Olga thought she was mature for her age, both in looks and in resolve.

Her thoughts were interrupted when the driver came on to the intercom and said, "When we cross the border, you're all going to have to exit the bus. Take all your belongings with you. You can't leave anything on the bus. After the border agents do their search, we will be on our way."

The buses slowed. Olga touched the cell phone in her bra, just as reassurance it was there, even though she could still feel it. Olga was glad her sister had chosen a very small phone, or it wouldn't have been so hard to detect.

The five buses pulled off the road and into a field and stopped next to train tracks. A train was stopped on the tracks. Freight train, not passenger. No one had mentioned that they were going to ride a train into Moscow, so Olga assumed they weren't. No place to sit on that train anyway.

A large fire was burning in a field next to the tracks. Probably to keep the soldiers warm while they waited. It seemed weird that they were stopping in the middle of nowhere. About ten armed soldiers carrying AK-47's were milling around. A number of other unarmed workers were standing with the soldiers. The men all stood to their feet and leapt into action as soon as the buses stopped.

The driver opened the door to their bus, and the girls filed out one by one to the soldiers' barking orders. Olga wondered why the men sounded so angry and rude. Belarusians came across the border to Russia all the time. This should just be a routine stop and search. She saw the other buses emptying as well.

The driver gave one of the soldiers the bags of passports and cell phones. The soldier took the bags and went over to the fire and threw them in. Flames burst higher into the air.

Several of the girls shrieked. Olga was stunned for a second. Not sure what was happening.

"Zatknis,"

"Shut up," Olga heard a soldier shout.

"Everyone. Get in a straight line," one man commanded. He seemed to be the leader.

The soldiers began to push the girls from the other buses together into one long line.

Why were they touching the girls? Olga's heart started racing.

The workers opened the luggage compartments and began unloading the bags. One by one they hauled the bags over to the fire and threw them in.

The girls screamed.

The leader fired several shots in the air.

Olga wanted to scream but nothing came out as she was suddenly paralyzed in fear.

What's going on? She tried to process it all. Anastasia gripped her hand like a vice. Was this a trap? Inconceivable that the whole thing had been a ruse. What were the men going to do to them?

Olga refused to believe the worst. Maybe they were getting new clothes in America.

But the girls had personal belongings. Keepsakes from home. All hygiene items for the plane. To freshen up before they meet their new husbands.

Nothing made sense.

The fire was raging as it consumed bags full of clothes, makeup, underwear, and personal effects. Several of the girls started crying. One girl was wailing.

A soldier slapped the girl across the face.

Olga wanted to cry but bit her lip, not wanting to do anything to draw attention to herself. The wails turned to whimpers as the soldiers' words became more threatening.

The girls were ordered to strip to their underwear. It was then that Olga realized they were *not* going to America. Something horrible was happening. Others must have realized it as well.

One girl from another bus took off running for a cluster of trees. A soldier easily caught her and tackled her to the ground and drug her by the hair back to the line.

Olga stood at the back end of the line the farthest away from the soldiers. She wanted to use her phone but didn't dare. She had to avoid being searched. She needed the phone. Suddenly glad the phone was so small. Olga barely filled an "A" cup as it was. The phone couldn't be readily seen through her bra.

If they were to pat her down, the soldiers would find it. There were so many girls. Maybe they wouldn't all be searched.

The phone was her lifeline to her sister. The only way she knew to get in touch with her. To let her know what was happening. She suddenly realized why the girls were told they couldn't contact their families for one year.

No one will know that we're gone! They may never know.

Olga dutifully took her clothes off so as not to draw attention to herself. She was shivering as much from the fear as the cold. Anastasia was watching her and did the same. The look on Ana's face was one of utter terror.

Some of the girls refused to disrobe at first and were beaten by the guards. Others weren't wearing underwear under their clothes and were using their hands to cover themselves.

Girls were bleeding, some had bruises and red marks forming on their faces. Eventually everyone complied. All the clothes were gathered and thrown into the fire. All personal belongings were taken off the buses and devoured by what had become a raging inferno.

The girls were given white gowns. Similar to a hospital gown that opened in the back and tied at the top. Olga was thankful for it. It was something to cover the humiliation. The night air nearly took her breath away as she was trying to catch her breath. The girls were shivering, even with the warmth of the fire nearby.

The gown would cover her bra and the phone. She slipped it on quickly and then helped tie Anastasia's in the back. The girl wasn't crying. She had a look of fear on her face, but she was being brave. Probably in shock. Too young to fully process all the ramifications of what was happening.

They were ordered onto the train.

No search. Thankfully.

Each soldier picked out one girl and made her stay behind. One man looked at Olga and started toward her but grabbed the girl behind her. He picked her up over his shoulder as she screamed and kicked her legs back and forth and hit his back with her fists.

Olga moved to the front of the line so she could get in as soon as possible. Whatever fate awaited them on the train had to be better than what the girls were going to face who were left behind.

The girls were forced on the trains, herded like cattle. There were no seats. They had to stand and hold onto the side or to each other. The looks on their faces were of shock and disbelief. Fear.

A few minutes before they were laughing and singing, imagining life in America as a rich housewife. Now they were fighting for their lives. For their souls. No one knew what awaited them. And no one in Belarus knew they were taken.

The doors closed. The train started to move.

Olga could hear the screams of the girls left behind. The soldiers' obvious rewards for completing the task at hand.

***

Ten minutes later

The doors were shut, and the girls were locked in the cars of the train. Packed in like sardines.

They began to move. Olga pulled out the phone. She had a signal. She dialed her sister's number. It went straight to voicemail. She left her a message.

"Daria. It's a trap. I'm on a train to God knows where. There is no American marriage. I think they are going to make us sex slaves or something. We're headed north. I don't know if you can help me or not. I hope you get this message."

She hung up the phone.

She thought about calling the authorities but paused. The Russians were probably in on it. She suddenly remembered her sister's American friend, Abbey ... Allie. More important to remember the number. She had put it in her contacts.

Her hands shook as she searched for it. She took a deep breath.

Dial 8 then wait for a dial tone. 10 then wait. 1 and the number.

The call went through but went to voicemail.

"This is Olga. Daria's sister. I'm in real trouble. Belles of Belarus is a scam. I'm in Russia. I think. On a train. We're headed north. Please help me if you can. There are three hundred of us girls."

The train lurched as it picked up speed.

The women screamed.

Olga turned off the phone and stuck it back in her bra. She looked around for Anastasia. She saw her across the boxcar from the sliver of moonlight that created a slight illumination through a crack on the side. She went to her as Anastasia's face lit up in recognition at seeing her.

Anastasia burst into tears. Olga clutched her tightly to her side.

"It's going to be all right," Olga said, stroking Ana's hair, having no idea if things were going to be all right. It sure didn't seem like it.

It was the only thing she knew to say.

26

Jamie checked her assailant for a pulse. It was strong.

Satisfied he was alive, she took his wallet so it would take the *Militsia* longer to identify him and then ran to the end of the tunnel the opposite way from which she had entered. She looked back in time to see a couple, holding hands, walking in from the other side.

"That's good. They'll call an ambulance."

Jamie looked at the man's ID, tore it up, and threw the wallet into the bushes. Confident she hadn't been seen, Jamie scurried up the hill, crossed the train tracks, and went down the hill on the other side.

Adrenaline still pulsed through her body from the confrontation. She took a moment to get her bearings, looking to the left and to the right. All she saw were a couple with kids, an older man walking with a bag in his hand, and a merchant loading some things in his car.

She scrambled down the embankment, and turned to the right toward Liberty Square, determined to get there before her contact and anyone else if they intended on setting a trap for her.

At the first opportunity, she slipped behind some trees to check the gun to make sure it was working properly. It had less than a full cartridge of bullets but appeared to be in good working order.

She counted the bullets. Twelve. Jamie liked to know the number. In a gunfight, she had an uncanny ability to count in her head the number of bullets she had fired.

Hopefully, there wouldn't be a gunfight. If there was, she felt better bringing a weapon to it. Another Russian-made Makarov handgun. Amazing that both young men were carrying military-style weapons, though she wasn't complaining. If she couldn't have her own Sig M11 A-1 compact in her hand, then this was as good as anything else.

She quickened her pace, almost running, and arrived in the square within five minutes. At the top of the hill on the south side in a clove of trees was a perfect spot where she could see the entire area but not be seen. She went around the square and entered the area from behind. Away from all the touristy spots.

Thankfully, no one was there. She had worried that someone else might've noticed that spot as well and may have already beaten her to it.

Her instincts told her the meet wasn't going to go well. It was a feeling she couldn't explain. Some might call it women's intuition in normal situations, but this wasn't a normal situation, and it was more than intuition.

Most men operatives in the field had it as well, although Jamie's discernment abilities were special. Curly had said as much. She had always had a knack for sensing a dangerous situation before it materialized. Something that had served her well in those types of situations and had saved her life more than once.

She scanned the square. No sign of her contact. She had a lot of questions for him and hoped he had the answers. The main question was the name of the man behind the pipeline. Jamie was told in her briefing the contact had that name. She desperately wanted it.

Her investigation was at a dead end, and a name would breathe new life into it. While she had a feeling Omer Asaf was involved in some way, she had no proof. If the contact could confirm it was him, her mission would be much simpler.

The square was basically empty. The church was closed and only a couple of people were milling around. No signs of any surveillance. She took a deep breath and focused on slowing her heartbeat. She suddenly remembered her phone rang during the confrontation with the man in the tunnel.

Was Alex calling back?

She should've blocked his number. Didn't need the distractions at the moment and decided not to check the phone in case it was him.

He was history. She had important and dangerous work to do.

Leave me alone.

Right at six o'clock, she saw an older man walk into the square carrying a briefcase.

His appearance helped her put Alex completely out of her mind. She studied the man closely, suspecting immediately he was her contact.

He walked across the square, past the carriage, and sat down on a bench next to the fountain. It had to be him. She had expected a younger man. He looked to be in his seventies. Frail. Walking slowly.

Jamie decided to wait a few minutes before going to meet him. She knew he had instructions to wait for fifteen minutes. She had time to make sure he wasn't being followed.

It didn't take much time. Jamie spotted the surveillance almost immediately.

He was being followed!

Two men. Black Jeep. Middle Eastern.

A jolt of fear shot through her. That could only mean one thing—someone was on to him.

Maybe them.

His life was in danger. Confirmed when she saw one of the men in the vehicle checking his rifle. She couldn't tell exactly what type of gun it was, but it wasn't long range. At least they weren't planning on assassinating him from a distance. If they got out of the car and moved against him, she'd have time to react.

Still ... *This can't be good.*

The Middle Eastern men were watching the square closely. On alert. Eyeing everyone who came in and out of the area. Clearly expecting something to go down.

The contact obviously didn't know he'd been followed. He'd led them right to the meeting. Not surprising, considering his level of training and his age and frail condition. How could he have known?

Jamie was thankful that she'd waited to approach him. Once again, her instincts were right. And her preparation had saved her. Her location was perfect for spotting the men and assessing the situation without being spotted.

Probably saved her life, and the life of the contact. She'd just leave. Live to meet another day.

Then she saw the man checking his rifle again. Like he was getting ready to use it. The driver was getting antsy. Looking around. Like he was about to move.

I have to warn him.

Jamie took the map out of her pocket and emerged from her hiding place. The men in the Jeep noticed her but didn't pay any particular attention. She made it appear as if she was just a tourist taking in the square.

The surveillance team kept their attention on the contact until she got closer when they suddenly became excited as she neared him. They didn't get out of the Jeep. Apparently, they wouldn't move as long as a tourist was in the vicinity.

"The train leaves at ten o'clock," Jamie said, when she got close enough for him to hear her.

The code phrase meant that the meeting was compromised, and ten o'clock was the direction where the danger was lurking. Her face was turned so the men in the Jeep couldn't see that she had said something to him. She hoped the contact was smart enough to know who she was and not give anything away with his reactions.

Jamie stopped in front of the bench and showed him the map.

"Point to the other end of the square," she said with a sense of urgency. "Pretend you are giving me directions."

It took him a moment to comprehend what was happening and who she was. He heard the angst in her voice, as she saw a concerned look cross his face as his eyes narrowed and he glanced around the square.

"Don't look around. Just pretend to give me directions," Jamie implored him. "There are men with guns here. I think they want to kill you."

He regained his composure and pointed the opposite direction from which she had come. Jamie looked up from the map toward where he was pointing, taking a quick glance at the men in the Jeep. The gunmen still hadn't moved so Jamie decided to see if she could gain any information.

"Do you have the name of the man in charge of the sex trafficking pipeline?"

"Omer Asaf," he responded.

Jamie was glad she asked. She now had confirmation. Just as she had suspected. Asaf was the Turkish businessman trafficking the women. The contact probably had more information, but she didn't want to risk any more communication.

She started to walk away.

"Briefcase," he said.

Jamie stopped walking and turned back toward him. She didn't want the surveillance team to see him talking but her not responding.

She let out a laugh, like he had said something funny. It didn't match the serious look on his face, but she hoped they were far enough away that the difference didn't register in their minds.

"You need to know about the briefcase," he added. "I brought it for you."

"Okay," Jamie said with a slight wave as she kept walking the direction he had pointed. She wasn't sure what he meant. He had a briefcase sitting next to him at the bench.

There was no way she could take it from him while they were being watched.

"I'll get it later."

She quickly formulated a plan. She would follow him out of the square and try to interact with him at another location. Find out where he lived. Then she could go into his house in the middle of the night, if necessary.

She walked to the end of the square and around to the back of the church. Out of the view of the men in the Jeep but in clear view of the contact still sitting on the bench. After a couple minutes, he got up from the bench and started to walk the other direction carrying the briefcase.

Jamie heard the Jeep before she saw it.

The tires squealed.

The engine roared as the man drove onto the sidewalk and into the square, speeding toward the contact coming to a screeching halt right next to him. The man on the passenger side jumped out of the vehicle and began shouting at the older man.

He sat the briefcase down on the ground and held his hands in the air. The gunmen grabbed the briefcase and stuck it in the back seat.

Jamie could hear the Middle Eastern man shouting but couldn't hear what he was saying. She could tell the tone was threatening. She pulled out her gun but was too far away to get off a shot.

The contact got down on the ground. He suddenly reached his hand under his coat.

No!

Don't do that. They'll think you have a gun. Even if you do, it's suicide.

Her worst fear materialized when the gunman took aim and fired.

Her contact's body lurched as the bullet entered it.

Jamie let out a scream and took off running toward them.

The man heard the scream and looked her way, turning his gun toward her. He fired six rounds.

Since she was too far away to hit him, it also meant she was too far away for him to hit her as well.

That didn't stop him from firing recklessly.

Jamie was unfazed and continued running toward them. A few more shots came her way, but none close enough to worry her as they banged off the concrete and off the side of a wall. She held her fire. Not wanting to waste a single bullet.

The man fired several more rounds. He was out of ammunition. He started to reload. The reason Jamie always wanted to know how many rounds she had in the chamber. Before he could finish reloading, she was close enough.

In full stride, Jamie raised her gun, took aim, and returned the fire.

One shot. *Tap.*

Hit the gunman right between the eyes.

He dropped to the ground, dead. The other man was still in the vehicle with his back facing her. Confused as to what to do. He looked at his dead partner on the ground then strained to look behind him at the danger approaching.

She saw several flashes from his gun as he sprayed bullets her way, shooting through his back window. He was so taken by surprise, he was panicking and not taking his time to get off a good shot.

Jamie fired two shots in his direction.

He revved the Jeep.

I can't let him get away. He had the briefcase.

Jamie stopped. Took aim as the Jeep started to move. She squeezed the trigger slowly firing three shots. The back of the man's head exploded into the windshield.

Jamie approached the vehicle cautiously. She made sure the second man was dead and then ran over to where the contact lay on the ground.

She checked for a pulse which was weak, but he was still alive. She carefully turned him over and checked for wounds.

A pain shot through her heart like an arrow through a target.

He was not going to live much longer.

"Stay with me," Jamie implored.

He coughed and blood oozed from the side of his mouth. He was trying to speak. Jamie leaned in, bringing her ear closer to his mouth.

"Briefcase. Take the briefcase," he said.

His last words.

One more breath. Then he died.

27

Jamie had no time to mourn. The contact was dead on the ground. The Director had said he was a valuable asset.

Nothing Jamie could do about it now.

It wasn't her fault. Somebody was already onto him. She hadn't led the men to him. They were already there when she got there.

She'd done the best she could to protect him.

Curly said not to analyze a mission until it was over. There'd be plenty of time to evaluate mistakes.

At this point, she didn't have the luxury of introspection. Machine gun fire erupted again in the square.

The shots startled her. Where were they coming from? Was it the police?

Rather than look to see, she sought safety first. Jamie dove behind the Jeep as more rounds pulverized the front of the vehicle. Glass broke and sprayed everywhere. She flattened herself against the side, protected by the engine block and the bullets were glancing off the other side of the vehicle.

When the men stopped to reload, Jamie stood up into a crouch so she could see over the vehicle. Two more Middle Eastern men had exited a sedan from the road and were running toward her. She was thankful they hadn't pulled up on the sidewalk like the other two men. They could've easily killed her.

She duck-walked over to the back of the Jeep, careful to keep her head down. Since they were running, they wouldn't be able to get a good shot at her unless they were highly trained. Which she doubted.

It wasn't a risk she was willing to take. She couldn't let them get closer. Not until she had a plan. So she peered around the back and fired five shots in their direction.

The men took cover behind one of the fountains. That bought her some time.

She quickly assessed the situation. This was why she had prepared so diligently before entering the square. She'd studied the exits and ran through all the options in her mind.

Only one made sense to her.

It wouldn't take the men long to come up with a plan as well. Probably try to outflank her. Which wouldn't be hard. One could easily circle behind her, and she'd be an open target. Trapped. With no place to run.

She wasn't going to wait around long enough for them to figure that out. She fired the remaining bullets in the gun she had taken away from the man at the train trestle and threw it to the side.

The men stayed behind the concrete barriers.

Sirens blared in the distance.

Oh great! I have to get moving.

The dead man's rifle was on the ground in front of her next to his dead body. Jamie was able to get it without exposing herself to more gunfire. She looked it over and found it was in good working order but out of bullets. She took a magazine out of the dead man's belt and reloaded.

She glanced around to make sure she had a clear path to her exit. Thankfully, no tourists were in the area. Or if they were, they had heard the gunshots and gotten safely away.

Staying and fighting wasn't an option. The best thing to do was to get away from there as fast as possible. She lifted her head up and saw confusion and indecision on the part of the assailants who were still behind the protective barriers.

Perfect.

She didn't bother wasting any bullets shooting at them. Instead, she took off running away from them. They opened fire but were wasting bullets.

Then it dawned on her causing her to stop in her tracks.

The briefcase!

She almost forgot it. Was it worth going back for? Her contact had risked his life to bring it to her. In fact, he had given his life to meet with her. She owed it to him. Something was in there he wanted her to have.

Jamie spun on a dime and ran back to the Jeep going at a different angle, so the vehicle was between her and the gunmen. She sprayed a few bullets toward them. Not expecting to hit anything, but enough to make them duck their heads.

As soon as she stopped firing, the men started shooting again, but held their position behind the barriers. The thud of rounds hit the metal on the Jeep and sent loud clanging noises echoing through the square.

The briefcase was inside the vehicle. It took several precious seconds to find it. She didn't find it right away. Then remembered the gunman had thrown it in the back seat. She couldn't just reach back and grab it. A stray bullet could hit her.

The men were peppering the car again. Glass was flying all around her.

She had to exit the vehicle, open the back door, and reach in and grab it.

The delay had given the gunmen an advantage. They were moving again. Trying to cut off her exit route. The first choice for an exit was no longer available to her.

Jamie was out of the vehicle now, clutching the rifle and the brief-case. Still crouched down. Before long, she'd be in the line of sight for the gunman circling around to get a position behind her.

She liked her odds. She could kill him before he killed her. But why take that chance. Now was the time to move and get away from there.

The sirens were getting louder. Soon, she'd have another problem to worry about when the Militsia arrived.

Jamie unloaded her rifle in the direction of the man coming at her flank. He fled for cover. That's all the time she needed.

She reached into the vehicle and got the other man's gun. She took off running the other way. The opposite direction she had run before.

The men weren't close enough to lock in on her, and she was moving quickly. She glanced back as they emerged from behind the barriers and started charging toward her, though unable to run and shoot at the same time.

This briefcase had better be worth it.

She had a head start, but they had the angle.

Her options were limited. The best option was to run to the left. That led to the main road. But it also led to where there were pedestrians. Cars. Shops. She couldn't risk the gunmen hitting an innocent bystander.

She doubted they cared, but she did.

She led them the other way, toward the river. The problem was that she could get trapped. The river was a natural barrier. It blocked her in.

Still the best option.

She ran downhill toward the bank. The hill was still manicured but steeper. She traversed it easily enough. So did the men.

At the river there were no streetlamps. Her dark clothes made it harder for them to see her. For a moment, she considered jumping into the river. But it was a cold night. She didn't know how cold the water would be. She would only last about two or three minutes before hypothermia would kick in.

Was that long enough?

What the man said next made the decision for her. They were close enough that she could hear them shouting at each other.

" *Omier skazau uziac jaho zyvoj.*" Omer said to take them alive.

The words sent a chill down her spine.

That changed things. A lot of information to process in that one sentence.

They weren't going to shoot her.

And they were working for Omer. The name of the man her contact said was responsible for trafficking three hundred women a month.

A rage rose inside of her.

Omer was the one who targeted her contact. She was determined to live to make him pay. As if she needed more incentive to get away.

Curly said the element of surprise was one of the best tactics to use in a dangerous situation.

"Do the unexpected. Create confusion among your enemy," he had said.

Jamie suddenly changed direction, running back toward the men. That startled them. They already said they weren't going to shoot. That created indecision. They raised their guns and began firing.

Jamie had already turned away from them. Into the trees, heading back toward the square.

Instead of going into the square, she headed toward a building. Past the area she'd used as a lookout point. Behind the building, she could disappear into the streets and away from the men. They'd be far enough away that no pedestrians would be in danger.

She heard them yelling instructions to each other. They were confused. Unsure what to do. Jamie would've easily gotten away, except she was carrying the briefcase, which slowed her down.

The terrain was also uneven. She didn't want to go full speed. Risk twisting a knee or rolling an ankle. In that instance, the gunfight would be to the death. No way she would let them capture her. The men saw the building and where she was headed.

They sounded frantic.

One screamed hysterically to the other, "Don't let her get away. Shoot her."

A volley of gunfire sprayed the ground around her. They then ran full out, so the shots weren't straight and hit close to her but off the mark.

Still, she was worried about a stray bullet or a lucky shot.

Just a little further.

The building was less than a hundred feet away. If she got to it, they'd never be able to find her in the maze of streets and alleyways on the other side.

She glanced back. They were closing in.

Suddenly she saw movement ahead of her. At the side of the building.

A person. A man. Tall.

He stepped out of the shadows. Holding a gun.

A light on the side of the building cast an eerie shadow over him.

He stepped into the light and shouted, "Jamie, stop!"

How did he know my name?

She came to a complete stop, her arms flailing from stopping so fast.

She was about twenty feet from him. Her eyes blinked in amazement. Trying to process the familiar person standing in front of her.

Alex.

Holding a gun.

Pointing it straight at her head.

28

"Jamie, stop!" Alex commanded.

Time took on a new dimension for Jamie in her mind. She suddenly saw everything in extreme slow motion. Her senses were so heightened, she saw and heard every detail. It had happened to her numerous times before. Now more than any she could remember.

Alex.

Standing just out of the shadows.

His right leg planted in front of his left. Two hands on a gun. Up and in front of him. The gun pointed right at her.

"Jamie, stop!" she saw his lips moving as he said it.

Her arms flailed as she came to an abrupt stop even though running full speed. Running from the gunmen chasing her.

Three flashes of light. Muzzle fire.

A concussion of sound that only gunfire makes.

Sirens in the background. Less than a minute away. Likely the *Militsia* racing to the scene. A bystander called it in.

Three whizzing sounds as the bullets flew by her ears.

A cracking sound as a bullet penetrated the skull of the person behind her.

A huge exhalation of air as two bullets penetrated the chest of the second assailant.

A thud as the first person fell and hit the ground. Like a tree falling in the forest. Probably the taller man.

A second thud. The other man down.

Crack! The sound of his head hitting the concrete. The least of his worries. Not that he had any worries anymore. He was dead.

Her mind spun like a computer. It all probably happened in that order. Too fast to know for sure. The end result, the same.

Alex wasn't who she thought he was. He'd just killed two men.

The next thing she knew, Alex reached out and grabbed the rifle out of her hand and threw it to the ground, shouting the words, "We've gotta get out of here. Now!"

Jamie couldn't hear the words clearly from the ringing in her ears from the gun blasts.

He pulled at her hand. Dragging her along. She was resisting slightly. Not sure what to do. Alex was bigger and stronger. She remembered that from the cruise.

She started running to keep up the pace. He was right. They needed to get away from there. And fast.

As she started to process things, she jerked her hand out of his. She didn't know what he was doing in Belarus or how he knew how to shoot. He must be CIA. Maybe a freelancer. Either way, she wasn't going to be dragged around like a dog on a leash or a child being saved from bullies by an older brother.

The sooner he learned she was his equal or superior, the better.

"This way. I have a car," Alex said, taking a right off the main road and darting down a side street.

Jamie started to run the other direction, away from him. She didn't for two reasons. The first one was curiosity. She had to find out what was going on.

She couldn't remember the second reason. All she could think about was the first one.

Jamie's dad was somewhat religious and had a saying, "Damn and hell are in the Bible. It's okay to use them if the situation warrants it."

This seemed like one of those situations.

"What the hell are you doing?" Jamie asked Alex, in a confused but stern voice.

They'd found his car on a side street and were driving away in the opposite direction from the square.

He didn't answer.

She had already figured out most of it in her mind. Alex was CIA. Brad had sent him on the cruise to check up on her to see if she was up for the mission to Belarus—to find out her state of mind.

Make friends with her, Brad had told him. Gain her trust. Don't let her know who he was. She's gullible. She'd fall for his charm. Wouldn't question anything. That's why he was chosen.

The CIA did that kind of thing all the time. Although usually they sent a pretty girl like Jamie to seduce a man. Get him to relax and give away information to the pretty lady. Many foreign agents had been recruited that way.

"Sleep with her if you have to."

I can't believe I kissed him.

Jamie knew Brad wouldn't say that. Alex made it physical on his own. She was so thankful she hadn't slept with him. At least she had some dignity left.

Anger was building as the picture became even clearer. Alex was the one following her around Belarus. She was sure of it. That's why she never heard from him.

He never called her when she could answer the phone. She'd know right away that the connection was local. That's why the tail seemed familiar. She'd seen his face in the background of the crowd, just couldn't process it fully.

He's good. She'd give him that.

Worse than Alex lying was that Brad didn't trust her. Thought she needed a nursemaid. For whatever reason, Brad hadn't believed enough in her to let her go on the mission alone. She suddenly remembered Director Coldclaw's objections raised at the first meeting. She was against Jamie going into Belarus alone. This must've been her call. She pictured Brad pushing back. Saying Jamie could handle herself. He had obviously been overruled.

Still . . . She couldn't believe she fell for it. She was verbalizing the words without even realizing it.

"I can't believe I was so stupid!" Jamie said out loud, hitting her forehead with the palm of her hand.

Alex kept his eyes on the road. His hands gripped the steering wheel firmly. They weren't speeding away, so much as maneuvering away. Smart. Alex obviously didn't want to draw the attention of the police.

He'd done this before, she assumed.

"Don't you have anything to say for yourself?" Jamie asked, loudly and roughly. Frustrated that he was ignoring her.

"Kind of busy here," he finally said dismissively, staring straight ahead, not even looking her way.

"You can't talk and drive at the same time? Pull over. Let me drive then. I can do both."

"I was saving your ass. That's what I'm doing here."

A burst of rage exploded inside her. She had to be careful. In a gunfight, adrenaline goes off the charts inside the body. It takes a while for it to come back down.

Her heart was racing. Every muscle in her body was tensed. If he said the wrong thing, she might strike him, before she even realized it. That's how mad she was at him.

"You weren't saving my ass. I had everything under control."

"Yeah, right. Whatever," he said, sarcastically, clearly trying to keep his response measured so as not to draw even more of her ire.

She punched him in the arm. Hard. Just once.

"Ow!" he shouted.

"I didn't ask for your help. I was doing just fine," she said smugly.

"You're welcome," he retorted.

"You're welcome? For what?"

"I was just responding to you thanking me for saving you from those two guys who were about to kill you, which ... I'm sure you'll do it soon. Thank me. When you calm down."

Jamie didn't respond right away. He had saved her. She probably would've made it out alive, but that wasn't a certainty. A number of mixed emotions ran through her mind. Embarrassment. Betrayal. Fear from what she knew was a close call.

Sadness. The contact was dead. He died right in front of her. Disbelief.

Neither of them said anything for what seemed like a good minute.

"What's your real name?" Jamie asked.

Alex didn't answer.

"A-hole," she muttered under her breath. "That's what I'll call you from now on."

Alex didn't respond. He probably knew this day would eventually come. She'd find out and would be mad. She was sure he assumed she'd eventually get over it.

"How about liar? Jerk?" she continued, regretting her tone but still letting her emotions get the best of her.

"Mike Seaver," he said, giving her a sideways glare.

Jamie rolled her eyes. " *Full House*?" she asked.

" *Growing Pains*. He was the son."

"Right. I know who he was. What's with you and sitcom characters?"

He just kept driving.

"Alex P. Keating! I can't believe I fell for that nonsense," she said sarcastically.

Remembering what Emily had said. Her friend had been right. Alex wasn't who he said he was. She should've known.

"My friend said that wasn't your real name. She said you were probably married with kids. I knew you were lying. I kept giving you the benefit of the doubt. I defended you!"

She said almost every word with emphasis.

"Whatever," he said again. Obviously, his fallback word when he had no comeback.

His cavalier attitude was only making her angrier. He owed her an explanation. Surely, he knew that. Though, now was probably not the best time. She needed to calm down first. She wasn't willing to drop it, but she did want to lower the rhetoric. She didn't want to come across as a crazy woman.

"What's your real name?" Jamie asked in a calmer tone. "I gave you my real name."

"Alex Halee."

"The writer."

"Yep. Roots."

"Seriously. Quit lying to me."

"That's really my name. Spelled H-a-l-e-e. Two e's. Not ey."

"So, your name really is Alex?"

"Yes. It's like Curly always said, 'Keep your lies as close to the truth as possible.'"

"You know Curly?" Jamie said in a questioning tone.

"Trained with him for nine months. Two classes after you. He said you were the best he ever trained. Until I came along."

"You're clearly the best liar he's ever trained."

"You're one to talk," Alex said, chuckling and with his own sarcasm mixed in. "Women's healthcare. Reproductive health. You were lying left and right. Don't judge me. That's what we do. You, of all people, should understand."

He had a point. She had lied to him. She wasn't lying about the feelings, though. She had really liked him.

The anger was starting to subside some. She was remembering why she had liked him so much. Even as angry as she was, she couldn't help but feel the attraction.

"Where are we going?" she asked more calmly.

"To a safehouse. We have to regroup. You've created a huge mess."

The anger returned with a fury.

"What do you mean, a huge mess?"

"You started a gunfight at the biggest tourist spot in all of Belarus. Our contact is dead. He's been outed. There are four dead gunmen in the square. You're probably marked now. You beat up another man in the alley. Have I left anything out?" he asked sharply.

"First of all, I didn't start a gunfight," Jamie retorted. "The contact was already outed. He was being followed. I was trying to save him."

Jamie stopped almost in mid-sentence. "How do you know about the man in the alley?"

"I was there. Watching."

"And you didn't think you should try to help me when he had a gun in my back?"

"No. You seemed to have it under control. That was a good move by the way. Impressive the way you disarmed him."

"I *did* have it under control. I didn't need your help then and I don't need it now."

The anger was now mixed with satisfaction from the compliment he paid her. The anger was still winning out, though.

"Thank you for helping me," Jamie said sarcastically. "There, you have your thank you. Now, let me out at the next block. I still have work to do."

"I can't. We have to call Brad. He's going to want to know about what happened. Probably already knows."

Before she could say anything more, Alex pushed a garage door button on the visor and pulled into the driveway of a house. On a side street. White siding. Modest looking. Typical safehouse. Away from everything so as not to be discovered.

Jamie was actually glad they were there. She needed a safe place to think. It would have in it a computer and a satellite phone. Food, weapons, and clothes. She needed to change out of the black clothes that had the contact's blood on them and into something dressier. So she could get back into the hotel.

Could she even go back to the hotel? She wasn't staying at the house with Alex. That was one thing for sure.

Alex closed the garage door, got out of the car, and walked into the house. Jamie grabbed the briefcase from the back seat and walked in behind him. He turned on the lights and went immediately to the refrigerator, pulled out two cans of soda and started pouring them into two glasses, mixing them with a green substance.

"Here, drink this," he said. "It will help calm you."

One of Curly's concoctions. Huge bursts of adrenaline can create a number of side effects that only someone who'd been through a gunfight could understand. The drink would offset the side effects but not hinder her thinking or performance. The caffeine from the soda would actually have a calming effect against the adrenaline.

Jamie drank it in one big drink. It felt good going down. Her mouth was parched with thirst.

Alex drank his quickly as well. She saw his hand shake slightly as he lifted the glass to his lips. She suddenly realized what he must be going through. He had just killed two men. Saving her. He was dealing with his own stress. Even though they were bad guys, taking a man's life was a difficult thing.

Jamie had killed two of them herself and put the man under the train tracks in the hospital. A tough business they were in. Few people would understand. Alex was one of them. She should cut him a break. He was just following orders. On the cruise. In Belarus.

And he was obviously good at what he did. Shooting those two men without hitting her was remarkable. Maybe his skills would come in handy.

A thought suddenly occurred to her.

Alex must have recognized the confused look that had come over her face. "What?" he asked.

"Did you call me when I was in the alley? When the man had a gun on me?"

"No. But I did get your message. That you broke up with me." He said the last line mockingly. "How do you break up with someone you aren't dating?" he said.

Jamie ignored it. Her mind was elsewhere. She pulled out her phone and looked at the missed calls. The most recent number wasn't familiar. A local number.

"If you didn't call me, then who did?" she asked almost to herself.

"Oh no! Oh no! Oh no!" Jamie said as panic filled her body, overriding the calming effects of Curly's drink.

"What?" Alex asked, his tone matching her concern.

"I think I know who called me."

29

The details were sketchy, but Jamie was beginning to believe that the mail order bride business was the sex trafficking pipeline. It made sense to her. Omer Asaf was the man behind the pipeline and also the one behind the mail order bride business.

If that was true, then Chastity's sister was in grave danger. She'd given her sister, Olga, Jamie's number. Now Jamie had a voicemail on her phone from an unknown number. Very few people had that number.

It had to be Olga calling for help.

"I think I know who called me," Jamie had said.

"Who? What's wrong?" Alex asked earnestly.

Jamie was holding the phone in her hand, waving it in the air, but not wanting to listen to the message she feared was there. Her mind was racing. Thinking through a number of scenarios. Hoping the worst one was not the reality.

"Olga. Chastity's sister."

"Who's Olga?"

"A girl I met. Actually, I never met her. I met her sister."

"What girl, Jamie? You aren't making any sense," Alex said.

"I met this girl at *Splash* nightclub," Jamie explained. "Her name is Chastity. I went back to a VIP room to talk to her."

"I know. I saw you," Alex said.

Jamie ignored him. She had felt his presence in the nightclub and had already assumed he'd been there. He'd obviously been following her for days. It made her wonder if he had bugged her room and phone as well.

It made her remember why she was so angry at him. Jamie took a deep breath, to settle her nerves and slow down the pace of her words.

"Chastity told me about her sister, Olga. She signed up to be a mail order bride through a company called *Belles of Belarus*. It's owned by a Turkish businessman. The contact said right before he died, that Omer Asaf was the one who was trafficking the women. He's a Turkish businessman. It's all coming together."

"When I met with our contact—"

"You met with the contact?"

"Yes. The contact said Omer Asaf was the one into terrorism and was a dangerous man."

"That's what he told me."

"He said I needed to warn you about him. I figured Asaf was somehow related to the trafficking somehow. But what does the mail-order-bride business have to do with sex trafficking?"

"That's how he traffics women. Through the mail order bride business. They sign women up, promise them they're going to America, and then sell them somewhere in Russia and Turkey."

"That sounds far-fetched. Even if Asaf owns the business, that doesn't mean it's not legit."

"It's not legit."

"You don't have any real proof that it's the pipeline."

It angered Jamie that Alex was pushing back. This was her area of expertise. Although, deep down, she was glad to have someone to talk with about it.

Alex continued his thought. "A lot of terrorists own legitimate businesses. I'm not sure a pipeline even exists."

"Our contact said it did."

"Still, I never believed the three-hundred-women number, anyway. Three-hundred women a month can't go missing without someone reporting it."

"That's what I thought," Jamie said. "But when we went back to the VIP room, Chastity told me all about what her sister was doing. That she's going to America to get married. I'm just figuring it out. There is no mail order bride business. It's a front for human trafficking. The girls aren't going to America."

"That's not possible. Their parents and family will know they're missing when they don't contact them."

"They aren't allowed to contact their families for a year. It's part of the contract. That's why they're never reported missing."

Alex nodded. "That's very clever," he said.

"They also aren't allowed to take their cell phones with them."

"Then how could she be the one calling you?"

"Chastity gave her sister an international phone and gave her my number. Wanted her to look me up when she got to America."

"She must've hidden the phone so they couldn't find it."

Jamie nodded. Then felt her mouth fly open.

"They're leaving tonight! Three-hundred women are on buses leaving this afternoon actually."

Jamie waved her phone in the air.

"Chastity told her sister to call me if she ran into any problems. I have a missed call and a voicemail. It's a local number. It has to be her. No one else has this number. Except Brad and you and a few others."

Jamie was pacing now.

"I have a weird feeling that those women aren't going to America. They're going to be sold into sex trafficking."

"Don't jump to any conclusions," Alex said. "Let's listen to the message."

Jamie dialed the voicemail and put it on speaker. A sense of dread overwhelmed her. A woman's voice in obvious distress blared through the phone.

"This is Olga. Daria's sister. I'm in real trouble. Belles of Belarus is a scam. I'm in Russia. I think. On a train. We're headed north. Please help me if you can."

They could hear women screaming in the background.

Jamie's heart sank to the bottom of her chest.

"Who is Daria?" Alex asked.

"Chastity. It's a fake name. She's a prostitute at Splash."

Alex nodded.

"I have to find a way to rescue Olga and the other girls," Jamie said.

Jamie was no longer pacing. She sat down on the couch and slumped backward.

A somber mood had come over them as the stark reality of what the girls must be going through was hitting them like a hammer hits a nail.

Alex sat down beside her and took Jamie's hand.

"That's not the mission," Alex said gently. "You know what Brad said. You are only to gather intelligence. You're not to intervene with the girls."

"I know what Brad said," Jamie responded angrily, pulling her hand away from his. Not angry at Alex, more frustrated with the helplessness of the situation.

Tears were welling up in her eyes. As much from anger as anything else. She turned away from Alex so he wouldn't see the tears. Not that it would matter. He certainly could hear the emotion in her voice.

"You heard the message," Jamie said, her voice cracking. "That's my friend's sister. The girl is scared to death. I have to do something to help her."

"What can you do, even if you wanted to do something? The message said they are already in Russia. You have no idea where they are."

Alex was right. She didn't know where the girls were, and even if she did, she had no way of getting them out of Russia. Not by herself. She couldn't ask Brad for help because he'd tell her to stand down.

"All I know is that I have to try. I don't expect you to understand."

"Look, your mission has been a huge success," Alex said. "You've found the pipeline. Brad can shut it down. Expose it for what it is. Belles of Belarus will never kidnap another girl again. Even if you can't do anything for these girls, you've helped hundreds of girls. Maybe thousands."

"I can do something for these girls," Jamie said emphatically. "Olga has a phone. I can call her and find out where she is."

Jamie took the phone in her hand and scrolled to the number. Alex stopped her.

"Think about this for a minute. Olga is obviously hiding the phone. So, her kidnappers don't know she has it. If you call it, and it's not on silent, it'll ring. They might discover it. You could put her life in danger without even knowing it. There are other ways to track the phone."

"Not without Brad knowing what I'm doing," Jamie retorted. "He can track it, but you and I both know he won't. If I tell him what I'm doing, he'll order me to stand down. They'll want to handle it through the proper channels."

Jamie mimicked Brad's voice when she said it.

"They'll contact Russia," she added. "The President or Secretary of State will make a big deal about it to Kuzman. He'll deny it. The girls will disappear. I have to think of something else."

"Well, I can't help you. I have my own mission to worry about," Alex said.

Jamie furrowed her eyebrows.

"What mission? I thought I was your mission."

Alex hesitated. "No. I was sent to Belarus to work the terrorism thread. You're gathering intelligence on the pipeline. I'm gathering intelligence to find out how the pipeline is funding terrorism. I wasn't sent here to watch you."

"Then why have you been following me?"

"I was worried about you. Like I said, I met with the contact yesterday. He gave me the name, Omer Asaf. He said that Omer was trying to buy a nuclear briefcase bomb. He also told me you were in grave danger. I followed you because I was worried about you."

"You were worried about me? You weren't sent to watch me?"

"Yes ... I mean, I was sent on the cruise to watch you. No, not watch you ... What am I trying to say? I was falling for you."

He was stuttering, probably afraid of making Jamie angry again.

"I admit it. I was sent on the cruise to meet you. To make contact. But only to see if I thought we could work together."

"You were falling for me?" Jamie stared Alex closely, looking for any indication he might be lying. Somehow playing with her emotions. Trying to get her to trust him again. He seemed sincere.

"I didn't know I was going to fall for you on the cruise."

He swallowed hard. Clearly nervous.

"You said you met with the contact yesterday and you followed me because you were worried about me. But you've been following me for several days. I could feel it."

She felt like a district attorney, deposing a witness. Looking for inconsistencies. Part of her still didn't trust him.

"I wasn't told to watch you here in Belarus. At first, I just wanted to see you. To be close to you. When the contact said you were in danger ..."

Her heart warmed. Jamie took Alex's hand again as emotions were clearly welling up inside of him. He refused to make eye contact with her.

"I never told Brad about us," he said. "I never told him that I have feelings for you. He never would've let me come on this mission."

"You have feelings for me?"

"Will you quit responding with a question to everything I say," Alex said, raising his voice in a playful tone.

"I'm just in shock. I didn't know you had feelings for me. I thought you did on the cruise. I felt it. Then you didn't call me back. But then when I saw you here and realized you were the one following me, I thought it was because I was your mission. That you were here because Brad didn't trust me."

"Brad trusts you. It's on me. I was trying to get close to you. Not for any reason other than I like you."

"You like me?"

"You asked another question."

They were both standing now. Too amped up to sit.

Alex had a wide grin on his face. He leaned toward her like he was going to give her a hug.

"You haven't answered any of my questions," Jamie said, playfully pushing him away.

"Let me answer it this way."

Brad put his arms around her, pulled her close to him, and kissed her on the lips. Hesitantly at first.

She didn't resist, so he kissed her more passionately.

"Wow!" Jamie said, letting out a huge breath when the kiss finally ended.

"So, you're not still mad at me?" Alex said.

"Oh yeah. I'm still mad at you. You lied to me. But I'm getting over it. Kiss me again."

He did.

30

Emotions were a strange thing. Kissing should be the last thing on her mind. She wanted to tell him to stop but couldn't make herself. Alex took her more deeply into his arms and kissed her again, stopping her from being able to talk at all.

All of her senses were still heightened from the events of the evening. The confrontation with the man at the train trestle. The contact dying in her arms. The shootout. Discovering Alex was a CIA operative. Uncovering the pipeline. Listening to the distress call.

Her senses were overloaded. She wasn't thinking clearly.

They made the kissing even more intense.

A satellite phone on the desk rang and echoed through the room. Alex's phone.

That ended the kiss abruptly. Just in time for Jamie.

A wave of guilt came over her. She felt bad that they were kissing while the girls were in trouble. It didn't seem like the right time to be making out.

"That must be Brad," Jamie said. "He probably knows about Liberty Square by now."

Alex walked over to the desk and picked up the phone.

"It is Brad. What do you want me to say?" he asked.

Jamie shrugged her shoulders.

Alex pushed the answer button and put the phone to his ear and said, "Shadow is dead."

Shadow was the name of the contact. Even on a secure line, they avoided using real names.

"She's all right. I saw the whole thing. She was amazing. Shadow was compromised. Those Middle Eastern men were sent to the square to kill him. She tried to save his life but couldn't. She did get all of them, though."

Jamie could only hear one side of the conversation. The phone wasn't on speaker.

"I don't know where she is," Brad said, putting his hand to his forehead and brushing roughly across it, obviously pained from having to lie to his handler.

"She probably went dark until everything settles down," he added, while looking at Jamie.

Jamie mouthed the words, "Thank you," to him.

He nodded in agreement and then turned his back to her. "I'll call you back once I find out more. I do know she's alive and wasn't hurt in the gunfight."

He hung up the phone.

"What did he say?" Jamie asked.

"He was relieved that you're okay," Alex answered. "That'll buy us some time until we can figure everything out."

Jamie walked into the kitchen and opened the refrigerator. She suddenly felt an intense hunger. The only thing in there was some leftover Chinese food and two six packs of soda.

"You can tell a bachelor has been living here. Do you have any food at all?"

"There's some power bars in the pantry."

Jamie opened the pantry. The bars were the only thing on the shelves. She took out three, opened one, scarfed it down, then threw one across the room to Alex.

He snatched it out of the air with no effort.

Jamie opened the other and finished it off in seconds. By the time she walked back across the room, Alex's bar was gone as well.

"Thanks for covering for me," Jamie said sincerely.

"What are you going to do now?"

"You mentioned a briefcase bomb," Jamie said, getting renewed energy from the bar. "The contact mentioned a briefcase to me. I thought he was talking about the briefcase he was carrying."

"No. Asaf is trying to buy one of their briefcase nukes. I told Brad about it, and he told me to keep gathering intelligence. He won't let me do anything else. I'm in the same boat as you. I can only gather intelligence. I can't intervene in the situation."

"I can't believe I risked my life for that briefcase," Jamie said. "I actually went back for it. It's probably filled with work papers. Although, for some reason, he wanted me to have it. Those were his last words."

"We might as well find out what's in it," Alex said, walking over to the briefcase still sitting by the door to the garage. He picked it up and carried it over to the table.

"It's locked," he said. "We don't have the combination."

He pulled out a knife like he was going to pry it open.

"Wait!" Jamie said. "The lock's no problem. You don't need the knife."

She pushed him aside, sat down in the chair, and set the briefcase on her lap as she would if she were going to open it normally. One latch was in the center with a combination to the right of it. She held the latch down in position with the thumb of her left hand, while lightly rolling her fingers of her right hand down over each numbered wheel to identify which one was the tightest. The way she gauged tightness was by gently tugging down on each one with her fingertip while applying pressure to it.

"What are you doing?" Alex asked.

"Opening the briefcase," she responded. "Shh. I need silence."

Once she determined which lock was the tightest, she set it to zero, and checked the other two wheels again for tightness. They still felt loose, so she clicked the zero lock to one and then felt the two wheels again. She kept increasing the number of the tightest wheel until another wheel felt tight. As soon as it did, she knew the tightest wheel was on the correct number.

She then set the second wheel to zero and checked the third wheel. Repeating the same process until the third wheel felt tight. The second number was then on the correct combination. Once the third wheel felt tight, then all three numbers were on the correct combination.

482.

Jamie released the latch, and it popped open. She raised her arms in the air in victory, shot Alex a satisfied look, and then shook out her hands to release the tension. Chin up, shoulders back, her lips were closed, and tightened together smugly.

"I'm impressed," Alex said. "Where did you learn to do that?"

She shrugged her shoulders and started going through the contents.

"What do we have here? A passport and plane ticket," she said, answering her own question. "He was getting ready to run. He already knew they were onto him."

"Denys Onufeychuk," Alex said, opening the passport. "I finally know his name," he said soberly.

"He's the Minister of Transportation," Alex added a few seconds later. He pulled up Denys' name on his phone and showed it to Jamie. It had a picture of Denys next to his title.

"And he almost made it out alive. He was a very brave man." Alex had a pained look on his face.

"Look at this," Jamie said excitedly.

She had fingered through dozens of pieces of paper. All in Russian. Most were marked with a red stamp at the top of the document.

SAKRETNY MIEMARANDUM

Top Secret Memorandum.

"Brad is going to want these documents. No telling what's in here. This could be a treasure trove of information."

Jamie held up a key.

"I wonder what this it to."

Alex took the key in his hand. "Looks like it's to a lock."

"How long did it take you to figure that out, genius?" Jamie said mockingly.

"I mean, a key to a storage locker." He gave her a playful glare.

"I wonder what's in the locker," Jamie asked.

"It might not have anything to do with us. It may just be his own locker with personal items in it."

"Maybe. Doesn't matter. We don't know where the locker is or the number of the locker. There must be several thousand around here. I wouldn't know where to begin finding it."

Alex sat the key down on the table as Jamie pulled a thumb drive out of the briefcase and held it in the air.

"What's on this?" Jamie said.

"Let's find out."

A high-end CIA computer system with a number of cords and accessories sat on the desk. Jamie made a mental note to look at the computer more carefully. She might be able to access information herself. Without Brad's help.

Alex plugged the thumb drive into the side. When an icon came up on the screen, he checked it for viruses. Satisfied, he clicked on the drive and started thumbing through the files.

"There's a video on here."

Jamie stood behind Alex, looking over his shoulder.

"Play it," she said.

He clicked on the file, automatically starting a video application. A few seconds later, Denys appeared on the screen. He was sitting in a chair in what looked like a personal residence. A bookcase was behind him, a picture of him and a woman was on the first shelf. He leaned forward and adjusted the camera and began speaking in English.

"I have been compromised. I am not proud of betraying my country. I love Belarus, and everything I did was for her best interest. Including now."

His voice cracked when he said it.

"When the Soviet Union fell, I oversaw the shipment of four brief-case nukes which were brought to Belarus and hidden inside of our country. They have been stored at UE Ekores which is a nuclear waste management facility located two km from Minsk."

He held up a document in the air.

"There is a map of the facilities and a layout on this drive. We have denied the existence of the briefcases for years. Omer Asaf has agreed to buy one of these nukes. He intends to smuggle it into the United States and to use it as blackmail to have the sanctions lifted against Russia."

Alex looked up at Jamie with his eyebrows raised.

Denys held up a key. It appeared to be the same one Alex had in his hand.

"This is a key to the storage area. The locker number is 156. If you can, you must go to the facility and take the nukes from the locker. In the briefcase is my badge. Use it. The handoff to Omer is to be on Monday. You must get them by then. They will be discovered missing, and the facility will be locked down. Time is of the essence. I wish you Godspeed. I hope you are successful. I've done everything I know to do."

What a brave man.

The screen went blank.

"What do we do now?" Jamie asked.

"I've got to get the nukes."

"Shouldn't you call Brad?"

"He'd tell me to stand down," he said as he gave her a sideways grin. "He'd have to get permission for me to go in and get them. I know what they'll say. The mission needs to be planned. They'll want to send in a team. Probably Seals. Undercover. A whole big operation. I can't call him. He'll say I'm only here to gather intelligence."

He shook his head. "No. I have to get them myself."

"How is that any different than what I'm doing?" Jamie asked strongly. "Before you were arguing that I can't go after the girls. I have to get permission from Brad. Now that it's your mission, you want to go off the tracks and disobey orders."

"They aren't the same thing. In your mission, we're talking about three-hundred girls. While that's important, with this, we're talking about nukes. The lives of three-hundred-million Americans are at risk. With all due respect, I think this is a lot more important."

The words stung Jamie like a dozen wasps. She bit her upper lip to keep from saying anything. Alex must have realized it because he stood from his chair and took her hand. She looked away, unable to look him in the eye.

"I didn't mean it that way."

"Those girls may not be important to you," Jamie said with intensity, "but they mean everything to me. That's my job. I get that yours is more important. I hope you get the nukes in time. But I have to go after the girls. That's who I am. If you don't get that, then we can never be together."

"I do get it. Totally. I wish there was something we could do. We don't know where the girls are. But we do know where the nukes are. You heard the man. We have until Monday. Then the nuke is going to be in the wind. We might never find it. I have to go get it. I hope you understand."

"I do. Don't worry about me. I'll figure out something."

"I wish there was a way to get to Omer. He would know where the girls are."

"There is," Jamie said as excitement radiated from her demeanor and her voice.

"What do you mean?" Alex asked.

"I can get to him," Jamie said.

"How? He's always surrounded by bodyguards."

"Turns out, I happen to have a date with him," Jamie said smugly.

"A date!"

"Tomorrow night. He invited me to his hotel suite. At the *California Casino*."

"Well, you do get around. How did you manage a date?'

"He saw me at *Splash*. I guess he liked what he saw. He invited me over and then asked me out."

"You can't go to his hotel room. It's too dangerous."

"I can take care of myself."

"But he'll want to have sex with you."

Jamie hit Alex in the chest playfully with her fist. "You're jealous."

"I'm not jealous. I'm worried about you."

"This is the first time I've seen you jealous."

"I'm not ... I think you should tell Brad. Get his permission first."

"Why? I'm still on mission. I'm gathering intelligence. There's no telling what I might find in his room. His computer and his cell phone will be there. I'll take a thumb drive with me and download all his information."

"If we're going to do this then we need a plan," he said reluctantly.

"We?" Jamie said, taking a big leap in the air. "Does this mean you're going to help me?"

Alex rolled his eyes and let out another, louder, sigh.

"If you're going to his suite, then I'm going to help you. If he lays one hand on you, I'll..."

Jamie sidled up next to Alex, kissing him playfully on the neck. "You'll what?"

"I'll kill him."

"You're sexy when you're jealous."

"Like I said, we need a plan," he said, ignoring her comment and her advances. "The problem is not getting you into his suite, it's getting you out of it. Alive."

***

Alex went out and got some food. More Chinese. They were both starving and what was in the fridge was old. For two hours, they worked on a plan at the kitchen table. After it was cleared of the remnants of the meal, they went through each detail of the plan carefully. Meticulously.

Jamie was glad Alex was as attentive to the details as she was. They worked well together.

The plan had its risks, but they did everything they could to minimize them.

Alex yawned, causing Jamie to do the same. The plan didn't call for them to get any sleep that night. They would be leaving soon. For the storage unit. To steal the nukes.

They both jumped when the satellite phone rang again.

Brad.

Jamie looked at Alex. He returned the stare.

Alex picked up the phone and sent it to voicemail. "It's like Curly always said," Alex began.

"It's easier to ask forgiveness than permission," they both said in unison.

31

Liberty Square, Friday night, 10:00 p.m.

Lieutenant Petrov and Detective Fabi were standing in the middle of the square trying to figure out how the horrific scene in front of them had unfolded. A bullet ridden Jeep was in the middle of the square. A dead Middle Eastern man was in the driver's seat. He'd been shot in the back of the head.

The Minister of Transportation was lying on the ground, dead. Gunshots to his chest. Next to him was another Middle Eastern man. Shot.

The scene didn't make sense.

Two more Middle Eastern men were dead on the other side of the square. It seemed like they were chasing someone. The tables were turned on them.

Were they ambushed?

Fabi was the first detective on the scene. The Militsia arrived first after receiving a call of shots fired in the square. Once Fabi arrived, he called his Lieutenant. Petrov arrived within minutes and Fabi was going over the scene with him.

Between long drags on a cigarette.

Fabi immediately suspected that the American woman was involved. Petrov hadn't mentioned the possibility, but he didn't know everything Fabi knew.

Shortly after he arrived, Fabi questioned a man who was walking his dog on the sidewalk past the Holy Spirit Church just as the gunfire broke. He related that a slender man dressed in all black shot the two men in the Jeep.

He had been impressed with the unknown man.

"He shot the one guy while running," the man said.

"Where was he running from?"

"From over there." He pointed to the other side of the square.

"Show me," Fabi said.

The man showed Fabi where the man in black was when he fired the shots. It would take a tremendous marksman to pull it off. Either that, or the man was really lucky.

"What happened next?" Fabi asked.

"The Jeep started to drive away. The man in black shot the man in the back of the head."

"While he was driving?"

"Yep."

"From all the way over here?"

"Yep."

"That's impossible."

"That's what I saw."

He didn't see who had shot the man lying on the ground just off the sidewalk or who had shot the other two men on the other side of the square. But he did see them.

"Two more men jumped out of the sedan. Over there," the man said as he pointed to a four-door car parked on the street. They came out with their guns blazing. They chased the man in black down toward the river. That's the last I saw of them. That's when I took off."

Fabi had sent some Militsia down to the river to see if they could find anything. They came back empty. Although, they'd search it tomorrow morning in the daylight.

"Could the man in black have been a woman?" Fabi asked.

"I suppose," he said. "The person I saw was very thin. I saw him . . . or her running toward the Jeep. Running fast. He was shooting and so I ducked down."

Fabi relayed that information to his boss but left out the suspicions he had about the woman. He wasn't about to tell him he had been following her. Even confronted her at the restaurant. Where she threatened to kill him.

Petrov confirmed that the dead man on the ground off the sidewalk was the Minister of Transportation, Denys Onufeychuk. The same man Fabi had seen go into the American woman's hotel room, two nights ago. Well, he hadn't actually seen him go into her hotel room, but he did go up to the third floor. Obviously, to see her. Who else was he going to meet?

Another fact he was going to keep to himself.

Why was Denys in the square? To meet the woman? Maybe. Fabi didn't know. He knew the American woman was involved somehow but didn't know how. He was convinced the person in black was her.

Lieutenant Petrov bent over and picked up a handgun while holding it with a handkerchief.

"This is Russian," Petrov said. "A Makarov pistol. "What's it doing here? What do the Russians have to do with this?"

"I don't know."

"The four dead men are Middle Eastern. They all had machine guns near their bodies. Those aren't Russian guns."

"It's a mystery."

Petrov ignored him. Fabi knew from experience that Petrov was mainly talking to himself. Trying to process the scene verbally. He didn't really care what Fabi thought. Only what Fabi knew.

Which in this instance wasn't much, but more than he was willing to let on. Fabi intended to find proof that the woman was a spy and arrest him herself. So he'd get all the credit. So Petrov couldn't mess up his investigation.

Petrov continued to opine about the scene. Fabi pretended to listen intently, although his mind was on his next move against the girl.

"Denys didn't carry a gun," Petrov said. "Or at least that I knew of. Even if he did, this isn't what he would carry. Whose gun is it?"

Fabi thought he knew. A gang called the Red Spades had stolen a load of Makarov pistols from the Brotherhood, a Russian gang operating in Belarus. A member of the Red Spades was in the hospital with a concussion. The older brother of one of the boys attacked by the American woman.

He had been attacked earlier that evening under a train trestle not that far from here.

It couldn't be a coincidence. Fabi would bet a month's salary that the American woman took the gun off of the gang member and used it to kill the Middle Eastern men to make it look like a gang shooting.

More information he was keeping from the Lieutenant. More his speculation than anything. He needed proof and was determined to get it. This was his chance to make a name for himself.

"From the best I can tell," the Lieutenant said, "two men drove the Jeep onto the sidewalk, up to Denys, made him get on his knees and then shot him. Right over there. It doesn't look like the body has been moved or dumped."

Fabi agreed.

"The Jeep came from over there," Fabi said. He pointed toward the street. "There are tire marks on the street."

Petrov nodded but mostly ignored the remark. He had probably already seen the tire marks.

"That's where it starts to not make sense. Who are the two dead men over on the other side of the square?"

"Maybe the four of them were together," Fabi said. "You see that car over there, the sedan."

Petrov looked in that direction. Though dark, the street illuminated the car. Lamp posts every few feet lit up the square all night every night.

Fabi decided to speak up and share his own opinion.

"Here's what I think," Fabi said. "The two dead men over there by the building were in the sedan. They saw their friends get shot here by a third person. They came running and chased the man across the square. The man shot them over by the building, and then disappeared."

"That's very insightful, Fabi. I'm impressed. You keep working on that. Check out the sedan. Run the plates. And the plates on the Jeep. Let's meet first thing in the morning to discuss."

Fabi wished he hadn't spoken up. He scored some points with the boss, but now he was given a bunch of busy work to do.

At least, the Lieutenant had still kept him on the case. Now he had a reason to investigate the girl.

"I'm going to go call President Bobrinsky," Petrov said. "Someone has to tell him about the Minister. He's not going to like being woke up in the middle of the night. Can't be helped. You stay here and keep working the scene."

Petrov lit a cigarette and walked off.

Fabi welcomed being alone. He needed to think things through. The American woman was obviously extremely dangerous. She had killed four men, maybe five if you counted the Minister of Transportation.

Fabi had no intention of staying at the scene. As soon as Petrov was out of sight, he was going to go to the woman's hotel room and confront her. Search her room for black clothes. Any other evidence.

He touched his gun for reassurance. He might need it at her hotel.

He did have the element of surprise. She had skill. Hopefully, she was sleeping, and he'd catch her off guard. The last thing she would expect would be a knock on the door late at night from him.

The hotel wasn't far away. Fabi started walking that way when his phone rang, startling him. Who would be calling him in the middle of the night? It wasn't the Lieutenant. He could still see him at a distance walking toward his car. He had the cigarette in his hand, not his phone.

Unknown Caller.

"Hello," he said, hesitantly.

"Hello, Detective."

A woman's voice!

Fear pulsed through him.

The American!

"Do you want to know what happened tonight in the square?" she asked.

"Come into the station and let's talk about it," he replied, trying to sound confident, but his hand was shaking, his voice cracking.

"Meet me at the old water tower. Ten minutes. Come alone."

The line went dead.

Fabi stopped walking; his feet frozen in place. The woman was involved. Why was she calling him? Was it a trap? He couldn't go to the water tower alone. But he had to know.

He thought about calling his boss then decided against it.

I can do this.

Indecision scrambled his thoughts. He couldn't decide what to do. This might be over his head.

I should call for backup.

If he did, the Lieutenant would find out about it and take the case away from him. Take all the credit as well.

No!

He had to do this himself. This was what he'd trained for his whole life. Petrov had said to keep working on the scene. That's what he was going to do. Solve the case. Be a hero.

Fabi walked in the direction of his car. Excited, but scared to death. His hand shook as he tried to get the key in the lock and then into the ignition to start it. One glance in the rearview mirror confirmed the deep bags under his eyes. Sleep had been hard to come by since the American woman had come to town.

He took a deep breath, wanting to exhale slowly but letting it all out in one quick rush of air. Immediately, he wished he had the air back as a familiar voice shook him to his core, to the point he was unable to take a breath.

"Hello, Fabi," she said. "It's nice to see you again. Let's go for a drive."

She was in the back seat. He hadn't even noticed. How did she get into his locked car?

The American woman flashed a gun. It was now pressed into the back of his head.

Fear overwhelmed him.

From the scene at the square, she obviously knew how to use it.

She has to be CIA.

32

Friday night, 10:40 p.m.
Royal Presidential Palace

A phone rang, startling President Bobrinsky, waking him from a deep sleep. He looked at the clock. Only ten forty. It seemed later. He generally went to bed early. A phone call this late was never good. Usually meant some kind of national emergency. It had been a while since he'd been disturbed at night.

He pulled the phone off the table and hit accept, fully awake now. He had that ability. This wasn't the first time he'd been called in the middle of the night and wouldn't be the last. Came with the job. He'd more than likely have to get up, so he might as well wake up.

"Yes," he said, firmly.

"Comrade, this is Petrov." Petrov was the Lieutenant of the Militsia. *Local issue.*

Very unusual for the Lieutenant to be calling him. Especially at night.

"I'm sorry to call you so late, my friend," Petrov continued. "I'm afraid I have bad news. A mutual friend of ours is dead."

Petrov served with Bobrinsky years ago in the Russian forces, and they became good friends, although they rarely talked now that he was President.

"Go ahead."

"Denys was murdered tonight. Assassinated, apparently."

The three men were on a first name basis and had shared many drinks together over the years, although it had been a long time.

Hearing the name Denys caused his heart to skip a beat.

"What happened?" he asked, trying to not let his voice show any emotion.

"There was a gunfight in Liberty Square."

"Yes. I knew about that."

One of his aides briefed him before he went to bed. The press had been restricted from going to the scene or reporting on it. A statement would be released when he had more information. Hopefully, the worldwide press hadn't yet gotten wind of it.

At first, he thought it was probably gang related. Which made sense. That's why Petrov was calling him. How did Denys get caught up in it?

He was beginning to imagine the worst.

"There are four Middle Eastern men dead in the square."

Asaf! The fool.

Bobrinsky could barely contain his anger.

Asaf's men were to follow Denys. If necessary, they were to capture him and bring him in alive for questioning. He had obviously disobeyed his orders.

What was he thinking? A shootout in Liberty Square. What a disaster. If he didn't move quickly the fallout and information might not be contained.

No one could know that Denys was a traitor. That's why he had wanted Denys arrested and disposed of quietly.

"I'd like for you to keep me posted personally," the President said. "On the investigation."

"Of course."

Bobrinsky hung up the phone and immediately dialed Asaf's number. He answered on the first ring. As soon as he spoke, the President knew he hadn't been sleeping.

"I told you that Denys was to be taken alive," the President said, roughly.

"Those were the instructions I gave my men. I'm trying to figure it all out now. They were ambushed by someone in the square."

"Who?"

"I have no idea. My men are all dead. They can't say," Asaf said.

"Can they be tied to you?"

"Of course not. They can't be tied to either of us. But it does complicate things. I think we should conduct our business sooner."

The plan had been to transfer the nuclear briefcase to Asaf on Monday morning. Now Bobrinsky was having second thoughts. Maybe he shouldn't follow through on the deal.

They didn't know what they were dealing with or what the fallout from the shooting in the square would be. The President could easily cover it up, but he didn't know what he would be covering up.

Who killed Denys? Who killed Asaf's men?

Bobrinsky rubbed his eyes hard. Thinking. He didn't want to cancel the deal. The briefcase could be used to get the Russian sanctions lifted. He'd be a hero in the Russian President's eyes.

"I agree," he finally said. "Let's do the transfer Sunday morning instead of Monday. Nine o'clock. At the Ekores. You transfer the money then, and we'll give you the package."

Bobrinsky hung up the phone without waiting for a response and dialed another number. The man in charge of security at Ekores, Gyorky Guzmich.

"Commander," Gyorky answered on the third ring.

He sounded groggy. The President's number came up on the caller ID for all phones he called in Belarus. He insisted that everyone know it was him when he called so they would take it immediately and answer with the proper respect.

"There's been a change of plans," Bobrinsky said. "I need for the briefcase to be ready for transfer on Sunday morning, nine a.m., not Monday as we originally planned."

"As you wish. My men are working on the container to transport the device. It's not ready yet. But will be by tomorrow night. I will oversee putting the briefcase in the container myself."

"Excellent. Call me if there are any complications."

Bobrinsky hung up the phone, satisfied the situation was handled. Denys's death was probably the best thing. Now the secret of his treason would die with him, and there was nothing he could do to stop the transfer.

Maybe I can go back to sleep after all.

***

The following night, Sunday morning, 1:30 a.m.

For the second night in a row, Bobrinsky's phone rang and awakened him from another sound sleep—later this time. It took him longer to get his bearings. He'd had a little too much to drink the night before and immediately felt the effects of it when he sat up in bed. The call was from Gyorky.

Strange that he would be calling. He suddenly remembered he told him to call if there were any complications. There shouldn't be any. Gyorky was to work all day and night if necessary to get the briefcase ready for the handoff in the morning.

"Yes," Bobrinsky said wearily as he answered the phone.

"We have a situation," Gyorky said, his voice giving away his nervousness.

"What is it? Why are you calling me?" Bobrinsky asked, suddenly alarmed and more awake.

A brief pause and then Gyorky spoke. His words were slow and measured. "The briefcases are missing."

"What do you mean missing?" Bobrinsky shouted, fully awake now.

"They're gone. We opened the room where they were stored, and all four briefcases are gone."

"That's impossible! Who took them?"

"Last night, a few hours after you called me, Denys Onufeychuk entered the facility."

"Denys?" The last name he expected Gyorky to mention. "How do you know Denys was there, and what was he doing?"

"He used his government badge to get through security. We have a record of his badge being scanned."

"What time was that?"

"Twelve forty-three a.m."

"Thursday night?"

"No. Friday night. Actually Saturday morning. Right after midnight."

"I'm confused. Are you saying that Denys entered the facility last night and not the night before?"

"Correct."

The President knew that was impossible. Denys was killed more than four hours before then.

Asaf!

"I'll get back to you," the President said.

He hung up the phone and dialed Asaf's number. It went straight to voicemail. He got out of bed, found a number to the California Hotel, and dialed it.

"Get me Omer Asaf's room. This is President Bobrinsky." His name would have already come up on the caller ID so she would know it was really him.

"One moment please," the woman said and put him on hold. She came back shortly and said, "There's no answer in his suite."

"Send security to his suite right now. Enter his room. Have him detained. Call me back as soon as you have done so."

He gave the attendant the main number for the Royal Palace switchboard. A few minutes later, the phone on his desk rang. The hotel was calling.

"Commander, Mr. Asaf is not in his room. We don't know where he is. He was here earlier this evening. But no one has seen him for several hours."

Bobrinsky hung up the phone and calmly got the palace operator back on the line. He felt no fear, having dealt with difficult situations all his adult life. War. Revolution. His ascension to power. The breakup of the Soviet Union. He would not jump to conclusions until he knew the facts.

He suspected Asaf had Denys killed and stole his security badge. He used the badge to access the facility and then stole the briefcase nukes. If true, he would be trying to leave the country without having paid for them.

Asaf had a private plane at the airport. Bobrinsky hoped he wasn't too late.

"Mr. President," the operator said. "How may I help you?"

"Get me the head of security at the airport. Whoever's working tonight. I'll hold."

A few minutes later, Bogdan Yonaslovich was on the line.

"Is Omer Asaf's plane still at the airport?" the president asked.

"Let me check, sir."

Bobrinsky was put on hold.

"No sir. It left a few hours ago. I'm told a limousine came in at 11:43, and he boarded the plane at that time. It took off a few minutes later."

Bobrinsky himself had given instructions to the airport security that Asaf could come and go as he pleased and was not to be searched or harassed. He had no one to blame but himself.

"Where was it going?"

"I'll ask, sir."

The phone was silent, but he could hear Bogdan talking to someone in the background.

"It filed a flight plan for Turkey."

"Where is it now?"

"I have a man looking as we speak."

"Is it still in our airspace?" Bobrinsky asked, even though he knew the answer. It would already be halfway to Turkey.

Would there still be time to scramble planes and intercept it before it got to Turkey?

"I need its exact location," Bobrinsky said with urgency.

"That's strange," he heard the man say in the background.

A few seconds later, he came back on the line. "The plane is no longer on the radar system. We can't find it."

"What do you mean you can't find it? It didn't just disappear. Where is the plane?" Bobrinsky said, his voice raised in ire.

"I'm sorry sir, but I have no idea. The plane is not on that flight plan anymore. It's not even on the radar screen."

Bobrinsky hung up his phone. Feeling fear for the first time in years.

**

Sunday morning, 9:00, a.m.

The following morning, about the time the transfer of the nuclear briefcase was to take place, Lieutenant Petrov and Detective Fabi Orlov walked into the President's office.

Bobrinsky didn't rise from his desk to greet his old friend. He wasn't in the mood. He did shake Orlov's hand after Petrov introduced him. The only reason he was meeting with them was because Petrov said he had important information related to Denys and his death.

The President wondered if Petrov had found a link between Asaf and Denys.

Asaf was nowhere to be found. Neither were the briefcases.

This was spiraling out of control. He hoped he didn't have to kill Petrov and Orlov. That depended on how much they knew.

"What have you found out?" Bobrinsky asked, not offering the men a drink as was customary. He wanted to get to the bad news he knew was coming.

"Detective Fabi has been assigned to investigate the murder of our good friend Denys in Liberty Square on Friday night," Petrov said. "What he has found is very interesting. I will let him explain."

The President nodded his head acknowledging Fabi. "What did you find?" he asked.

Detective Fabi pulled out some papers and set them in front of the President. His hands were shaking as he did so. But when he spoke, he did so with confidence.

"I discovered bank statements from a Swiss bank account in Minister Denys's name. The payments appeared to come from the Americans."

Bobrinsky was already aware of those payments. He wondered how this low-level detective found that information. Rather than ask, he let Fabi continue. Better to act like he wasn't aware of the situation.

"At first, I thought they were proof that Denys was working with the Americans as a spy. Turns out, the payments didn't come from the Americans."

Bobrinsky sat up in his high-back chair. He was very interested to learn why Fabi believed that stunning news.

"The payments were traced to an account owned by one of Omer Asaf's companies," Fabi continued. "In your hand are also bank statements from Asaf's accounts."

Bobrinksy looked them over.

"Asaf made those payments to make it look like it came from the Americans."

"Denys was working with Asaf?"

"No. Asaf was making it look like Denys was a traitor."

Bobrinsky threw the statements down in disgust. Asaf had brought those same statements to him to make him think Denys was a spy. So he could kill him, steal his badge, then take the briefcases.

He'd been tricked. Asaf would pay with his life.

"There's one other thing," Fabi said. "If I may?" Fabi stood and pulled one of the statements off of the desk and handed it to the President.

"What's this?"

"It is a transfer of more than eight million dollars out of Denys's account. It happened after he died, so Denys obviously couldn't have made the transfer," Fabi explained.

"Who did then?" Bobrinsky asked, already knowing the answer to that question.

"The money was transferred back to Asaf's account. We assume it was done by Asaf."

"That scoundrel."

Petrov interjected and stated what Bobrinsky already knew. "It would seem that one Mr. Asaf was trying to make it look like our comrade was a traitor working for the Americans, when, in fact, he wasn't. He was loyal to the motherland and was murdered for it."

Bobrinsky slumped into his chair. Solemn. With tremendous regret. He'd trusted Asaf. Now his good friend was innocent. Wrongly accused. Killed over lies. Not only had Asaf stolen the nukes, but he had murdered one of his best friends. Besmirched his name in the process.

"Asaf is going to pay," the President said, resolve returning. "I want a warrant out for his arrest. We will seize all of his assets. Close down all of his businesses."

"Of course," Petrov said.

"Well done, Detective Orlov. Give this man a promotion and a raise," Bobrinsky said to Petrov as he stood and held out his hand to Fabi, shaking it strongly.

"Let's all have a drink."

He walked over to the cabinet and poured three drinks.

The President raised his glass and said soberly, " *Da nasaha zahin-ulaha tavarysa, Denys.*"

The other two men repeated the toast. "To our fallen comrade, Denys."

33

Sunday Morning, 9:00 a.m.

Alex sat in front of a computer and dialed Brad's secure number for a video conference. The screen flickered, and Brad and Director Cold-claw's images appeared, staticky at first, but slowly coming into focus until they could see and hear each other perfectly.

Alex had a big grin on his face. The tone was not reciprocated by the two on the other end of the call, who were about to demand answers.

"Hi Alex," Brad said, in a semi-friendly manner.

"Hello," the Director added.

That was as friendly as the conference was going to get at the moment. They were probably dealing with all kinds of fallout from the shootout, and they had no answers to tell anyone.

"I guess the first question is, where are you?" Brad asked, in a serious, but not confrontational, tone.

Typical Brad, he would withhold judgment until he knew the facts. He was also going to take the lead in the conversation, try to set the tone, although the Director would, no doubt, interject anytime she wanted.

Brad was Alex's supervisor. His neck was sticking out a mile as well.

"I am somewhere over the North Sea," Alex answered. "I think I just passed over the Faroe Islands."

"And what, exactly, are you doing there?" Brad asked. His eyes widened some in surprise, but he kept the same tone. Alex could see them clearly now on the video screen.

"I'm headed home."

"You're not on a commercial flight. From the background noise and what's behind you, I'd say you're on a corporate jet. A nice one, at that. Commercial too good for you now? I see my pilot must have shown up."

Alex had sent Brad an urgent message late Friday night, early Saturday morning. The message had asked for a commercial pilot and a limousine to be at the safehouse by midnight Saturday night.

Something Brad had managed to do, even though he wouldn't have known why. Another good thing about Brad. He trusted the people in the field. If they needed something, he provided it, if at all possible, no matter how strange it seemed.

Especially if the word urgent was associated with it. The operatives weren't to use that word unless it was a real emergency.

It had been.

Alex answered. "Yes. I'm on a private jet. And yes, your pilot arrived on time. Thank you very much."

"That wasn't easy to do," Brad said. "Do you care to explain, or do you want us to guess why you are on a private jet, flying over the Atlantic?"

"I borrowed it from a friend. He'd like to say hi."

Alex turned the camera to Omer Asaf lying on the couch, his hands and feet were tied, and his mouth gagged. Alex was in Asaf's private jet. One of the nicest planes in the world with a fuel range of 8500 miles. Enough to get him to America without stopping for fuel.

After Jamie and Alex kidnapped Asaf Saturday night, they brought him back to the safehouse. When the limousine and pilot showed up, they put him in the back seat, went to the airport, and Alex and the pilot boarded the jet and took off.

Alex hacked into the computer controls and gave the plane a new identity number so it couldn't be tracked. It was now traveling under an entirely different number and code that no one else knew.

He took the most northern route, where there would be the least amount of traffic. Likely no one would even see his plane until it got to the destination.

Which was something they needed to discuss. Where should he take Asaf?

"Who is that?" Brad asked.

"Omer Asaf."

"The billionaire? You kidnapped him?" Director Coldclaw asked, her voice suddenly raised to a questioning tone. "Are you crazy?"

"The man is bad news," Alex retorted. "He was trying to buy a briefcase bomb from Bobrinsky. We stopped him just in time."

"You were told not to intervene," Brad said. "Your mission was to gather information. You had no authority to act on your own."

The Director glared at Brad. Her shoulders tensed. Alex could almost see steam coming from the top of her head.

"I gathered the information," Alex said, casually, knowing they wouldn't be mad for long. "We learned that the transfer was going to happen this morning. We had to stop it. Before you say anything else, let me show you something."

Alex had set up the camera to work wirelessly. He took it in his hand and walked to the back of the plane, opened a door in the floor and took stairs down to the cargo hold. A light was on in the area and Alex hoped it was enough for them to see the reason he was acting so confidently.

Four briefcases were lined up against the wall. Alex turned the camera on the nuclear briefcases he and Jamie had stolen late Friday night from the storage unit in Ekores.

"What are those briefcases?" Brad asked.

"Are those what I think they are?" the Director said right after him and before Alex could answer.

Alex could no longer see them since he wasn't by the computer, but he could hear them and was trying to picture their surprised faces.

"Are those nuclear?" Brad asked.

"You got it!" Alex answered excitedly, turning the camera on his face so they could see the wild grin on it. "Those are the four missing nuclear briefcases that Bobrinsky has been hiding."

"Are you serious?" Director Coldclaw asked. "Do you have confirmation those are really the nukes?"

The CIA had been trying for years to figure out how to secure those nukes. Short of military action, they hadn't been able to come up with anything.

Director Coldclaw's first concern would be deniability. Even if she was excited. Bobrinsky had claimed they didn't have the nukes. Our stealing them could create an international incident.

It was complicated.

They didn't need to be concerned. Alex and Jamie had worked all that out brilliantly in Alex's estimation. He couldn't wait to tell them the whole story.

"I would open them and prove it to you, but I don't want to risk any nuclear leakage," Alex said. "But those are the real thing. We used Denys's badge to go in and steal them from the storage locker where they were hidden."

Alex walked back up the stairs, closed the hatch, and sat down at his computer. He affixed the camera back on the top so they could see him. The Director still had a stunned look on her face. He could tell her mind was spinning as she tried to process all the ramifications in her mind.

If steam was coming from her head, it was from her mind working too fast. The thought made Alex smile even more.

"If you used Denys's badge, then he's been outed," Brad said with concern.

"Actually, Denys was already outed. Asaf outed him. He somehow got ahold of bank statements showing the CIA payments into Denys's Swiss bank account. He showed those to Bobrinsky. Asaf had his men follow Denys, who had a meet scheduled with Jamie in the square. That's when all hell broke loose."

"What happened?" Brad asked.

"Jamie saw Denys was being followed. She tried to warn him. You know. Follow protocol. Let him know he was being followed. She approached him and used the phrase for danger. After she cleared the area, Asaf's men came into the square to kidnap Denys. They would have tortured him. Jamie saw them come after him, re-entered the scene, and that's when the gunfire broke out."

"That's when Denys was killed," Brad said soberly.

Alex knew Denys was a valuable asset. It had taken years to develop him. But the risk of the agent being outed came with the territory. Fortunately, Denys hadn't died in vain. With the four nukes and all the classified information, he might go down as one of the most effective agents in history.

"That's when he was killed," Alex said. "Jamie did everything she could to save him. She was remarkable."

"She shouldn't have gone back in," Brad said.

"It's a good thing she did," Alex retorted.

"There was a huge shootout in a tourist area," Brad responded, in an angrier tone. "Our contact is dead. How could that be a good thing?"

"That's how we got the nukes," Alex said, defensively. "Along with a boatload of other intelligence. Brad, check your files. Denys was carrying a briefcase with a lot of classified information. I downloaded them and sent them to you. He also had a key to the storage unit and a map where the nukes were hidden in the briefcase. Jamie grabbed it before she got out of there. Took a lot of courage to do what she did."

"There was nothing she could do for Denys, I guess," Director Coldclaw said. "In a way it's better. If he was already outed. They were going to kill him anyway. Torture him until he talked. Then make him suffer more. Probably better that he died in the square rather than be tortured to death."

"Here's the most amazing part of it," Alex said. "Denys isn't outed. Bobrinsky thinks Asaf was lying about Denys."

"What do you mean?"

"We made it look like Asaf was behind everything. I went into Denys's bank account and made it look like the money came from him and not the CIA. Then I transferred the money, eight million dollars back out of that account, and made it look like Asaf stole it back."

Part of Alex's training was on computer sabotage and surveillance. He had the reputation as one of the best hackers in all of the CIA.

"What happened to the money?" Brad asked.

"About that," Alex said hesitantly.

"Alex … What are you not telling us?" Brad said, a little more sternly.

"We have a new agent in Belarus to take Denys's place. I transferred the money into an account I set up for him."

"Who did you recruit to be a new agent?"

"Actually, I didn't do it. Jamie did. She recruited him."

"Regardless of who did it, who is he … or she?"

"He's a he. His name is Fabi Orlov. He's a Detective in the Minsk Militsia. He's meeting with Bobrinsky in a few hours. Giving him the proof that Asaf was lying about Denys. Bobrinsky will put two and two together. Asaf lied about Denys, had him killed, used his badge to steal the nukes, and then left the country in his jet before he could get caught."

Alex paused to let that sink in. When they didn't ask a question, Alex continued.

"Denys is going to be a hero in Belarus as far as Bobrinsky is concerned. He'll get a martyr's funeral. Fabi will be a hero too, for that matter. And a rich man. Bobrinsky will have no idea what happened to Asaf. He's in hiding as far as Bobrinsky is concerned. Fabi will be a good agent. Not as high level as Denys, but who knows. Maybe we can help him get promoted up the ranks."

"You weren't authorized to give him eight million dollars," Brad said.

"Don't worry about it," the Director interjected. "The money was already spent. Well spent. Sounds like we are getting double use out of it."

"And this jet I'm on is worth at least seventy million dollars," Alex added. "It's now the property of the United States of America. And Asaf's got bank accounts with billions of dollars in it. I've already looked at most of them. All of which we can freeze or seize. Say the word, and I'll take it out of his account right now."

Alex looked over at Asaf. A final look of resignation came over him as he slumped into the couch and let out a moan, probably realizing life as he knew it was over.

"I don't know what to say," Director Coldclaw said. "I should be mad at you for disobeying Brad's orders. But how can I argue with the results? You deserve a lot of credit."

"Jamie's the one who really deserves most of the credit. She's the one who got the briefcase so we could steal the nukes. She flipped Fabi. And she arranged it so we could kidnap Asaf. By the way, we have his computer and cell phone. There's a treasure trove of intelligence on it. Bank accounts. Money laundering. Terrorist contacts. He's into all kinds of things. He's the one behind the sex trafficking as well."

"How did Jamie arrange it so you could nab Asaf? We've been trying to get close to him for years."

"She got him to ask her out on a date."

"A date!" Director Coldclaw said with exasperation. "That's against the rules. Are there any rules in the handbook that the two of you didn't manage to break?"

"I'll get back with you on that," Alex said with a grin. "There may have been one, but I'll have to try to remember."

Brad and the Director both laughed. Their moods had improved considerably since the beginning of the conversation.

"Anyway. She had a date with him," Alex said. "In his hotel room."

"Dear God!" Director Coldclaw said. "I don't know if I want to hear this."

Alex couldn't wait to tell her.

34

"Jamie went to Asaf's hotel room," Director Coldclaw said, with exasperation. "I can't believe it."

Alex felt the huge grin on his face. The look on their faces didn't match his. They weren't amused.

"Here's the story," Alex said. "Jamie went to his hotel room. Saturday night. About 9:30 in the evening. Asaf invited her there."

"How did she manage that?"

"She met him at his club. It's called *Splash*. Somehow, Jamie finagled her way into a meeting with him alone in his hotel room."

"Good heavens!"

"She's good."

"Yep. Asaf took one look at her and was smitten. He asked her to his suite."

"And, of course, she accepted," Brad said.

"That sounds dangerous," Director Coldclaw said.

"You know Jamie. She's fearless. Anyway, she went there. Right on time. It's a big suite. Asaf owns the *California Hotel and Casino* in Minsk. So, he's got the whole top floor. Of course, she gets by security. Because she has a date. Asaf is expecting her. She gets in with no problem. So, she's alone with him in the suite."

Director Coldclaw buried her head in her hands in obvious disbelief.

"They order room service. Asaf thinks he's about to get lucky."

"My word!"

Alex forced back a laugh.

"I dressed up as a waiter and brought the food and champagne up to the room. Then I left. Jamie proposed a toast, and he drank it. The drink has a sedative in it that put him to sleep. Why wouldn't he drink it? He thinks Jamie is going to have sex with him after they eat."

The Director gasped.

"She didn't have sex with him. Obviously. He fell asleep. When I came back to get the trays, I put him in a compartment underneath the cart. The guards didn't think to search it. Why would they? I'm leaving the room, not bringing anything in. I took him out to my car and to the safehouse. Jamie waited a few minutes, then walked right out the hotel entrance. Just like normal. She told the guards Asaf left and went to *Splash*. The guards believed her."

"Ingenuous plan," Brad said.

"You said Asaf was behind the sex trafficking," the Director said. "How's that?"

"I meant to ask about that too," Brad added. "Do you know what Jamie found out?"

"Asaf owns a company called *Belles of Belarus*."

Alex could see Brad looking down and could hear him typing something—probably pulling up the website.

"It's a mail-order-bride business," Alex explained. "A front for sex trafficking. They recruit women. Promise them a husband in America. Then they load them on buses and take them to Russia, where they sell them into the sex trade."

"How do they get away with it?" the Director asked. "I would think the families would report the girls missing."

"The girls sign an agreement saying they won't contact their families for one year. They tell them it's part of the confidentiality agreement. They can't contact their families until they become US citizens. The girls don't know any better. They're just trying to get a better life."

"That's horrible."

"They confiscate their passports and phones. The girls are easily trapped with no way of escape."

"We need to figure out how to get Belarus to shut that down," Coldclaw said.

Alex continued. "We're on it. Later today, Fabi Orlov, our new agent, is going to raid the offices of the company in Pinsk. Everyone associated with it will be arrested and questioned and all the files confiscated. Fabi is going to get us the names of the girls who were kidnapped and make it a high-profile thing. Get it some publicity so it can't be covered up."

"Good idea."

"President Rutherford needs to call Kuzman and Bobrinsky and put pressure on them to find the girls who have been trafficked and return them home," Brad said.

Rutherford was the President of the United States.

"He can make it a congratulatory phone call to Bobrinsky," the Director said. "An attaboy for cracking down on sex trafficking and uncovering the ring. We can put a reward out for the arrest of Asaf. Actually, put him on the ten-most-wanted list. Pretend he's still on the loose."

That sounded like a good idea to Alex.

"That reminds me," Director Coldclaw added, "Alex, you need to take the plane to Guantanamo Bay. We can't bring Asaf here. We'd have to get him an attorney. He'd have rights. There we can interrogate him. At the right time, we can announce that we arrested him."

Alex figured that was the best option, but it wasn't his call.

"We'll decide what to do with him later. For now, I don't want anyone to know we have him. Let Bobrinsky think he was behind the theft of the nukes. We can make them disappear altogether. I can't tell you how happy I am about this mission. The President is going to be very pleased. You did good, Alex."

"That sounds great. Jamie will be excited too."

"Where is Jamie?" Brad asked.

"She's still in Belarus."

"Why? She finished her mission. She found the pipeline. And a whole lot of other things. Why isn't she with you?"

Alex took a note from Jamie out of his pocket and held it in his hand reading it to himself.

Alex. You know I have to do this. It's who I am. Love, Jamie.

When he woke up Sunday morning, the note was on her pillow, and she was gone.

"Alex . . . Where is Jamie?" Brad demanded.

"She went to save the girls."

***

Earlier that morning
Sunday Morning, 1:30 a.m.

Jamie left the safehouse feeling bad about not saying goodbye to Alex. It had to be done. He would've tried to talk her out of going. Pointed out all the risks. The dangers. The fact that she had no idea where her friend's sister had been taken.

She wouldn't have any good arguments to refute him. So she left.

All she knew was the girls were somewhere in Russia. She didn't even know that. Asaf could've put them on flights going to the Middle East or any other parts unknown. If she'd had more time with Asaf, she might've gotten it out of him, but she had to get moving.

Alex thought the best plan of action was to regroup and call Brad. He was right. That's why she went ahead and left. Like the note said, it's who she was.

She wouldn't abandon her friend. Alex had also pointed out that Chastity could hardly be called a friend. They met once at *Splash* nightclub. But her sister, Olga, had called her on the train after being kidnapped. Turned to her for help.

Jamie couldn't get the fear in Olga's voice out of her mind. She'd want someone to help her if she were in that situation. Once it crossed that line of emotional connection, Jamie had to do everything she could to help her. But she had no idea how.

Three days had gone by, so finding Olga would be like finding a lost cell phone in the state of Texas. But she had to try. She needed some luck. Curly always said luck was when skill crossed the path of opportunity.

The skill was there. She now needed the opportunity. He also said people make their own luck in life. She intended to.

Finding Olga would have to wait a few hours. She had to do something else first.

Jamie walked several blocks to a main road and caught a cab to her hotel. After packing her possessions, she checked out then drove the three miles to the *Splash* nightclub. In her trunk was a large satchel she'd taken from Asaf's hotel room. Filled with what she estimated to be about a million dollars in cash.

Luck played a part in her even having the satchel. After Alex took Asaf out with the tray of food and drink, she scoured the room for anything that might be useful for intelligence. She took Asaf's phone and computer and left the rest. As she was leaving, she saw the satchel hidden in a closet. Figuring it was just clothes, she almost didn't look in it. She couldn't believe it when she saw it was filled with cash.

That's when the idea came to her. She had to hurry to the nightclub before the girls' shifts ended.

The bouncer at the door let her into the club without looking in the satchel after she slipped a hundred-dollar bill in his hand. The club was barely half full. Not nearly as packed as it had been the last time she was there.

Chastity wasn't hard to find, since she was standing around along with a hundred or so other women, clearly bored, without much to do. Her face lit up when she saw Jamie and came over to her immediately. Jamie hugged her and tried to match her enthusiasm, but her mood was more serious.

It was apparent that Chastity had no idea what had happened to her sister. Jamie would have to tell her.

"We need to go back to the room," Jamie said, referring to the VIP room they'd gone back to the first night they met.

"Sure," Chastity said. "Come this way. It's been a slow night. I'm sure it's available."

They walked back toward the curtain in the far corner. Jamie couldn't help but grin as she walked by the roped-off area where she met Asaf for the first time. She took great satisfaction in the fact that he was tied up on a couch in the safehouse and would soon be on his own airplane back to the U.S. or wherever Director Coldclaw decided to send him for interrogation.

The man at the entrance to the VIP rooms waved them through without so much as a second look. Turns out their room was in use, but the bigger one next to it wasn't. Even better. They went inside and closed the door.

Jamie sat the satchel on the table, opened it, and took out some documents.

"What are those, Allie?" Chastity asked.

"My real name is Jamie. I'm not an American tourist. I can't tell you who I work for, but I can tell you it's for the good guys, and I'm here to help you."

"My real name is Daria. Not Chastity."

"Daria, I have here a legal document, signed by Omer Asaf, the owner of *Splash*. It releases you from the contract you signed with *Belles of Belarus*. All you have to do is sign it, and you are out of the contract."

Jamie had typed up the agreement on the safehouse computer and printed it out. She then persuaded Asaf to sign it. Technically, it wasn't a document that would stand up in the court of law.

Any contract signed under duress was invalid. Asaf was definitely under duress when he signed it, but he wouldn't be in a position to contest its validity anytime in the near or distant future.

Daria took the document in her hand and said, "All I have to do is sign this, and I'm out of my agreement? Sounds too easy."

"You also have to agree to never go back into prostitution again."

Jamie took a pen out of the satchel and handed it to her. Daria signed her name without any objection or without even reading it.

Jamie opened the satchel and took out some money wrapped in a paper seal.

"This is five thousand American dollars. It's yours. Consider it a severance package."

Daria's eyes widened and her mouth opened into a confused look.

"This is for me? That's amazing. I can go back to school. I can go to America and see my sister."

She threw her arms around Jamie and said thank you several times. Jamie bit her lip. She wasn't ready to tell Daria about her sister yet.

"Listen carefully," she said. "Go out into the club and bring as many girls as you can back to this room. I want to talk to them."

"Sure. I can do that."

"Hurry," Jamie added. "We don't have much time."

A few minutes later, more than a hundred girls were cramped into the room. Several were still with men and Daria had left word with the bouncers to have them come see her when they were finished.

Daria instructed the girls in the water area to get dressed and come to the meeting as well. The room was buzzing. Something like this had probably never happened to them before.

The room was actually more of a suite. Large table, king-size bed, one nightstand with a clock on it. A couple of lamps and track lighting on the ceiling. A large picture on the wall above the bed.

It also had a couch up against the far wall, although it seemed out of place and looked like it was hardly ever used. Jamie stood near the couch, her back against the wall so she could face all the girls.

She quieted the group and began speaking.

"I am here to announce that *Splash* is permanently closed, effective immediately."

A groan went through the room.

"Why? What's going on?"

Jamie could hear the questions and confusion in their voices.

"I have it on good authority that the government of Belarus is seizing control of the nightclub, and the police will be raiding it at first light."

Jamie could feel a wave of fear go through the girls. The reaction she wanted. What she said was true. Fabi was going to bring the Militsia to the club early in the morning and take control of it.

Bobrinsky would likely seize all of Asaf's properties in Belarus after what had happened.

Jamie waved one of the documents in the air. Same as what Daria had signed. After Asaf had signed it, she had made 150 copies. Enough for all the girls.

She told them the same thing she told Daria. Sign the document and they would get $5,000 each. They had to leave immediately and agree not to go back into prostitution. Jamie knew some of the girls might eventually go back into it, but most wouldn't.

The money was an opportunity for them to start a new life. Courtesy of Omer Asaf.

Daria distributed the documents to the girls, everyone signed it and Jamie distributed $5,000 to each one of them. The girls could hardly contain their excitement.

"The agreement also has a confidentiality clause. That means you can't tell anyone about it," Jamie explained.

"We won't," she heard them saying.

"Go get your things and leave out the back entrance," Jamie said. "Good luck to all of you."

The girls filed out of the room. Daria went to get the rest of the girls who were probably finished by now, and they stayed until every girl signed the document and received their money. Jamie felt a great deal of satisfaction.

She counted the number of contracts. One hundred and thirteen girls were rescued that day. They were working at *Splash* voluntarily, but she considered them rescues anyway. They'd been exploited for money by rich men. This was their chance to get free from it. She only wished she could've helped the girls on the day shift.

As Jamie and Daria were packing up to leave, the manager of the club walked in, highly agitated.

"Where are the girls?" he asked, roughly.

"They left."

35

The manager of Splash was furious.

"Who told them they could leave? I have men out there who are clamoring for them."

"They aren't coming back," Jamie said.

"Yes, they are," he retorted angrily. "I'm going to call Asaf."

"Be my guest," Jamie said, sarcastically. "Doesn't change the fact the girls aren't coming back. They all quit."

"We'll have them arrested. For breaking their contracts."

"You're the one who should be worried about getting arrested," Jamie retorted sharply. "My sources tell me the police are going to raid the club at any time and close it. They might even be on their way here now. I suggest you and your men get out of here as soon as possible."

He started to object, but something stopped him. A fear or panic, judging by the look on his face. Probably some illegal things going on he didn't want anyone to know about.

He left the room without saying anything further.

Jamie and Daria didn't wait around to find out what happened next. They grabbed their things and went out the back entrance and ran to Jamie's car. Daria was laughing hysterically as they drove away. Her nightmare was finally over.

Jamie looked at her friend and forced a smile, knowing the happiness would be short-lived.

She'd have to tell her about her sister. Sooner rather than later.

***

Jamie drove the two of them to Daria's apartment, where she invited Jamie to spend the night, and she accepted.

Daria poured them both something to drink. A plan was starting to form in Jamie's head, and she needed Daria. First, she had to tell her the bad news.

"Your sister has been kidnapped," Jamie said.

The words sent a chill through the room.

" *Belles of Belarus* was a sham. There were no American men to marry. It was a front for sex trafficking."

Daria's look went from jubilation to panic in the blink of an eye.

"Where is Olga?" she asked, her voice cracking and tears starting to form in her eyes.

"I don't know. I was hoping you could help. Has she called you?"

"She called a couple times and left me messages," Daria said.

Her eyes were darting back and forth. She stood and went and got her phone. Her whole body was shaking. It was clear she was trying to hold it together. Jamie knew she could burst into tears at any time.

"The messages were so garbled, I couldn't make out what she said," Daria explained further. "She called me again tonight, but I was at work. I have another missed call from her."

A flicker of hope leapt up inside of Jamie. Her kidnappers must not have discovered the phone yet. They'd be ready the next time she called.

"Let me see your phone," Jamie said. She played all three voicemails, but the messages were unintelligible. "Did you set her phone up on a family plan?"

"Yes. It's on my account."

"Good. Let me go into your settings."

Jamie scrolled through the settings until she came to the location application. There was a feature on phones that would let her see the location of other phones on her family plan. Daria's feature was on. She hoped Olga's was as well.

She went into the sharing setting. Olga's phone was in there. It was on.

Jamie looked at the history which recorded the location of all calls between the phones. It showed the three calls.

"Do you have a computer?" she asked.

"Yes. It's in my bedroom."

They went into the room and Daria sat down at her desk and powered it on. An older model, but it would work. She entered the password and stood up from the chair so Jamie could sit in front of it.

Jamie pulled up a map of Russia. The first call Olga made was from Savitskiy Log. Just across the border into Russia. A set of train tracks was nearby. Olga mentioned they were on a train headed north.

Jamie hadn't told Daria that she got a call from Olga as well and might choose not to. She'd want to listen to the message. No way she'd let her. It was too chilling.

Savitskiy Log had to be the location where the girls were taken off the buses and put onto the trains. They had a starting point.

The second and third calls were made from a location further north. Probably after the girls were removed from the train.

Obninsk.

A small town an hour or so outside of Moscow. That's where Olga was a few hours ago. Or at least that's where her phone was. Jamie considered calling her but resisted the urge. Alex was right. The phone was the best link to her. Better if Olga could keep it hidden as long as possible.

The important thing was they now had a lead. A location.

Jamie told Daria what she found.

"I want to go with you," Daria said.

"I want you to. I need you to," Jamie responded.

"When do we leave?"

"Let's leave in the morning. I need to get some sleep and eat something."

Curly always said to eat and sleep when you can. On a mission, you never know when the next opportunity will come. Jamie had been up almost nonstop for three days. With little naps in between intense missions.

"I don't think I'm going to get much sleep," Daria said.

"I understand."

Jamie curled up on the couch. Those were her last words of the night, as she was out as soon as her head hit the cushion. She didn't remember anything else until the smell of coffee woke her up the next morning.

They scarfed down some breakfast and headed out as soon as they could. The first stop was a car dealership nearby that Jamie had found on her phone. They needed a better vehicle than her rental car. One that couldn't be traced back to her. She didn't know what they'd run into in Russia but was sure there'd be some trouble.

The dealership was closed since it was early Sunday morning, but Jamie called the number, and told the owner who answered she would pay cash. All she needed to say to get him to get up early and open the showroom.

They picked out a black, four door, Volvo Turbo SUV. After a little haggling, they settled on a price. Jamie counted out $60,000 American dollars and told him to keep the change for his trouble.

Part of the deal was that he signed over the title but didn't fill in the name of the buyer. That way it couldn't be traced to them in case they did something to draw the attention of the authorities.

He put a temporary sticker on the back.

The drive to Obninsk took nearly eight hours. Jamie considered going to Savitskiy Log first, but Olga wasn't there. She wanted to head straight to the last known location of the phone.

Olga drove most of the way so Jamie could research where they were going. She pulled up satellite images and found Savitskiy Log. She followed the train tracks all the way to Obninsk.

The tracks crossed over the road they were traveling on several times. Knowing Olga was right at that spot at one time was a sobering thought.

They made good time and pulled into the location just before dark. The locator indicated the phone was still there. She could feel optimism rising inside of her. Also, nervousness and adrenaline as she prepared for what they might find.

Jamie was ready to bolt into action and was much better prepared for this mission than she had been in Minsk. She had taken from the safehouse a gun, a rifle, a submachine gun, smoke bombs, grenades, and a two-way communication system so she and Daria could talk to each other.

And a few other things she might or might not need.

They made a couple passes by the building so she could check out the location. The complex wasn't as large as she expected. But everything else she envisioned in her mind was the same in every other way.

Located next to the railroad tracks, it had a fence all the way around it. Not a tall fence. Or a security fence. Just a chain link. Something easy to jump over. That told Jamie the girls were not at that location for very long.

Right off the road was a makeshift gate secured by a chain and padlock. Inside the fence was one building. Older. More of a warehouse but probably contained offices.

And buses. Several With color-coded cards in the windshields. Before they left Pinsk, Olga had sent Daria a text from her phone with a picture of her bus. She was in a blue bus she had said in the text.

The buses with the cards confirmed they were in the right place. The girls had ridden the train to this location. Also, a ten-to-twelve-seat passenger van was parked next to the buses.

No lights were on, and no cars were parked in front or in back. Obviously, the girls weren't there. Jamie related to Olga what she was thinking. Olga's optimism turned to disappointment.

Not for Jamie. She knew the ebbs and flows of missions. Nothing was generally this easy. Too much to expect to drive straight to the location and find Olga right off the bat.

This was a process. Almost like driving on the GPS route on a phone. Stay on the blue line. They were on the blue line. They'd tracked the girls from Pinsk all the way to a location in Russia. Where they were dropped off the train. Clearly, right there.

That was significant progress.

The phone was still showing the phone was at that location, which told Jamie that the phone had been found or Olga had left it behind. A long shot chance Olga was still there. Maybe hiding in the building.

Time to go find out.

36

Warehouse, Obninsk, 5:17 p.m.

Jamie easily slipped over the gate and into the compound, fairly certain no one was there. The road in front was not heavily traveled, but enough so that she hurried to make her way around to the back of the building.

The front had a door that appeared to be the main entrance, but she was sure there'd be a back entrance. The railroad tracks were in the back, and there was no way three-hundred kidnapped girls exited the train and walked around to the front entrance.

She tested her communication headset linked to Daria who was in the SUV parked a little way down the road. Far enough away where she wouldn't be associated with the building, but close enough that she could watch the entrance to warn Jamie if anyone happened to come by.

"Can you hear me?" Jamie asked.

"I can hear you great," Daria said.

"I'm entering now. Let me know if you see any hostiles."

"Will do! Good luck," Daria said, excitedly. The sound quality was good. The devices had been improved considerably over the years.

Jamie picked the lock to the back door in less than forty-five seconds. She'd expected it to take longer. The building had little to no security. No alarm. No deadbolts. No bars on the windows.

That told her the girls weren't there for very long. This was just a transition point.

The door opened into a large open room. She flipped on a pocket flashlight and took a quick glance around the room. A couple doors on the left side were probably closets, Jamie assumed. A door to the right was open and looked to lead to another section of the building.

Trash littered the floor. Water bottles, food wrappers, and some white hospital gowns were piled in a corner. A few had blood on them.

Jamie didn't spend much time looking around. While it confirmed the girls were there, she wouldn't find anything that might lead to where they were taken. That would be in an office, if there was one.

She went through the door off the right side of the room and found it led to a hallway and four offices. Two were empty of furniture. The only thing they contained were supplies, water bottles, and more of the white gowns.

The third had a desk and a phone but no files or papers. She skipped looking for anything in any of those three. The last office on the left was larger. It had a desk, a chair, one file cabinet in the back corner, and a safe.

She found what she was looking for on the desk. Right in plain view. A list. Three actually. On Belles of Belarus letterhead, its logo on the top right-hand corner. Definitive proof she was in the right place. The pages were professionally typed, and very well organized. Three pages.

A phone lay on the desk. A quick glance through verified it was Olga's. The battery was almost dead. They had obviously found it. She slipped it into her pocket and turned her focus back to the lists.

She hoped Olga hadn't paid too great a price for having it and that none of the blood in the other room was hers.

Jamie studied the pages in detail. Each page had a different heading on the first line: Red Buses, White Buses, Blue Buses. The Red and Blue lists each had a hundred and twenty names on them. The White bus list had sixty names.

She scanned the names on the Blue Bus list. There were three Olgas.

She suddenly realized she didn't know Daria's last name. She thought about asking her on the headset, but it wasn't necessary. Her sister was one of the three. For sure. She'd find out which one soon enough.

Someone had written on the top of each page. A man's handwriting. He wrote A-Mon on the red bus list, G-Mon on white, and Z-Mon on the blue in big letters. Jamie deduced that the writing was the location where the buses took the girls.

She had already decided the buses out front were not the same ones that came from Belarus. If they were, why transfer the girls to a train? They would've just stayed on the buses.

Those were likely back in Belarus. These took the girls somewhere else. Somewhere close enough for the buses to come back there.

Five names were scratched through and written on a yellow pad. At the top of the page was the word airport. The names were Sofia Invanova, Anastasia Eltsina, Elisaveta Smimov, Yonna Kutznetsov, and Ksenya Alexeev.

It was obvious those girls were sent somewhere out of the country. Probably flown to the Middle East. Why those particular girls were chosen wasn't apparent. Could've been by looks, age, or by random selection.

One of the Olgas on the blue list had a star beside her name and the initials M.E. written next to it. There were three girls with the initials M.E. beside their names. That probably meant those three girls were singled out and taken to a separate location from the others.

One girl on a red bus had the word "mine" written beside her name.

Some thoughts were coming together in Jamie's mind. She had a feeling the girls on each list were all taken to the same location. The blue bus girls went to Z-Mon.

What did that mean?

She pulled out her phone and took a picture of each page. Then she went to the file cabinet, opened it, and found four other files.

Each file contained the same thing with the same handwriting on the top. An abbreviated letter, a dash, and Mon.

What was a Mon?

Dates were also on top of the pages. Jamie was thankful that Belles of Belarus was so organized and had left such a good paper trail.

According to the dates, five groups of three hundred girls had been brought to Russia.

Fifteen hundred girls! The number was staggering. All thought they were going to America; instead, they were sold into the sex trade. An anger built in Jamie as each piece of information brought the picture more into focus.

She took pictures of each file and put them back in the cabinet in the same order so it would look like they weren't disturbed. She pulled up her phone and googled Z-Mon Russia Obninsk.

Nothing meaningful came up. She really didn't expect it to. She needed more information.

Jamie scrolled through her contacts and called one of them. A woman answered.

"Jill, it's Jamie. I don't have much time to talk. I'm on a mission. I need your help."

Jill Vanderbilt was the director of *Save the Girls* for the Eastern European division. She was located in Brussels, but the organization had locations throughout the world. They were the largest rescue organization in the world.

As a non-profit, they were well respected. Ninety percent of their donations went to rescuing girls, and thousands were helped each year.

"How can I help you, Jamie?"

They had worked together long enough that Jill knew to skip the small talk and get right to the problem at hand.

"I'm onto something big. There's a bear outside my door."

Jill would know Jamie was either in Russia or an adjoining country. The bear was the symbol of Russia and a code name they often used for it.

Save the Girls had an office in Russia and did a lot of work there. The government let them exist to give the appearance they were helping in the fight, even though the government was part of the problem.

"If you were going to kidnap fifteen hundred girls, where would you take them in Moscow?" Jamie asked. "In groups of one hundred."

"I don't know off hand. I've never heard of such a thing."

"It's happening. I have proof. I just don't know where they are. Think. What facility would house a hundred girls and keep them isolated with no way to escape?"

"A prison obviously."

"I don't think many men are going to go to a prison to pay for sex," Jamie said.

"An abandoned prison. Renovated."

"I don't think so. It has to be nicer than that. I still don't think guys would go there. The stigma. Are they going to do it in prison cells? Not going to happen."

"A school," Jill said. "An abandoned school. They obviously couldn't operate out of a functioning school. Even a college wouldn't be feasible."

"Schools don't have living quarters. It would cost too much to renovate."

"A hotel?"

"Not secure enough," Jamie answered. "Too many windows. Exits. No way to guard the girls. They could put bars on the windows, but hotels are right out in the open in high traffic commercial areas. If there were bars on the windows everyone would see them and ask questions."

Silence on the line as both of them were thinking.

"What about a church?" Jill asked. "An abandoned church? Maybe. Couldn't be an active church for obvious reasons."

"There are no living quarters," Jamie responded. "Does Mon ring a bell to you? What would it be short for?"

More silence as Jill was clearly thinking.

"Never mind," Jamie suddenly said, excitedly. "I know what Mon stands for."

"What?"

"No time. Jill. Can you get me thirty men or women in short notice? In Russia. Near Moscow. Obninsk to be exact. They need to be experienced," Jamie added. "There might be some danger. They also need to be able to drive a bus."

"I can try."

"Don't try. Do it. I need them fast. Have them go to the Hotel Na Mirnum. Check in under the name we always use."

Jamie froze. She heard a sound.

"I've got to go. Get me the thirty people," she said as she ended the call.

A faint sound.

Coming from another room.

Somewhere in the building.

Most people probably wouldn't have heard it. Sounded like a chain. Rattling, at slight movement. Accidental probably. The person didn't want to be heard.

Jamie knew that sound. She'd heard it before.

37

Jamie listened intently. She heard the sound again.

She put her phone in her back pocket and took out her gun. She peered around the corner. The lights were all out. She moved slowly toward the sound or at least where she thought it was coming from.

Off the main room. Jamie had assumed they were storage rooms. She was kicking herself for not clearing the building. It seemed empty.

Jamie crept up to the door. She heard whimpering. Light sobbing. A girl.

The door was locked. She put her gun back in the holster attached to a belt at her waist and picked the lock easily. She took her pen light out of her pocket and opened the door, shining it into the room.

More a closet than a room. Empty except for one old-looking mattress on the floor, and a girl lying on it. Squinting trying to adjust her eyes to the light.

Her hair was mussed. A chain was around her ankle secured by a key lock. The other end of the chain was attached to the wall.

A bowl of water was on the ground next to her. It looked like a dog's bowl.

The sight broke Jamie's heart.

The light brown-haired girl was wearing a white gown. She still had makeup on. Smeared from the crying. Barefoot. Her ankle was bleeding from the chain rubbing against it. Not Olga. She looked nothing like Daria.

"It's going to be okay," Jamie said gently. "I'm here to help you. What's your name?"

The girl didn't respond. Jamie knelt down beside her and pushed her hair out of her eyes. She wiped the tears off of her face with her fingers. Kissed her gently on the forehead. A gesture to earn her trust.

"Are you hurt?" Jamie asked.

The girl said no, meekly.

It took almost five minutes for Jamie to pick the lock on the chain around the ankle because it was an older, rusty key lock. Jamie imagined the key actually stuck when inserted. Once free, the girl clutched Jamie, gripping her arms, as if afraid Jamie might leave her.

"I'm going to get you out of here," Jamie said.

A voice in her headset erupted. "Hostile just pulled up to the entrance," Daria shouted, with panic in her voice.

"How many?"

"One man. From what I can tell. He's getting out of his car. He's opening the lock on the gate. He's opening it. You've got to get out of there! He's driving in."

"Calm down," Jamie said. "I'm going to sign off for now. You won't hear from me for a few minutes."

Jamie turned to the girl. It pained her to say it, but she had no choice.

"I'm so sorry. You're going to have to stay in this room. Just for a few minutes."

"No!" she shrieked. "You can't leave me here."

She gripped Jamie's arm like a vise. She tried to stand and used Jamie's arm to pull herself up.

"I'm sorry. It can't be helped. I have to go. It will only be for a few minutes."

Jamie forced her back onto the mattress. Gave her the pen light so she'd have light in the room.

"You have to stay really quiet. I'm going to come back for you. I promise. Trust me. I won't leave you."

Jamie closed the door, her heart breaking for the girl. She locked it. Hoping the girl would stay quiet.

She turned on all the lights in the main room, walked through the side door, down the hallway, and back to the office where she turned on every light in the hallway and in the office. She put her elbows on the desk, her phone to her ear, and started talking in a loud voice.

Jamie heard the man open the back door which she had left unlocked. She imagined the look on his face was one of disbelief when he heard a voice and saw all the lights on..

"Gav-no!" she heard the man say.

The literal translation for the Russian word was cow excrement. In that context, the man meant it as a four-letter curse word. Americans had a similar word.

Jamie started speaking louder. In Russian. Loud enough for the man to hear her. She pretended to be having a heated discussion on her phone.

The man stormed into the office. Jamie was glad he didn't have a weapon. If he did, it probably would have been drawn. She had no idea if her plan would work. She'd thought about taking him out when he walked through the door then interrogating him. But that would take time. She needed information and needed it fast.

Confirmation really. She thought she knew where they'd taken the girls, but if she could pull off the acting job, she might gain his trust and find out what she needed to know much faster.

" Ты кто," the man said roughly. "Who are you?"

Jamie held up her hand to silence the man and gave him a glare at the same time. She continued to talk into the phone like she was angry at the person on the other line. She hung up the phone abruptly, stood, and held out her hand.

"I'm Candice. With *Belles of Belarus*."

The man tilted his head to the side with a confused look and didn't immediately shake her hand. Jamie held up one of the papers on the desk. She pointed to the name on the letterhead.

"Candice Smith, CEO. That's me. There's been a huge mistake. The girls that came in Saturday morning on the train. They went to the wrong place."

The man's eyes narrowed. His eyebrows furrowed. His lips tightened. Clearly confused. Probably wondering what to do next.

Jamie surmised that the girl in the closet was the one with the word "mine" next to it. Either his payment or a girl he stole to keep as his own slave, figuring no one would notice. He'd come to spend time with his prize.

"What monasteries did these girls go to?" Jamie asked. She'd quickly learn if her theory was right.

He didn't answer.

"What does A, G, and Z stand for?"

She handed the man the lists of girls. He still seemed unsure of himself.

"The A is Arkzysheskya Monastery, G is Gorissky, and Z is Zaissonapassky," he finally said.

The confirmation she needed. She was right.

Russia had dozens of monasteries around the region that were abandoned years ago as fewer and fewer people became monks and the older ones died off. Jamie had read that young people in Russia were abandoning the Russian Orthodox Church in droves. No one wanted to be a monk anymore.

The facilities were a perfect place to hide and imprison girls. They would have living quarters, offices, a chapel, and most importantly, large walls, built to keep people out and the monks in. Their lifestyle was one of complete isolation from the world.

Jamie assumed Asaf purchased them, had them renovated, and the girls were taken to each one.

The men probably came to the chapel, made their payments, then went back to the living quarters with the girls, where they had sex.

The men had privacy; the women were trapped; and tens of thousands of dollars were made out of each monastery every month.

Ingenuous plan considering the depravity it would take to come up with such a scheme.

Jamie's own ingenuous plan was forming. Time to ratchet up the rhetoric and put it into action.

"No! No! No!" Jamie said, raising her voice considerably.

"What?"

The man seemed genuinely concerned. So far, the ruse was working.

"They weren't supposed to go to monasteries," Jamie said. She had raised the tension in the room several more notches. "They were supposed to go to the *Palace of the Idokopas Cape.*"

Jamie started pacing around. Her hands and arms animated as she spoke.

The man's eyes widened in fear. She got the reaction she wanted at the mention of the Palace.

"I didn't know," he said, stuttering his words. "It's not my fault."

"Whose fault is it then?" Jamie said angrily.

The Palace was better known as Dacha Kuzman or Kuzman's Palace. It was a large Italianate Palace built on the coast of the Black Sea for President Kuzman. Estimated to cost more than a billion dollars to build. A massive complex complete with shops, restaurants, and recreational facilities.

"The girls were supposed to be taken there so they could entertain President Kuzman and his guests," Jamie explained. "This is a disaster."

The mention of the president struck fear in every citizen, especially those who had dealings with Kuzman that went bad. The man standing in front of Jamie would be wondering if he was in real trouble. Thoughts of prison, torture, and Siberia were probably running through his mind. Especially since he had stolen one of Kuzman's girls, or so she would lead him to believe.

"We've got to get the women back," Jamie implored. "And to the right place. Sit down. What's your name?"

"Yuri," he said, as he dutifully sat in the chair in front of the desk.

"I need your help. Let's go over the lists," Jamie said.

The man was extremely helpful.

Slightly less than three hundred girls were taken to the monasteries. Fortunately, they were all within thirty minutes of their location.

Yuri had a man in charge of each facility. He called each one and told them that a fleet of buses would be coming to pick up the girls to transport them to a different location. They were to see that the girls were ready to go by tomorrow.

"What about these girls that went to the airport? Where did they go?" Jamie demanded to know.

"I don't know. I swear. They got on a private plane."

"What about these girls that have a star by their name? It says M.E next to it."

"M.E. stands for Mordo Estate. Three girls went there."

Jamie knew of the estate from her research driving over. It was a large residential complex owned by Vagit Mordo, an oligarch who was the Deputy of Fuel and Energy for Russia. One of the world's richest men.

Yuri explained that the girls were taken to his estate to be his personal servants and escort companions for ninety days. Then they were to be replaced with new women.

She didn't want Yuri calling the estate. The oligarch was a powerful man with contacts in the government. The bogus story worked with the imbecile in front of her but wouldn't work with a sophisticated government official who could easily verify it wasn't true.

I'll have to go there myself.

Thirty minutes later, Jamie exited the building, turned out all the lights, and locked the back door. The girl from the closet was with her. Yuri had taken her place in the closet. His ankle was chained to the wall. The door to the closet was locked. The light out.

A bowl of water sat in the dog bowl next to him.

38

Mordo Estate,
Obninsk, Russia

Jamie received confirmation that the last bus carrying the last group of girls had just arrived in Belarus. Jill, the Director of *Save the Girls*, had managed to find enough people to aid in the rescue of the fifteen hundred girls and Jamie's plan had worked to perfection.

She went to a tour bus company and ordered a fleet of buses which were delivered to the warehouse where the girls were originally brought by train from Belarus. Jill's team arrived shortly thereafter, and Jamie went over the mission with the drivers.

They were to drive to a monastery, fill their bus up with girls, and drive them to Pinsk, Belarus. Jill had contacted Detective Fabi Orlov who would be there to meet them and gather their statements as more proof against the employees of *Belles of Belarus* and Omer Asaf.

Save the Girls and Detective Orlov would share the credit for rescuing the fifteen hundred girls. No one would know Jamie was involved, which was how the CIA liked it.

Yuri, the man who oversaw the operations at the warehouse in Obninsk, was extremely helpful once again. He called the guards at all of the monasteries instructing them that the girls were going to be picked up and transported to another location and not to provide any resistance or question their actions.

Jamie found most people helpful when they had a gun to their head.

Yuri was now in Belarus. He'd traveled with them on the bus in the underneath luggage compartment, his hands and feet bound, and his mouth gagged. Probably being arrested by Fabi about that time.

He was a Russian citizen, and his family in Russia would probably wonder what happened to him, but they would likely never know. People had a way of disappearing in the Belarus prison system.

Jamie didn't know if Bobrinsky knew about the sex trafficking, but he'd no doubt be at the forefront of reveling in the success of its demise. He'd do everything in his considerable power to shut it down and even take credit. Spout off to the world his resolve to end human trafficking in his country.

Jamie despised politicians for this reason. Many were downright corrupt. All were opportunistic. Hypocritical and insincere. They did what was politically expedient. Fifteen hundred girls kidnapped right under Bobrinsky's nose was a huge stain on his leadership. He had no choice but to turn it around and take credit for the rescue.

Act appalled. Even if he wasn't.

Jamie couldn't care less at this point. She was relieved that the girls were safe. Now she could focus on the mission at hand.

A number of girls had been sent to Mordo Estate. Including Daria's sister, Olga. She had to figure out how to rescue them. Even if Olga hadn't been one of the girls sent there, Jamie had no intention of leaving any of the girls behind.

So, she had to quickly devise a plan to get Olga and two other girls out. Preferably without a gunfight.

First came the surveillance. Curly ingrained in Jamie the need for preparation when you had the time. In this instance, she didn't have much time. She did decide to wait until the other girls were out of the country, before she acted.

It was a delicate balancing act and a roll of the dice. Word would eventually get back to the owner of the estate and the girls would be moved or killed. She hoped and prayed it wouldn't be until after the fifteen hundred girls were safe. At this point, she had to consider them first.

Missions were fraught with these types of moral dilemmas. She wanted to rescue the three girls, but the greater number took priority.

That didn't mean she couldn't use the time wisely and scope out the estate. It became immediately clear that the rescue had several complications.

The compound was a fifteen-hundred acre sprawling fortress. Jamie expected guards but didn't expect a bastion. An electric fence surrounded the entire estate. Security cameras and motion sensors ensured that no one could enter the area by way of the fences without detection.

One single road led in and out and was manned by a security guard who carried an assault rifle with a thirty-round magazine. Ten to twelve other soldiers were interspersed throughout the estate.

A covert operation, by herself, was not going to work. A direct assault with gunfire was out of the question. Jamie had to come up with a different plan.

If she somehow managed to get inside the compound, her biggest challenge would be finding the girls. She didn't even know for sure that they were there.

The main house was forty-thousand square feet. Two swimming pools, three tennis courts, a bath house, a fitness center, and a building that housed offices.

A separate four-thousand square foot two story house in the back was the most likely place to house them. An armed guard stood in front of the house twenty-four hours a day. Why would a soldier be guarding a guest house?

It gave her hope that they were still there.

Soldiers were stationed around the main house, which made sense. Mordo would require around-the-clock protection. But Jamie figured Mordo wouldn't want three sex slaves living in his primary residence.

The guesthouse was the next likely alternative.

Jamie learned from surveillance that the guards at the gate worked three eight-hour shifts. Six in the morning to two in the afternoon; two to ten and then ten to six.

After a long think, Jamie finally decided on a plan. She'd actually considered it back in Belarus. It's the reason she wanted to bring Daria with her to Russia. Under any other circumstances, she never would've considered bringing a civilian into such a dangerous situation. Even if it was the victim's sister.

Now was the time to share her plan with Daria.

"How are we going to get inside?" Daria asked Jamie.

"We're going to drive right up to the gate," Jamie answered.

Daria's eyes widened.

"Won't they arrest us?"

"Maybe."

"I don't understand."

"We'll arrive at the gate right after the two o'clock shift change."

She explained the plan fully to Daria.

"Do you think it'll work?" Daria asked nervously.

"You don't have to do this," Jamie responded.

"I want to. She's my sister. She'd do it for me."

"It's very dangerous. We may not make it out alive."

"I know. What are we waiting on? Let's do it," Daria said.

They were about a mile down the road from the estate hidden in a cluster of trees. Standing outside of the black SUV.

Once Daria was willing to go along with it, Jamie said to her, "Hold out your hands and put your wrists together."

Daria did so.

Jamie had some bindings in her hand and used them to tie Daria's wrists together. To where they looked snug, but Daria could squeeze her hands out of them if she had to.

Jamie helped Daria into the passenger seat. They drove to the entrance of the estate. Daria was surprisingly calm.

Jamie made a mental note to slow her own heartbeat. She'd soon know if the first part of her plan was going to work. If it didn't, she expected a shootout.

Arrest wasn't an option. The guards would never take them alive. If things went south, she'd try and shoot her way out of safety.

Jamie felt confident that she could kill the guard at the front gate before he killed her. She was not as confident that she could make it to the guest house. Even if she did, how was she going to find Olga and get her and the other girls out?

While she was well armed, one gunman was no match for a small army of guards with machine guns. She needed to get them to voluntarily let her in.

She approached the entrance and the guard motioned for them to stop. A large, fortified gate blocked the entrance anyway. She couldn't have penetrated the guard gate, even if she wanted to.

If the guard didn't let her in, she'd shoot him, then abandon the car, and sprint to the house. Killing whoever got in her way. She'd find the girls and do her best to lead them back to the car.

Daria was instructed to run back to the cluster of trees. Jamie would pick her up once she had the girls safely out of the compound.

If she didn't return, then Daria was to assume the worst and go back to Belarus.

Let's hope it doesn't come to that.

Jamie rolled down her window and greeted the guard in a friendly manner.

"I'm bringing the girl back from the doctor's office," Jamie said.

The soldier peered through the window. Jamie was praying he'd seen Olga before. A look of recognition flashed across his face. Daria and Olga were identical twins. Jamie couldn't tell them apart in pictures and doubted the soldier could either, or at least that's what she hoped.

"I didn't know the girl wasn't in the estate," he said.

"She got sick and had to go to the doctor. I'm the doctor's assistant. They called me to pick her up and bring her back. I don't remember you. There was a different guard here when I arrived."

"We just changed shifts. Let me check the records. He should've written it down."

The soldier went back to the guard station and flipped through some papers. He came back to the car scratching the side of his head, confused.

"There's nothing written down."

Jamie just shrugged her shoulders.

"I'll just leave her here with you," Jamie said. "I don't have to go in. She can be your problem."

The guard looked down the road. It was more than a mile to the house.

"I can't leave my station," he responded. "Take her in and drop her off and come right back out."

" *Spa-see-ba.*" She thanked the guard.

The guard raised the gate, and the concrete barrier went down into the ground. Jamie drove through the entrance, down the main road, and around the back of the main house to the guest house.

If the girls weren't there, Jamie would have to improvise. At least they were inside the compound, and she had a weapon. The guard hadn't bothered to search them. Probably a breach in protocol.

She let out a sigh of relief when she was safely away from the guard house. Daria squealed with delight. Thankfully, after they were out of the guard's sight.

Jamie pulled up to the guest house and got out of the vehicle. She went around to the other side and opened the door to help Daria out. A guard standing at the front door of the house was looking at them in an alert but relaxed state.

He seemed to have recognized Daria as well. Jamie figured he wouldn't ask any questions since they had already made it past the main gate.

"I'm bringing the girl back," Jamie offered even though he didn't ask. "She went to the doctor."

She'd soon know if this was where they kept the girls. By the reaction of the guard, it was.

He stepped away from the front door and motioned for them to go into the house.

Jamie led Daria through the door and into what was a large hallway. The downstairs appeared to be the main living area with a full kitchen and dining room. The upstairs was likely where the girls stayed.

No one was downstairs. They needed to move quickly before anyone got suspicious.

Jamie took the bindings off of Daria's wrist and then bolted up the stairs, two at a time. She counted at least eight bedrooms in the upstairs section.

She called out Olga's name.

No response.

Daria ran past Jamie, frantically looking in each room.

They heard a sound coming from the end of the hall. Daria was already running toward it. The girls were in an upstairs living area, watching television. Jamie spotted Olga immediately.

Daria threw herself at Olga, hugging her tightly, crying. Olga rubbed her eyes as if she didn't believe what she was seeing. The other two girls stood there with their mouths opened in disbelief.

Jamie took control. There'd be time for celebrating later. They weren't out of danger, yet. Far from it.

"Each of you get a blanket," Jamie said. "Put shoes on. Leave everything else behind. Then follow me back downstairs. We're getting out of here."

"Don't worry," Daria said to Olga and the other girls. "You can trust her."

The girls scrambled to find blankets.

"Hurry. Wrap the blankets around you," Jamie said. "Especially you, Olga. I don't want the guard to see your face."

This was the tricky part.

How was she going to get the girls in the car without the guard out front stopping them?

39

Jamie took the girls downstairs and staged the living room the way she wanted it. She put Olga in the first room in the hallway nearest the entrance. One girl laid down on the couch, the blanket over her. Daria and the other girl stood next to her, looking concerned.

Satisfied, Jamie walked down the hallway, opened the door, and called for the guard.

"Hurry. I need your help." Jamie said. "The other girls are sick."

The guard rushed past her. Olga emerged from hiding in the first bedroom and slipped out the front door. Jamie ran behind the guard to block his view if he should turn around. Olga was told to go straight to the car and get in the back seat on the floor out of sight.

"Help the girl on the couch," Jamie said to the soldier. "Get her in the car. I have to get her to the hospital."

The soldier helped the girl to her feet. He walked her down the hallway, out the door, and over to the car. Daria and the third girl followed behind.

"Put her in the front seat," Jamie said.

Daria opened the door for him. The other girl got in the backseat on Jamie's side.

"These girls are going to have to be quarantined," Jamie said to the guard. "I'm taking all of them to the hospital."

The soldier started to object. Jamie cut him off.

"I suggest you go wash your hands. She's very contagious."

The guard's eyebrows raised, and he looked at his hands. Then went back in the house.

When all four were safely in the SUV, Jamie backed out of the driveway, and began driving to the entrance. She sped up slightly. Still trying to maintain a reasonable speed so as not to alert anyone. She approached the guard gate and rolled down the passenger side window.

"This girl's really sick as well. I've got to take her to the hospital. All the girls have to be quarantined. They have infectious typophacus."

He hesitated.

"I wouldn't get too close," Jamie said. "It's really contagious."

The guard stepped back and looked like he was holding his breath.

"Don't forget to write it down," Jamie said emphatically. "The girls will be in the hospital for a minimum of three days. I don't want the same problem when I bring them back."

"No problem," he said, as he went back to the guardhouse and raised the gate. Jamie could see him writing on a clipboard.

Once they were a good distance away, the girls started cheering wildly.

Jamie couldn't stop grinning either. This was her favorite part of her job.

They drove to the Hotel *Na Mirnum* in center city Obninsk. The hospital ruse would buy them time. Not much but a little. Word could've already gotten out about the monastery girls disappearing. Mordo would come investigating.

The girls were laughing and having a good time as they got out of the car and went into Jamie's hotel room.

"Infectious typophocus," one said. "Is that a real disease?"

"I made it up," Jamie admitted.

"It was brilliant," Daria said.

Jamie made sure all the girls were okay. They were physically. Emotionally it would take time. Fortunately, she had gotten to them before they had suffered too much pain.

She told the girls to sit on the bed. She wanted to discuss something with them. She had the title for the SUV in her hand. She signed Daria's name on the buyer's line.

"It's yours," she said, handing it to her.

Daria's mouth gaped open.

"I don't know what to say. Are you sure? Is that legal?"

"If anybody asks, just say your rich uncle left it to you."

Jamie took $5,000 in cash out of the satchel and gave it to Olga and then gave the other two girls the same amount. She didn't bother having them sign any agreement.

"Nothing will compensate you for what happened," Jamie said. "At least this will help you get a new start in life."

The girls started crying and thanked and hugged Jamie.

"Get on the road and drive straight home. Don't even stop for food or gas. Wait until you're out of the country."

"Were all the girls rescued?" Olga asked.

"Not all of them," Jamie replied. "There were some girls taken to the airport."

"Do you know their names?"

Jamie pulled up the list on her phone. She had sent the original files back with one of the bus drivers.

"Here are the names," Jamie said, handing Olga her phone.

Olga began to cry.

"Oh no! Anastasia is on this list. She's only fourteen."

One of the other girls was looking at it, standing next to her, "I know Sofia. She's only fifteen. She's from my hometown."

Jamie now knew how they picked the girls for the airport. They chose the young ones.

"You have to find Ana," Olga implored. "She was already scared to death. No telling what they're doing to her."

"I don't know where she is," Jamie retorted.

"Can't you find her?"

Jamie let out a loud sigh.

"Yes. I can find her, and I will. I promise. You girls get going. The sooner you're out of here the better I'll feel."

After several hugs and a few more tears, the girls were on their way.

Jamie walked back into the hotel room and fell backward on the bed. Exhausted. Frustrated. Knowing she had to go back to work.

How am I going to find them? They could be anywhere in the world!

She had to try. It's who she was.

***

Jamie allowed herself a two-hour nap. When she woke up, she felt worse. She grabbed a power bar and an energy drink from a convenience store next door then called Jill to arrange a ride for her. A man met her at the door. She insisted on loading the bags herself.

The satchel was still full of almost $400,000. The cache of weapons from the safehouse were heavy, but she didn't want anyone else handling them. Her backpack was the only other thing she was carrying.

He drove her to a nearby local rental car place. Easier to load her equipment into a car there than at the airport. She left the rental car place and drove to the CIA safehouse in Moscow. After unloading her equipment, she called Brad.

"Hey, Denworthy," Jamie said.

"Lynda Carter, good to finally hear from you. You've been busy."

Jamie let out a chuckle. Lynda Carter played Wonder Woman on a television show back years ago.

She didn't feel like Wonder Woman. She felt a little hopeless at the moment. She couldn't get her mind off the young girls who still needed rescuing.

"It's been a productive week I'd say," Brad said.

There's no way he could give her a hard time for disobeying orders. What Jamie had accomplished looked as good for him as much as it did her. A lot of people would be really happy about this mission.

"Good work," he added.

Jamie was shocked. Brad didn't give out compliments often.

"When are you coming home?"

"About that ... I'm not coming home. Not yet, anyway."

"Why am I not surprised?"

"There are five more girls missing. They were taken to the airport. I want to find them."

"You've already saved more than fifteen hundred women and girls. You can't save all of them."

1643 actually.

Brad didn't know about the hundred and forty-three at *Splash* nightclub. He'd never know about them, but she did, and they were in her count.

"I may not be able to find them, but they were the youngest girls. Fourteen and fifteen years old. I have to try."

"I thought sixteen was the minimum age for the mail order bride business."

"Me too. They probably lied or something. Or were recruited because of their age. But they were specifically singled out and put on a private plane. I'm going to find them."

"Okay. Good luck. Let me know if I can help."

Jamie hung up slowly. Brad couldn't help, but she knew someone who could.

The call with Brad had been easier than she imagined. Brad didn't put up a fight at all. The success of the mission gave her some capital. It would run out eventually, but she would keep using it as long as she could.

She dialed another number.

"Well, hello," Alex said, with excitement in his voice.

"Hey, to you too," Jamie replied sweetly.

"I delivered the package," Alex said. He didn't know she was on a secure line.

"I knew you would. You're probably taking all the credit too. We're secure by the way."

"Okay. Of course, I'm taking the credit. The terrorism thread was my side of the mission. Tough luck kid."

"I think I did all right on my mission. I found the girls."

"You did? That's great."

"All of them," she said.

"All three hundred of them?"

"No. All that were kidnapped over the five months. Fifteen hundred of them. I'm so glad I didn't listen to you and went and found them."

"Ouch!"

"I'm just kidding. Seriously. We did it. This was a huge success. We got Asaf. We got the girls back. I couldn't have done it without you. You were amazing."

"Back at you."

"I need a favor."

"Legal or illegal."

"Does it matter?"

"No. I just wondered."

"Legal if you are in the U.S., illegal if you're in Russia. I'm in Russia right now. So, you're in the clear. My neck is the one on the line."

"That's the way I like it."

"Shut up and do me a favor."

"What's the favor?"

"A plane left the Ostafyevo International Business Airport last Sunday. Private plane. Rich businessman. I need to know where it went."

There was no response from Alex.

"How soon can you let me know?" Jamie asked.

"Hang on."

She could hear typing in the background.

About a minute later, Alex came back on the line. "The plane went to an island in Turkey. The plane and island are owned by Emin Patel."

"What took you so long? I've been waiting for nearly a minute," Jamie said sarcastically.

"I had to take a drink of soda first."

"What's the name of the island?"

"Do I have to do everything for you?"

"Never mind, I can look it up," Jamie retorted.

"I already have it. Guzellik Cay. Guzellik means *beauty* in Turkey. Beautiful Key is the literal translation."

"Is there anything you don't know?"

"The island is one-hundred-fifty acres. It has a landing strip. Who says crime doesn't pay?"

"Tell me about it."

She looked over at the satchel full of four hundred thousand dollars. Walking around money for Asaf. Pocket change.

Alex continued. She could hear him typing on the keyboard in the background.

"That's where he landed the plane. The island is a hundred miles from the mainland. That's a good place to enslave women. They aren't going to swim to safety, but it's close enough for a helicopter ride over. He probably entertains guests on the island."

"They aren't women," Jamie said in a serious tone. "They're young girls. Fourteen and fifteen."

"Oh ... That type of island. There's a Muslim temple. With a gold dome. Beautiful beaches. What's your next move?"

"I'm going to go there. To find the starfish on the beach."

40

Jamie rented a private jet from the Ostafyevo International Business Airport and was on her way to the island in the Aegean Sea to rescue Ana and any other girls being held by Emin Patel. She had satellite images up on her computer and studied the small island to determine a strategy.

A plan had formulated in her mind.

Alex had hacked into Patel's cell phone and found that he was in the Mediterranean Sea on his private yacht on a likely course back to his island from Athens, Greece.

Jamie was on a race to get back to the island before him.

The ruse of her posing as Candice Smith, the CEO of *Belles of Belarus* had worked so well in Obninsk, she decided to use the same strategy on Patel's island. She'd pretend that she was there under Patel's instructions to pick up the girls and take them to him.

Hopefully, whoever was on the island would be gullible enough to fall for it. If everything went well, she could land and get the girls out without a gun fight. More than likely, only one or two armed guards were on the island anyway—maybe none.

No reason for guards when the girls had no way to get off the island anyway.

The pilot interrupted her preparations when he came on the intercom and said, "Jamie, we are nearing the island. You should come up here and look at this."

Jamie had called Jill at *Save the Girls* and asked her to find a pilot preferably experienced in rescues. She thought about hiring a private pilot but didn't want to put an unsuspecting person in that kind of danger.

Calling Brad was not an option. He'd nix the operation altogether. Mike Mertens, one of Jill's employees out of Brussels, had twenty-years of experience as a commercial pilot and had been with the organization for two years flying Jill around the world.

He was aware of the risks and more than willing to take them to save the girls. Jamie took the co-pilot seat next to him.

"Look over there," Mike said.

On the island was a building with a gold dome on top. Alex had said that Patel had built a Muslim temple on the island. A strange sight for an island paradise.

Jamie concluded that more than likely Patel used it for more than religious purposes by using the girls to create some kind of sick religious, sexual experiences for him and his guests.

"Let's circle the island a few times and see what we see," Jamie said. "Without making it too obvious we're there."

Mike made a broad sweep around the island, and from their vantage point they weren't able to see any armed guards. One woman was sitting on the beach. She appeared to be reading a book.

"I hope the girls are still here," Jamie said. There were no signs of them.

"He might've moved them if he got word of what happened up in Belarus," Mike said. "Or they might be on his yacht."

"Let's hope not. Make one more pass."

Mike circled around. He suddenly pointed off in the distance.

"Look! Over there," he said with a sense of urgency.

A large dot. A boat.

Patel's yacht?

Still a long way away, but it appeared to be heading in the direction of the island at a normal speed.

"In my briefcase behind you are some binoculars," Mike said. "Grab those and let's take a look."

"It's clearly a yacht," Jamie said, peering through them. "No way to know if it's Patel's or not."

Jamie handed the binoculars to Mike to look through.

"I think we've been spotted," he said. "There are people on the deck pointing in our direction. I also see men with machine guns on the deck."

A jolt of adrenaline powered through Jamie.

"How long will it take them to get to the island from their position?" she asked.

"Fifteen minutes is my guess. Maybe twenty. Maybe ten. Hard to say. Especially if they speed up from seeing us."

"We have to hurry then. Land this bird as fast as you can. I'm going to go in the back and get ready."

Within three minutes, they were on the ground, taxing to the end of the runway just off of the main house. That proximity to the house would save them time.

Jamie looked out the window, and the woman who'd been sitting on the beach was standing now, walking toward the plane. No apparent sense of urgency or alarm. No other people were coming their way.

No guards. Still, no sign of the girls.

Jamie stuck her head in the cockpit and said, "Keep the engines running. You stay here. Be prepared to get us out of here as quickly as possible."

"As soon as you're clear, I'll turn the plane around, so it's heading in the right direction for take-off," Mike said, excitement building in his voice.

"If anything happens, you take off. Go and get help. Do not leave the plane under any circumstances. Okay."

Mike nodded reluctantly. She wondered if he really would leave her there. No use arguing with him about it. Hopefully, they'd be leaving there with the five girls.

Jamie lowered the steps and exited the plane. The woman was getting closer, almost to the runway. Jamie put a big smile on her face and extended her hand in a friendly manner.

The woman returned the smile and said hello in English. She was clearly American.

"Hi. My name is Candice," Jamie said. "I'm with *Belles of Belarus*. Mr. Patel asked me to come and pick up the girls and take them to his yacht."

Jamie saw a look flash across the woman's face. Obvious, but not discernable as to what it meant. Not a look of recognition. Something else. There wasn't enough time to figure it out.

"He's supposed to be here sometime this morning," the woman replied, looking out toward the ocean.

"Change of plans. He was coming here. Now he's going to another island and wants the girls with him."

Jamie looked out the same direction. The yacht was not yet in sight from the island.

"I think I should call him," the woman said, pulling her cell phone out of her shorts pocket. She started dialing a number.

"That's strange," she said. "I'm not getting a signal."

Jamie brought with her a cell phone jammer from the CIA safehouse. She had activated it before she got off the plane. The woman wouldn't be able to get a signal. This was a response she had anticipated.

"Oh well," Jamie said. "I need to hurry. I'm running behind as it is."

"There he is!" the woman said excitedly. "He is coming here."

Jamie looked in the direction she was pointing. Though still a good distance away, they could clearly see the yacht. When Jamie looked back toward the woman, she had a gun in her hand pointed at her.

"You're not Candice," the woman said. "I know Candy. She's the one who recruited me. Years ago. Who are you?"

That's what the strange look was all about.

Jamie held her hands up in the air and in front of her.

"I've come to get the girls," Jamie said strongly. "It's over. Candice has been arrested in Pinsk. Belles of Belarus is no more."

Jamie took a step closer to the woman still keeping her hands in the air.

"Don't move," the woman said. "Don't come any closer."

"Jamie, what's going on?" Mike said. He was still on the plane but standing at the steps. Looking out on the runway where the woman had a gun pointed at Jamie.

Just the distraction Jamie needed.

The woman looked that way, startled.

Jamie bent her knees, lowered her upper body, and moved slightly to the right so she was out of the line of fire. She brought both hands up and wrapped them around the gun, pushing it up and back. In seconds, she had the gun in her hand pointed at the woman.

"Where are the girls?" Jamie shouted.

The woman didn't respond right away. She looked in two directions. Toward the temple on the north side of the island and back toward the main house on the south side.

The girls were clearly in those two locations.

She had to hurry.

Jamie grabbed the woman around the waist, threw her up over her shoulder, and carried her over to the plane, kicking and screaming, which Jamie ignored.

"Tie her up inside," Jamie said to Mike. "Get the plane turned around. We're going to have to get out of here in a hurry."

Jamie bolted to the main house in a full sprint, still carrying the woman's gun, not knowing what she'd find inside.

The house had a wing that had clearly been added on and was not part of the original construction. Jamie deduced that the girls were in there. The house was large but square, so she was able to make it to that area through one hallway.

The door was locked. She pounded on it and heard girls scream on the other side of the door.

No time to pick the lock. One swift kick at the doorknob, and the door splintered, the lock separating from the jamb. A louder scream went up from the room as the girls ran into a closet.

Jamie followed them to the closet door.

"I'm not going to hurt you. I'm here to take you home," Jamie said.

The girls were huddled in a corner clutching each other.

"Are any of you Ana?" Jamie asked.

They didn't answer, but one girl looked at a girl hiding behind another. Clearly Ana. She appeared to be the youngest of all of them.

"Ana," Jamie said. "Olga sent me to help you. But we have to hurry."

"You know Olga?" the hiding girl said meekly.

"Yes. I'm going to take you back to Belarus. All of you. We have to hurry. See that plane." Jamie pointed out a window.

They could see the runway from their vantage point. Jamie could also see the yacht coming toward the island. Faster. Patel had obviously spotted the plane and was hurrying to find out what it was.

Jamie estimated in her head that she had less than five minutes before they would be in range of the guns.

"Follow me," Jamie said.

The girls hesitated. Jamie grabbed one of their arms and started pulling her out of the closet and toward a door that was off of the annex and closest to the runway. The other girls followed. A flimsy lock was on the door and Jamie easily kicked it open.

"Run to the plane. All of you. Get on it. Now!"

The five girls ran across the sand, to the runway. Mike was at the top of the steps motioning for them to come toward him. He helped them into the plane as Jamie sprinted toward the temple.

The building had four large columns, and two massive iron double doors, padlocked and secured by a heavy chain. She turned her head and fired the gun at the lock, concerned about a ricochet bullet, so she fired it at an angle. It penetrated the lock but didn't immediately separate the lock from the chain.

She fired again. At closer range. This time the bullet shattered the lock, sending shards of metal clanging against the door and the concrete portico and a couple off her hand and arm, causing slight burns.

Jamie ignored the searing pain and unwrapped the chain and heaved one of the big doors open. Inside was the entryway or foyer to the temple.

She called out for the girls.

No response.

There were two doors to either side of the altar. She ran to the door to the right. The only one that appeared to have a lock on it. She fired her gun into the lock and the door swung open. No girls were there.

She ran across the room to the other door and opened it. Nothing but supplies. Maybe there weren't any girls in the temple after all.

She started to leave but then heard a noise in the other room. She ran back to it. Inside the room was a curtain. She hadn't noticed it before. Behind the curtain was a door. It wasn't locked.

Inside were three girls. They looked to be seventeen or eighteen. They weren't huddled together, but all had a terrified look on their faces. They were in a living quarters. No windows and only the one door.

Jamie shouted, "We have to get out of here! Now! Patel is coming. I'm here to help you escape. Follow me."

Jamie ran out the door, through the temple area and out the two double doors. She glanced back and the girls were following her. She could see in the distance the yacht closing in on the island.

Jamie lagged behind to let the girls get ahead of her.

"Run to that plane. As fast as you can. I'll cover you."

Mike had the engines gunning. A large whirring sound was deafening as they neared the plane.

The yacht was less than a mile out. It had stopped. A boat was being lowered from the side. The gunmen were climbing into the boat. The moor for the yacht was on the other side of the island. Patel must have thought they would get to them faster by using the smaller boat.

Jamie bolted up the steps of the airplane.

"Are there any other girls on the island?" she shouted once inside, hoping the answer was no. She wouldn't be able to save them without a gunfight. If there were, she'd already decided she'd stay behind and let Mike leave with the girls. Save who they could.

Several shook their heads no. One of the older ones spoke up and said, "This is all of us. There were more but Patel took them off the island several months ago and brought the new girls in. We don't know where he took them."

Jamie thought about going back into the house to see if she could gather evidence against Patel but quickly rejected the thought. Instead, she went back to the steps, raised them, and secured the door.

"Let's get out of here!" she shouted to Mike. "Everyone's on board."

The plane lurched forward. Jamie was thrown backward, knocked to the floor. She grabbed the railing next to the cockpit door. The girls were already in their seats with seat belts around their waists. The woman was in the corner, her hands and feet bound. A blank stare on her face. Probably not sure exactly what was happening.

The nose tilted, the plane lifted from the runway and made a quick ascent to a higher altitude.

Jamie slumped back on the ground. She let out a huge sigh of relief. She glanced out the window and could see the yacht just off the island and the gunmen standing on the runway looking up at the plane.

A wide grin came on Jamie's face.

All we have to do is get this plane to Belarus, and this mission finally can be over.

I hope nothing else goes wrong.

41

The plane landed in Minsk safely.

Jamie thanked Mike profusely. "I couldn't have done it without you," she said several times.

He'd made it easier for her when he distracted the woman holding a gun on her, and his piloting skills getting the plane off the ground that fast were amazing. *Save the Girls* was lucky to have him, and she'd tell Jill so the next time she saw her.

Jamie gave each of the girls $5,000 and explained to them what would happen when they arrived in Minsk.

After landing, they all exited the plane so appreciative of what Jamie had done for them. None really talked about their experience on the island. That would be for another day. *Save the Girls* would have counselors who would spend time with each one to help them through the physical and emotional trauma.

Jamie stayed on the plane. She was still a CIA officer, operating covertly in Belarus. Her identity needed to be hidden.

Mike escorted the still bound woman down the steps and into the custody of Detective Orlov who had met the plane. They learned the woman's nickname was Hollywood. They called her Holly for short.

She grew up in southern California where she went to school with Candice at UCLA and was recruited by her to work for Asaf who then gave her to Patel. Her job was to recruit and coordinate young girls and lure them onto the island. Promising them anything to get them there.

Technically, Holly wasn't a Belarusian citizen, but her crimes were against Belarusian girls and women, and Jamie doubted she'd ever see the outside of a prison again in her life.

Jamie sat in the back of the plane out of sight, away from the windows, though she allowed herself the satisfaction of watching the girl's reunions with their friends and families from a back window where she couldn't be seen. A deep sense of accomplishment flooded her soul. Her heart was warmed by the success of the mission.

All that was left to do was to take the plane back to Obninsk, and then she could go home.

She suddenly felt total exhaustion. This had been the most trying of all her missions. She allowed herself to close her eyes and almost dozed off when she was awakened by a familiar voice. Jill had entered her cabin and was standing at the doorway.

Jamie motioned for her to come in. She mustered up the strength and stood, and they hugged and kissed each other on the cheeks. Tears were in their eyes. Tears of joy.

"You are amazing!" Jill said with sincerity. "I can't tell you how thankful we are for you. You rescued more than fifteen hundred girls. Our fundraising is through the roof from all the publicity."

"That reminds me," Jamie said. She walked over to the closet and pulled out a satchel and handed it to Jill.

"What's this?" she asked.

"An anonymous donation."

Jill opened the satchel, and her mouth flew open at the rolls of cash.

"There must be a hundred thousand dollars in here," Jill said.

"$353,000 to be exact," Jamie replied. "Don't ask where it came from."

Jill sat down in a chair across from where Jamie was sitting. "You know God is using you to do incredible things," she said.

"I know. I can sense God's presence in these missions. Guiding my steps. Protecting me."

"You have a gift. A calling."

"I never really saw it as that until now," Jamie said, using her hand to wipe away a tear. Jamie was saved in a revival at her church as a young teenager. While she'd always been strong in her faith, she was starting to see what she was doing as a call of God on her life.

"I do feel like this is what I'm supposed to be doing. I just wish I could do more. I wish I could save all the girls."

"You can't save everyone," Jill replied. "There was only one person who could do that as you know. But you're doing your part."

"Thank you for all you do," Jamie said. "I couldn't have done this without you."

"There are two people who want to see you. Can I send them inside?" Jill asked.

"Sure."

A minute later Daria and Olga entered the cabin. They were so excited to see Jamie, and the feeling was mutual. The girls were talking so fast Jamie could hardly keep up. The exhaustion was making it hard to concentrate, even with the happiness they were bringing her. Fortunately, they did most of the talking.

"I've enrolled in school," Daria said.

"We've applied for visas to America," Olga said. "Can we call you if we get there?"

"Of course."

"Ana is going to live with us," Daria said. "Her stepfather would just take her money anyway."

"That sounds like a good idea."

After a few more minutes of conversation, they said a tearful goodbye.

"We'll never forget you," they said.

"I'll never forget you, either."

The girls left after more tearful goodbyes. Jamie dozed off again.

Mike stuck his head in the cabin waking her from the slumber. He informed Jamie they weren't allowed to take off yet.

"There's someone who wants to talk to you, first."

"Who?" Jamie asked.

"Me," a familiar voice said from behind Mike.

"Detective Orlov," Jamie said, rising from her seat and extending her hand. "What a pleasant surprise."

She was fully awake now.

He sat down in the chair, so Jamie sat across from him, wondering what he wanted.

"We're taking statements from the girls. It's going to take a few days. There's so many."

He said it matter-of-factly. In a monotone voice. Concern started to rise inside Jamie. Moe was acting strangely.

"You know what this means?" he finally said in a solemn tone.

"What?" Jamie asked.

"I'm going to have to arrest you! You're operating here illegally," he responded.

A bolt of panic suddenly overwhelmed her. Adrenaline shot back through her veins, overcoming the exhaustion. She sat up in her chair.

She didn't have a weapon near her. Other than her hands. She wasn't thinking clearly anyway. This was so out of the blue.

A grin suddenly came on his face.

"I'm joking," he said, laughing hysterically. "You should see your face. Remember when you said you were going to have to kill me?"

"I remember."

"Two can play that game."

He stood to his feet. "I got you! That was a good one, wasn't it?"

He grabbed Jamie's shoulders and kissed her cheeks with great affection.

"That was a good one," Jamie muttered. "You're right. You got me."

"So much for getting sleep," she thought to herself as she tried to slow her racing heartbeat.

It wasn't until they were finally in the air and out of Belarusian airspace, that she finally let herself relax.

42

Jamie had been home for three weeks and spent a lot of that time with Alex. Turned out he didn't live in San Francisco. He lived in Arlington, Virginia, in a condo about ten minutes away from her.

They spent the last week of the three at Camp Peary, better known in CIA circles as "The Farm." A nine thousand-acre CIA training facility for covert officers located near Williamsburg, Virginia.

Curly made it his personal mission to make it as difficult and intense a week as possible, and Alex and Jamie did their best to turn it into an obsessive competition. They worked on tradecraft, counterintelligence, surveillance, firearm instruction, hand-to-hand combat, obstacle course, and some classroom language training.

The competition got so intense they were barely talking to each other at the end of the process. Besides their bodies being extremely sore, they were sore at each other.

Back in Arlington, Virginia, they decided to call a truce and meet for dinner. The conversation was pleasant but forced.

Superficial. Casual. Not much warmth.

At least compared to what they had experienced on the cruise and in Belarus. They were both trying hard to recapture some of the spark, but it wasn't working.

"Alex, I like you," Jamie said.

The meal was finished, and they had allowed themselves to order dessert. As a treat. For surviving the week with Curly.

"But," he said, recognizing she hadn't completed her thought.

"I think we were taking things a little too fast."

"I couldn't agree with you more," Alex replied. "I really like you too. With what we do, things can get really intense in the field. It's normal for passions to get intense as well."

"Don't get me wrong," Jamie explained. "I had a good time with you. I don't want to date other people. I want to take it slow. We barely know each other. I still want us to be together ... and I hope you feel the same way."

She had dreaded talking to him about it. Wondering if they would even be able to remain friends much less date.

Surprisingly, Curly hadn't tried to dissuade them from pursuing something. He thought they were meant for each other. If they didn't kill each other first, he had quipped.

"For sure," Alex said sincerely. "The problem is that we have no idea what our next mission will be. I could get a call from Brad tomorrow and be gone for three months. Same thing with you. It's hard to have a relationship like that. But we can try. You know. See where it goes."

The rest of the evening went pretty well. They went for a walk. Held hands. Sat on a bench under the stars. Laughed some for the first time in a week.

It seemed to Jamie like the ice was cracking a bit. They had an understanding. They would date but take it slow. See what developed.

Alex drove them back to Jamie's house and walked her to the door. She decided not to invite him inside. It wasn't that late, but this was what taking it slow looked like to her.

Alex seemed fine with it. He gave her a kiss. Not just a peck, but not an intense, passionate, knock your socks off, kiss. As they ended the kiss, both of their cell phones pinged at the exact same time.

A text from Brad. They both got the same message.

In my office. One hour.

Jamie and Alex sat in Brad's office in the two chairs across from his desk. Brad had excused himself to use the restroom. Both of them fidgeted nervously. Generally, those messages meant they were about to get an assignment. Neither of them knew why he had wanted to meet with them so late in the evening.

Strange.

"I wonder where I'm going," Jamie said.

"Me too," Alex replied. "I guess he has a mission for each of us. I hope I go somewhere warm."

"I hope I go someplace where I don't get shot at," Jamie said.

They both laughed.

"I'm so glad we cleared things up tonight," Jamie added. "Before I have to go away."

"Oh, I know," Alex replied. "I feel good about our conversation. This break from each other will actually help that. A few months apart will do us good. Give us a chance to see how we feel about each other. You know what I mean?"

Jamie did know what he meant.

Alex wasn't trying to be rude or evasive. Like he was looking forward to being away from her. She didn't get the feeling he was acting like a typical man who wanted to take it slow because he was afraid of commitment.

They were both intense people. If they did form a relationship, they probably needed to be away from each other for a few weeks at a time periodically to be able to make it work.

"I mean. I'll miss you," Alex said. "Some. But this will give me a chance to clear my head."

"You'll miss me some?" Jamie said laughing, punching him in the arm playfully.

"Maybe a little more than some," he retorted, hitting her back. More of a pat than a hit.

This will be good.

Maybe Alex would evolve into being a good friend. Maybe it would become more than that. She was happy with where things were.

Brad reentered the room.

"I have a mission for the two of you," he said, getting right to the point.

"Both of us?" Alex asked. "You mean, you want us to go together or you have a separate mission for each of us?"

"One mission. The two of you. You'll go together." He said the words slowly.

"Where?" Jamie asked.

"Singapore."

They looked at each other. Alex shrugged his shoulders, and Jamie gave him a slight smile.

"Singapore's nice," Jamie said. "There are worse places to go on a mission. I've never been there. Sounds good. What's our cover?"

"You're going to pose as a married couple. On your honeymoon."

"What?" Alex said.

Jamie's response was right behind his.

"Honeymoon? I don't think that's a good idea," she said.

"You're both perfect for it. You are already dating. You obviously have chemistry. You work well together. Perfect match. You'll have to share a place. Two-bedroom apartment so you'll each have your own room. Act all in love. It's very important for the mission that you pull off the cover. You have to make the targets believe you really are married."

"How long is the mission?" Alex said.

"Plan to be gone for at least six weeks. Probably more like three months."

"We have to pretend to be newlyweds for three months?" Jamie asked.

"That's right," Brad replied. "You leave in the morning. 8:00 a.m. Sharp. I want you to go to the prop room tonight."

The prop room was a large room in the basement that housed all kinds of items used by officers in the field to make their cover more believable.

"What do we need from the prop room?" Alex asked.

"You need to pick out your wedding rings," Brad responded.

So much for taking things slow.

Not The End

Thank you for purchasing this novel from best-selling author, Terry Toler. As an additional thank you, Terry wants to give you a free gift.

Sign up for:
Updates
New Releases
Announcements
At terrytoler.com

We'll send you a copy of *The Book Club*, a Cliff Hangers mystery, free of charge.

READ MORE BOOKS FROM TERRY TOLER

Jamie Austen Thrillers

Read all the Jamie Austen Thrillers. They must be good.
They've been number one on Amazon in ten different countries.
Click on the link below.

THE JAMIE AUSTEN THRILLERS (12 book series)
Kindle Edition (amazon.com)

https://amzn.to/3vmPUy7

Cliff Hangers Mystery Series

Who wants to read a good mystery? We've got you covered! Read the Cliff Hangers where homicide detective, Cliff Ford, solves crimes in Chicago, with help from his wife Julia. These books have everything Terry Toler is known for. Page turning suspense, a hint of romance, and an ending you won't see coming.

The Cliff Hangers Mystery Series (4 book series)
Kindle Edition (amazon.com)

https://amzn.to/36WX3go

About Terry

Terry Toler is an Amazon international # 1 best-selling and award-winning author. He writes clean fiction with a message and life-changing nonfiction. He's a public speaker, entrepreneur, and has authored more than forty books.

Sign up for his newsletter where you'll get free stuff, exclusive content, and news of releases and promotions. He can be followed at terry-toler.com.

If you like his books, please take a few minutes to leave a review on Amazon. We really appreciate it. It helps draw more readers to his books. Thanks!

Printed in Great Britain
by Amazon

34316597R00209